Meet the players in

Partners

Bobby Von Marron—The handsome, charming partner in the prestigious firm La Tourraine, Durant, and Von Marron, he believed winning was everything . . . then he discovered what it was like to lose.

Lulu Von Marron—Beautiful and spoiled, she lived in the rosy glow of Valium, champagne, and dreams—until her world came crashing down.

Gloria Von Marron—She was the last of the Von Marrons—and determined to be the best. Until she realized winning meant nothing without love.

Win Durant—He wanted all of La Tourraine, Durant, and Von Marron. And nobody—especially Gloria—would stop him.

Gardner Durant—He defied his father to pursue his own dreams. But his love for Gloria would forever alter his life.

PARTNERS

Carolyn Bransford

FAWCETT GOLD MEDAL • NEW YORK

A Fawcett Gold Medal Book
Published by Ballantine Books
Copyright © 1989 by Carolyn L.L. Bransford

Library of Congress Catalog Card Number: 89-91219

ISBN 0-449-13442-3

Manufactured in the United States of America

First Edition: September 1989

To my parents and my grandparents who paved the way for this good life.

I wish to thank Maggie Osborne whose writing expertise was essential to the completion of this novel, and Maria Carvainis, my agent, whose support and enthusiasm were equally important.

Prologue

THE PAPARAZZO SHIFTED on the sea wall and adjusted his telephoto lens. It was a gorgeous New England day. A hundred yards to the north, grass that reminded him of emerald velvet rolled down from the mansion to the shore. Autumn sunlight sparkled off the waters of the Sound. He was glad to be here. His photo—if he got a good one—would appear in *The Times*.

Raising the camera to his eye, he scanned the water until he found the boat, then zoomed in on the man standing at the rail. Good-looking son of a bitch. Expensively casual. White shorts, navy shirt open to the waist, great tan. Probably somebody; he'd check it out later.

Following the man's gaze, he tracked the lens down to the water, skimming the waves until he found her. Over the years he had taken hundreds of photographs of Gloria Von Marron, but he still experienced a small intake of breath each time he saw her.

She was one gorgeous woman. She reminded him of Grace Kelly in Grace's heyday. Blond, beautiful, cool and patrician, yet smoldering underneath. Not many women had that quality, that exciting combination of fire and ice. There wasn't a man alive who wasn't turned on by it.

Lovingly, he moved the camera to view the length of her body. It would have been great to catch her frolicking naked in the water, but that wasn't her style. She was wearing a black, one-piece swimming suit, but it was some suit, sexy as hell. Cut high on the thighs and plunging nearly to the waist in front, the suit was held in place over her breasts by a thin gold chain. Class all the way; the genuine article. As he clicked the camera, she arched her throat and spread her arms, floating on the water like a treasure yielded up by the sea. He would have sacrificed

1

ten years of his life to step into her world and spend the night with her.

The water was cold against Gloria's back, the sunlight warm on her face and breasts. The contrast was as sharp and well defined as the contrasts in her life. The thought amused her, and a smile touched her lips. As a rule she avoided examining herself too closely; long ago she had learned the result was too painful. Instead, she had trained herself to live for tomorrow.

Now, the tomorrow she had worked toward, had schemed for, was finally about to dawn. The skeins of the past would knit together into a carefully woven tapestry of revenge. It required but two phone calls, which she would place tomorrow morning. Then all the threads would tie together.

Savoring the thought, she lifted her face to the sun and closed her eyes. Whoever claimed that revenge was a dish best served cold was wrong. Her hurts were long-standing, yes, but the desire, the obsession for revenge, had never cooled. It had burned like a bright flame to fuel the years of hard work and denial, had cast a bitter light over the many sacrifices. Now, finally, the score would be evened, the flame extinguished. Perhaps now she could begin the life she should have had.

It all depended on Gardner. Which side he chose. Conscious that he watched from the boat, she extended her arms in a lazy backstroke, the relaxed motion in conflict with the turmoil stirring her thoughts. She had never intended Gardner to be caught in the middle. That he had been was a constant raw ache.

They had agreed not to discuss business this weekend. Selfishly, she had made the request in order to give herself one perfect weekend, one cherished memory in the event she had to live her life without him. Would that sacrifice be required of her, too?

The sharp chill of the water invaded her body and, turning, she cut through the waves with a clean strong breaststroke. When she pulled herself up the ladder, water flowed off her body and streamed from her hair, sparkled on her eyelashes like tears.

"Hold me," she whispered, looking up at him, letting him see the love softening her eyes. "Please hold me."

Pressing into his warmth, she clung to him, tasting the salt on her lips before he kissed her. Their bodies meshed, the fit perfect and exciting.

"I love you," he said against her wet hair.

"I know. That's what makes this so terrible."

against him and rested his chin on top of her hair.
ything I can say to make you reconsider?"
he said softly. It was too late. Years too late. The
she would unleash tomorrow had been set in motion

she opened her eyes, she saw the blue flag fluttering
pole near the steps leading from the lawn to the shore.
could ignore it," Gardner said, smiling down at her.
"Pretend we don't see it."

They both knew that was impossible. William didn't raise the
blue flag unless one of them was urgently needed. Smiling, she
touched his cheek, letting her fingers linger, then she donned a
terry robe while Gardner hoisted anchor and fired the auxiliary
engine.

"It's probably nothing," she said. But she knew that wasn't
true when she saw William standing on the jetty. As Gardner
cut the engine and the boat swung toward the posts, she looked
at William's seamed face and the warm breeze suddenly turned
icy.

He helped her out of the boat. "There's an urgent call from
Lewes, Miss. You're to phone back immediately."

For a moment she stood paralyzed. Then she was running
toward the house, cutting up a hidden path she hadn't used since
childhood. Once inside, she paused briefly to catch her breath,
then hurried to the nearest phone.

A dozen possibilities played through her mind as she dialed
with shaking fingers. Please, don't let it be any of them, she
thought, as the line clicked through the overseas relays. One
minute, two. Her gaze swept the room as she waited. Sunlight
streamed through the tall windows, casting bars of illumination
across the Portuguese carpet, the cut crystal vases, across the
polished grand piano, now unused. She looked at the piano. So
many memories.

The line crackled then came alive in her hand. "Margaret?
Margaret, what's wrong?"

Hysteria garbled the words, but she heard them in her heart.
"They've taken him, Gloria! They've taken Robby!"

Margaret's sobs crowded her mind as Gloria's knees buckled
and she sat hard, oblivious to the wet print she was leaving on
the Queen Anne settee. "Oh, my God. No."

She knew it happened, kidnappers snatching up the children
of the wealthy. But not Robby, never Robby. He was safe. Be-

cause he was her secret; no one knew. But someon
did know. "When? How did it happen?" she said.

"This afternoon." The words were choked by sobs
park. One minute Robby was there, the next minute . . ."

Gloria's throat closed, and she could hear her heart hammer
ing against her ribs. "Have you . . ." She wet her lips and tried
again, struggled to make the words audible. "Have you heard
from anyone? What are the demands?"

"A man telephoned thirty minutes ago. I wrote it down."
There was the rattle of paper being smoothed, the faint sound
of a dog barking. Then Margaret's drowning voice. "He said:
'Tell the bitch the boy is in his father's care.' "

For an instant the room went dark. From what seemed a vast
distance she heard Margaret's sobs breaking against her ear as
she tried to understand that he could be that desperate, that
cruelly ruthless. "No police," she whispered.

After hanging up the phone, she doubled over, fighting nausea. Oh God. How far would it go? Would they hurt him? Was
he calling for her? He would be so frightened.

"Gloria? Darling, you're white as chalk!"

She looked up to see Gardner standing in the doorway. So
loving, so trusting. A mist of tears blurred the sunlight around
him. She had always known that someday she would have to tell
him. But she had wanted to choose the moment, had wanted to
tell him in the least painful way. Now the choice had been taken
from her.

Standing, she faced him and her expression stopped him from
taking her in his arms. This, then, was how hell began. "My
son has been kidnapped."

"Your son?" His eyes were blank, uncomprehending. Despair washed over her like a wave. In a moment he would ask
who her son's father was. The answer would shatter him. From
this moment forward his life would not, could not be the same.

She closed her eyes against a rush of pain and wondered if it
had always been like this. Had the Von Marrons always destroyed those they loved most . . . ?

Book One

1973

Chapter 1

$\mathcal{G}$LORIA VON MARRON was thinking about sex. The subject fascinated her.

A sensual breeze teased her silvery hair and brushed across her long tanned legs as she descended the stone steps leading from the parterre gardens to the sand. It was difficult to concentrate with so many people in the house. Remy was home from Princeton, her father seldom went into the city during the summer, and her mother was perpetually surrounded by a coterie of caterers, florists, decorators, and secretaries. Then there was Margaret, William, and the remainder of the staff.

The wide expanse of private beach was gloriously empty, groomed and raked clean of any reminders of last week's Regatta Ball. By facing toward the water, Gloria could blot out all evidence of civilization and pretend she was Eve, waiting for an experienced Adam to sail over the horizon and introduce her to adult mysteries. Her sigh would have been embarrassing had there been anyone to overhear; it was so blatantly a sigh of longing.

Kicking at the sand, she wandered idly along the edge of the water, brooding, wondering when and if she would ever be kissed and if she would be good at it. That she stood poised impatiently on the brink of womanhood, she knew. Finally her body had shown signs of catching up to a mind that had never really been that of a child. But it wasn't happening fast enough, she thought, frowning. She still didn't have any breasts to speak of, and she despaired that perhaps she never would.

It would have been comforting to speak to her mother about kissing and developing breasts and all the rest, but Lulu Von Marron wasn't the type of mother to welcome that sort of chat. Gloria couldn't even imagine such a discussion. Bending, she sorted among the pebbles on the beach, then stood and brushed the loose sand from her bare legs, enjoying the tactile pleasure of touching smooth warm skin. This was the summer she had begun to shave her legs.

After selecting one of the pebbles, she weighed it in her hand then flung it hard toward the waves rushing up the beach, imagining her mother's cool patrician face.

"No doubt about it, squirt. You hit whomever you were aiming at."

Spinning, Gloria faced away from the water and shaded her eyes, blinking until she spotted her brother, Remy, sitting in the shadows beneath the sea wall.

"I didn't see you there."

Slouched against the stone wall, Remy exuded the careless aristocratic elegance characteristic to the Von Marron men. He smiled at her with an engaging smile that concealed more than it ever revealed. But Gloria knew all Remy's secrets, or thought she did. His smile hid a vulnerability and a puzzling lack of confidence that sometimes made her feel older than he was.

Remy was the favorite, the heir and the future of the Von Marrons. Bobby and Lulu Von Marron doted on him, fought over him, focused what attention they were willing to give squarely on Remy. Occasionally Gloria suspected her parents forgot they had a daughter. When she thought about it, it seemed Remy should have been the one to possess confidence and self-assurance.

He patted the sand beside him, smiled and waved her over. She settled beside him, but her pleasure at his invitation faded when she noticed the joint between his fingers.

"Are you crazy?" Lifting on her knees, she cast an anxious glance over the stone wall. "Mummy and Daddy will kill you if they catch you smoking."

"They'll kill me anyway, one way or another." He shrugged, sucked at the smoke, and held it inside.

"Why do you say things like that?"

"Because it's true." Remy looked at her and then closed his eyes. "I can't win, you know that. If I continue with my music, father will feel betrayed. If I give it up, Mummy will feel betrayed. It's killing me."

"Isn't there some way you can go into business and still keep your music?" The skirmish over Remy's future had waged for years, but this summer the war had escalated toward a decisive battle.

"That's not what I want." A vapory stream of smoke leaked from his mouth and nose. "You see, squirt, the Von Marron heir doesn't give a rat's ass about the family empire. Not about Home Limited, not about La Tourraine, Durant and Von Marron." He peered at her shocked expression and grinned. "I see you recognize heresy when you hear it. Face it, the Von Marron heir is a fuck-up in all areas but music. The jury is still out on that one. But we'll know soon, won't we?"

She hated it when he fell into one of his moods. "You're not a . . ."

Smiling, he watched her struggle to speak the words. "A fuck-up." Holding the end of the joint between his thumb and forefinger, he inhaled deeply before pushing the stub into the sand. "Sure I am. You know more about the Von Marron holdings than I'll ever know. Or want to know."

Everything he said was true, but it embarrassed her to hear him say it. The problem of Remy's future ran through Goose Point like a dark undertow tugging at all of them. Every glance and every word contained a reference, a nuance that established a position or attacked a position. Sometimes Gloria sided with her mother's views, sometimes with her father's. No matter what she did, she betrayed someone she loved.

"When is the competition?" Everything hinged on the De-bussy Competition. If Remy won the competition, he could pursue a career in music, as her father had grudgingly agreed. If he lost, Remy had agreed to enter one of the family firms immediately after graduating from Princeton.

"In three weeks." Remy turned his long slender fingers in front of his face, staring at them.

"Shouldn't you be practicing?"

"And compete with Watergate? Even in the music room I can hear the damned TV blaring."

Gloria took his hand and gripped it. "I know you'll win."

"I have to." After a minute he rolled his head along the sea wall to look at her. "Have you seen the framed *Life* Magazine cover in my bedroom?"

"The one of Daddy and Georges La Tourraine? Of course I have."

Remy nodded then turned his face toward the water. "Father saved La Tourraine's life."

"During the war, I know." Puzzled, she watched him.

"La Tourraine was blinded and father talked him across the

channel. He kept his Mustang on La Tourraine's wing, talking all the way. Landed him on a grass field outside Dover.''

''I know all that.'' Remy's expression worried her. ''Remy, why are you thinking about this?''

''Our father was a hero, a genuine, fucking hero. How many heroic deeds do you think I'll be able to pull off on a keyboard?''

''It's not the same thing.'' The conversation had shifted toward depths Gloria recognized but couldn't follow. ''Are you saying you want to be a hero?''

''Oh God, Gloria. You're so young. Every man wants to be a hero in his father's eyes, but I never will be. Can you understand that?''

She understood better than he would have imagined. But she didn't say so because it would have sounded as if she envied Remy's future. Perhaps she did.

''Bobby Von Marron is the best polo player, the best tennis player, the best rider, the best shot. The best everything. How do I compete with that?''

''I don't know.'' She had no answer. But she had questions of her own. ''Remy?'' she glanced at him then lowered her head and pretended to study the sand. Heat rose in her cheeks. ''Have you ever . . . I mean, when you go out with a girl, do you ever want to . . . ?''

When he grasped what she was asking, he laughed and her blush deepened. ''This topic isn't the sort of thing a gentleman discusses, squirt.''

''I need to know and there's no one else to ask. Have you . . .'' Her face turned scarlet. ''Have you done *it*?''

On the lawn above Margaret called, her voice almost on top of them. ''Gloria? Have you forgotten your fitting?''

''Saved by the nanny.'' Remy grinned.

''Margaret's not a nanny, she's a companion now. I'm too old for a nanny.'' Frustrated, Gloria poked her silvery head above the sea wall. ''I'll be there in a minute.''

Margaret smiled and waved. ''Don't be too long. Mr. Attenbury is here from London to fit your school wardrobe.''

''I'm coming.'' She looked down at the top of her brother's head. ''I'm showing Parker's Muncy on Saturday. Will you come? Mummy can't, she's having her hair done for the Duchess's reception, and Daddy is planning to meet with Uncle Win about the oil embargo.''

''Of course I'll be there.'' Reaching, he squeezed her hand.

"I have to win!"
was the only thing that

"Winning is the Von M

"I'll just die if I don't win.
blue ribbons she had to win befor
only that she didn't yet have enough.
the sunlight as she lifted her head and fr
bles.

"You're fourteen years old, squirt. There's ple
win."

"You don't believe that. Second place is the same as
She watched him tap something from a leather pouch over a t
paper, then roll the paper and moisten the edge. "Remy?" A
light blush returned to her cheeks. "I started menstruating last
New Year's day. Everyone else started before me."

"Hey, that's great." When Remy smiled, he was as handsome
as their father. "Is that what I'm supposed to say?"

"You don't have to say anything. I just wanted to tell someone." After brushing the sand from the seat of her shorts, she
walked to the steps, then looked back and waved.

Remy's misery was so profound she could see it and feel it.
But she didn't fully understand it. If her parents had lavished
the same attention on her that they focused on Remy, she would
have blossomed like a flower drenched in sunshine. And if her
future had included Home Limited or a position at La Tourraine,
Durant and Von Marron, she would have grasped it eagerly and
considered herself blessed.

"Mummy?" Gloria leaned into the sun room, relieved to find
only her mother and Etta Nelson, Lulu Von Marron's social
secretary. Sunlight poured through the windows, illuminating
Lulu's golden hair, shimmering across the soft pleats of her red
silk skirt.

"Etta and I are planning Remy's celebration party, Gloria.
You know I don't like to be interrupted when I'm worrying about
the seating arrangements." Lulu Von Marron spoke with a cultured Boston accent that sounded deceptively incapable of rage
or hysteria, a voice calculated to garner the bearer whatever she
wanted. She pressed back a wave of shining hair. "You can't
imagine the difficulties when the Duke and Duchess are expected."

"I won."

that habit.
h Margaret
riday, I want
ve?''

e,'' Lulu said,

look today.''
oothing a frown
over Etta Nelson's
ther permits. If not,

PARTNERS

Second place
counted.
ton way.''
Gloria didn't know how many
her mother took an interest,
Her bright hair swung in
wned toward the sta-

Gloria wasn't good enough, winning

11

ny of time to
ast.''

the archway, Gloria
war Etta's dark chignon.
By the day o... be in a state of nervous
exhaustion, hysteri... know why the flowers
weren't exactly matched o... gements had been made
to keep the photographers out. Etta would call Dr. Barbeau to
administer vitamin B shots and Valium. That's how it always
was. Vitamin B and Valium were more important to her mother's parties than the caterers.

Following the notes of a Debussy prelude, Gloria entered the
music room. The chords were light, dreamy, seductive, drawing
her forward. Crossing the room, she stood behind Remy and
placed her hands on his shoulders.

''Thanks for being there today,'' she said, dropping a self-
conscious kiss on his cheek.

''You made those other girls look like clumsy peasants. Where
on earth did you learn to ride like that or to look so damned
haughty? You absolutely captivated the judges, squirt.''

Her throat drew tight. She wished she could tell him how
much she loved him for caring enough to be there, but she would
have cried if she had tried to capture the emotion in words.

''Let's hope I do as well at Carnegie.'' He replaced his long
fingers on the keys. ''Listen carefully and tell me if I have a
chance. This is my first selection.''

She tilted her head and screwed her face into an expression
of concentration, then laughed as she recognized the piece. It
was an Elton John song, ''Don't Shoot Me I'm Only the Piano
Player.'' Sunlight sparkled in her gray eyes. ''You can't lose.''

"Carnegie, here I come. The other competitors might as well concede right now."

"I know you're going to win."

"Pressure, pressure. Mummy is already planning a victory celebration, and you're handing out blue ribbons." Grinning, he watched her pin her ribbon on his sleeve.

"I want you to have it."

His music followed her to the door, but it wasn't Debussy. "You Are the Sunshine of My Life" reached out and wrapped around her as she knew he intended. She blew him a kiss then waited outside the music room until he shifted again to Debussy. The prelude was brilliant, exquisite.

After the sunlight flooding the music room, her father's study seemed like a cave. When her eyes adjusted, she saw Bobby Von Marron in front of the television, his long legs elegantly draped in front of him. He was as carelessly handsome now as he was in the framed *Life* Magazine cover, perhaps more so, she thought. When Lulu complained that half the women in their set were in love with Bobby Von Marron, the accusation was only partly in jest.

Dropping to the arm of his chair, Gloria leaned to give him a quick kiss. "Have I missed anything?" The TV cameras moved in on Archibald Cox's frown.

"Win Durant and I both advised Cox not to accept Nixon's appointment. This thing is going to blow wide open and when it does, neither side is going to come up clean. Pour me another gin and tonic, will you, honey?"

"Nixon thinks he has Cox in his pocket."

"He's in for a surprise. Dammit, Whitehall couldn't have died at a worse time. If Whitehall were alive, he'd be in Washington now and we'd know what's really going on."

Gloria leaned against her father's shoulder, inhaling the warm rich scent of an English aftershave. "Hasn't the firm replaced Whitehall?"

"With whom? Whitehall was worth ten of anyone else. With Edison in Washington, the firm knew what Nixon was thinking before Nixon did."

"How did Edison Whitehall really die?" If she didn't look at him and if her tone were casual enough, perhaps she would learn the truth.

Her father lifted an eyebrow. "Edison died at his desk of a heart attack. You know that."

She knew this was the official explanation, but she also knew it wasn't true. Gloria recognized every expression, every nuance in her father's repertoire, and she knew when he was lying. The reason mystified and intrigued her as much as the drama unfolding on the television screen.

"Will you and Uncle Win and Georges La Tourraine take in another partner to replace Mr. Whitehall?"

"More likely we'll buy in Whitehall's interest according to the partnership agreement and leave it at that." He tasted his gin then looked at her and laughed. "Good God, sometimes I forget how young you are. So. What did my precocious daughter do today? Was the steeplechase this afternoon?"

"No, the show."

"I forgot. I'm sorry, honey. Did you win?" When she nodded, he raised his glass in a toast. "That's my girl, a winner. I'll order champagne with dinner. We'll celebrate."

Champagne would be nice, she thought. She hoped he remembered this time.

Everyone at Goose Point relaxed when Winthrop and Chissie Durant came for the weekend. With Chissie as a soothing influence, Lulu was less nervous, less likely to lapse into one of her moods. Without being aware her smile had assumed a wistful quality, Gloria stood on the porch and listened to the drift of laughter floating from her mother's opened bedroom window. Someday Gloria would be old enough to join them, Chissie had promised.

Leaning backward, she stretched against the porch railing and concentrated on the music floating through the house and out into the summer day. This was the summer of Debussy, that was how she would remember her fourteenth summer. Not Watergate, not the emotional undercurrents, but Debussy. The music saturated her days, irrevocably Remy.

Now leaning forward, she crossed her arms on the railing and tried to decide how she would spend the day. If Gardner Durant had accompanied his parents to Goose Point, the decision would have been easy, but he had not. And if Gardner had come, he probably wouldn't have noticed her anyway. He would have spent the weekend with Remy.

Gloria knew what she wanted to do right now, and she knew she shouldn't do it. Still . . .

After swiftly scanning the lawns and glancing toward the stable to make certain no one watched, she stepped off the veranda and slipped behind the lilacs that grew close to the house. Behind the shrubbery lay a narrow expanse of ground where nothing grew. If she bent double and followed the foundation, she could nearly circle the house concealed behind the lilacs and forsythia.

She really was too old for this sort of thing, but it was the only way she knew to learn anything important. And she liked to know things.

Bending low, she followed the contours of the foundation until she heard the sound of the television from the window above her head. When she heard Win Durant's voice, she settled herself on the ground and removed an apple from the pocket of her shorts.

Although she and Remy referred to Winthrop Durant as Uncle, he was not a family member, though he often seemed to be. Gardner and Remy were best friends; Chissie and Lulu had grown up together; and Win Durant and Gloria's father had been in the war together and later were roommates at Princeton. The families were as interwoven as genuine relatives. They shared stories that dated back to the war when Win Durant had saved Bobby Von Marron's life just as Bobby would later save La Tourraine's life. Only Durant hadn't made the cover of *Life* Magazine.

Winthrop Durant was her father's business partner and closest friend. He was also the driving force behind La Tourraine, Durant and Von Marron, the more glamorous end of the Von Marron holdings. Her father was quick to give Durant credit for the firm's success. It was Durant's unquestioned genius that had built the firm into a powerful force. A profile in *The Wall Street Journal* had lauded Durant as a financial legend, and Bobby Von Marron publicly agreed. Gloria's father was fond of joking that his role at La Tourraine, Durant and Von Marron was to lasso clients off the polo fields and ride them into the firm; Durant did the rest. This statement always drew a laugh, but Gloria sensed it was true.

Patiently, she bit into the apple and waited for news of Home Limited or La Tourraine, Durant and Von Marron. Either of the Von Marron interests would do.

"Nixon is going to push Cox too far. That's when the shit hits the fan." Although Gloria had never seen Win Durant lose his temper, he generally spoke as if he were on the edge of doing so. His deep voice contained a controlled quality as if he were guarding something explosive that might erupt if he relaxed.

"Then you believe Nixon is definitely involved in the cover-up?"

"Christ, yes. We've got people at the firm figuring this thing every conceivable way, up to and including impeachment."

"That silly bastard, Whitehall, picked a lousy time to die. What in the hell was he doing in an East Side bathhouse at two in the morning?"

Gloria heard a rustle that might have been a shrug, then Durant's voice. "What does any fairy do in an East Side bathhouse? He went there to get laid. It must have been good. Good enough to cause a goddamn heart attack."

"Who would have figured it? We were there when he married Helen. Of course I heard things, but I didn't believe them."

So Nixon wasn't the only one involved in a cover-up, Gloria thought, straining to hear. The circumstances of Edison White-hall's death had to be concealed; even she could understand that. A powerful, prestigious firm like La Tourraine, Durant and Von Marron would not want a hint of scandal to reach its clients.

She missed the first part of her father's reply. ". . . if you hadn't been with Helen Whitehall when the call came. We'd have been facing one hell of a blowup." There was a pause. "How did you happen to be with her? At two in the morning?"

Durant laughed. "Edison wasn't the only Whitehall wanting to get laid."

"Jesus, Win. Helen has lunch with Lulu and Chissie. They work on the same charities."

"How much you drink is none of my business, Bobby, and who I fuck is none of yours."

Chissie Durant's warm eyes and soft smile leapt into Gloria's thoughts, and she wished she hadn't eavesdropped. Against her will, she imagined Win Durant and Helen Whitehall in bed together kissing and doing whatever else lovers did. After a moment, she pressed a hand to her hot cheeks then pushed the apple core between the lilac branches. Quietly, she slipped back to the veranda.

Winthrop Durant stared steadily at the television, but his mind wasn't following the Watergate weekend wrap-up. It infuriated him that a man as brilliant as Edison Whitehall could have been so goddamn stupid as to die the way he had. Tied to a massage table wearing a studded dog collar and a pair of tasseled leather briefs. Someone had drawn lipstick circles around his nipples and balls. Christ. For years Durant had known about Edison's apartment in Washington and the succession of young men who passed through it, but he hadn't known Edison was fool enough to risk dives like the Bacchus.

After swallowing his Scotch, he shifted his glance to Bobby Von Marron. Who the hell was Von Marron to lecture him? Or to focus on the least significant event of that night? Bobby hadn't been there. He hadn't walked into the Bacchus and smelled the sour odor of sweat and sex, the stink of perfume and musky heat. Von Marron hadn't looked at Whitehall's hairy paunch hanging over those idiotic tasseled briefs or seen the stains on the table. Von Marron sure as hell hadn't been there to help wash and dress Whitehall and haul his dead ass downtown to the firm to arrange a more respectable death scene.

Van Marron's manicured hands were clean; the dirty part of the business had fallen to Durant. He drained his Scotch and poured another. If he had known at the beginning that he would spend twenty years carrying Bobby Von Marron, would he have accepted the partnership?

Hell, yes. Although he had the brilliance and the expertise, Von Marron had the connections and the wealth. It was that simple. Without the Von Marron millions and the Von Marron social connections, La Tourraine, Durant and Von Marron would have died. Brilliance wasn't enough.

Patience, he reminded himself. Eventually the firm would be his. The other partners were merely window dressing; Durant had built the firm. It was his in all but name and assets. All he had to do was outlive the bastards.

Plus, he had Gardner. La Tourraine had sired only daughters. Whitehall's sons had no interest in business. Von Marron's son didn't bear thinking about. The little prick wanted to be a musician, for God's sake. It didn't surprise Durant. Remy Von Marron lacked the barest hint of a killer instinct, he had no feel for business.

But Gardner. Christ, now there was a kid. Gardner had all Durant's good qualities and none of his liabilities. He had inherited Chissie's classic good looks and Durant's powerful physique. And he had an instinct for blood; he was a competitor. Watching Gardner command a polo field or seeing him dominate the tennis court at the club was sheer joy. Gardner went for the win, and winning was a drive Durant had cut his teeth on.

If Durant didn't outlive Von Marron and La Tourraine, Gardner would. Then the firm would belong solely to a Durant. As it always should have.

"As long as we're discussing Helen Whitehall," he commented, "We may have a problem."

"What kind of problem?"

"She wants an appointment with both of us. No attorneys, no outsiders."

"Did she say why?"

Von Marron's innocence never failed to astonish Durant. "Knowing Helen, it involves money."

Bobby crossed his ankles atop a Moroccan leather hassock and returned his attention to the television. "The buy-back is clear-cut. Let the attorneys handle it."

"I think we should hear what she has to say." Briefly Durant considered a word of preparation then discarded the thought. It was possible he could have figured it wrong. "Can you come into town the week after next?"

"If you think it's necessary."

Both Win and Bobby were forty-nine years old, but Bobby looked a decade younger. The gray that had begun to streak Durant's temples was hidden in Bobby's light hair. Pound for pound, Durant believed he was in better physical shape, but he would have traded that advantage instantly to possess the elegant Von Marron carriage, the result of generations of breeding. Winthrop Durant had no patrician background. He was not an elegant man. He wouldn't dream of leaving his home dressed as Bobby was now. Durant couldn't wear slacks, a pullover, and loafers minus socks and still manage to project the image of a country gentleman.

That realization summed up the vast difference between himself and Bobby Von Marron. Von Marron belonged and had always belonged. Win Durant never had. It didn't matter how much money he made, or how many boards he sat on, or how many endowments he presented, he was and always would be a redneck from Oklahoma with no background and no social standing. He was a curiosity, an upstart who had married far above himself and who had traded on the Von Marron name to build a power base. Durant didn't deceive himself; he knew that was how his detractors regarded him. He looked the part, he acted the part, but he played the role on sufferance.

"Well, if the girls are ready, we're due at the club for drinks," Bobby said, standing and stretching.

"You go ahead, I have some calls to make. Tell Chissie I'll catch up later."

In his present mood he didn't need a lengthy dose of Lulu

Parker Von Marron. After cleaning up behind the Von Marrons for twenty years, he merited better than the cool reserve with which she treated him, as if he were one of the servants who needed to be kept safely at arm's length lest some contamination occur.

The truth was, and it was a continuing sore spot as irritating as an aching tooth, Lulu Von Marron was the only woman Durant had ever wanted but hadn't had. The only woman who had ever said no to him and meant it. He got an erection just thinking about her. She was nervous and unstable, a lousy mother, selfish and spoiled, and probably frigid. But if Lulu Von Marron had given him the slightest encouragement, he would have taken her to bed in an instant.

He was one of the most powerful figures on Wall Street, handled billions of American and foreign dollars, was a self-made millionaire twenty times over. He sat on the board of a dozen Fortune 100 companies and was respected and feared in every financial capital throughout the world. Yet Lulu turned those cool gray eyes in his direction and once again he became a hick kid fresh off the Oklahoma rigs wearing grease under his nails. A nobody. He would have surrendered half his portfolio for one hour in bed with the bitch.

Chapter 2

*L*ULU DECIDED THE GALA was progressing nicely. There had been that irritating contretemps in the kitchen earlier, something about the household staff not cooperating with the catering staff, but Etta Nelson had smoothed it over, thank God. The ice sculpture, a life-size baby grand, had proven a sensation and the flowers were splendid. Champagne was flowing freely and the canapes were a brilliant success. If Bobby hadn't insisted on acting like such an ass, she could have relaxed and enjoyed the party and Remy's triumph. Bobby's behavior enraged her. God only knew what everyone would be saying tomorrow.

Shifting slightly, she scanned the dinner jackets and pastel gowns crowding the Rose room, seeking Mocton-James from *Woman's Wear Daily*. Had the reporter noticed Bobby hadn't offered a single toast? Of course he had. The slimy little ferret didn't miss a thing.

Accepting a champagne glass from a passing tray, she raised it above a dazzling smile. "To my talented, talented son!" Those clustered about her lifted their glasses to Remy's victory. "Now where has our genius run off to?" Turning in a calculated swirl of petal shaped silk, a Valentino, she moved through the rooms, seeking Remy. He was behaving as churlishly as Bobby, undoubtedly wounded by his father's behavior. Definitely, she had to find a moment to speak to Bobby.

"Darling, there you are!" Remy was nearly hidden by the terrace doors, standing with Gardner Durant and Gloria. Gardner Durant was deliciously handsome, Lulu could admit it. But Remy—Remy was magnificent, so perfectly a Von Marron. "Darling, have you presented yourself to the Duchess?" She couldn't resist touching her beautiful, talented son, smoothing back his golden hair, stroking those long, gifted fingers. Remy was her creation, her statement to the world. "I know Wallis wants to congratulate you."

He lowered his head. "Mother—please."

Pride flushed her cheeks. Remy was her accomplishment and her conceit. Wrapping her hand around his arm, she tugged him forward to stand before the glistening ice sculpture. "To the maestro!" she called gaily, lifting her champagne.

The glitterati of the world's most fashionable social set smiled and applauded and flashbulbs exploded as Lulu touched her cheek to Remy's. "Smile, darling. This is our night. Don't be so modest." She didn't understand modesty, but she found it rather endearing in her son.

Bobby appeared, but instead of joining her toast, he bent near her diamond earrings and his fingers bit painfully into her smooth flesh. "I want a word with you."

"And I want a word with you," she said between clenched teeth. Smiling into each other's eyes, the perfect couple, they moved through the crush toward Bobby's den.

The instant the door closed behind them, Lulu whirled on him. "You selfish bastard! You're so goddamn fascinated with Bee Bee Halston's breasts that you've forgotten your only son!"

"Christ, Lulu, you're humiliating him! This idiotic party is bad enough. Do you have to compound Remy's embarrassment by making those ridiculous toasts?"

They had taken positions facing each other across Bobby's Louis the Fifteenth desk. Lulu leaned over the gleaming wood. "I'm trying to honor him. Is that so hard for you to understand?"

"He lost the competition! He took third place."

"Obviously the judges were bought." Irritated, she waved a hand of dismissal. "You know Remy was the best. You were there."

"He lost. Everyone here knows he lost. By pretending otherwise, you're making a fool of yourself and making Remy miserable!"

She stared at him, beginning to grasp the implications of what he was saying. "You really believe that, don't you?" Her eyes widened. There had been her hair and gown to see to, last minute disasters to avert. There had been no time to reflect on Bobby's interpretation of the competition's result. Her skin tightened. "Next year we'll demand impartial judges who can't be bought."

"There won't be a next year. We agreed. You and I and Remy." Bobby met her eyes across the desk. "I was prepared to honor my end of the bargain, Lulu. Remy must honor his. He accepts a position at Home Limited or with La Tourraine, Durant and Von Marron after graduation.''

"No." Her face paled beneath her rouge. She couldn't believe he was saying these things. ''You're glad he lost, aren't you?'' Gradually the situation was becoming clear to her. She began to understand. ''You wanted him to lose because you're jealous. All your life you've been the best at everything. But Remy's doing something you can't do. That's it, isn't it? You don't want to believe Remy won because that means you lost.'' Bobby had to win, had to have everything his way. She followed this thought through and her expression twisted. ''It was you who paid off the judges!'' Of course. She saw it now. Lunging forward, she slashed at his eyes with her fingernails.

Catching her wrist, he gripped it so hard that tears jumped in her eyes. ''We agreed, Lulu.''

"You wanted Remy to lose so you can take him away from me." She wrenched her arm free and tried to catch her breath. "Well, I'm not giving him up. Do you hear me? You're not going to take my son away from me.''

''What the hell are you talking about?''

''We'll see. We'll just see about that.'' No one ever refused Lulu Von Marron anything she wanted, and she wanted Remy to have his music. She wanted to be the mother of the maestro. Rubbing her wrist, she stared across the desk at her husband and calculated what her strategy would be. She had a year to change his mind.

Each time her mother dragged Remy forward, Gloria shared her brother's anguish. Witnessing his torment was unendurable. Turning her eyes away, she made a choking sound.

''Third place is no small change, squirt,'' Gardner Durant said, misunderstanding her expression. ''When you consider the quality of the competition, just making it into the finals was a triumph.''

''He didn't win.''

Gardner's dark eyebrows lifted. ''What is it about you Von Marrons? Is there a rule that states a Von Marron has to win every round? If so, that's unfortunate because life doesn't work that way.''

''Remy was the best.'' The lie, prompted by loyalty, stuck in her throat. Remy's performance had been undeniably flat and had lacked passion.

...lace is no disgrace."

...rejected his attempt at consolation. She had watched
...Durant play polo and, like her, Gardner played to win.
...one of the things she admired about him. But then, she
...ased because she had had a crush on Gardner for years.

...rdner Durant was tall, handsome, and carried himself with
...less ease. Gloria recognized glimpses of Uncle Win in
Gardner's features, but Gardner was more polished, less abrasive than Uncle Win. He possessed warmth and humor that she did not associate with his father, as well as a sense of confidence and self that she did. Once again, she wished she were old enough for him to notice her, wished he would stop calling her squirt.

"Oh Lord, Mummy's doing it again." She bit her lip, hesitated, then hurried forward hoping to rescue Remy before her mother made another toast. "Remy, Senator Jamison asked to speak to you." He looked terrible. His face was ashen and his mouth trembled.

Lulu's grip tightened on Remy's arm and she leaned to his ear. "Don't listen to your father, darling. Everyone knows you won. You were the best." Remy stared at her. His eyes seemed too large for his face. "Be gracious. Accept your accolades. For heaven's sake, darling, enjoy our triumph."

There was something very wrong with her mother's smile. Uneasily, Gloria wondered if anyone else had noticed. Lulu's cheeks were feverish, her eyes shone with a strange heat. With a tiny shock, Gloria wondered if Lulu genuinely believed Remy had won first place.

"Mother, I have to go to my room."

"No, darling. We'll be sitting down to dinner in ten minutes. I've placed you at the head table beside the Windsors."

"Mother, I'm sorry, but . . ."

Eyebrows lifting, Lulu watched him bolt through the crowd and then up the staircase. "I can't imagine what . . ." Noticing Gloria, she glared at her. "Now don't you vanish, too."

But Gloria was already moving through the glittering crowd and up the staircase. 'Remy, wait!" Catching up to him, she leaned against the corridor wall. "Mummy means well. She's just proud of you, that's all."

"I lost." The despair behind his whisper hurt Gloria to hear. "The only person who seems to realize what happened is father. You can fucking well bet he knows I didn't win!"

"Third place is nothing to be—"

"Shut up!" For one shocking instant Gloria thought strike her. They stared at each other as the color drained Remy's face and his hand dropped to his side. "Not you, too His hopelessness devastated her.

"You did your best," she insisted helplessly. Oh God, she wanted to say something to make it better, but she didn't know the right words.

"My best wasn't worth shit. It never has been."

"That isn't true!"

"Liar." The dark fire in his eyes drove her backward. "Just leave me alone, okay? Just go away. You're only making it worse."

The terrible fire continued to burn in his eyes as she slowly backed away from his anger, then suddenly the heat died and his shoulders dropped. "There are no more Von Marron heroes. No more *Life* Magazine covers. Just pale carbons. Redundancies. Go away, Gloria."

Before she stumbled down the stairs, she heard his bedroom door slam.

She was still upset when Lulu's fingers dug into her bare shoulder. "Where is your brother? This is unforgivable. I told him we'd be seated in ten minutes. It's been twenty. How could he embarrass me like this?"

"Mummy, Remy—" The words dried on her lips as the world splintered into slow motion.

First came the explosion.

Then a strange silence as conversation ceased abruptly and polished heads turned toward the staircase. Afterward, Gloria remembered watching Lulu's hair and earrings fly backward as if she were turning swiftly, but in actuality time had slowed. Gloria felt as if she were fighting through knee-high syrup to move forward, a thick sticky substance that sucked and pulled at her legs. Slowly, slowly, she and Bobby and Lulu pushed through the crush of people and converged on the staircase.

They pulled themselves upward, the ascent endless, then Bobby burst through Remy's bedroom door and his heel slid in the blood. Continuing to move in slow motion, he turned and extended his arms to prevent Gloria and Lulu from following, But it was too late.

Now time accelerated, *gathering speed* until the images sped past at an *appalling rate*. Gloria clung to her father's arm as the *horror* ripped through her mind too swiftly to assimilate. She couldn't grasp what she was seeing.

First there was blood. Blood everywhere. On the floor, on the striped wallpaper, soaking the French bed linens. Bright crimson. She saw the shotgun lying between Remy's legs. Saw his bare toes. Then she saw Remy. The top of his head was red and pulpy. Pink and gray matter splattered his pillow and the wall behind the bed frame. Glass fragments crunched beneath her satin slippers and she looked down, blinking at a shattered frame and the *Life* Magazine cover. At torn strips of sheet music. The magazine cover and the sheet music were speckled with tiny red dots.

Then her mother screamed. And screamed and screamed.

Bending forward in the darkness, Gloria clasped her hands around her legs and ground her forehead against her knees. Oh God, oh God. Tremors rippled through her body, her jaw ached from clenching her teeth together.

She didn't know how long she had been here, sitting on the floor of the stone terrace, leaning against the base of the ice sculpture. Numbing cold invaded her where her bare back pressed against the ice. Her skin burned and felt as if it had blistered. When she could not bear the pain a second longer, she leaned forward over her knees until the fire on her skin cooled, then she clenched her teeth and pressed back against the ice.

She kept seeing it. The horror gripped her mind. The blood, the shotgun, Remy lying twisted on the bed. She remembered her father thrusting her away from him and rushing to her mother. She remembered falling in the glass and blood. Because it was easier to grapple with small events than to face the horror of the larger event, she sat on the floor and stared at the speckled *Life* cover, wondering insanely if her mother's screams were orchestrated to follow the bloody scale of tiny red dots.

Her mother's screaming went on and on and on until Dr. Barbeau arrived. From that point, Gloria's memory blurred. People arrived; people tried to depart. There were screams, shouts, a rising hum of whispers. And Debussy playing in her mind behind the strains of ''You Are the Sunshine of My Life.''

Oh God. God. A sob ripped upward from her stomach. The summer of Debussy. He would never play Debussy again. She would never again tell him she loved him. That moment on the staircase—why hadn't she said the words? Why hadn't she simply told him she loved him? Her fingernails dug into her scalp.

''There you are.'' Margaret dropped to her knees on the terrace stones, oblivious to the melting ice water soaking into her dress. "Thank heaven. We've looked everywhere for you. Darling, you're freezing. Come inside now." Shock pinched Margaret's mouth when she looked at the shivering girl. Watery trails of mascara streaked Gloria's face, a rusty stain had dried across her cheek. But it was the agony in her eyes.

"Why? God, God. Why?"

"I don't know. Hush, darling. Come inside and we'll get you warm." She winced as Gloria's nails bit into her arm.

"Where is he? Where did they take him?"

"The coroner's office came with an ambulance, darling. Don't you remember?" Margaret dipped her handkerchief in a puddle forming at the base of the ice sculpture and rubbed at the bloody streak on Gloria's cheek. "Mrs. Durant and Mr. Von Marron are with your mother. Dr. Barbeau gave her a sedative. Mr. Durant has been on the telephone; I think he's with the police now."

"Where's Gardner? And Etta?"

"Shh, it's all right. Etta saw the guests out; now she's with the catering people. Gardner went with Remy," Margaret said, as though it were true. "Darling, the police wish to speak to you. Are you up to it?"

"They want to speak to me?"

Margaret helped her stand and gasped as she saw Gloria's back. Oh Lord. She hoped Dr. Barbeau hadn't left yet. Placing her arm around Gloria's waist, she led her inside then glared at Captain Moore. "You can see for yourself," she snapped. "Miss Von Marron is in no state to be questioned." The girl's body shook uncontrollably.

"I'm sorry, but a statement is necessary. Miss Von Marron was the last to speak to him."

"I was the last . . . oh, my God!" Gloria's voice was thin, and her body went rigid. Hysteria darkened her gray eyes, and her fingernails raked at Margaret's sleeve. "It's my fault!"

"Gloria, no!"

"If I had said the right things—if I hadn't gone back to the party—if I had stayed with him!" Her eyes were wild; she was panting for breath. "He said . . . he said I was making it worse!"

Margaret enfolded her in a fierce protective embrace. "No, darling, no! It's not your fault!" She met Captain Moore's curious stare over Gloria's shoulder. "You little shit," she hissed. Never in her life had she said such a thing. "See what you've done? Get the doctor, she's hysterical."

"We must have—"

"Margaret, take Miss Von Marron upstairs at once."

Winthrop Durant's authority cracked across the room, and Margaret shot him a look of gratitude. She had never been so glad to see anyone in her life.

"You there," Durant's stony gaze fell on one of the uniforms. "Send Dr. Barbeau to Miss Von Marron's room."

"I think the doctor left, sir."

"Then get him back here," Durant said coldly. He turned to Captain Moore. "Miss Von Marron will give no statement." His expression did not change when Gloria fainted into William's arms as William rushed forward, his butler's tie opened for the first time in memory. "I believe it's time we had a little chat, captain." Durant removed a cigar from his breast pocket and examined it. "What we have here is a hunting accident."

Captain Moore swore. "A hunting accident?"

"Precisely. The newspapers will phone for confirmation." Expecting the captain to follow, Durant moved toward Bobby's study. "We'll have a drink and prepare your statement."

The day of the funeral dawned hot and overcast. A thin deck of clouds filtered the heat; the air was so humid it tasted liquid. Before nine o'clock the temperature had soared into the eighties, wilting the flowers that arrived every few minutes. Their thick, cloying fragrance pervaded the house and collected in the stairwell.

Gloria swallowed a rush of saliva and pressed her hand to her waist. The heavy sweetness of the wilting flowers sickened her. All she could think of was trying to control the churning in her stomach until Durant and her father entered the foyer where she waited.

"Daddy!" Running forward, she threw herself into his arms and clung to him, pressing her face against the lapels of his black silk suit. This was the first time she had seen him since that terrible night. Margaret and Chissie Durant had kept her away from Bobby's study and away from Lulu whom Dr. Barbeau kept heavily sedated.

Bobby patted her shoulder awkwardly. Finally he lifted her face and tried to speak but failed. Bewildered, he gave Gloria a gentle push toward Margaret, then turned aside and fumbled for his handkerchief. Winthrop Durant cleared his throat in the silence.

"William will drive the family. Chissie, Gardner, and I will follow in our car. Bill Smith will drive the household staff. After the service, we will return to Goose Point for the interment. The site service will be brief and should conclude before any guests arrive. A light buffet will be served on the terrace.'' Pushing back his dark sleeve, he glanced at his watch. ''Etta, will you see what's keeping Mrs. Durant and Mrs. Von Marron?''

Gloria stood beside Gardner at the door, looking outside. She focused steadfastly on the limousines and did not glance toward the mound of raw earth atop the spit of land that jutted into the Sound. She didn't yet know how she felt about Remy being buried at Goose Point. It was what her mother wanted. Lulu had insisted.

''Margaret said you're going to deliver the eulogy,'' she said to Gardner as he slid an arm around her waist. Outside, William rubbed a piece of flannel over one of the limousine's fenders. He wore a black band over his uniform sleeve.

''Yes.'' Gardner answered in a thick, moist voice she didn't recognize.

Then everyone turned to face the staircase.

Chissie Durant descended first. Her pale lips were pressed into a line, and she glanced first at Bobby and then at Durant with a tiny shake of her head. At the foot of the stairs, she took Durant's arm and looked back up the staircase.

Gloria sucked in a breath and felt her stomach cramp. Lulu paused above them as she always did when making an entrance. But she was wearing red. She wore a scarlet satin dinner suit and a tiny matching cocktail hat with a veil that reached to her brows. Red, red lipstick slashed across her mouth like a smear of blood.

A brilliant smile curved her bloodred lips. ''Hello, darlings. Did we keep everyone waiting?'' Gloria's shocked gaze dropped to the rag doll cradled in her mother's arms. It was one of hers, taken from the shelf above her bed where it had been forgotten years ago. Lulu adjusted a limp yarn curl on the doll's forehead. ''Naughty boy. We're late.''

Gloria bit down on the fingers of her gloves. She couldn't move, couldn't breathe. She felt frightened and sick.

''God.'' Bobby closed his eyes then drew a breath and stepped up beside his wife. Lulu moved backward. ''Darling,'' he said, ''you look lovely, as always. But don't you think something in a darker color would be more appropriate?''

For a moment Lulu looked confused. ''Red is Remy's favorite color. I don't want to disappoint him.'' Clasping the doll to her breast, she leaned forward to inspect Bobby's attire. "You look rather drab, darling. So funereal. A striped tie would be better, don't you think? Perhaps something in rose or green."

"Lulu," Bobby leaned against the polished bannister, touched her shoulder. "We have to leave now. If you'll give me the doll, I'll take it back upstairs."

"No."

"You don't want to take that thing to the church. If you'll just give it to me, I'll—"

A long sound hissed from her throat. "You'd like that, wouldn't you?" Her lips pulled away from her teeth. "But you aren't going to take my baby. Not this time. Remy is mine!"

Win Durant stared. "Jesus Christ," he said softly. Chissie covered her eyes.

Watching her father, Gloria suddenly knew how he would look in twenty years. He looked older than Gloria had ever seen him.

"If it means that much, we'll take the doll with us," he said.

Lulu made soft crooning sounds. She rocked the doll against her red satin breast. "You aren't going to take my baby?" Mistrust narrowed her eyes.

"I won't take your baby."

After she had considered his promise, Lulu straightened her shoulders and examined the small group standing at the bottom of the staircase looking up at her. A dazzling smile illuminated her features when she spotted Gloria. "Chissie! Did you come to play?"

"Mummy?"

Lulu swept down the steps and embraced her, enveloping her in a cloud of musky perfume. She wrapped her arm around Gloria's and led her onto the veranda then toward the first limousine. "The tea set you liked so well is broken," Lulu confided brightly. "But Mama promised us another."

Wide-eyed, Gloria peered over her shoulder as Lulu bent into the car. "Daddy?"

"Oh, God. I don't know, I just . . . Christ!"

The drive into the city seemed endless. Gloria pressed into the corner of the seat and listened to her mother's silvery voice babbling nonsense that frightened her.

"After the party, we'll stop by the Palm Court for tea. Remy adores the Palm Court." Lulu smiled down at the doll cradled in her lap. "I know! We'll have a party to celebrate Remy winning the competition! Yes. The Duke and Duchess will be at

Pauline's that weekend; the Duke has always admired Remy. Chissie? Do you have my purse?'' Gloria shrank into the seat and twisted her gloves. ''There's a note pad and pen in my purse. Oh, never mind, I'll remember.''

She couldn't take her eyes off her mother. She whispered, ''Daddy?''

''Where is Remy?'' Lulu demanded suddenly, interrupting her plans for the party. ''Bobby, I insist you speak to him. He should be here with us, it's his party after all. Where is he?''

The ride went on and on. No one spoke except Lulu. ''He should be here,'' she repeated in a petulant voice. Her long fingers, never still, stroked the doll, pulled and tugged at its clothing and yarn hair.

''Daddy?'' Gloria swallowed hard. ''I think I'm going to be sick.''

''An ice sculpture,'' Lulu exclaimed brightly. ''Something grand, I think.''

''Don't be sick, Gloria.'' Leaning forward, elbows on knees, Bobby covered his eyes with both hands. ''I can't handle anything more.''

She closed her eyes and concentrated on forcing the sour taste back into her throat. Finally, William eased the limousine to the curb in front of St. James Church, followed by the Durants and the household staff. They stepped to the pavement and waited while Bobby attempted to coax the doll from Lulu's arms. People paused on the church steps to stare at Lulu's scarlet satin dinner suit and the dirty yarn doll she held clutched to her breast.

''You always tried to steal him from me!'' Lulu bent into a protective crouch. Spittle flew from her red lips. ''From the first you were jealous that Remy loved me more than you!'' Bobby glanced at the audience gathering on the steps. A dark flush rose from his collar. ''You'll never get him away from me. Never!''

Gloria was certain her knees would have collapsed if Gardner Durant had not taken her arm. She leaned on him and tears filled her eyes as Uncle Win moved between her father and mother. He pulled Chissie forward.

''Let her keep the goddamn doll. Just get her inside,'' Durant said quietly. Turning, he offered his hand. ''Henry, good of you to come. Arthur, the family appreciates it.'' Kissinger and Burns peered at Lulu over Durant's shoulder.

''Jesus,'' Bee Bee Halston said, loud enough for everyone on the steps to overhear. ''Look what Lulu is wearing.'' She paused a beat. ''Imagine—wearing red to a funeral. Doesn't she own anything pink?'' The purred remark would be repeated with gleeful relish for weeks to come. A few muffled snickers erupted. Icy hatred hardened Gloria's eyes; she would not forget Bee Bee Halston.

At last, thank God, they moved inside the church. Remy's closed coffin gleamed under the soft lights above the altar. Artfully positioned spots illuminated an acre of flower arrangements. Hidden speakers played Debussy.

Gloria remembered snatches of the service and the interminable drive back to Goose Point. She remembered Gardner Durant standing at the velvet-draped lectern looking young and handsome and devastated. She remembered the soft rose-colored light glowing across the casket's brass fittings. And the sober young men wearing navy blazers and Ivy Club ties who carried Remy to the car waiting outside. She remembered Lulu humming through the service, her red-tipped fingers continually caressing the rag doll.

She recalled a few words from the interment atop the land spit at Goose Point, remembered masses of hushed people moving through the house. Then, finally, it was over, and she was standing alone in the living room, pulling petals off a spray of white roses while William moved around the room emptying ashtrays. Lulu was upstairs, collapsed in drugged sleep; Bobby was drunk in his den.

''William?'' She examined the petal in her palm. ''Do you think Mummy is crazy?''

''I wouldn't know, Miss.''

Because she couldn't bear his pity, she crushed the petal in her hand and flung it from her, then she ran from the room and up the stairs to her bedroom. After throwing off the black linen dress Chissie Durant had bought for her, Gloria pulled on a pair of shorts and a light sweater. If she remained in the house another minute, she would start screaming, and she didn't know if she would be able to stop. Running, she sprinted across the veranda, through the gardens, and down the stone steps to the beach.

Twilight shadows tinted the water a deep lavender. Without pausing, Gloria strode directly to the edge of the purplish water and sucked in a sharp breath as the cold waves washed over her toes.

It would be so easy, she thought, closing her eyes. All she had to do was walk forward then swim until she was too exhausted to think about Remy's empty room or Lulu's craziness or Bobby's hollow eyes. No one would notice a swimmer in the deepening darkness; no one would miss her. Hypnotized by the waves, she stepped forward.

"I thought you had more courage."

Heart pounding against her ribs, she spun toward the sea wall and the sharp voice. "Gardner?"

"A life for a life, is that the plan? You drown and Remy magically reappears?" She heard the disgust thickening his voice. Water spilled around her calves, icy against her hot skin. "Go ahead. Another death will make your parents feel a whole lot better, won't it? Just what they need. Two suicides to cope with. Sure. That will solve everything."

Now she saw the shadowy bottle of Scotch pushed into the sand beside him. "You're drunk," she said.

"You could say that. But not drunk enough to do something as stupid and futile as walking into the Sound. And I thought you were a bright girl."

Anger forced a rush of adrenaline through her body. "Shut up, Gardner, just shut up! You don't know what you're talking about."

"Okay, then suppose you tell me."

She couldn't read his expression. He was only a dark shape against the darker stones forming the sea wall. Hysteria welled up in her throat, and she shouted at the shadows draping the sand and wall. "Are you too drunk to guess? It's my fault! I was the last one to speak to Remy. I could have stopped him!"

"Oh, I get it. Because you didn't stop him, you deserve to die, too." The Scotch bottle lifted, then descended to the sand. "Exactly how would you have stopped him?"

"I should have said what he needed to hear." Her hands flew outward in a helpless gesture. "If I had said the right words, Remy would be alive now!"

"What are the right words, Gloria? I need to know. Because I could have said them, too. I was there. I talked to him backstage at Carnegie; I talked to him at the party. Tell me the right words. What should I have said that would have saved Remy's life?"

Finally she heard the anguish and the guilt, as sharp and piercing as her own. "You, too?" she whispered.

"Of course, me, too. Did you think you were the only person beating yourself? You're goddamn right, me, too. I was Remy's best friend. I knew him better than anyone else. But I didn't stop him from blowing his fucking head off, did I?''

"Oh, God.'' She covered her eyes. Despair pushed against her shoulders. "I wish to God it had been me instead.''

"That's very good, Gloria. Now we move from guilt to self-pity.''

Shock snapped her head upward. When she could speak, she screamed at him. "Damn you! Just shut up! If I died no one would notice. No one would go crazy or make scenes. Remy was the golden boy, the family's future.'' Striding up the sand, she stopped and glared down at him. "The world revolved around Remy. I envied him, did you know that? And can you guess how it makes me feel now? I wanted Remy's life. I wanted my life to count for something, too. I wanted Mummy and Daddy to notice *me*!''

"If you want Remy's life, then take it. I understand there's a vacancy. At least do something better with your own life than throwing it away by walking into the Sound.''

Tears of anger and helplessness spilled over her lashes. "Remy's death doesn't create a vacancy I can fill. Do you want to know what's expected of me? Planning and attending parties, then a suitable husband and a suitable heir, then a lifetime of planning and attending more parties. Just like Mummy. Just like . . .'' Sobs tore upward from her chest.

"Oh, Christ,'' Gardner said softly. "Come here.'' Reaching out, he caught her wrist and pulled her down on the sand beside him. Overcoming her resistance, he pressed her head against his shoulder. "I apologize. I'm mad at the world, and I'm taking it out on you.'' He stroked her hair away from her face, patted her back. "I've had too much to drink, and I probably won't say this well, but listen anyway, okay?'' For a moment, he rested his chin on top of her hair. "I'll tell you what I told Remy; maybe you'll hear it. Your life is your own, Gloria. You can throw it away like Remy did, or you can make it into whatever you want it to be.''

"It's not that easy.''

"I'm not saying it's easy. If Remy were here, I think he'd tell you to say the hell with all those parties if you don't want them. Build a life that's satisfying to you. What do you want?''

"I don't know yet,'' she said eventually. This conversation would have been impossible anywhere but here, in the dark, with his arms around her.

"Think about it. Is there a rule that says you can't have Remy's life? I don't believe it. Go ahead, take over Home Limited someday. Grab Wall Street by the throat if that's what you want. Who says you can't do it?''

"Tradition, society, my parents."

"Those are excuses. If no one expects anything from you, then start expecting things from yourself."

His words carried the solemn conviction of drunken profundity, well intentioned, but more easily voiced than acted upon. Still, listening made Gloria feel better than she had in days. Abruptly, she realized Gardner's arm was still around her waist. She could hear his steady strong heartbeat beneath her ear. His breath stirred her hair. Scarlet blossomed in her cheeks, and she was glad it was dark.

"Thank you," she said stiffly, easing away from him. Bending forward, she pretended to slap at sand fleas.

"Feeling better?"

Oddly, she was.

Gardner caught a strand of hair that had pulled loose from her ponytail and gave it a tug. "We aren't going to punish ourselves with any more guilt. And we aren't going to stay angry at Remy for what he did."

Her head jerked. She had believed she was the only person in the world small enough and mean enough to be furious at someone who had died.

"He shouldn't have done this to us, but we'll forgive him." Bending forward, Gardner looked at her, and Gloria had the impression he was seeing her, really seeing her for the first time in years. "You are going to be very, very beautiful, Miss Von Marron. A real heartbreaker." When he spoke again, his voice had thickened and dropped in register. He gripped the neck of the Scotch bottle and turned his head away. "I think you should return to the house, squirt. Now."

The words stung. She had been so certain he would kiss her. Awkwardly she scrambled to her feet and brushed the sand from her legs. "Thank you for trying to help."

"Think about what I said."

"I will."

Gardner Durant had not convinced her that she was blameless for Remy's death, but he had shown her a way to atone for her fault. For that, she would always be grateful.

Chapter 3

 *F*ROWNING, DURANT LOOKED AT Bobby Von Marron and then cursed beneath his breath. Clearly, he should not have insisted Von Marron be presented for the meeting with Helen Whitehall. Von Marron looked like shit. His pale eyes were red-rimmed, strands of hair dropped across his forehead, and there was a spot on his tie.

Stepping backward on the thick mauve carpeting, Durant glanced up at the floor indicator above the elevator doors. "How is Lulu?"

"She's still obsessed with that doll. She eats with it, sleeps with it, takes it to visit Remy's grave. I wish to Christ I'd never agreed to have Remy interred at Goose Point."

"She needs therapy," Durant said bluntly. "You knew it a year ago when she lifted that bracelet from Tiffany's and when she wandered through Bergdorf Goodman wearing only a slip." The elevator doors slid open. "Think about it."

"Hello, Win. Bobby." Helen Whitehall stepped off the elevator and extended a kid-gloved hand. A fur hat covered her auburn hair; fur draped her shoulders.

Only Helen Whitehall would wear sable before the leaves had turned color, Durant thought, amused. Dropping his gaze, he studied her silky legs as she preceded them into the small, elegantly posh room he had chosen for the meeting. Cut crystal and imported Tudor paneling glowed softly beneath carefully recessed lighting. He remembered those long legs wrapped around his waist. Helen Whitehall was one hell of a lay; he almost regretted dropping her.

Coffee was served in the firm's gold-rimmed Sèvres cups and condolences were exchanged. The idea of Helen as a grieving widow brought a smile to Durant's lips. The Whitehalls hadn't

35

lived together in years, not that Helen had permitted herself to become lonely. Her latest interest was an Argentinian polo player who had attended Yale with her son.

Ordinarily Bobby would have opened the conversation with a concoction of social chitchat that gradually led toward business, at which time Durant would have taken over the meeting. But today Bobby sat slouched in a wing chair, more interested in doodling across the pad propped on his knee than in learning how Helen Whitehall planned to rob them.

"Small talk isn't my strong point," Durant said, turning away from Bobby. He kept his voice pleasant, conversational. "What's the agenda, Helen?"

Dark lashes swept her cheeks as she opened her purse and withdrew a gold cigarette case. "I'm unhappy about the partnership buy-back agreement."

"Talk to the attorneys." He lit her cigarette.

"They say the buy-back is ironclad."

"It is."

"But, darling, I don't want to be bought out." Leaning back, she crossed her legs, drawing his attention to the seductive expanse of dark-tinted silk stockings and the hint of creamy flesh above. The fur slipped from her shoulders and exposed a collar draped to display the tops of her breasts. "I'd like to propose an alternate arrangement."

"Such as?" So far she wasn't saying anything he hadn't expected. Enjoying himself, Durant stared at her breasts as he was intended to do. He listened and agreed that Edison Whitehall had been brilliant, had made a significant contribution to the firm, and, as one of the four partners, had added prestige and credibility to the firm. It didn't surprise him when she suggested retaining Edison's partnership interests in a trust fund for Edison's sons.

"With you as interim beneficiary, of course." Maybe he would drop by her country place one weekend and fuck her for old times' sake. One for the road.

"Of course." A feline smile lit her eyes. "I'm so pleased we're thinking along the same lines, darling." Neither of them included Bobby in the conversation.

"The firm would never agree to your proposal, Helen. The buy-back agreement stands." Not for a moment did he believe they had reached the main event.

Helen's eyes narrowed and she regarded him through a curl of cigarette smoke. "Tell me, Win. How high was the partner's

bonus last March? Two million each? Three or four million?"
A polished finger tapped her cigarette over the ashtray.

"Forget it." Amused, he pretended to listen as she continued
the argument, but they both recognized that she argued without
genuine conviction. "This is entertaining, my dear," he said,
glancing at his watch, "but I have another appointment in thirty
minutes. Let's cut to the bottom line, shall we?"

"You're a nasty bastard, Durant," she said, smiling. "All
right, bottom line. The poor widow wants a bonus of five million on top of the partnership buy-back. Cash."

He stared at her. "Bobby? I want you to hear this." This time
he didn't offer to light her cigarette. "Or what?"

"Or I go to the newspapers with the truth about how and
where poor dear Edison met his unfortunate end." She released
a stream of smoke toward the chandeliers. "And where you
were at the time, dear Win."

"You're bluffing."

"Wouldn't the newspapers just adore it? Wouldn't Chissie? A
nice, juicy sex scandal involving the partners at La Tourraine,
Durant and Von Marron. While partner A is screwing partner
B's wife, partner B is getting it off in a homo bathhouse. It's so
damned good he dies mid-orgasm. Then, and the papers will
love this bit of skulduggery, partner A gets out of partner B's
bed and spirits partner B's dead body out of the bathhouse and
back to the firm, to make it appear as if partner B died harnessed
to his desk instead of to a massage table. Now gentlemen, how
do you suppose the firm's cherished blue-chip clients will react
to this sordid little tale?"

Durant stared. If a man were powerful enough and successful
enough, he could bugger twelve-year-olds so long as he did it
privately. Half the Street might snicker over drinks, but business
went on as usual. But let a whisper of a man's personal perver-
sions go public and the rules changed abruptly. The public demanded that Wall Street maintain the fiction that the world's
power brokers were men of unbending dignity and integrity.
When the public's confidence was shaken, heads rolled and
money dried up. Clients evaporated and old-line houses crashed.

Bobby startled them by speaking. "Win is right. You wouldn't
put your sons through a nasty personal scandal."

"Wouldn't I?" Coolly, Helen met his eyes. "Try me, Bobby.
Do you really suppose anything I did would surprise them?"

"You'd get tarred with the same brush, Helen." Durant looked
at her. "I'd make certain of it."

"The way I see it, gentlemen, La Tourraine, Durant and Von Marron owes me for fifteen years service. The only reason I didn't divorce Edison fifteen years ago is because it would have embarrassed the firm. I'll be angry, very angry, Win darling, if the firm denies that debt. If you think I won't go public, you're wrong. I'll create a scandal like this town hasn't enjoyed in a long, long time. Before I'm finished you won't have a dozen clients willing to admit they ever knew you or did business with La Tourraine, Durant and Von Marron. And, Win, I'll love every minute of it."

Bobby spoke into the lengthening silence. "Pay her."

Durant jerked. Angry knots jumped along his jawline. "She's talking through her ass," he said coldly. "The minute a story like this hits print, she's persona non grata on both sides of the pond. As dead as Edison."

"Pay her." Losing interest, Bobby dropped his head and studied his doodle pad.

"You heard the money man," Helen purred. "Darling, this meeting is happily adjourned."

"Fuck you."

"Anytime." Laughing, she dropped her cigarette case into her purse. "You have my number." A plummy French perfume enveloped him as she stood and adjusted her furs. "When may I expect my bonus?"

"Ask Von Marron."

"I'm asking you."

Five million above the millions required to buy in Edison's stock? "I'll need some time."

"I'm a reasonable woman. Let's say Christmas, shall we?"

After she had gone, Durant reached for the telephone beside his chair. "Mrs. Ivory, call the chairman of the New York Federal Reserve and cancel my appointment. Also, reschedule the lunch with Lehman and Morgan, and postpone the meeting with Troubridge's arbitrage group. Send up some Scotch and ice."

"Look at me, Von Marron." The control for which he was famed wavered on the edge. He heard it in his voice. "If ever again you countermand me in front of a third party, I will see that you regret it for the rest of your fucking life. Is that understood? I will not tolerate another incident like this one."

Bobby blinked. "Threats, Win?" he asked softly.

"If you disagree with my decisions, we will discuss your objection privately. You do not overturn my decisions publicly. Not ever."

''Have you considered what Helen's revelations would do to Chissie?''

''Helen was bluffing,'' he said flatly.

''Can we take that risk?''

Every day the firm accepted risks that made Helen's threat trivial. If Bobby didn't understand that now, he never would. But Von Marron had no interest and no understanding of the technical side of business. What he did, and did better than anyone else, was lunch. Bobby Von Marron could extract more information over a couple of martinis and a poached salmon than Durant's best floor man could discover in three twelve-hour days. And Von Marron was on intimate terms with old money on two continents; he was unequaled as a client source. But the guts of investment banking were as alien to him as an empty pocket.

''All right.'' Durant drained his Scotch and ran a hand through his hair. ''It's done. Now the question becomes: where do we find an additional five million dollars? And does La Tourraine take an equal share of this?''

''Georges didn't figure in Edison's death. Helen is our problem.''

The reply was tactfully phrased. But if Bobby Von Marron was willing to take a piece of Helen's blackmail, so should La Tourraine. Leaning back in his chair, Durant pinched the bridge of his nose. Georges La Tourraine accepted the prestige of heading the Paris office, and he sure as hell accepted his yearly bonus; he should damned well accept his share of the firm's problems. But the argument was futile. La Tourraine was one of Von Marron's blind spots.

In point of fact, Georges La Tourraine was too lucky to live. It wasn't enough that he possessed one of the oldest aristocratic names in Europe, or that he had been born swaddled in wealth and privilege. The bastard also had luck. Georges should have died during the war, but Von Marron had been there to save his ass, and Von Marron had been carrying him since. Durant carried them both.

From the day it opened, the Paris office had lost money or had shown only marginal profits. Investment banking didn't prosper when the man presumably in charge couldn't trouble himself to take an interest. La Tourraine's reckless theory that business could be conducted from the bed of a client's wife had proved so much horseshit.

Gall flooded Durant's mouth. Each time he looked at the firm's letterhead, acid poured into his stomach. As long as he lived he would resent that La Tourraine's name took precedence over his own. Now the bastard was going to take another free ride.

"We can't take the money out of the firm," he said finally. The doodle pad enraged him; he wanted to slap it out of Bobby's hands. "Putting the accountants aside for the moment, we're not as strongly capitalized as we have been in the past, or as we should be. We put ten million into the back office, and last spring we spent eighteen million upgrading the trading room systems." Moreover, the bond market had collapsed, and the firm had taken a beating on the last two syndicate books.

"Perhaps we're trying to expand services too rapidly."

Durant made himself look away from the doodle pad. "If we remain a specialty boutique, we won't be able to compete."

"Then maybe it's time we took the firm public."

And make La Tourraine one of the world's richest men? "I don't think so. In the future, yes, but not now. Going public is an ace we aren't ready to put on the table."

More and more privately held firms were going public, usually prompted by the need for an infusion of capital. The possible sums were enormous, and the money poured in seemingly overnight. But restructuring meant the formation of a board, and in many cases the original partners found themselves squeezed out. Going public made sense as the privately held houses were moving in the direction of the dinosaurs. But not yet. Among the blue-chip houses, La Tourraine, Durant and Von Marron ranked above First Boston and just below Goldman Sachs. The firm still had an edge.

"Then we'll have to use private funds." Bobby bent over the doodle pad and meticulously drew a star above an inverted U that reminded Durant of a tombstone.

"Christ." Von Marron made it sound childishly simple. "Neither of us are that liquid."

"Sell some of my shares in Home Limited."

Just like that. Durant leaned back. "You missed another Home board meeting Tuesday. Because you didn't show, they had to postpone. Don't miss next Monday, Bobby. There's a situation brewing in Uganda; the North Sea drilling leases need to be reviewed; and a new head of the South American mining and lumber division needs to be appointed."

"Vote my proxy."

"Bobby, your grandfather created Home Limited, your father gave his life to it. Is it too much to ask that you occasionally appear for a board meeting?'' Now wasn't the time for a lecture. Moreover, they had already had this conversation too many times to count. "Shit." Durant released a breath. "All right. I'll vote your proxy."

"This thing with Helen . . ." Standing, Bobby dropped a heavy hand on Durant's shoulder. "Take care of it, Win."

Von Marron committed them to a five-million-dollar ball breaker, then dropped the problem in his lap. "If I raise the money by selling shares of Home, Bobby, that will take your family position down to about sixty-five percent. Give or take."

For the first time in days Bobby's lips curved in a thin smile. "The sound you hear is my father and grandfather spinning in their graves."

The day after the funeral the gardener planted a beech tree beside Remy's grave. Yesterday, a marble bench had been delivered and positioned beneath the tree a few feet from the marble rectangle that covered Remy. Approaching quietly, Gloria sat on the bench, clasping a spray of garden roses in her hands.

For the third consecutive day, Lulu was lying on top of the grave. Watching her mother made Gloria feel hot and queasy inside. Today Lulu wore a straw hat that had crushed against the slab and the flowing organdy Scaasi she had worn to the Regatta Ball. Yesterday, she had chosen a satin peignoir trimmed with Valenciennes lace, arranging the folds across the grave slab while workmen cemented the bench in place. The day before, she had worn an exquisite lace point Balmain.

Gloria bit the inside of her cheek and turned her face toward the water. Everyone said her mother would get better. No one hinted that Lulu was crazy. No one suggested it was odd or abnormal to spend all day lying on top of a grave. As long as no one said anything, Gloria could make herself believe everything might turn out all right.

"Go away." Lulu flicked a look toward the bench then returned her gaze to the cloudless sky.

Gloria gripped the roses a little tighter. "Mummy, I was wondering . . . when are we going back to New York?"

School had already started. For the first time she was eager to return. She longed for routine hours and routine tasks, for a regimen that could be predicted.

"You're just like your father. You and Bobby may be willing to leave Remy and forget him, but I'm not." The organdy sleeve swept up to cover Lulu's eyes. "I won't leave him. He's the only person who ever loved me."

"Please don't cry, Mummy. Everyone loves you." The moment reminded her of that night in the hallway with Remy. She wanted desperately to help, to say the right words. But she didn't know the right words. "I love you."

"You. You don't count."

Pain and shock stopped the words on her lips. It was one thing to think something, another to hear it confirmed. Gloria gripped the roses so hard that petals fluttered to the ground.

"I'm so tired," Lulu murmured beneath her sleeve. "Play Debussy for me, darling. Play Debussy so Mummy can rest."

"I count," Gloria whispered.

"Who's there?" Lulu lifted her sleeve a short distance. "I told you to go away."

"I count!" The roses spilled to the grass when she pushed to her feet. Deliberately, she crushed a blossom under her heel then ran toward the house.

Gloria learned about Helen Whitehall's blackmail the way she learned about everything of importance, by eavesdropping. The moment Uncle Win's car rolled away down the driveway, she ran into her father's study and confronted him, her cheeks flushed with anger.

"You can't do it. Daddy, you can't sell off Home Limited to pay Uncle Win's blackmail!"

"You were listening?" Looking up from his gin and tonic, he frowned at her.

"The blackmail is Uncle Win's problem, not ours. Why should you have to sell Home stock to bail him out? He's the one who screwed Mrs. Whitehall, not you."

"Good God. What kind of talk is that from a fourteen-year-old?"

Kneeling beside his chair, she clasped his hand and looked up at him. "Daddy. Grandpa Robert took Home partly public to expand the overseas divisions, but I heard him tell Remy a dozen times that he regretted it and that Remy should never let the family percentage fall below seventy." Tears of anger and frustration brimmed in her eyes. "If Uncle Georges isn't part of this, why should you be?"

"Jesus Christ. How long have you been listening at doors? Gloria, you don't understand any of this."

"I understand you're paying the full five million."

"Win signed a note for his half."

"At two points under the current interest rate."

Bobby stared at her and swore. "How do you know these things?"

"Daddy, please. I understand why Uncle Win has to pay the blackmail. The firm stands or falls on its reputation. But why do you have to be part of it? Uncle Win is using you."

Her father slapped her.

They stared at each other in shock. Then Gloria lifted a trembling hand to her cheek. No one had ever struck her.

"I will not hear a single word spoken against Winthrop Durant. Not ever." Bobby's face had paled and his voice was unsteady, but he continued. "Win Durant is the finest man I have ever known. The most brilliant, the most loyal, the best. He has done more for this family than you will ever know. You wouldn't be here now if he hadn't saved my life during the war."

"Grandpa repaid that debt. He sent Uncle Win through Princeton." Her own voice emerged thin and nearly inaudible. She sounded very, very young.

"Nothing can repay the debt this family owes Win Durant. Win is my business partner and my oldest and dearest friend. I will never believe a word against him. To suggest his honor and integrity could be questioned is reprehensible! Go to your room, Gloria."

"Daddy, please listen—"

"Now!"

For one terrible instant, she thought he would strike her again. Slowly she backed from the room, then ran blindly up the staircase, choking on a rush of tears, struggling with the shock of the last few minutes.

Holding her cheek, she lay on her bed and wept. Eventually, she conceded everything her father had said was true. Uncle Win had always been there for the Von Marrons and he always would be. The family owed him much.

But Gloria sensed she was right also. Win Durant was using her father. For the first time she admitted what she had known for a long time but had refused to acknowledge. Her father was not a businessman. Bobby Von Marron was handsome, cultured, a gifted athlete, and a man possessing tremendous old-school charm. He made a perfect outside man for the firm. But he was not a businessman.

Finally she began to comprehend why her father had pushed Remy so hard toward the family firms. He wanted a Von Marron at the helm of the Von Marron holdings, but he knew it could never be himself. He had wanted Remy to succeed where he had failed. The hopelessness of it freshened her grief.

After a time she rose from her bed and stood at her bedroom window staring down at her mother lying on top of Remy's grave.

Later, Gloria washed her face, combed her hair, and went downstairs to apologize to her father.

"Remember this, darling," her father said when she lapsed into an uncomfortable silence. The sharp smell of gin punctuated his words. "Win Durant is the best friend this family has or ever will have. If you ever need help and I'm not there, go to Win. You can count on him."

"I'll remember." Neither of them mentioned the slap.

"She's worse, isn't she?"

"Yes." Bobby stood before the window, looking toward the beech tree and the marble bench. "Barbeau keeps her so drugged she can't put on her makeup. Etta Nelson does it for her. Every day she goes out there and lies on Remy's grave." Letting the draperies fall, he reached for the decanter on his desktop. "She blames me for Remy's death."

"Maybe she blames herself." Durant folded his hands across his waist, watching as Bobby refilled his glass.

"Who knows? She can't sleep, won't eat. She's lost fifteen pounds. I suggested we visit Georges and Thérèse in Paris, get away for a while. But she won't leave Remy. Last night she accused me of having an affair with Bee Bee Halston or Delores McClaire."

Durant smiled. "Maybe Bee Bee is just what the doctor ordered."

"This is my vice." Bobby raised his glass. "Lulu won't believe it, but I've never been unfaithful to her. She's the only woman I ever wanted or cared about."

"I drove out to tell you about the Home directors' meeting," Durant said, opening the portfolio on his lap.

Bobby looked at him, then laughed. "It's true, Win, you have all the charm of a mongrel dog."

"I've never pretended otherwise."

"Do you know what they say about you on the Street? They say Win Durant would walk over his crippled mother to cut a deal. They say pure poison runs in your veins."

Durant grinned. "Who says that?"

"Your friends. Your enemies are less kind."

"As one friend to another, aren't you hitting that pretty hard?" Durant nodded toward the gin decanter.

Bobby's shrug was eloquent. "Not everyone is as admirably detached as you. Some of us have to wallow in the pain. We have to punish ourselves with it. This helps."

"For how long, Bobby?"

His laugh was harsh. "For as long as it takes."

For some reason eavesdropping was worse in someone else's house than in her own. Uncertain how to handle the situation, Gloria gazed down the corridor, wishing she were on the far side of Uncle Win and Aunt Chissie's bedroom door. She had to pass their door to reach the staircase. Pausing, she stood quietly and wondered if she could slip past without being seen or overheard.

"I imagine you've had a few flirtations over the years." It was Chissie's soft voice. Gloria looked at the door and held her breath. She wished she had remained at Goose Point instead of coming into town.

"Oh for Christ's sake, Chissie. You find a diamond clip in the car and build an entire scenario around it. I told you—the clip belongs to Mrs. Aldridge, a client. She's older than Methuselah, a crone."

"I've suspected a few times, but there was never anything concrete."

"Chissie—"

"No, Win, let me say this." In the ensuing pause, Gloria tried to slip past the door, but her shoe creaked and she froze. Above the sound of her heartbeat, she heard Chissie draw a breath. "I know I've never been exciting in bed. I guess I couldn't blame you much if you had someone else." Durant swore. "I just—no, let me say it—I just don't want you to rub my nose in it. Don't embarrass me, Win."

"The clip belongs to Mrs. Aldridge. I don't know what else to tell you."

"I can't endure the thought of my friends sitting over lunch saying, 'poor Chissie'. If I believed there was any possibility of that happening, Win, I'd divorce you. You have to understand that I mean it. The firm wouldn't matter, nothing would matter. I can't bear the idea of anyone laughing at me or pitying me."

"Chissie—the only woman I care about is you."

"I know you care about me. I also know you're a man with

large appetites.'' A pleading note entered her voice. ''I just don't want to know about it. No more diamond clips, Win. If I know, I'll have to do something about it.''

Carefully, quietly, Gloria retreated down the corridor, opened the door of the guest room and slammed it. She dropped her purse, then dropped it again for good measure. Making as much noise as possible, she passed the silence behind Uncle Win and Aunt Chissie's door, then hurried down the staircase.

Once outside the building, she jammed her hands in her coat pockets and drew a long breath of cold air. Some Thanksgiving this was going to be, she thought, turning toward the traffic rushing along Fifth Avenue. Uncle Win had been in New York less than an hour and already he and Aunt Chissie were arguing, Gardner wasn't expected until just before dinner, and her parents hadn't arrived yet.

She had stayed overnight with Aunt Chissie because Uncle Win was in London, and Aunt Chissie had insisted she didn't like to stay in the penthouse alone. Gloria suspected this wasn't true. She thought it more likely Chissie had wanted to get her away from Goose Point and, as guilty as it made her feel, she had jumped at the chance to escape. Aunt Chissie had taken her to the Russian Tea Room for dinner and then to Lincoln Center to the ballet. Gloria had loved every minute.

Ducking her head and steadfastly not allowing herself to recall the conversation she had overheard, she strode toward Fifth Avenue, crossed against the light, and entered Central Park.

At the first bridge she stopped and crossed her arms on the stone railing, frowning toward the twin towers of the San Remo.

Everything was wrong. Her mother wasn't getting better. Her father didn't go into the city anymore. Even though Margaret had discussed the matter with her father, Gloria still wasn't in school; and the first term had almost ended. This was the first year she could remember when they hadn't closed Goose Point at the end of August and returned to New York.

The worst thing—the terrible, disloyal, worst thing—was that she had begun to secretly wonder if the Von Marrons had ever been a normal, happy family. She wanted to think so, and sometimes she remembered it that way. But deep inside she wasn't certain. If they had been the happy, close family she longed to remember, could everything have gone this wrong? Unconsciously, she lifted a hand to the cheek her father had slapped.

''There you are. Mother said I might find you here.''

''Gardner! You arrived early.''

They stood together holding hands and studying each other. Gloria decided he looked older, more handsome, if that was possible. He was wearing his hair longer than she remembered, and he seemed taller.

He tucked her hand through his arm and they crossed the bridge. "I don't suppose it would do any good to tell you it's not a terrific idea to come here alone."

"Our house is only a few blocks from here. I practically grew up in the park."

They lowered their heads against the brisk November wind, and Gardner adjusted his longer stride to hers. The weather had been unseasonably mild until today, only two light snows since the end of October. Gloria glanced toward the heavy sky, praying it would not snow. The plan was for her to return to Goose Point with her parents; she didn't want anything to disrupt the plan and add to her guilt.

"Do you remember the Thanksgivings at Goose Point?" she asked Gardner, holding to his arm. In the past, Lulu had opened Goose Point for the holidays. Remy had brought friends from Princeton and Gloria had invited friends from Chapin. The Durants and the Whitehalls had come, and Georges and Thérèse La Tourraine had flown in from Paris. Lulu had organized hunts and card parties and dancing and, when they had been younger, she had hired a magician to entertain the children.

"Would it make you happy if mother hired a magician for today?"

"That isn't funny," she said sharply.

"Sorry, squirt. I was trying to coax a smile."

"Well, don't."

He tightened his grip on her arm when she tried to pull away. "In a bad mood are we?"

"Wouldn't you be?" She stopped walking so he would have to stop. "Your mother has been wonderful, but I'd rather be at Goose Point for Thanksgiving, like always."

"Don't tell Mother. She wants to keep you." Leaning against the wind, he tugged her forward, making her walk faster than she wanted to. "What did you think about the article in last week's *Times*?"

The pink deepened in her cheeks. "You saw it?" She had hoped he hadn't. The lead to the article had read: VON MARRON HEIRESS, RICHEST GIRL IN THE WORLD? Beneath the lead was a photograph of her standing on the steps of the Metropolitan Museum. The photograph was flattering, but she didn't recall when it might have been taken or by whom. "The reporter knew I'd placed first in my French section last year, and he knew I collect antique dolls." Dolls were an uncomfortable subject, and she looked up at Gardner expecting him to comment. When he said nothing she released her breath. "How do reporters find out about such things?"

"You're big news, squirt. Very rich and very eligible." Gardner grinned into her upturned face. "From now on everything you do is going to make headlines. Where you go, what you wear, who you're seen with. A lot of young gentlemen are going to be checking you out with a view to the future."

"Checking me out. Like a library book." She made a face. When was he going to stop treating her like she was the village idiot and he was a sage old man of the world? "I don't want to be news."

"I'm afraid it goes with the territory."

"And I don't want boys interested in me just because I'm an heiress."

"Believe me, that won't be the only reason." He smiled at her and winked.

The compliment and the wink pleased her. They emerged from the park and wandered toward the fountain in front of the Plaza, drained now for winter. Sitting on the rim, they tossed popcorn to the pigeons.

"Gardner, do you have a girlfriend?" The blurted question horrified her as did the violent blush that followed. Bending abruptly to conceal her fiery face, she fumbled with a shoelace.

"I'm saving myself for you, squirt." Leaning backward, he tossed a kernel of popcorn in the air and caught it on his tongue, looking to see if she had noticed.

"Don't tease me."

"What makes you think I'm teasing?" When she glared at him, he shrugged and smiled. "I date occasionally. No one special."

Still bent over her shoe, unable to stop the words, she said, "Aunt Chissie hopes you and Bitsy Morgan will get engaged." She despised herself for saying these things.

"Bitsy Morgan?" His laugh made her feel instantly better. "Having worshiped at the feet of a Von Marron, how could I settle for a mere Morgan?"

Her spirits sank again. "Dammit, Gardner. I don't tease you."

"When did you start swearing?" Standing, he pushed back his coat sleeve and glanced at a gold watch. "Come along, Miss

Von Marron. Mother's having people in and we're expected to perform as the wonderful children.''

Gloria stood slowly. "I'm going to grow up someday," she announced. The words emerged midway between a threat and a challenge and she instantly regretted them.

"I don't doubt it. I can see the headlines now." Smiling, Gardner drew a line in the air with his glove. "Von Marron heiress grows up at last. The civilized world rejoices.''

She tried not to laugh, then gave it up and grinned. "You're hopeless, do you know that?" Grabbing his arm, she pulled it down to his side. "Aren't you ever serious?" The moment she spoke, she remembered the night on the beach after Remy's funeral and her expression sobered.

He tucked his hand into his pocket, trapping her arm close to his body. "You have a wonderful laugh," he commented softly, smiling down at her. "I have an idea you don't laugh nearly enough. That's too bad. You're very beautiful when you smile.''

"And ugly the rest of the time?" she asked, keeping her tone light. Looking at his eyes and mouth did strange things to her nervous system.

"I've never seen an uglier girl," he said, grinning and dodging the punch she landed on his arm. Before they entered the Durant's building, he stopped and turned her to face him. "Look, squirt. We're going to make this a terrific Thanksgiving. Okay?''

"Okay."

"You could manage a little more enthusiasm. I've been looking forward to today. But I don't want to spend the holiday looking across the table at an ugly girl with a sour face.''

He sounded so like Remy that sudden tears sprang into her eyes and her throat closed. She leaned her forehead against his shoulder. "Oh God, Gardner. I miss him so much.''

"I know, squirt. So do I." His arm slid around her waist and he gave her a hug, then he led her inside out of the cold wind.

Bobby waited until the last minute before he telephoned. "I'm sorry, Chissie, we aren't going to make it. Go ahead and serve dinner," he said when she came to the phone. "Lulu's been screaming for hours. Etta finally got her settled down about thirty minutes ago.''

Leaning his head against the back of his chair, he closed his eyes and blessed the silence.

"I'll bring Gloria home tomorrow, Bobby. I'd like to talk to you about her. She really should be in school."

He was drunk. Not as drunk as he wanted to be, not as drunk as he needed to be. But he was getting there.

"Bobby? What does Dr. Barbeau suggest?"

"He wants to institutionalize her." At the far end of the line he heard Chissie weeping. "I can't do that to her."

"Maybe it's the best thing," she said through her tears.

After he hung up, he poured more gin into his glass and placed the decanter on the floor beside his chair within easy reach.

This wasn't a Thanksgiving for the memory books. His wife was hysterical, his son was dead, and he couldn't remember exactly where his daughter was. He only remembered that he had struck her. Christ. He wanted to turn the goddamn clock backward. He wanted to be sitting at his Thanksgiving table with his wife and his daughter. He wanted his son returned to him.

There was no way to understand it. He had tried until his head felt like whirling blades were chopping at his brain. And he still didn't know why.

A terrible anger shook his body. For one blinding moment he hated Remy more than he had hated any single thing in his life. In one careless, selfish moment Remy had destroyed everything Bobby valued—his marriage, his family, his image of himself. And he didn't know the hell why. He only knew Remy had loaded him with more guilt than any man should have to endure.

He poured another drink, then made himself think about Lulu. From the beginning they had been the perfect couple. Handsome, charming, fitted to one another like pieces of a jigsaw puzzle. Now a hand had reached out of the grave and snatched the perfect couple off the top of the cake.

He wanted his wife back, the way she had been before Carnegie and the Debussy competition. Pushing unsteadily to his feet, he walked to the mirror in the foyer. He looked old, and that surprised the hell out of him. There were grooves across his forehead, lines framing his mouth. He looked like his father.

"Christ."

Turning away from the mirror, he leaned against the table beneath it and looked up the stairs, listening to the silence. Was it a good sign? He thought it might be. Maybe she was feeling better now. Maybe she would like a cream sherry. They could sit on the bed and talk like they used to, then later, if she felt up to it, maybe they would make love. It had been weeks.

The longer he considered the idea, the more reasonable it became. Smiling for the first time in days, he found a silver tray and loaded it with the gin decanter and a cream sherry for Lulu and then a bowl of caviar he found on the table that William had set up for him.

He was drunk enough that carrying the tray required all his concentration, and he moved up the staircase with meticulous care, not glancing at Remy's closed door as he passed. Lulu's door opened easily when he pushed against it with his shoulder.

"Lulu? Darling?"

The only illumination in the room came from the flicker of the television set and a slice of pale light shining past the bathroom door. Etta Nelson snored gently in front of the stripes across the TV. She looked exhausted.

After placing the tray on the table beside her, he touched her shoulder. "Etta? I'm here. You can go to bed now."

She woke with a start and blinked at him before she jerked toward the rumpled empty bed. "Mrs. Von Marron?"

He heard it then, the sound that had been flowing under his thoughts since he entered the bedroom. The sound of steadily running water.

"Oh my God," Etta whispered.

"Lulu!" He crossed the room in three strides and halted abruptly when he could see into the bathroom. Water spilled over the top of the tub and streamed down the side onto the carpet. Pale pink water. Then he saw her dangling arm and the deep red gash across her wrist. With a terrifying sense of déjà vu, Bobby sagged against the bathroom door and stared at the bright crimson drops falling from her fingertips. Then he heard Etta's scream, and it all began again.

Chapter 4

*W*HEN THE DURANT'S LIMOUSINE arrived at Goose Point, a half-dozen cars jammed the gravel drive that circled in front of the veranda. An ambulance blocked the steps; spinning red lights atop the police vehicles chased the darkness across the face of the house.

Captain Moore waited beside the car door until Durant stepped out. The two men examined each other. "It appears we have another hunting accident."

"Tell your people to turn off those flashers," Durant snapped. "Is she dead?"

Chissie made a small choking sound and slipped her arm around Gloria's waist as Gardner assisted them out of the car.

"Mrs. Von Marron is alive."

Gloria sagged against the limousine's dark fender and covered her eyes. Relief drained the energy from her body.

"All show and no go," Moore said with a shrug. "The cuts weren't deep—the husband found her within minutes."

"Any reporters?"

"Not yet."

The sterility of the exchange was numbing. Gloria didn't wait to hear more. Pulling free of Chissie, she ran inside and bolted up the stairs. Margaret caught her outside Lulu's door.

"Gloria, she's resting now."

By leaning to one side, Gloria could see past Margaret's shoulder into her mother's bedroom. Dr. Barbeau and her father were there, and Etta, who had been crying, and one of the maids. Her mother lay propped against a mound of pillows, her eyes closed, her bandaged wrists resting atop the counterpane.

"Please, just for a minute." Her mother resembled a beautiful, lifeless doll.

"She's heavily sedated, darling." Margaret peered into her eyes then sighed. "All right. But just for a minute, mind."

One of the maids worked in the bathroom. Water had soaked the carpeting several feet into the bedroom, and Gloria carefully walked around the damp section. Biting her lip, she held her breath and approached the bed slowly. Someone, presumably Etta, had combed her mother's hair and had dressed her in a fresh, blue silk nightgown. Lying against the pillows, Lulu looked pale and porcelain and elegantly lovely. It didn't seem possible she had attempted to kill herself. Gloria reached toward her mother's hand, then withdrew her fingers, uncertain if she should touch her or not.

"Further delay would be unwise," Dr. Barbeau said at the foot of the bed, speaking in a hushed voice. "She has to be institutionalized."

"Oh God." Bobby raked a hand through his hair. "Those places are so—"

"Not all of them." Gesturing to Etta, Dr. Barbeau instructed her to send the ambulance away. "There's a commendable sanitarium outside Geneva. The care at Les Eaux is excellent and the staff noted for discretion. Mrs. Von Marron will have a private suite and her own maid if she prefers. Or one can be provided for her."

"I don't want to hear the details. Make the arrangements with Win Durant."

"Les Eaux is very exclusive, very expensive. You should be aware that Mrs. Von Marron may be there for a lengthy stay."

"Win will take care of everything."

Gloria wet her lips. The family was disintegrating. There was only her father and herself now. To show her support and because she felt a need to do something, she straightened her shoulders and moved to stand beside her father. "We want the best for Mummy," she said to Dr. Barbeau. When she saw the hint of pity behind his spectacles, she looked away from him and lifted her chin.

Barefoot and wearing only a nightgown, Gloria stood in the darkness outside the door to her father's study. Shock pinched her expression. In the last hour she had learned more about her mother than she wanted to know. The shoplifting sprees, the manic bursts of activity followed by lethargy and periods of incapacitating depression. Episodes of neurotic behavior that dated back several years, that had been concealed and smoothed over. Tears rolled down her face and wet the lace collar of her nightgown.

"Bobby, we have to discuss Gloria."

"Not now, Chissie." Gloria heard the clink of ice dropping against crystal, a splash of liquid. "My life is falling apart. I can't cope. Everyone wants something from me, and I don't have it to give. First there was Remy." His voice wavered and cracked. "Now Barbeau insists I put Lulu away."

"There's no alternative," Win Durant said. "The only choice in this mess is what happens to you."

"I'll stay with Lulu, of course."

Chissie cleared her throat, the sound delicate and filled with discomfort. "I wish there was a tactful way to say this, Bobby, but there isn't. Right now you seem to be part of Lulu's illness. As harsh as this may sound, I think Dr. Barbeau was right when he suggested the Les Eaux people will insist that you don't see her for a while. It might be wise."

"If they won't allow me to stay with her, then I'll open the Paris house and wait there until she's better."

"And Gloria?"

There was a pause. "I don't know. Right now I just can't cope with a teenage daughter. . . ."

A hand touched Gloria's shoulder and she jumped, her heart banging against her ribs. "Oh Margaret!" she whispered. "You scared me to death."

"Come back to bed. You know you shouldn't be listening at doors. And you're barefoot. Do you want to catch cold?"

"Please, just another minute. They're talking about me."

Margaret led her firmly toward the staircase. "If you're meant to know, you'll learn about it soon enough."

At the top of the stairs, they paused and looked down the length of the darkened corridor toward the thin strip of light shining under Lulu's door. A nurse was with Lulu and would remain until she was delivered to Les Eaux.

Margaret opened the door to Gloria's room and Gloria followed her inside. "Will you sit with me a minute? Please?" She slipped between the sheets and pulled them up to her chest. "Will you come with us if we go to Paris?"

"You're really too old for a nanny," Margaret said gently. She dimmed the light near the bed. Seeing the shine of moisture in Gloria's eyes, she added, "But we'll always be friends, won't we?"

"That means you aren't coming with us." When she could

speak past the lump lodged in her throat, she asked, "Where will you go?" Losing Margaret was almost worse than losing her mother. As long as she could remember Margaret had always been there for her. Blindly, she reached for Margaret's hand and squeezed her fingers.

"I imagine I'll return to Lewes, and you'll come to visit me. Remember how lovely England is in summer? We'll bicycle through the lanes and I'll show you the cottage where I was born and the house where I grew up."

Later, when Margaret, believing she was asleep, had tiptoed from the room, Gloria rolled onto her back and stared at the row of dolls sitting on the shelf across the room from her bed.

If the summer had been the summer of Debussy, then this was the winter of silence. The accusing silence behind Remy's closed door. The confused silence behind Lulu's door and the drunken silence from her father's study. The brooding hush that had descended over Goose Point. It was the silence of snow, silence that concealed whatever lay beneath.

She had always believed when the world shattered, if such a thing were possible, the event would be accompanied by catastrophic noise. It hadn't occurred to her that worlds and eras could end in closed doors and silence.

Without Chissie Durant's quiet assistance, Bobby Von Marron could not have gotten through the next two weeks. Bewildered and angry, he wandered through the days in a stupor, groping for inner resources that had shriveled years ago. When Chissie gently suggested he needed to officially close the New York town house and dismiss the servants at Goose Point, he looked at her from blank eyes. The directive was obvious, but he hadn't thought of it. It was Chissie who telephoned Paris and asked Georges and Thérèse La Tourraine to open the Paris house; Chissie, working with Etta, who began to close Goose Point.

The nights were the worst. Wrapped within an alcoholic mist, he sat in the dark in his study, away from the drugged specter of his wife and the bulldog Barbeau had hired to watch over her. He stared at the television until the stations signed off, then he pretended to read the memos and reports Durant continued to send him.

Most nights he drank until he passed out in his chair. Other nights the alcohol didn't perform and he came face-to-face with Bobby Von Marron. At such times his anger and despair clotted into rage. None of this should have happened. Life should have treated him more kindly or should have provided him with stronger armor. It was a goddamn travesty for a man to discover at age forty-nine that he lacked substance.

Opening his desk, he removed the blood-stained *Life* Magazine cover. He had had substance then. How old had he been? Remy's age? Flying a Mustang like it was part of his body, flak exploding on his wing, the sky black with smoke and debris. And the joy of it. Good Christ, the joy of it. He had never felt so alive, not before or since. Had not felt anything approaching the same sense of worth and purpose.

Falling back in his desk chair, gripping his drink in both hands, he remembered how it had felt to walk into White's or into the Savoy wearing his lieutenant's uniform. He and Durant and La Tourraine, London's white knights, as different as men could be but alike in their swagger of heroism and promise. Saviors of the world. And when the war ended, they understood they would conquer the world they had saved.

Where had the heroism and the promise gone? When had he lost them? Or had he ever really possessed courage and strength? It occurred to him that possibly those qualities existed only in a bottle.

"You have my address at Princeton," Gardner said.

"And you have the address of the Paris house."

They sat on the marble bench in front of Remy's grave. Earlier, William had swept the snow off the slab and filled the stone urn with yellow roses. Now tiny flakes of fresh snow drifted like powdered sugar over the slab and frosted the rose petals.

Gardner took her gloved hand. "I'll miss you, squirt." Gloria lowered her head, not trusting her voice enough to answer. "But you'll be back." Lifting her chin with a finger, he smiled into her eyes. "Europe isn't big enough to hold a Von Marron."

"Daddy says he doesn't know when we'll come home. It could be as long as a year. Maybe two."

"By that time you'll speak French like a native."

"I already speak French like a native. And Italian." She gave him a shy smile. "Are you impressed?"

Shifting so he could see her better, Gardner lifted his hand to brush the snow from her cheek. "Very impressed," he said quietly, and she understood he didn't refer to her facility with languages. "So much has happened in such a short time. It must seem as if the world has collapsed around you. You've been dealt a lousy hand." She didn't know how to respond. Instead of answering, she inspected her gloves. "You've handled everything with dignity and courage."

"No I haven't," she whispered. "Maybe it looks that way, but that's not how it is. That's my public face. Remy's gone and Mummy's crazy. Daddy's here but he isn't. Etta has accepted a new position, and Margaret is going home to England. And I . . ." She didn't want him to see her cry, and she turned her face toward the gray water tossing in the Sound and waited until the tightness receded from her throat. When she was confident her voice had steadied, she looked at him again and made herself smile. "Tell me about you. What will you do after graduation? Will you take a position with La Tourraine, Durant and Von Marron?"

Gardner leaned forward, elbows on knees, his hands clasped in front of him as he looked at Remy's grave. Snow had collected in his dark hair. "No. I've given the future a lot of thought, and I've concluded I'm not cut out for investment banking."

Gloria stared, surprised. "Have you told Uncle Win?"

"Not yet."

"Gardner—"

"I know. Remy and I discussed it endlessly." He spoke in a quiet tone, continuing to regard Remy's grave. "My father isn't going to take it well. It's going to be a hell of a battle."

Margaret's voice called through the falling snow and they looked toward the house. "It's time," Gloria said in a strained voice. Standing, she pulled her cap over her ears. White-coated attendants moved to the back of the ambulance and shut the doors. William was closing the limousine's trunk over a pile of luggage. "Oh, Gardner. I don't want to go."

"It won't be forever," he said, rising beside her.

"Will I see you again?" The melting snow had dampened his hair and caused it to curl.

His laugh wrapped her in warmth. "Of course you will, squirt. I'm not going anywhere. I'm just hanging around, waiting for you to grow up." Taking her arm, he turned her up the path leading to the house and the waiting cars. "I have a combination Christmas-going-away present for you."

"You do?" Surprise filled her eyes, then dismay. "I don't have anything for you."

They stopped beside the veranda steps and he smiled down at her. "I bought you a subscription to *The Wall Street Journal*. I have high expectations for you, Miss Von Marron."

"A subscription to . . ." For a moment she was afraid her

disappointment was obvious, then she understood and a radiant smile illuminated her face. "Thank you!" She looked into his dark eyes, already missing him. "For the gift. And especially for the expectations."

He hugged her and she clung to him until he passed her to Chissie, then Chissie was weeping against her cap, talking about her mother. Uncle Win turned from her father to give her a quick, distracted embrace. She managed not to cry until Margaret opened her arms; then the tears came, thick and scalding.

"I love you, Gloria," Margaret said against her ear. "If you ever need me—"

"I'll miss you so much! I love you too."

Someone pulled her away from Margaret's embrace and assisted her into the limousine. The ambulance carrying her mother and the bulldog nurse crunched down the driveway, and the limousine glided after it, moving away from the house. Twisting on the seat and blinking furiously, Gloria peered back and waved to the group assembled on the veranda steps. Then the snow closed behind her and Goose Point disappeared from view.

Durant had given instructions that Home Limited's private jet be renovated to accommodate her mother. The bedroom had been enlarged to provide space for Miss Kolchec, and the mirrors had been removed because Lulu had developed an aversion to them. Lulu's screams rose above the sound of the jet's engines.

"Where are you taking me? I won't go! I won't leave Remy! And these straps . . . what are these straps? Release me at once, you bastard. I want Remy!" The sound of her mother's shrieks shredded Gloria's nerves.

When Bobby emerged from the bedroom, he dropped onto the sofa and rubbed his temples, then he called the attendant and ordered gin on the rocks. When the drink arrived, he drained it in a single gulp. For a moment his eyes met those of his daughter. Then he turned his face to the window. When it became obvious they wouldn't discuss it, Gloria turned to the window, too.

Thérèse La Tourraine did all she could to make Christmas in Paris as pleasant as possible for the Von Marrons. The task proved daunting. Lulu, whom she had never cared for, played the role of bereaved mother to the hilt, weeping and screaming for Remy. One tried to understand, but it had been four months after all. Of course Lulu Parker Von Marron was neurotic and had been when Thérèse first met her years ago at Le Rosey in Switzerland. True, jealousy mixed in and shaded her opinion. It was difficult not to envy Lulu. As a young woman Lulu had been a stunning beauty who had worn her pedigree like a string of antique pearls, and later there had been Bobby Von Marron and all the columns and society pieces celebrating the perfect couple.

Standing in the doorway to the Von Marron's living room, Thérèse watched the lights on the Christmas tree blink shadows across Bobby's face. She wondered if Georges, that bastard, would look as ravaged if she were in Lulu's situation. More likely he would seek immediate consolation in the arms of his latest mistress, where he no doubt languished at this moment. What a pity Frenchwomen were expected to behave with civility. Her inclination was to telephone the de Simone residence and leave a message reminding her husband of the dinner engagement at the Von Marrons and demanding that he leave Diana's bed at once. Unfortunately, one did not indulge such inclinations.

Entering the living room, she chose a seat beside Gloria and took the girl's cold hand in hers. "Will your mother be joining us tonight?"

"No."

Although everyone focused on Lulu, as Lulu undoubtedly intended, in Thérèse's opinion it was young Gloria who was the genuinely tragic figure in the Von Marron drama. It tugged her heart to look at the girl. Gloria Von Marron was as stunningly beautiful as Lulu had been at the same age, slender and elegant, silvery-haired and gray-eyed. Like her mother before her, Gloria would inspire envy in women and yearning in men. But there was pain and vulnerability in the girl's eyes which had never marked Lulu's expression. And beneath that vulnerability, a deep inquisitive intelligence which Thérèse did not attribute to Lulu. Shrewdness, yes; brilliance, no. And Lulu Parker Von Marron had never been neglected a day in her pampered life.

But this one, this forgotten child—Thérèse had taken Gloria Christmas shopping, a small courtesy anyone would have extended, and the child had been embarrassingly grateful, as she was for any small attention paid to her. Thérèse hoped Bobby took her advice—and soon—and placed Gloria in school among others of her own age. A teenage girl should be laughing and flirting and experimenting with lipsticks and clothes instead of hovering at the elbow of a man too shattered to notice.

Paris provided a picture postcard Christmas, but it was the worst Christmas in Gloria's memory. Snow drifted gently past frosted windows, and inside, the warmth of the fire enhanced the pine scent of the tree. Carols filled the room. But silence flowed beneath the music, profound and painful.

After days of anxious discussion, it had been decided that Lulu would join them downstairs. When Miss Kolchec brought her mother into the living room, Gloria tensed, waiting for the screaming to begin. Instead, Lulu had not spoken a single word, had not made a sound, and in the end that had been worse. She sat like a porcelain doll in the wing chair where Miss Kolchec had placed her and she stared at the Christmas tree with a bewildered expression. Silent tears ran down her face. She didn't move, didn't glance at the presents Bobby hopefully placed on her lap. The gifts slid to the carpet. She didn't look at the boxes Bobby and Gloria unwrapped. She stared at the Christmas tree and wept her silent, anguished tears, and after a time Miss Kolchec led her away.

The silence in the living room deepened and became inviolate. After her mother had been taken upstairs, Gloria tried to unwrap another gift, but the noise of the paper pulling from the box crackled across the silence like small ripping explosions. She glanced toward her father who sat staring into the fire, then she set the gift aside. A German choir filled the room with *Silent Night*, and Gloria swallowed an hysterical impulse to laugh at the utter appropriateness of the selection.

When her father finally spoke it was as if he had suddenly remembered she was present, although he didn't look at her. He continued to stare at the flames in the grate. "Thérèse and Georges will take you to Aigmont on Friday," he said. "I'm assured Aigmont is an excellent school."

The news came like a crash of lightning from a cloudless sky. She wasn't prepared for it. Yes, she knew Chissie and Thérèse had spoken to her father about placing her in school, but because nothing had come of it, she had assumed nothing would. She had assumed her father needed her as much as she needed him.

"I'd rather stay with you and wait until next fall instead of entering school in the middle of the term." She clasped her hands in her lap and willed the moisture to recede from her eyes. At some point during the last months she had learned to control the tears that seemed only a word away. Tears upset her father, making further conversation impossible.

"Everything is arranged."

No one had requested her opinion. "I want to stay with you, Daddy."

"Gloria, please. Don't be difficult. There's nothing to discuss." Finally he looked at her with eyes so dull and weary that she had to bite her lip to keep the tears away.

"I won't get in your way or be a problem, I promise. You won't even know I'm here. Please don't send me away." Despite her efforts, a tear welled over her lashes and rolled down her cheek. She couldn't stop it. All the people she loved had scattered and gone. Her father was all she had left. "Please," she whispered. "Please, don't do this to me. Let me stay here. I could go to school in Paris."

"Oh God. I can't tolerate a scene."

Blinking rapidly, trying not to cry, she watched him approach the cart by the Christmas tree and mix a fresh drink. His hands were shaking, and he refused to look at her.

Contempt as deep as only the young can feel swept over her. This golden man, this god whom she had worshiped and adored, her father, had less strength than she. Less backbone and more self-pity. Her mouth tightened in sudden, shaking anger that was easier to bear than pain. More than anything, she suddenly wanted to create a scene to end all scenes. Then he would notice her. She wanted to scream and throw things and smash the tree to the floor. But of course she did not. At some point, without realizing it, she had rejected physical scenes as a show of emotionalism more suited to her mother than to herself.

"Then you've decided. I have to go to Aigmont," she said flatly. "You don't care what I want."

"There's no choice."

"There are choices, but you don't want to hear about them." After setting aside her gifts, she stood and stared at him and at the drink in his hand. Her mouth twisted and her gray eyes were unforgiving. "I'm the one without choices, not you. So I'll go because I have to." Her chin lifted and anger mounted behind her stare. "I'll succeed at Aigmont. Then you can tell yourself you did the right thing by abandoning me." He closed his eyes and winced, but she felt no pity. "I will never forget this, and I will never forgive it."

The statement was forged partly from the strength of adulthood, partly from the liquid heat of youth. Because she was gifted with an analytical mind, Gloria recognized this and felt an impatient embarrassment for her age. She understood she had struck out with the intention of wounding, and she had succeeded. She recognized the shock and hurt in her father's expression. No apology sprang to her lips.

Raising her head, she turned her back to the fire, to the Christmas lights, to her pile of gifts, and to her father. Naively, she had believed that because it was Christmas, they could be a family again, just for this one day. But Christmas had lost its magic. She climbed the stairs to her bedroom and swore if she ever had children of her own, they would never endure a Christmas as lonely and as silent as this one.

Few realized Thérèse La Tourraine was not a beauty, which was precisely as she intended. Long ago she had discovered that what most people considered beauty was largely illusion. One required only wit and wealth to create that illusion. As Thérèse lacked neither wit nor wealth, she created and maintained the illusion, assisted by some of the world's famed experts. Her clothing was by Chanel, with a dash of Guy Laroche when she wished to be whimsical; her makeup and perfume were custom-blended; her hair was by Alexandre. No detail was too small to be part of the ultimate illusion. Her nails were lacquered to perfection; every ensemble was exquisitely accessorized.

But Thérèse herself was never, not for a moment, deceived by the illusion. She knew who she was. And between beauty and a shrewd mind, she understood which would last longer and in which to place her faith.

Curving beautifully made-up lips, she smiled at Madame Geroux, the headmistress of Aigmont, and silently congratulated herself on having chosen emeralds for today. Madame Geroux's small dark eyes continually strayed to Thérèse's earrings and bracelets throughout the interview. The tiny flicker of envy coupled with a generous serving of obsequiousness told Thérèse that Madame Geroux could be managed.

"We must discuss Mademoiselle Von Marron's room assignment," she said, arranging her expression into one of pleasant expectation.

A furrow of distress appeared between Madame Geroux's brows. "I am so sorry, Madame La Tourraine. Aigmont allows no parental interference with room assignments. Surely you understand. We know our young ladies and gentlemen best and make every effort to arrange a compatible match."

Surprise lifted one elegantly penciled brow, followed by a hint of doubt which Madame Geroux was intended to observe. "Of course. But, in view of recent events . . . I must know whom you have in mind." Again the expectation, more insistent now.

Madame Geroux hesitated. "Well—I thought to pair Mademoiselle Von Marron with Mademoiselle Gabrielle Devet."

Naturally, Thérèse understood the arrangement. A Devet at Aigmont was as great a coup as a Von Marron would be. Devet and Von Marron would be the shining jewels in the school's crown. Both were renowned heiresses; both came from similar backgrounds; both had already attracted considerable media attention. Thérèse recalled young Devet from a country weekend. Pale and handsomely arrogant, blood so blue the redness had all but vanished. One could cut a franc note on Devet's cheekbones, sculpted to patrician height and sharpness.

"I think not," she decided after a moment. Why she had taken an interest in this matter, she could not have explained. Except Gloria had no one else, and perhaps because it gave her pleasure to overpower the Madame Gerouxs of this world. "I'll have a look at the student roster, if you please."

"Oh, I'm afraid that is not possible!"

Thérèse glanced idly at the diamonds surrounding the gold face of her watch and allowed a trace of impatience to form at the corner of her lips. "I'm certain you are as interested as I am in settling the matter. I'm equally certain Mademoiselle Von Marron will be a credit to Aigmont if the arrangement is concluded to everyone's satisfaction. Therefore, Madame, I must see the roster. If you please." It was all in one's manner and tone, she thought absently, watching as Madame Geroux reluctantly produced the student roster. The word *privé* was stamped in red letters across the top of the folder.

The Aigmont roster read like a social register of the world's aristocracy. "This name," Therese said, pausing over a frown. "I don't recognize it. Holly Drake?"

Madame Geroux cleared her throat and touched the silk scarf draping her small bosom. "You must understand, Madame La Tourraine, my predecessor was not always as discriminating as one would hope. Mademoiselle Drake is the daughter of," she drew a breath, "the film actress, Elfie Drake."

Thérèse's lifted eyebrow was eloquent. But she found herself returning to Miss Drake's name in the register. "An American?"

Distaste thinned the line of Madame Geroux's lips. "Indeed. A . . . difficult . . . girl." Madame's hesitation spoke volumes.

"Rebellious, perhaps? Angry?" An emphatic nod confirmed the assessment. A tiny smile softened Thérèse's mouth. She hoped she was not making a mistake. "It's settled then. Mademoiselle Von Marron shall be assigned to Mademoiselle Drake."

Madame Geroux's mouth fell open. She looked appalled.

Gloria hated Switzerland, despised Chamonix, and she especially loathed Aigmont. Sitting outside Madame Geroux's door, waiting for Thérèse, she glared at the dark paneling and tried not to breathe the heavy scent of age and herbal furniture polish. Beyond leaded glass windows and aging draperies now faded to a venerable rose color, a snowy landscape dropped toward the valley and the resort village of Chamonix. Filled with resentment, she scowled at the rooftops until Thérèse La Tourraine and Madame Geroux emerged from Madame's parlor. They led her up two flights of worn stairs to a room smaller than her bedroom at Goose Point.

Madame gazed at the pale wallpaper and ancient furnishings with pride. "This was once Princess Sophia's room." When Gloria made no response, she rubbed her hands together and cleared her throat. "I shall excuse Mademoiselle Drake from her literature class and ask her to come to you immediately."

"I'll meet her soon enough." Gloria shrugged, knowing she was being difficult and not caring."

"It is the custom, Mademoiselle."

"Madame is something of a dragon," Thérèse said when Madame Geroux had gone, "but manageable." She opened the closet near one of the gleaming brass beds. "Oh dear, so much leather. How vulgar. But what can one expect from the daughter of a film star? You must request a reassignment the minute a vacancy is available. Mademoiselle Drake is completely unsuitable, of course. You must request Devet. It is what your father would wish."

Her father cared nothing for her wishes, why should she care about his?

"Hello." A short, plump girl appeared in the doorway, wearing a winkled skirt and sweater and a sullen expression. "Geroux said I had to come up here." She returned Gloria's stare and responded to Thérèse's polite comments with replies bordering on rudeness.

"Well, my dear," Thérèse said. She gave Holly Drake a lingering appraisal then enfolded Gloria in a perfumed embrace. "If you need anything . . ."

Gloria clung to Thérèse La Tourraine, holding fast to the last familiar face. When Thérèse departed, her final connection to safety and comfort would disappear. Unwilling to watch Thérèse close the door behind her, she turned blindly to her closet.

"Oh Christ, wouldn't you know I'd get stuck with a crybaby. Shit."

"I'm not crying."

"Oh sure."

The anger she had been trying to control rushed to the surface. "Don't you dare judge me!" Turning from the closet, she ran a pointed glance over Holly Drake's wrinkled skirt and sagging knee socks and her mouth twisted. "What I do is none of your business. If I want to cry, I will."

"Like all the other weak sisters who have been abandoned in exclusive Swiss schools. Poor you. You're breaking my little heart."

No one had ever spoken to her like this. "You don't know anything about me. So just shut up."

"How stupid can you get? I know all about you. You're the media's newest poor little rich girl. Big time heiress—I'm so impressed—whose mother is nutty as a squirrel and living in a looney bin, and whose brother blew his brains out. Now big daddy wonderful has dumped you."

Gloria gasped. "That . . . that isn't . . . my father did not dump me, he—"

"Save it, kiddo. I've been there. Lie to yourself if you're that dumb, but don't lie to me, because I'm not buying a word of it. My mother has dumped me in more places than you can name. This is my sixth school in four years. I know when someone has been dumped. Big deal." Tossing herself across one of the beds, Holly Drake pushed her hand under the mattress and came up with a package of American cigarettes and book of matches. She lit a cigarette, expelled a cloud of smoke, and gave Gloria a challenging look.

"Listen, the minute my mother is well, my father is going to take me out of here."

"Dream on. But at least you've got a father. Me? I've got more uncles than you ever heard of. Elfie should install a revolving door for all my uncles. Elfie, in case you didn't know, is my mother. The film star. She says she's twenty-five years old. I'm fifteen. Figure that one out.''

"It's against the rules to smoke."

"So? What are you going to do about it? Turn me in to Geroux?'' Holly blew a stream of smoke toward the window she had opened a crack. "Go ahead. If I get expelled, so what?''

"You can be expelled for smoking?''

"They ain't going to give me a prize, kiddo.''

Gloria's lips curved in a slow smile that didn't soften her eyes. "May I try one of those?''

"You're kidding." Holly's eyes narrowed. "Seriously? You don't look like the type."

"Move over and give me one.'' Gloria climbed on the bed and settled her back against the wall. She accepted a lit cigarette from Holly and inhaled as Holly had done, then burst into a fit of coughing. "God, that's terrible!''

"So put it out.''

"No.''

When Holly laughed, she sounded like her famous mother. "I didn't think I was going to like you. But maybe you're okay.''

"Don't make any snap decisions.''

"No, I can tell. You're mad at the world. You got crapped on just like me.''

Gloria puffed at the cigarette, coughed, and made herself keep smoking. "Will they really expel us for this?''

Holly shrugged. "Is that what you want?''

"I don't know." She wanted her father to miss her as badly as she missed him. She wanted him to come after her begging forgiveness. She wanted life to be the way it used to be before the summer of Debussy. And none of that was going to happen. She waved at the smoke collecting in front of her face. "I want my father to feel sorry for dumping me.''

"Not a chance. They don't feel sorry; they feel relieved. Face it, kiddo, you're here to stay. If not at Aigmont, then someplace just like it. You're on your own now.''

Leaning her head back against the wall, Gloria closed her eyes. "On my own,'' she whispered. Panic closed her throat, and she struggled to breathe. Then she realized she had always been on her own.

"It's not so bad,'' Holly said. "After awhile you learn you don't need all those other people.''

But she wanted them. She wanted to love and be loved. She drew on the cigarette, exhaled slowly.

"Tell me about this place," she said finally, looking around the room they would share for the next three years. The room was small but well-appointed, the furnishings were genuine antiques. She and Holly each had a desk and a private bathroom. Their window overlooked the valley and one of the ski runs. They had laundry service on the weekends, and Chamonix was only an hour by train from Geneva. All in all, she decided, things could have been much worse.

The first quarter of 1974 ended on a down tick. Win Durant took the spiral in stride; he had been through the cycles before. Eventually the market would reverse its southern trend. His primary concern at the moment was the Paris office. The Paris bourse remained open only a few hours a day, a continuing frustration to American-based firms. His greatest cause for worry was the Paris staff. Von Marron and La Tourraine were both outside men and the *agent de change* was a weak link. What was needed were a half-dozen suits on the inside, savvy people who knew their asses from their assets. After glancing at the clock, Durant leaned away from his desk and tapped the end of a pen against his cheek.

If the firm were solely his, he would close Paris and open an office in London. At the very least, he would sweep the dead weight out of the Paris office and bring in some new blood. Some hand-picked brilliance.

He glanced at the clock again as Lucille Ivory, his secretary, buzzed to notify him that Gardner had arrived. Smiling, he stood and gripped his son's hand as Gardner entered his office. Durant had waited a long time for this day.

"That's a new lithograph, isn't it?" Gardner asked, leaning over Durant's leather sofa. "A Morell."

"Your mother selected it. Along with the others." Although he and Chissie attended the major art showings, he had never been interested to the extent of pursuing genuine knowledge in the field. It pleased him to know Gardner enjoyed and understood art. The background he and Chissie had provided their son was one he envied. Christ, if he had come from a similar background, he would have owned the world by now.

For this special day, he had decided they would lunch in the firm's dining rooms on the twenty-eighth floor. He wanted Gardner surrounded by opulence, by reminders of the promise La Tourraine, Durant and Von Marron extended, by the power the firm exerted.

When they were seated and Sedrick had flicked linen napkins across their laps, Durant made himself exchange trivialities until they had been served. He inquired about Gardner's classes, asked if he were still rowing and playing polo, asked if he had stopped to visit Bobby Von Marron during his recent trip to Paris at spring break.

"Yes, I saw Bobby. We had a lengthy discussion in fact." Gardner lowered his gold-rimmed coffee cup. "I want to speak to you about it."

"But first—happy birthday. I've waited a long time for your twenty-first birthday." Sentimentality had never been Durant's strong suit; the moment was emotional and difficult. He congratulated himself on his foresight in selecting one of the private dining rooms. "I want you to have this." He watched Gardner open the portfolio he placed in front of him. "I've started you with basic blue-chips with a Street value of fifty thousand. A year from now, before you begin your apprenticeship, I'll want to see what you've done with them. I'm confident the results will be impressive."

Gardner's shoulders stiffened. He glanced at the portfolio, then closed it and raised his eyes to the Monet above the sideboard.

"This summer we'll create a position for you in the back office. I want you to learn the business from the ground up. Next year after graduation, we'll place you in the bull pen for a while, then I want you to consider the Paris office. A few years in Paris, and—"

"Dad, wait." Gardner looked at him and Durant recognized the expression of a man preparing for battle. "I spoke to Bobby Von Marron in regard to the fellowship offered by Home Limited. Bobby believes the Home board will award the fellowship to me if I want it. I do."

For the first time in a decade Win Durant was speechless. His shock was worse than anything he had experienced in years. When he could speak, he stared at his son in appalled disbelief. "Home Limited is   privately held corporation. A Von Marron corporation."

"Home shares are traded on the exchange."

"A portion is traded. Von Marron owns sixty percent, he has control." His voice was flat, expressionless. But it enraged him to state the obvious and realize it was necessary. "I want you here. I have always expected you to accept a career position with La Tourraine, Durant and Von Marron. You know that."

"Please try to understand." Gardner noticed his hands were clenched into fists and he opened his fingers. "I'm not interested in investment banking. I never have been."

"Are you saying you're not interested in money?"

"I'm interested in money. I'm not interested in this arena. Companies like Home Limited are an exciting challenge. How they're managed and the direction they go will determine a large part of the world's future development. Industrial companies are impacting the environment. Some are raping the earth to supply the world's demand for fuel and mineral supplies. I think it can be done without irrevocable destruction. That's part of the challenge."

"Who the hell do you think you're talking to? I sit on Home's board of directors, for Christ's sake. La Tourraine, Durant and Von Marron earns a quarter of its annual fees from transactions enacted for Home Limited. Do you think I don't know what the industrial conglomerates are doing? I know more about it than you'll ever know!"

Dark color rose in Gardner's face. "Maybe you do. I won't argue with you. My point is, I believe I can make a difference at Home Limited. It's what I want to do."

"You don't know what the fuck you want to do. You're only twenty-one years old." He saw his son trying to control his voice and his temper, felt his own rising.

"I know I'm not interested in investment banking. I don't want to spend my life working twenty-four hours a day in an office with windows that won't open, fighting an ulcer every time the market takes a slide."

"Is that what you think investment banking is? Do you think it's that simple and boring?" Incredulous, he waved a hand to encompass gleaming crystal and polished wood, the priceless paintings, the Sèvres china, the sterling flatware. "Investment banking is about money and power. It's about picking up the telephone and hearing the president's voice asking your advice. It's having brunch with Kissinger in the morning and playing tennis with the prime minister of Japan in the afternoon. It's knowing what's happening before anyone else. It's having the entire world bend its knee and say, yes, Mr. Durant, or no, Mr. Durant. Think about that. That is what investment banking is all about. It is not about some fucking windows!"

Gardner's face was pale, but his eyes were steady. "I want a life outside my career. There has to be more to life than amassing paper profits."

"Like shit there is! Bottom line—that's the only thing that counts. The *only* thing. Did you win or did you lose? That's all there is!"

"If I enter La Tourraine, Durant and Von Marron, I'll never have a success. Wait a minute, hear me out, I'm talking bottom line. Whatever I accomplish, people will say I couldn't have done it without you and your help. I'd have to be twice as good as anyone else just to be considered half as good. I'd never be Gardner Durant; I'd always be Win Durant's son."

"That is total and absolute shit!" And if it wasn't, was it so terrible to be known as Win Durant's son?

"If you treated me differently, I'd think it was because you didn't believe I could make it on my own. If you didn't treat me differently, I'd resent it." Gardner spread his hands. "I want to succeed on my own. Not because my father owns part of the firm, not because I'm under your wing—but because I'm good at what I do. The best. I'll never know how good I can be if I work for you."

"You'd rather offer yourself up as a Von Marron lackey instead of taking your rightful place here? Like hell. I won't allow it!"

Durant's voice had risen until he was shouting, something he had not done in years. Feeling the blood in his face, his pulse in his neck, he forced himself to sit back in his chair. He clenched his teeth and swallowed the bile rising in his throat. "What did Von Marron say to you in Paris? Did he offer the fellowship or did you ask for it?"

"I'm not asking permission to accept the Home Fellowship, Dad. I'm informing you of my decision."

A line had been crossed. Suddenly Durant understood his son had stepped into adulthood. At any other time he would have felt proud. Instead, he felt sick. All his dreams, all he had worked toward and struggled for was being rejected by a kid still wet behind the ears. He covered his eyes with his hand and fought for control. He tried to remember what it was to be twenty-one and too stupid and too arrogant to understand that you didn't know shit from shoe polish.

If his own father had lived and if his father had tried to hand him the world when he was twenty-one, would he have had the sense to take it? Christ, yes. He would have grabbed it and wrung it dry. Instead he'd had to make his own way, force his own opportunities. And that is what he had done. But he hadn't battled his way to the top only to have his son reject everything he represented.

"You're making a mistake. I want you here, at La Tourraine, Durant and Von Marron."

"I know. This has been the most difficult decision I'll ever make. I'm sorry to disappoint you."

"Think it over. We don't have to decide the future today."

"I have thought about it. Dad, I'm sorry, but if Home Limited offers the fellowship, I'm going to accept it."

They stared at each other. Acid poured into Durant's stomach. "I vote Bobby's proxy," he said finally. "If you accept a position with Home, I can promise you every shit job Home Limited has. If a piece of logging equipment breaks down in Brazil, you'll find your ass sweating in a jungle. If the price of diamonds falls, you'll be on the next plane to South Africa. If Home needs a coal study, you'll be the asshole standing under a mountain." Gardner's eyes glittered. Anger? Sorrow? He couldn't tell.

"Do what you think you have to. We'll both find out what I'm made of. But threats aren't going to change anything." They stood then, facing each other across the china and antique silver. Gardner looked very young. "I'm sorry, Dad. I know how much—"

"Get out."

The stem of his wine glass snapped between his fingers. With dulled eyes he watched the wine seep into the Holland damask, then he swept his hand across the table, sending the china and crystal crashing to the Brussels carpet.

It wasn't enough that he had given Bobby Von Marron twenty-four goddamn years of his life. Or that he had quadrupled the Von Marron fortune. Now Bobby Von Marron had stolen his son. He had been the cause of Gardner's defection.

The rich took what they wanted; that was how the game was played. They took. He wanted to know when was it his turn? How much money and how much power did he have to have before he was one of them?

"Mr. Durant?" Sedrick stared at the linen and broken china shattered across the carpet.

"He'll change his mind."

"Yes, sir." Sedrick looked over his shoulder and wet his lips uneasily.

"He'll be back."

* * *

"Durant? Gardner? I thought it was you."

"Pull up a stool and sit down, Whitney. Have a drink."

Pont Whitney lifted a brow. "Looks like you have a head start, buddy."

Gardner leaned forward and signaled the bartender. "It's emancipation day. I always get drunk on emancipation day. Haven't you heard? It only comes along once in every twenty-one years."

"I get it. Today is the day you kissed off your old man. How did it go?"

"Not well." Gardner stared at his image in the back mirror then drained his Scotch. "Picture shouting and threats and you'll have some idea."

"At least you did it." Pont frowned and pushed at his drink. "Me? I'll end up running an international shipping concern when I'd rather own a dive shop on a Mexican beach. And you know why? Because I don't have any guts. No guts, Gardner, old man. It's a medical anomaly, a very sad case." He slid off the stool. "I'm not the man to drink with. Right now I envy you too much."

"I feel like shit."

"You'll get over it. The point is, you have your life, you lucky bastard."

"I have my life." He looked in the mirror and thought about Remy Von Marron before he ordered another double Scotch.

Book Two

1977

Chapter 5

MORNING WAS THE BEST TIME of the day. Gloria pulled a thick sweater over her head and down over her turtleneck, then stepped to the bedroom window. The first light of dawn brushed the needle tips of the Aiguilles and transformed the snow draping Mont Blanc into glistening flows of pink and gold. A few lights winked on in Chamonix, a haze of sweet-smelling wood smoke overhung the valley.

A snowball splattered against the glass, and she drew back. Laughing, she opened the window and leaned out to smile at Nicholas de Beauharnais-Rolland standing below. He pushed his skis into the snow and blew her a kiss before he cupped his hands around his mouth and shouted up to her. "Hurry up, we're almost ready to leave."

Plumes of exhaust puffed behind the Aigmont bus; Eliot Grenel, the athletic and expedition director, supervised the loading of equipment and students.

"God, he's handsome!" Holly said, leaning over Gloria's shoulder.

"Nicky?" Heat rose in her cheeks as she looked down at him.

"Him, too. But I meant Eliot. Look at the cool way he moves. Jesus, did you ever see anything so sexy?"

Gloria smiled. "As a matter of fact . . ." A tremor of sensual pleasure ran through her body and she gripped the window sill, thinking about the inn at the far side of the valley. Images flashed through her mind: Nicky's firelit eyes, the touch of his naked skin beneath her fingertips, the moist warmth of his tongue licking drops of wine from between her breasts.

Her stomach tightened and she swallowed, aware of the heat

turning her cheeks scarlet. "We'll be right down. Don't leave without us."

Grinning, Holly stuffed her curls beneath a knit cap. "No chance of that. I've got Eliot wrapped around my little finger. He says I've got the best tits he's ever seen." She caught the parka Gloria tossed to her and opened the door.

"Not so loud. You know Devet would love to catch us and tell Geroux." Gloria's silvery hair disappeared beneath her cap and she pushed her hands into brightly colored gloves. "I'm already worried someone is going to recognize us at the inn or check the theater to see if we're really there."

They were the last ones to board the Aigmont bus. Letting Holly step inside first, Gloria stopped to inhale the sharp icy air. She loved it here. Whenever she recalled her first impression of Aigmont, she smiled with regret. Aigmont was the best thing that could have happened to her.

Eliot Grenel winked and ran a slow glance over the dark ski pants molding her hips. "There'll be plenty of time to admire the view. If we ever get out of the parking lot. Are you coming or not?"

The way he said "coming" brought a flush to her cheeks. She didn't like Eliot Grenel. He was older and handsome in an oily way, but half the school believed he was servicing Geroux when he wasn't chasing after the students. Gloria hadn't told Holly, but she knew Holly wasn't the only girl Eliot took to the inn.

"I don't know what you see in him," she said, dropping into the seat beside Holly. "He's got slimy eyes."

"You're kidding! Eliot can make me come just by looking at me. You don't know what he can do with those eyes!" Putting their heads together, they spoke behind their gloves. "What's Nicky like in bed?"

"You know I don't talk about that."

"Come on, give. I tell *you* everything."

Later, Gloria wished she had paid more attention to their route, but she didn't stop laughing and gossiping with Holly until the bus halted at the embarkation lot midway up the mountainside. Mont Blanc rose above them in icy, daunting splendor.

"Why did I agree to this?" Holly groaned while they waited for their equipment to be unloaded from the bus. "I hate cross-country."

"What a glorious day! You'll have plenty of opportunity for downhill."

"God. What I hate most about you, Von Marron, is your relentless optimism."

"I'd like to think that smile has something to do with last night," Nicky said, moving up beside her. Looking at her mouth, he gave her a smile that did wild, pleasant things to her nervous system.

"It does." From the corner of her eye, Gloria watched Holly roll her eyes. In Holly's oftstated opinion, there was no hope for Gloria as a flirt. Playing games wasn't her style. Either she was attracted to someone, or she was not. She saw no point pretending otherwise on either side of the equation. Moreover, it seemed a cheat to flirt with Nicholas; she loved him and he loved her. Their relationship had transcended games.

"Really stupid," Holly commented, moving up beside her as they left the parking lot for the trail. She nodded toward Nicholas who skied in front of them taking the lead. "You have to keep a man guessing. Take Eliot and me. You know he expects me to hang back with the others so I can be near him. He's wondering why I'm up here with you and Nicky. He's wondering if he did something wrong last night. You have to keep men off balance."

"Why should I be dishonest? Nicky wouldn't play games with me." Nicky looked back at them over his shoulder and winked at her. Immediately she wished Holly had stayed behind with the rest of the group and felt guilty for it.

A puff of vapor underscored Holly's exaggerated sigh. "That's puppy love talking, Von Marron. When you've had more experience . . ."

The group caught up for midmorning chocolate and biscuits, and Eliot admonished the three of them for skiing ahead. "Stay with the group," he cautioned sharply, looking at Holly. Holly shrugged and grinned.

Afterward, she set out after Gloria and Nicky. "You see?" she crowed, cutting beside Gloria. "Keep 'em guessing."

"He's just worried about us. We're several minutes ahead of the others."

"Oh Christ. Trust you to take the romance out of it."

"Nicky said he'd wait for us by the ice bridge."

"An ice bridge? Shit! I hate this!"

Holly skied up beside Nicky and examined the ice bridge, then cautiously peered into the crevasse. Shadows shaded toward blue down the jagged sides. "Oh God. There's no bottom."

"If you want to see the bottom, you'll have to ski closer to the edge," Nicky said, laughing.

"Not a chance. Isn't there some other way across? Or a way around it?"

"Nope." He looked at Gloria. "Shall we cross or wait?"

Holly answered promptly. "I vote to wait. I don't want to go across at all. What if I fall and slide off the edge?"

"Then it's good-bye Holly Drake." Nicky grinned at her. "Come on, it's wide enough to take four people. Don't be such a chicken. We'll ski across and wait for the group on the other side."

"Nicky, maybe Holly's right. If we ski across, Eliot will be furious." The minute she spoke, Gloria realized he would interpret her hesitation as a challenge.

"Screw Eliot. I'm going."

He pushed off, thighs straining against his dark ski pants. Nicholas de Beauharnais-Rolland was a strong skier, his form nearly perfect. She loved the look of his long, athletic body. Loved the way he smiled, the arrogance in his eyes, the stubborn set of his chin.

After halting with a flourish on the far side of the crevasse, he shouted back at them. "Are you coming, ladies?"

Good sense indicated they should wait for Eliot Grenel and the others. Eliot was going to explode when he discovered they had crossed the ice bridge before receiving his permission. But Nicky had crossed safely. If Gloria didn't follow, Nicky would suffer the full blast of Eliot's anger alone. Plus, he would think she was a coward or that she didn't trust his judgment. She cursed softly under her breath, beginning to feel the cold now that she had stopped moving. She studied Nicky waiting on the other side and understood this was some kind of test. Whether she approved or not, game playing existed.

Leaning forward, she thrust her poles into the snow and shoved off. The ice bridge was longer and narrower than she had first estimated. Through her peripheral vision, she glimpsed sharp-edged walls glistening in the afternoon sun, and she could feel the bottomless empty space beneath her. Relief dropped her shoulders when she straightened beside Nicky on the other side of the crevasse. He grinned and gave her a thumbs-up sign then they both looked back at Holly.

"Shit, shit, shit!"

Laughing, Nicky called to her. "Wait for the others. I hear them coming."

"That's the surest way to coax her across. She's determined to annoy Eliot."

Holding hands, they watched as Holly drew several deep breaths, looked behind her at the first parka emerging from between the slopes of the cut; then she straightened, swore loudly, and pushed off. When she drew up beside them, she closed her eyes and sank down on the backs of her skis.

"I don't ever want to do that again! God. My heart is pounding so loud I can't hear a thing." When Nicky, smiling, explained they had to cross the ice bridge to get back to the bus, Holly looked horrified. "Stop laughing. I was seriously terrified. If I ever agree to this sort of lunacy again, will the two of you please throw me back in my room and lock the door? I despise skiing. I wanted to go to school in Hawaii, but no. It had to be here."

Still laughing, Gloria turned from Holly to watch the others emerge from the cut and approach the ice bridge. It was a small group, two girls from her form and a friend of Nicky's. Plus Eliot Grenel, who was furious.

He removed his goggles and shouted across the crevasse. "Stay right where you are. I want to talk to you three." With no more than a glance at the tracks they had cut across the snow covering the ice bridge, he skied forward, the others following close behind.

Gloria heard the first crack without understanding what it was. Her first thought was that someone had fired a pistol. Before she could turn to inspect the mountain and attempt to locate whoever had fired the shot, a second loud crack followed immediately upon the first. This time there was no mistaking the source. Eyes wide with horror, Gloria jerked toward the ice bridge and gripped her poles. The group on the bridge slowed nearly to a halt, looking to either side and then at each other.

"Move!" Eliot screamed. His poles clawed into the ice. "Go!"

The ice bridge broke loose in a single piece, the sides snapping free within a pulse beat of each other. For an instant the ice bridge appeared to hang suspended in air, then it collapsed in the center and the pieces tumbled into the crevasse spilling chunks of ice and brightly colored parkas. Screams lifted above the roar of cracking, smashing ice. Seconds later there was nothing. Only a spiraling spindrift of loose snow through which Gloria could see the sparkling sides of the crevasse. Then silence. A terrible sudden silence as profound as death.

"Holy Christ!" Nicky whispered.

Gloria's pulse crashed in her ears, her stomach looped in long, queasy rolls. Placing her hands on her knees, she leaned forward and swallowed repeatedly against the nausea burning her throat. This could not have happened. It had to be a nightmare. Please God, let me wake up in my bed at Aigmont.

"Holy shit!" Holly, still sitting on the backs of her skis, stared in bewilderment at the settling plume of fine snow. "This is some kind of joke, right? I mean—they didn't, they couldn't have just . . ." Her voice thickened and froze.

Doubling over, Nicky vomited between his ski tips. He pulled his cap from his head and wiped his lips, swallowing convulsively. "Jesus. One minute they were there, and the next minute . . . shit! Oh God."

Tears clouded Holly's unblinking stare. "Did you see Eliot's eyes? God! He was looking at me when it happened. Oh God!" She covered her face and shuddered. "It could have been me! I was the last to cross before—Christ! It could have been me! I could be down there right now! I could be dead!"

"Holly, stop it!" Moving to Holly's side, Gloria knelt in the snow. "It wasn't you. You're safe."

"But it could have been me. I wanted to wait. I almost did. Then I would have been down there, too!"

"Listen to me. What's happened is terrible, but we have to stay calm." She spoke as much to herself as to Holly. Behind her eyes she continued to see the bridge collapsing and the parkas tumbling among the ice chunks. A scream built at the back of her throat; she closed her eyes and took several deep breaths, swallowing hard.

When she had battled down the scream and the images, she lifted her head and looked toward Nicky, hoping he would help her with Holly who continued to babble, on the edge of hysteria. But Nicky stood motionless, staring into the crevasse as if hypnotized. She returned to Holly and touched her cheek. "Don't think about it, not now. Think about us instead." It was the only way. "Holly. We have to decide what we're going to do."

"Do? What is there to do?" Hysteria thinned Holly's voice. She flung a mittened hand toward the crevasse. "They are fucking dead, Gloria. We can't *do* anything! All we can do is wait for someone to rescue us!"

Except it wasn't going to be that easy. Grateful for something to take her mind from the horror of the disaster and deliberately not looking toward the crevasse, Gloria brushed the snow from her sleeve and examined her watch. It was two o'clock. When would someone miss them and start to worry?

"I need to speak to Nicky. Will you be all right?" When Holly didn't respond, she touched her cheek again, then skied to Nicky's side. "Nicky, I need your help. Were we going directly back to Aigmont, or were we supposed to have dinner in the village first?"

Nicky didn't answer. He stood without moving, letting the spindrift of snow settle on his face and hands.

Gloria bit her lip and tried again. "Think about something else, Nicky. Help me." Paralyzed, he stared into the crevasse watching the snow floating where the bridge had been. She skiied back to Holly.

"Holly, try to remember. Were we planning to return to Aigmont, or were we to have dinner first?" She wanted to ask if Eliot had announced their schedule, but she couldn't bear to speak his name. A rush of weakness turned her knees to straw. "Holly?"

"I don't know! Why are you babbling about dinner, for Christ's sake? Eliot is dead! So are Isabelle and Susan and Eric. Don't you care? Don't you give a shit? What's the matter with you?" Tears ran down her cheeks, and her body shook uncontrollably. "You didn't like Eliot, did you? You're glad he's dead!"

"Oh Holly, you know that isn't true. I'm as devastated as you are. But if I let myself think about what happened, I'll go crazy." She raised her voice to include Nicky. "It's easier to think about us. Please listen to me. It will be hours before we're missed. Geroux won't realize anything is wrong until late tonight. No one is going to look for us in the dark; it will be morning before they send a search team. We have to talk about what we're going to do."

They couldn't survive a night on the mountainside. Already the afternoon shadows had raced across the crevasse and Gloria could feel the temperature steadily dropping against her face. She rubbed her glove over her cheek and glanced at the sun sinking behind the peaks.

"Nicky? Nicky, talk to me."

"Eric's down there. And Eliot," he whispered. "Maybe they're still alive. Maybe they're hurt, waiting for us to help them."

It wasn't possible. Tears came to her eyes, and she brushed at them with her glove. "No," she said after a moment. She took his sleeve and turned him to face her. "Think about us, Nicky. We can't stay here or we'll freeze."

Finally, he understood. "We're going to die."

"Nicky—"

"We can't get back to the bus, and no one is coming for us. Oh Jesus, Jesus! I don't want to die." A sound like a sob tore from his throat, then he looked down at himself. Gloria followed his gaze. A large, wet stain spread and darkened the front of his ski pants. He tried to cover it with his gloves then his hands fell away, and he stood in front of her, weeping.

"Oh Nicky, don't. Please don't." Embarrassment deepened the icy pink in her cheeks. She tried to tell herself it didn't matter that he had wet himself or that he was crying. "Please, I need you. Holly is hysterical and I feel like going to pieces and— Nicky, help me."

He tried to speak then dropped his eyes and helplessly shook his head.

"It's getting colder," Holly sobbed. "Do you feel it? I'm cold. Are we going to die? We're going to die, aren't we?"

"Nicky—please."

"Goddamn it, Gloria, leave me alone! I don't know what to do! We can't go forward and we can't go back. All we can do is wait."

He was right. The bridge was gone. And the mountain behind them was daunting. To cross it in daylight was newsworthy; to attempt it in approaching darkness was unthinkable. Nausea rose again in her throat, and she felt her stomach cramp.

"There's no choice," she whispered. She peered up at the peak and clenched her fists. If she had her bearings correctly, Chamonix lay in the valley on the other side. "We have to go over the peak."

Nicky and Holly stared at her incredulously, then dismissed the suggestion in a single voice.

"Do you want to kill us, too?" Holly buried her head between her knees and rocked back and forth. A thin, keening noise issued from her lips.

"That's insane. We'd never make it." Nicky turned away from her to look into the crevasse.

She didn't argue. The mountain was overwhelming, impossible. Gloria sank down on the backs of her skis. They couldn't ski over the mountain in the darkness, not even in moonlight. It was too dangerous. It would make any rescue attempt much more difficult. Icy wind whipped eddies of snow across the face of the mountain as she watched, swirled around her body and stung her cheeks.

So they would sit here and wait. In all probability they would be frozen when the search team found them tomorrow morning. The press would have a field day. Cold wind sliced through her parka like flying needles as she imagined the headlines.

"We have to try," she said after a minute.

"Shut up, Gloria!" Holly raised a tear-stained face. The tears had begun to freeze on her cheeks. "If we go up there, they'll never find us. We have to wait."

"Holly's right."

Staring up at the mountain, she thought it through. "Do you know what's wrong with us?" she asked, speaking to herself more than to either of them. "Someone has always taken care of us. All we have to do is make a phone call or speak a word and someone makes our problems vanish. Except that's not how it's going to happen this time."

"Bullshit!"

"Don't you see? This time no one is coming. No one is going to make our problem disappear. By the time anyone misses us and assembles a search party, we'll be dead. The only way we have a chance to survive this is by helping ourselves." She looked at Holly. "Remember when you said we were on our own? We have to try." Standing, she studied the mountain and felt her heart drop to her toes. "Trying is better than sitting here waiting to die. It's better than giving up."

The need to do something, anything, was woven into a dozen personal images and emotions. Remy, her mother, the past two summers with her father, the helplessness of having no choices, of having no voice in her own life. And there was the need to win. She couldn't give up. If she was going to die, then she preferred to die having tried to win. She attempted to explain her feelings to Holly and Nicky, but neither understood. They didn't want to hear.

Looking at Nicky, she felt a deep sadness. Only this morning she had loved him. "I'm going."

"For Christ's sake, don't be so stupid!"

"When I reach Chamonix, I'll send someone back for you." Bending over her skis, she tightened her bindings, then drew a long breath and prayed she had the courage for what she needed to do. She started sidestepping up the slope.

"Gloria, come back here!" Holly dashed a glove over her eyes. "You'll never make it."

One step at a time. She wouldn't think about the mountain or the cold or the parkas tumbling among the ice chunks, just the next step. She would think about the people she loved. Margaret. Gardner. Her parents. Uncle Win and Aunt Chissie. Remy. She would think about winning.

"Gloria!"

Freezing wind flowed over her cheeks and lips, but exertion had heated her skin. A trickle of sweat zigzagged down the inside of her sweater. Good. Up this rise, then down the other side. Up the next rise, then down. Don't think about the shadows or how cold it would be when full darkness descended. Keep the rock outcropping on her left. Win.

"Goddamit, Gloria! Come back." She heard them calling below her.

In the end there was no one but herself. Nicky and Holly couldn't help her any more than her father could have helped when Remy died and her mother went to Les Eaux. She understood that now. She had only herself.

Her mouth set, and she placed one determined foot and then the other, rising another yard. Never again would she look to other people for guidance, for a measure of her own worth. Never again. The words became a litany, setting the rhythm for her ascent.

When she gained the top of the first rise, she stopped to catch her breath and turned her heated face into the wind. Beneath her, she saw Nicky and Holly struggling to follow. There was no triumph in the sight, only an additional weight of responsibility. She waited until they had nearly reached her, then she skied down a short slope and began the long sidestep up the next rise.

Exhaustion transformed her feet into unwieldy lumps of concrete. Blisters formed inside her boots, broke, then formed again. Pain shot upward with each dragging step. Gloria had never been so cold in her life. Long ago she had ceased to feel her cheeks; her lips felt as if they would split if she tried to speak.

"I can't go on." It was Holly.

Stopping, Gloria peered dully at the pale shadows strewn by a quarter moon. The sky and trees were black; their clothing appeared dark gray; the snow and her breath were shaded a paler gray. Black and gray. The shadings seemed significant.

She made herself turn back and watch as Holly slid into a boulder, then fell to the ground beneath a shower of snow dislodged from the rock. The quarter moon emitted enough light that she could see the broken tip on Holly's right ski. Ice clung to Holly's brows and had formed around her mouth.

Following in Holly's tracks, Nicky glided to the boulder and sagged against it before he, too, slipped to the ground. He curled into a ball beside Holly. "No more. I have to rest."

Each step toward them sent darts of pain stinging toward her thighs. Her knees were rubbery, her voice blunted by fatigue. "Get up," Gloria whispered.

"I can't," Holly moaned. Helpless tears had frozen near her lips. "I can't feel my feet."

"Get up."

A tide of rage choked her, shocking in its intensity. She hadn't believed she still had the energy to feel anything. "You're always telling me how goddamn tough you are—now get up!"

Holly turned her face into her mittens.

"All you two have done is bitch and complain every damn step of the way!" Tears heated her eyes. They had fought the mountain and her, fought each other, fought survival. "I don't care anymore, do you hear me? If you're expecting me to pull you up again, forget it. I'm through begging you to live!" Contempt stacked atop her rage. If they died, she would be free of them. And, God, she wanted to be free of them. She didn't want to wait anymore or plead with them one more time.

"Get up or you'll die!" Dashing at the tears in her eyes, she told herself to leave them. Instead, she lifted her pole and swung it hard across Nicky's buttocks. "Get up, goddammit! Move!" He was weeping again, not even attempting to protect himself from her blows. Hours ago she had decided she loathed him.

"Go on without us." Holly curled forward in the snow and pushed her face into her arms. "Go on and leave us alone."

"You'll die if you stay here." Didn't they know she craved rest, too? Didn't they know she yearned to tighten into a ball, too, and just go to sleep? She was so tired. Somewhere she had read that freezing was an easy death, that you felt warm near the end. It was so simple. Just close your eyes and go to sleep. Like walking into the Sound and swimming until you slipped beneath the waves. Gardner's voice rose in her memory, taunting her, telling her he had believed she had more courage than to give up so easily.

"One more rise," she murmured. "Then if you want to give up . . . all right." She hated herself for pleading, for wasting what energy she still had. They ignored her.

"I'm leaving."

When they didn't move, didn't open their eyes, she stared, hating and envying them, and she hesitated. Continuing was hopeless, she had understood that several miles ago, several hours ago. But she wouldn't give up. She would not give up until she could no longer lift one boot in front of the other. Turning to look at the moon-shadowed slope rising before her, she wondered if she could do it. God, she was tired. Her boots and gloves felt like marble weights. The anger bled from her system and despair rushed in to replace it.

The tears on her cheeks congealed to slush and she wiped at them with her glove. Then she dragged herself forward and made herself begin the slow painful sidestep up the slope, sucking gasps of icy air as old blisters popped and new blisters formed. One step at a time. Never again. One more step. Win. Never again. Just one more.

At the top, she leaned over her knees, panting and weeping, swaying. The larch forest in front of her seemed inpenetrable. But the ground sloped down. Just a little further. She would give it up at the next slope. Groping, she grasped a branch and pulled herself forward, no longer caring about position or direction. The only thing that mattered was to win a few more yards. Then, never again.

She emerged from the trees suddenly, unexpectedly, and stopped, staring stupidly at a scattering of lights below. What she was seeing didn't immediately register. When it did, her knees collapsed and she fell in the snow and wept. Great heaving sobs mixed with laughter scraped her throat raw. Adrenaline burst through her body when she finally struggled to her feet. Every instinct urged her forward, toward the safety of the lights. Instead, she turned and forced herself back through the larch forest, made herself return down the slope.

"You're lying," Nicky groaned when she shook him awake. "Go away."

"I saw the lights! We can make it. I swear it, we're almost there. We won! We beat the mountain!"

Two hours later, they skied into Chamonix, stumbling with exhaustion, wooden with cold, and they fell against the door of the first house they reached. Blood had frozen on the gash on Gloria's forehead, Nicky and Holly had frostbitten fingers and toes. They were too fatigued, too numb to speak. But they had made it. They had won.

* * *

Someone placed a steaming mug of chocolate between her fingers, but she was too exhausted to raise the cup to her lips. When she next opened her eyes, Madame Geroux's chalky face was bending over her, and Aigmont's doctor stood beside her. Their voices sounded slurred and distant. It was excessively hot in the room, but she couldn't stop shivering. She remembered someone carrying her outside to Madame's touring car, then, when she stirred again, she was in her bed at Aigmont. A wide bandage covered most of her forehead. Blinking, she pushed up on her elbows to touch the bandage, remembered to look to see if Holly was in her bed.

Holly was propped against her pillows, staring though the darkness. "I hated you. I wished you were dead." The early dawn shadows hid her expression. "You saved my life." When Gloria said nothing, Holly began to weep. "Why did you do it? What drove you?"

Gloria dropped her head onto the pillow and slept.

The press conference was the second ever permitted at Aigmont. At Madame's direction, an array of pastries had been set out on a buffet along the west wall of the dining room, complimented by silver urns of Swiss coffee and chocolate. Newsmen and newswomen from two continents demolished the refreshments in less time than Madame would have believed possible, leaving napkins and crushed cigarettes behind as they rushed to the windows to observe Elfie Drake's arrival. Elfie emerged from a white Mercedes, wearing dark glasses and a knee-length lynx.

From their bedroom window Gloria and Holly watched the press surround Elfie.

"That's my new uncle," Holly commented, studying the man who supported her mother's elbow. "He's producing Elfie's new film. Maybe she'll marry this one."

For the press conference and her mother, Holly had wrapped gauze around her breasts, flattening her generous figure. She wore a high-necked, drop-waisted plaid dress and no makeup. Green ribbons tied the braids that fell over her shoulders.

"She's so beautiful, isn't she?" Holly pressed her forehead against the window glass. "You know something? One day soon I'll be older than she is. She's still twenty-five."

"Right now you look about twelve." Standing next to Holly, Gloria felt and looked several years older. She touched the pearls at her throat, deciding she looked matronly in gray wool.

"Do you know what she'd do to me if I showed up with tits? If I looked my age? I'd never see her again."

"You don't see her now." Though Gloria spoke in a quiet voice, she instantly regretted the words. She thought of the blue ribbons in her bedroom at Goose Point and the trophies she had accumulated to please Lulu. "I'm sorry, Holly. You really do look about twelve years old. Elfie will be pleased."

"Really?"

The naked hope in Holly's eyes was painful to observe. But for a moment the closeness between them returned. They hadn't talked much during the last three days. Unless it was necessary, they avoided looking at each other. The night on the mountain had carved a gap between them which they seemed unable to span.

Turning from the mirror, Gloria lifted the pile of telegrams on her desk and reread Gardner's. There were messages from nearly everyone she knew, including her father. That telegram she wadded and threw into her wastebasket.

"Maybe he'll surprise you and come after all," Holly said, taking Gloria's place before the mirror. She stared at her braids and her flat chest and sighed.

"No."

According to the telegram, her father was urgently needed in New York. Business. He said he looked forward to seeing her for the summer. He said he was glad she had been rescued, glad she was unhurt. He did not say he was proud of her. He did not say he was missing her.

"He probably didn't know Elfie was coming, or Nicky's father."

"Probably not." Gloria told herself she didn't care.

Madame Geroux escorted them to the dining room and watched with distaste as Elfie Drake kissed the air beside her daughter's cheek while flashbulbs exploded. Hastily, Elfie removed herself to the far end of the dining room, drawing most of the press with her. Ensconced on a wooden stool which quickly became a throne, Elfie tossed back the lynx to expose her famous breasts, then held forth on her latest film, which she had deserted in order to support her "poor baby daughter who almost died." Her trademark shudder was exquisite.

Madame had a word with Paul de Beauharnais-Rolland, Nicky's father, then stepped to the lectern and cleared her throat into the microphone. Briefly she described the accident and provided pertinent information on those who had perished. Standing behind Madame, Gloria watched the furious scribbling. She blinked as cameras flashed in her eyes, and unconsciously she stepped backward when Madame finished and a chaos of shouted questions erupted.

"Whose decision was it to ski out?"

"Will you lose any fingers or toes?"

"How did it feel to watch your friends die?"

"Look this way for the cameras!"

Madame Geroux rapped a pen on the side of the lectern. "We will progress more smoothly if each provides his own statement." She glanced toward Paul de Beauharnais-Rolland then touched Nicky's sleeve, urging him forward.

Nicky explained he had crossed the ice bridge and Gloria and Holly had followed. He told the scribbling reporters how the bridge had collapsed, told them of the shock and horror he had felt.

"I knew we couldn't remain at the crevasse. We would have frozen before anyone found us. So I convinced Miss Drake and Miss Von Marron that we had no choice. It seemed obvious. We had to ski out."

Gloria's silvery hair swung across her cheek as her head jerked up. Holly clasped her hands and stared at the floor.

"There were moments when they—we—wanted to give up."

"But you persuaded Miss Von Marron and Miss Drake to keep going?"

"I felt responsible for them, naturally."

"Miss Von Marron and Miss Drake owe you their lives." Flashbulbs popped and cameras whirred.

Nicky gave the reporters a boyish grin, at once proud and modest. "Both girls acted with courage." His tone suggested gallantry rather than truth.

Fury displaced Gloria's initial incredulity. Heat pulsed in her cheeks, cheeks the reporters had already labeled as being as delicate and patrician as a Sèvres cup.

"That is a lie."

Until this moment, she had not grasped the power of a quietly spoken word. Cameras and faces swung toward her, but she was unaware. This was between herself and Nicky. Or perhaps the confrontation was between herself and whom she had been before. Whatever it was, something had happened on the mountainside. She had accepted that she was alone. That she had no champion but herself.

"You were paralyzed with fear," she said to Nicky, leaning

past Holly. "You wept and told me I was stupid to even think about skiing out. You insisted we wait by the crevasse to be rescued."

"That isn't true!" Nicky threw a quick look toward his father, then spread his hands in a pleading gesture. "Gloria, you know what happened."

"I know you were so frightened you wet your pants. I know you wanted to give up. You laid down in the snow and told me to go away and let you die." She stared at him. "I should have done it."

Shouts exploded over the dining room, and the press surged forward. Flashbulbs blinded her. Lifting her chin high, Gloria walked to the door and left the room.

"It's a scandal." Bobby Von Marron dropped the newspaper beside his chair and rubbed his eyes. "I suppose I should take her out of Aigmont."

"The term is nearly finished, isn't it?" Win Durant had directed Lucille Ivory to hold his calls, but his gaze continually strayed to the row of screens on his desk terminal. A steady line of figures flowed across the glass. He hoped to Christ someone on the trading desk had picked up what was happening to IBM.

"Madame says Gloria is being ostracized. She says she spoke to her about withdrawing but Gloria refuses. I wonder if Lulu has seen the headlines. I keep meaning to ask if she's allowed newspapers." He dropped his head. "Of course, Beauharnais-Rolland will take his business out of the Paris office."

"Tell La Tourraine to romance Beauharnais-Rolland. The Beauharnais-Rolland account is too substantial to lose. Tell Georges to look for the weakness. I'd suggest he begin with the tankers Beauharnais-Rolland has in the Caribbean. I suspect he'll find some leverage there."

The shock in Bobby's lifted brow annoyed him. "Surely La Tourraine, Durant and Von Marron would not resort to blackmail. If Paul wishes to place his business elsewhere, that is precisely what he should do. We don't want someone with the firm who doesn't want to be with us."

"The Beauharnais-Rolland portfolio generates a quarter of a million dollars in annual fees. Considering the profit record of the Paris office, I should think this is an account you and Georges would wish to save."

"Certainly. And I'm convinced Georges will mount a persuasive effort, but without resorting to questionable tactics."

"I'm leaving for D.C. in an hour, Bobby. I don't have time to argue the point. Tell La Tourraine to do whatever is necessary to placate Beauharnais-Rolland."

"One of the reasons I came in today, Win, is to tell you Georges isn't well. He's seeking a second opinion, but it looks like cancer."

"Cancer." Durant leaned back and studied the shine of moisture filming Bobby's eyes. "How long does he have?" The firm had only recently recovered its capital position after buying back Edison Whitehall's partnership interest. After three years. Still, a step backward at this point could mean a giant step into the future. He thought of his son and the taste of soured dreams closed his throat.

"We'll know more after next week."

He didn't open his briefcase during the flight to Washington, D.C. Instead he frowned out the plane's window, nursed his drink, and thought about Gardner. Goddamn him. Three years hadn't lessened the pain he continued to feel when he thought about Gardner's betrayal. He had genuinely believed Gardner would tire of chasing after Home Limited's problems and would appear in his office begging for forgiveness and for a position with the firm.

He had done what he could to effect that resolution. He had used his position on Home's board of directors to assign Gardner every unpleasant job that came across the table. He had sent his son to the North Sea, to the Antarctic, to mosquito-infested regions of the equator. He had given Gardner tasks no one else would accept. Each time Gardner had emerged triumphant, returning stronger, leaner, more determined. If Durant had not been poisoned by his son's betrayal, he would have been proud.

He rolled an unlit cigar between his fingers and ordered another drink. When La Tourraine died, he would be a step closer to having it all. Eventually Gardner would regain his senses and shake free of Von Marron's influence. He would return to claim the empire Durant had built.

Chapter 6

$\mathcal{I}$T WAS COOLER in the lake country outside Butiaba than it had been in Kampala, but still hot enough that Gardner's shirt clung to his back as he and Lars Trumby moved out of the shade. The copper pit opened in front of him, but for the moment he was more interested in the buildings north of the administration offices. Last year, at his urging, Home Limited had opened a medical clinic and a school at Butiaba. The clinic issued quinine every morning and administered emergency first aid; the school offered day classes to the miners' children and adult classes following the last shift. Only seven children had entered the school building this morning.

"All right, Lars, cut to the bottom line. What's going on here? You're running light shifts; a quarter of your equipment is sitting idle; the school is nearly empty."

Lars Trumby looked toward the pit. "You've read the reports. Africa's at war. Uganda is surrounded by insurrection. There's fighting in Ethiopia, fighting in Zaire." He shrugged.

"I didn't come here to learn what I can discover by reading a newspaper. I doubt fighting in Zaire has much to do with Butiaba's idle trucks. What's happening here is local. I want to know about it."

Trumby studied him, then nodded. "There's Scotch in my trailer. I've got ice."

The trailer was shaded by a cluster of mvuli trees. The thin shade and a laboring air conditioner made it almost pleasant inside. Gardner took a seat in the small living room, noting the careless clutter of bachelor living. "Where's Susan?"

"I sent her home to the States." Lars handed him a drink. Already the ice had begun to melt.

"It's that bad?"

"It's that bad."

"Amin?"

"What you're reading in the newspapers isn't half the story. Amin is a bloodthirsty lunatic, a military butcher without conscience or morals, who's trying to put a hard squeeze on the world. I thought Home would pull out of here last year after the Entebbe thing. Now I'm starting to think whoever is running this outfit has his head up his ass. You can tell Tobler I said so. Except Tobler isn't going to listen to you or read your reports either. Hell, Gardner, I was stripping ore when you were still in diapers. If Tobler won't listen to me, he sure as hell isn't going to listen to you."

"If he would, what would I tell him?"

Lars scrubbed a hand through graying hair. "You'd tell him to get the fuck out of Uganda. Yesterday." After a moment he looked up from his drink. "Walter Tobler doesn't want to hear that Home should abandon a thirty-million-dollar investment. Not while there's an ounce of profit still to be had. Tobler is going to work this pit right up to the minute a mob of blood-crazed savages come running out of the bush wielding hoes, machetes, and machine guns. Profit, that's all that counts."

"Then you think the mine should be abandoned?"

"Damn right I do." Leaning his elbows on his knees, Lars Trumby met Gardner's direct gaze. "Amin wants foreign investment out of here. He wants the whole pie for himself. And if we won't go politely, he'll give us a shove. Shit, the only thing keeping this operation going is a network of bribes starting with two thousand shillings a month to a Neanderthal named Omuta."

"Two hundred and thirty-eight dollars, American."

"Sounds cheap. But they're just getting around to us; this is only the beginning. And Omuta is only the local guy. We're paying fifty thousand shillings to the government and have been since Obote's regime. It's part of the cost of doing business. But things have changed. The heat's on, and money is only part of it. Amin wants us out. Think about it. The kickbacks don't mean shit. What does Omuta need money for? Hell, there's nothing to buy. We could pay him ten grand a month and he'd still live in a tin shack and eat garbage. The kickbacks are meant to hit us in the pocket, but they're just one step in the program. The rest of the pattern is taking shape. Labor intimidation, equipment sabotage, shipping foul-ups. We're starting to see it."

Gardner nodded. He had seen some of it himself. "How much of this does the board of directors know?"

Lars freshened their drinks. "I've sent Tobler a blizzard of paper, but who knows what he's done with it. I've told him fifty thousand Asians have packed it in and gone home. Amin has slaughtered one hundred thousand Ugandans in the last five years. I've told Tobler fourteen thousand and two hundred tons of ore were shipped last year—from all the mines. We shipped that much ourselves three years ago. You want production figures? Come over to my office and I'll show you figures. We're taking a hit." He drew on a cigarette. "You know what kind of response I get? Tobler's people say increase production. Shit, how am I supposed to do that? Two days before you arrived, my first shift came to work and found three heads nailed to the front gate. A supervisor and two day laborers. A third of the shift took one look, then disappeared."

Gardner stared. "Did you speak to Omuta about it?"

"You don't get it. We aren't paying protection—we're paying to keep the doors open. Omuta shrugs and says, sorry, B'wana. He says he doesn't know who's hacking off heads. It's not his problem if my men piss in their pants when they come to work. Not his problem that more and more workers aren't showing up. He doesn't care shit about schools or clinics. Doesn't care about employment or what happens to these people when the mines close. The party line says foreign investment goes. When the natives storm the palace, pal, you can bet your ass Omuta will be the first bastard through the gates with a machete in each hand."

Following a hot, restless night, Gardner accepted Lars's invitation and studied the production figures and charts in the cramped office. He examined a row of disabled equipment, observed the shifts dwindle to a trickle of men. The tension in the compound thickened as the days passed until it became as tangible as the heat and dust overhanging the mine pit. He saw fear in the faces of the miners, read it between the lines of the production reports. But it wasn't until he stood before a row of severed heads spiked to the entrance gate that the reality drove home. Butiaba's problems weren't open to the quick fix he had been sent here to apply.

"Christ." This time there were four heads. One had belonged to a child.

"I want the school closed," he said to Lars as they walked across a grassy landing strip toward Home's plane. "Give the instructor a year's wages and get him the hell out of here." He tossed his bags up to the pilot and glanced back toward the gate.

As long as he lived he would see that boy's bloodied face and want someone to pay for it.

"No offense, Durant, but do you have the authority to close the school and authorize a year's wages?"

"The truth? I don't know. We'll find out." His expression was grim. "Meanwhile, assume I do and get that man out of here before his head shows up on the gate. And watch out for yours." They shook hands then he swung up into the plane. "I'll be back to close you down," he shouted.

"I hope to Christ you are."

During his three years with Home Limited he had not requested a favor of his father or sought any advantage from his father's position on Home's board of directors. But now he thought of the row of bloodied heads and knew it was time to use whatever influence he possessed. He needed to bypass Tobler and gain access to the full board.

Winthrop Durant gave way to his son's impassioned speech. He arranged Gardner's presentation to Home's board in full knowledge the precedent would send angry ripples racing down the chain of command. He was equally certain Gardner would waste the board's time and embarrass himself.

Five minutes into Gardner's Uganda presentation, Durant forgot his reservations and forgot that Gardner was his son. His mind reeled with facts and figures; his thoughts jumped forward to access Home's tenuous position.

"In closing, Mr. Tobler," Gardner addressed a perfunctory nod to Home's president, then returned to the full board, "I'll repeat: Home is going to lose Butiaba. The only question is when. You can see from the figures I've provided that production is down. These figures reflect a wound, gentlemen. At this time next year we'll be looking at a hemorrhage. And a great number of our employees will be dead." He looked at each man sitting around the table. "I recommend we cut our losses and get out. Last year Zaire National made an offer for Butiaba that was rejected by this board as being too low. Gentlemen, I urge you to reconsider. Sixty cents on the dollar, if you can still get it, is looking better every day. The alternative is to wait for Amin's henchmen to seize the mine, in which case we're looking at a dead loss."

Walter Tobler stood. "Very impressive, Mr. Durant. Thank you. The board will consider your recommendations."

Win Durant watched Gardner gather his materials and leave

the board room. The presentation had been controlled and professional. Gardner's passion was evident and exerted an undeniable effect, but emotion had not overshadowed the presentation, not even when the row of severed heads had flashed across the screen.

At the end of the day, Durant was empowered by the board to inform Gardner that Home would reopen negotiations with Zaire National. Butiaba was to cease production immediately; all personnel were to be flown home.

"We're sending you back to Uganda to supervise the shutdown," he told Gardner over drinks in Harry's Bar. Before they left, he announced Gardner's promotion, the words sticking to the roof of his mouth. When Gardner smiled in anticipation, he turned aside, knowing his son hoped for a word of congratulation. He could not speak that word. Instead, he raised his eyes from his drink and said, "You just cost Home Limited several million dollars. You had better be right."

What infuriated Gloria was how obvious they were. They didn't attempt to conceal the fact they were sleeping together.

She handed the menu to the waiter and tasted her Chablis, hating the wine, hating Maxim's, resenting her father for insisting she have lunch with Bee Bee Halston. There was nothing Bee Bee could say or do to make Gloria accept the affair. Aside from disliking Bee Bee, she would have rejected any woman who attempted to replace her mother.

"Well," Bee Bee said brightly. She bared her teeth at her compact mirror, removed a spot of lipstick from her front tooth with her little finger, folded the compact into a Cartier purse. "It's been a busy summer, hasn't it? Does it seem to you there have been more parties than last year?"

Even Bee Bee's voice irritated. She spoke in a flat midwestern twang which a decade on the East Coast had not softened. When she attempted French, as she had done with the waiter, Gloria felt like cringing. Plus, Bee Bee seemed incapable of sitting still. She bounced, bubbled, crossed, and recrossed her legs. Finally, she was younger than Lulu Von Marron, voluptuously animated and alive.

"Too busy for Daddy to visit Mummy, apparently," Gloria said, glancing at her watch.

"Ah yes." Bee Bee's heavily mascaraed lashes narrowed. "And how is dear Lulu? You saw her—when was it?—two weeks ago?"

"She's as beautiful as she always was," Gloria said truthfully, watching Bee Bee. "I imagine she'll be coming home soon." This was a lie.

She dreaded the trips to Geneva as her mother didn't appear to be improving. Les Eaux itself was lovely, situated at the edge of the lake. Each guest—Les Eaux didn't call them patients—occupied a beautifully appointed suite, and the staff wore uniforms designed by Dior. But nothing could obliterate a pervading ambiance of quiet despair. It overtook one the moment the car moved beneath Les Eaux's scrolled gate. It was there in the brooding silence, in the distraction and emptiness glimpsed in the eyes of the guests. Gloria had recognized the despair behind her mother's feverish gaiety, had recognized it in the sudden drop of her mother's shoulders. Lulu had settled into a permanent state of melancholy. She believed Remy played Debussy for her while the staff slept.

"Bobby and I think it's time we discussed your debut," Bee Bee suggested over the poached salmon. "I think New York, don't you? The Plaza or the Pierre, whichever you prefer. Of course we'll select your gowns while you're still here in Paris."

Gloria's debut had been planned for years. Somewhere among Lulu's papers was a lavender and blue book containing lists of guests, decorations, designs for Gloria's gowns.

She lowered her fork. "Mummy will expect me to wait until she's better and can be present."

"That could be a very long time. I thought Bobby told you. I've decided to sponsor your debut."

Gloria's eyes deepened to a darker gray. "Aunt Chissie or Aunt Therese will sponsor me if I ask. But a debut without Mummy is out of the question. I'll wait until she can be there."

"Gloria, don't be difficult. You know as well as anyone that Lulu isn't coming out of Les Eaux."

"Then I won't have a debut." She shrugged.

"Don't you think that's foolish? There's no reason to sacrifice your debut. Everyone knows the situation. They'll understand." Bee Bee touched her napkin to her lips. "Let me put it this way. Don't be an ass, Gloria. I've already told people I'll be your sponsor."

"Then you made a mistake, didn't you?" The sudden coldness in her eyes extended beyond her years.

"Your loyalty is admirable and duly noted." Bee Bee inspected her lacquered nails. "But I think you're too smart to hold onto a foolish position. You have responsibilities, family obligations. You're expected to come out.''

Bee Bee's confidence that Gloria could be managed infuriated her. ''There's no point discussing this. I won't be manipulated.'' Like her father was being manipulated.

''I see.'' Bee Bee studied her from beneath the brim of her summer straw hat. ''Your directness is refreshing. It seems I've underestimated you. Our little Gloria is growing up.''

''I can't think why you haven't noticed, as you're all but living in our house.''

''I do live there, my dear. Except when you come to visit.'' They took each other's measure across the silver and linen. ''You may as well accept it and make an effort, Gloria. I'm not going to vanish. I'm going to marry your father.''

Heat rushed into her face. ''I don't think so.''

''Indeed yes. Surely you didn't imagine a man like your father would live as a monk all these years. Why should he? He needs a wife, a hostess.''

''I'll never agree.''

''I'm not asking your permission.''

Bee Bee's lazy smile made her clench her fists. '' 'Look what Lulu is wearing,' '' Gloria quoted softly, the memory as fresh as yesterday. '' 'Imagine—wearing red to a funeral. Doesn't she own anything pink?' ''

Bee Bee was beyond blushing, but at least she had the grace to appear uncomfortable. ''You weren't meant to hear that.''

''Everyone was meant to hear. You dined out on it.''

''We're not going to be friends, are we?'' Bee Bee said finally. When Gloria refused to answer, she fluttered her fingers at the waiter. ''At least we understand each other. Ours is not going to be a close little family.'' Standing, she drew on her gloves. ''Sign the check to Bobby's account.''

Gloria's immediate inclination on leaving Maxim's was to rush directly to the bourse and confront her father. But after a moment's thought, she dismissed her driver and chose to walk off her anger instead.

It was a warm Paris day, saturated with summer sounds and smells, alive with young girls in bright cotton dresses strolling to the music drifting from open car windows. Ordinarily, Gloria would have inhaled the dusty summer scent of the chestnut trees with pleasure, would have happily occupied the afternoon examining the new fall lines ornamenting the shop windows. But today, she longed for Goose Point and summers past. She had walked several blocks before she could make herself look forward.

Was she behaving foolishly as Bee Bee insisted? Pausing, she studied her reflection in a shop window, recognizing her mother's high cheekbones and silvery hair. The slim, elegant body. To make her debut without Lulu would be an admission that Lulu's illness was incurable. It would be the final acceptance that her mother was lost to her. Intellectually, she understood Lulu was not coming home; she had known it for a long time. But emotionally, it would feel like a betrayal to come out without Lulu. Finally, the rounds of parties and balls and teas would have been for Lulu's sake, not her own. In her view debuts were archaic, part of a tradition that had vanished with the robber barons.

Reassured on that point, she directed her thoughts to Bee Bee and her father, feeling her body tense. A hundred questions troubled her. Had her father been seeing Bee Bee before he put Lulu in Les Eaux? Did he love her? Would he divorce her mother to marry Bee Bee? If he needed someone, why hadn't he turned to her? With the hurt came anger. Anger at her father's weakness, anger at Lulu for abandoning them, anger toward the forces that split families and people.

Eventually she would question her father about Bee Bee, but not until she was certain they were alone. Until then, she decided to ignore Bee Bee and ignore the sleeping arrangements at the Paris town house. From this moment forward, Bee Bee Halston would cease to exist.

When she returned home, she placed a photograph of Lulu in every room, positioning the frames where her father was certain to see them. The gesture was childish, but she did it anyway. Then, because she needed a connection to happier times, she spent the afternoon writing to Margaret.

The fire in the wastebasket made the office seem hotter. Gardner read through the papers in his hand, then dropped them into the flames. "That's it for me. Are you about finished?"

Lars nodded without looking up from his charts. "This is the last. What's going on out there?"

Without the noise of heavy equipment, the compound seemed eerily quiet. The dust and rattle of the two jeeps delivering personnel and baggage to the landing strip didn't fill a silence that had begun to fray everyone's nerves. Gardner stood beside the window and looked toward the low brush growing up to the chain-link fence enclosing the mine's perimeters.

"I thought you said Simli and John Moku were coming in to help close up."

"They didn't show."

"I don't like this. It's too quiet out there." Realizing what he had said, Gardner smiled. "Sounds like something out of a B movie."

Lars tilted his head toward the Uzis lying across the desk. "Except those aren't props, friend." After dropping the last of the office papers into the fire, Lars gazed around the office. "That's it. Let's blow this pop stand."

Holding the Uzis across their laps, they settled into the jeep waiting outside. "Has the plane arrived?" Gardner asked the driver.

Chip Glaston, an engineer from Ohio, shook his head. "Not yet. If it doesn't get here soon, I know half a dozen people who are going to have heart attacks." The jeep surged forward, and Glaston glanced over his shoulder. "I know this sounds stupid, but I keep imagining I'm seeing people creeping through the brush."

It didn't sound stupid. For the past hour Gardner had sensed they were being watched. He exchanged a glance with Lars Trumby, understanding Lars was feeling the same thing.

"Have you fired one of these things?" Lars asked.

"Not before yesterday." At his insistence, they had organized an impromptu target practice in the pit before the first shift arrived.

Lars swore. "Where the hell is the goddamn plane?"

Glaston parked the jeep at the edge of the strip where they had decided to leave the vehicles. They walked toward the cluster of people and baggage waiting near the center of the field, feeling the heat and the unnatural silence.

Gardner wet his lips and gripped the Uzi. The group at the center of the strip was exposed and vulnerable. If he was Omuta, he would attack now. Before the plane arrived, while the Home group was standing together without a stick of cover. Narrowing his eyes, he studied the mvuli trees and the brush, imagining he saw movement, imagining man-sized holes cut in the fence. He wiped his palm on his pant's leg and tightened his grip on the Uzi.

"Here it comes!" They cheered as Gerda Heber pointed to the sky. The Home plane tipped a wing at them then nosed toward the field. Gerda gave Gardner a look of immense relief. "I can tell you now, I wasn't as brave as I pretended. I am damn glad to see that plane."

He smiled. Gerda was a tough old bird who had insisted on staying to the end, despite his efforts to persuade her to leave on the first plane out.

"And here come the bad guys," Lars muttered, swinging up the Uzi. "Right on schedule."

"Shit."

Dozens of men brandishing knives and spears poured through the holes in the fence, screaming as they ran forward. Gardner spotted only two or three antiquated pistols. No machine guns. Behind him, the plane hit the strip, taxied past them, and began the turn at the end of the field.

"Glaston! Get these people on board." He adjusted the Uzi in his arms, planted his feet, and wondered what the hell he was doing here.

"Christ," Lars muttered. "There must be a hundred of them. Some are our people. The big, nasty bastard with the rifle is Omuta."

They were shouting and screaming, running toward the plane that had halted behind Gardner. He heard Chip Glaston screaming above the whine of the propellers and the din of the shrieking savages sprinting toward them. It was like every bad African movie he had ever seen. Except this time it was real. A spear chunked into the ground five feet in front of him, and he stared at the quivering shaft. The ping of a bullet slapped into the plane's fuselage.

When the wave of half-naked men reached the verge of the strip, Gardner raised the Uzi and felt it jump in his hands. Dirt and grass sprayed up from the ground in front of them. To his astonishment, the rush stopped. A few men looked toward Omuta, and Gardner had the absurd idea they had never seen a machine gun before.

"Get the hell on board," he shouted to Lars.

"What about you?"

"Don't leave without me. Forget the baggage, just get inside. Let's get the fuck out of here!"

They were coming again. Sunlight flashed on blades that looked two feet long. They were close enough that he could smell them and could see the hatred in their eyes. A sting nipped his thigh like an insect bite, and a shower of spears sliced into the grass in front of him. Christ. The Uzi shook his body as he fired. A half-dozen men fell and others ran forward to take their place.

"Gardner! Now!" Lars shouted over the mounting whine of the propellers.

Gardner swung the Uzi toward the strip and fired before any of them could run forward and block the path of the wheels. Three men went down. Then he flung the Uzi through the cargo door, caught Lars's hand and swung himself up and inside. Bracing against the door, Lars continued firing as the plane rushed down the strip, then finally lifted.

"Let me see that," Gerda demanded, kneeling beside him.

"What?"

"There's a knife in your leg."

Now he noticed the hilt of the penknife protruding from his thigh. The stenciled words, Butiaba Mine, Home Limited, appeared on the handle.

"I hope they pay you a lot, boss." Gerda reached for the plane's first aid kit. "This strikes me as service above and beyond."

He stared at the knife handle, feeling sick inside. "I killed a dozen people," he whispered.

"I wish you'd killed a hundred more," Gerda said briskly. She cut his pants away and wound a strip of gauze around his thigh. "Those bastards would have nailed our heads to the schoolroom door." When she finished with his leg, she rocked back on her heels and peered into his eyes. "You're a hero. I don't want to think about what might have happened if you hadn't been there."

Lars instructed the pilot to radio ahead for an ambulance and a doctor. Gardner spent two days in the Kampala hospital before Home's jet arrived to fly him back to New York where Chissie checked him into Lenox Hill. The wound wasn't as serious as it might have been. Still, he would carry a permanent reminder. His doctor predicted he would limp after strenuous physical exertion or when he was unusually tired.

"Otherwise, I'm as good as new," he told his father when Win brought him the paperwork that had accumulated on his desk.

"They burned the buildings. Destroyed the equipment."

"I was right." He said it quietly, with no real sense of triumph. He said it because his father didn't, and because he was beginning to grasp his own worth.

Winthrop Durant stood at the window looking down at the

parked cars on Seventy-seventh Street. "No one dies in a Wall Street blood-letting," he said. "Isn't it time you reevaluated your situation?"

"I'm doing what I want to do." The statement was still valid.

He thought about his father after Win departed, understanding his father had not forgiven his defection. Win Durant wanted a family empire. But the sun had set on the great family dynasties and had risen on a generation of individualists who felt an urgency to carve their own empires. He did not regret his choice, only the strain that existed between his father and himself.

The empire he had chosen to conquer was Home Limited. Eventually he wanted Tobler's seat. He wanted to make a difference in the industrial world, and he believed he could.

"So how's the hero?" Lars Trumby leaned his head in the door and grinned. "When are you going to stop malingering, get your ass out of bed, and get back to work?"

"Lars! What are you doing here?"

"I came to say good-bye. The company's sending me to Brazil. Susan and I are leaving at the end of the week. I understand you're getting North Sea duty out of London. Tough."

"This is the first I've heard about it. Is that a bottle of Scotch under your arm?" When he saw it was, he laughed.

"I wish to hell you'd hurry up and get some years on you, Durant, and take over this outfit. You want to know what Home Limited is doing in Brazil? It's shit. Listen to this. . . ."

The choice had been Vassar or Radcliffe at Harvard. Finally Gloria chose Harvard because her father preferred it. It irritated her to realize she still sought his approval. For a time she considered switching her registration, but in the end, hating herself, she stayed with Harvard.

"I'd like to get this settled before you leave," Bobby said over drinks. They were in London at the Connaught Grill, waiting for Gardner Durant to join them. "I'm not going to marry Bee Bee Halston. I know what she told you, but it isn't going to happen." He sounded weary. They had discussed the subject a dozen times before. "You're old enough to understand—"

"I don't want to hear about you and Bee Bee."

"Gloria, you have to understand that I love your mother. If Lulu were well, I . . . there's Gardner." The relief in her father's quick smile made her angry.

Telling herself she had no choice but to believe her father's assurances, Gloria concealed her anger and studied Gardner Durant while he shook hands with Bobby and then bent to kiss her cheek. He was older, deeply tanned, stronger, and more handsome than she remembered. Suddenly she felt fourteen again, all arms and legs, needing the reassurance of a quick glance toward the wall mirrors.

"Good Lord," Gardner murmured, staring at her after they had ordered drinks. "I don't think I would have recognized you. You've grown up, squirt. And you're gorgeous. How old are you now? Nineteen? Twenty?"

"Eighteen." The pleasure of his approval and obvious admiration was tempered by his use of the word *squirt*. It indicated he still regarded her as green and unformed.

"What are you doing in London?"

"Shopping," Bobby answered. "Gloria preferred to purchase her college wardrobe here instead of Paris."

"Sensible girl." Gardner looked at her and smiled. She wondered if he knew about her father and Bee Bee Halston. "And a heroine. The newspapers reported you had a head gash, but I don't see any scar."

"That was six months ago, old news." She had dropped the curtain on Aigmont and everything that happened there. "Tell us about you. I understand you single-handedly held off a rioting mob of bloodthirsty savages and saved Home Limited."

His laughter came easily, warm and robust. "The reports are exaggerated. But I'll admit this—working for you Von Marrons is never dull."

Throughout dinner she listened quietly as Gardner and her father discussed business, Gardner with enthusiasm, her father with thinly concealed boredom. Until now, she hadn't realized how much she had missed seeing Gardner Durant.

"What do you think of Walt Tobler?" Bobby asked over coffee and brandy.

Gardner hesitated. "My father is in a better position to judge."

"I'd like to learn your opinion."

"If profit is the sole, bottom-line objective, I doubt you can find a better man than Tobler."

"But?"

"Tobler is too shortsighted on occasion, too focused on the immediate. For example, at present Home has a substantial interest in North Sea oil and in the Alaskan pipeline. Personally, I'd advise Home to dilute those investments. Carter's position on energy conservation is the tip of an iceberg that will rise and damage oil prices in the long run. Tobler also favors a short position in timber. We're harvesting more than we're replanting."

His intensity was impressive. And Gloria enjoyed watching his hands. Gardner's hands were tanned and strong, and he used them effectively to make a point or to underscore a statement. She also enjoyed hearing news of Home Limited. Without realizing it, she had been hungry for news from America.

Bobby declined more coffee and looked at his watch. "I'm tired, and I have some calls to make. So, if you two will excuse me."

When Bobby had left the Grill, Gardner focused his attention on Gloria. "Did all that business talk bore you?"

"Not at all." She watched her father leave, knowing he was hurrying upstairs to telephone Bee Bee. "I enjoyed it."

"No, yes, yes, and yes," Gardner said, grinning.

"What?"

"No, I'm not seeing anyone special; yes, I've missed you; yes, you're extraordinarily beautiful; and yes, I'd like to walk. Those are the questions you wanted to ask, aren't they?"

She laughed, remembering why she liked him so much. "I saw your photo in the *London Times* last week. You were gazing into the cleavage of Lady Someone. You only write at Christmas, so how can I guess if you miss me? I'm not as beautiful as I'd like to be, and yes, I do want to walk."

When they stepped outside, she inhaled the damp night air with a sigh of pleasure before she tucked her arm through his. "Seriously, are you going to marry Lady Whoever? The papers predict you will."

"I plan to marry you someday, squirt. After you've had a few affairs and conquered the world, come see me. By then we'll both be ready."

"We're agreed then," she said lightly. "That's the plan." She wasn't sure if she felt flattered or stung by his teasing tone.

"How about you? Are you seeing anyone special?"

"I was. It didn't work out." Tilting her head back against her collar, she gazed at the darkness overhead. "Daddy's living with Bee Bee Halston."

"I know."

"I suppose everyone does. It's never going to be like it was before, is it? Holly was right. In the end you have to go it alone."

"That's not always such a bad thing."

"So I'm learning."

Because he didn't trust himself to take her to her door, Gard-

ner said good-bye to her in the Connaught lobby. Seeing her
again had been a shock. Without thinking about it, he had frozen
Gloria's image at the age of fourteen. But she was a woman
now, a very beautiful woman. He hadn't been the only man to
notice; Gloria Von Marron attracted considerable attention. The
ever-present paparazzi had snapped their photographs when they
left the Connaught and again as they returned. He suspected he
would find himself and Gloria in the papers tomorrow morning.
Gloria, laughing up at him; him, gazing down at her with a
besotted expression.

Shaking his head, he walked toward the phone on the concierge's desk. Prudence suggested he mention the photographs
before Elizabeth saw them.

"I'd feel more assured if you'd come by for a drink," Elizabeth said after he told her about the pictures.

He hesitated. It was early and he felt like making love. He
turned to look toward the elevator Gloria had taken upstairs and
remembered the curve of her breast, the scent of her perfume.

"I'd love to," he said into the telephone. "But I'm leaving
for Scotland early, and I still have to pack. I'll take a rain check."

After he hung up the phone he cursed under his breath. Lady
Elizabeth Boden was warm, witty, and practiced in bed. He had
no idea why he had turned down her invitation. Irritated, he
pushed his hands into his coat pockets, looked toward the elevators as if he expected the doors to open and Gloria to emerge,
then pushed through the Connaught doors and walked into the
night air.

Perhaps it was time he quit calling her squirt.

Chapter 7

*G*LORIA FELL IN and out of love during her freshman and sophomore years, bought strawberries and Carr's biscuits at Sage's Market, drank sherry through the snowy dusks and long weekends. She did the things Harvard girls did. She bought croissants at Au Bon Pain, prowled Schoenhof's for foreign editions, attended the teas and lectures hosted by the Brattle Street Brahmins. She dressed her hair simply, wore little makeup, and unconsciously assimilated the scrubbed, casually elegant look so covetously identified with Cambridge.

After ending a frustrating on-again off-again relationship with a Harvard business grad near midterm of her second year, she put together a stock portfolio and used the hours previously occupied by the Harvard grad to manage the portfolio. What began as a much-needed diversion swiftly became an all-consuming fascination.

Shortly after placing her first stock order, Gloria found herself hurrying directly home after classes to read and absorb as much financial information as was available. Weekends were devoted to a meticulous study of *The Wall Street Journal* and the trade magazines. Gathering and analyzing information became an obsession, one she preferred to studying or attending social engagements.

She immediately comprehended that possessing information was the key to winning. A hint of an impending merger, a whisper of government gossip, when applied correctly these translated into a win. The market was the greatest sweepstakes on earth, the world's most passionately played game. And Gloria excelled at it. By the end of her sophomore year she had nearly doubled her portfolio. If she had been privy to better and swifter information, she believed she could have tripled her initial investment.

"I've decided to remain in New York this summer," she informed her father after numerous abortive attempts to persuade him to return to the States and open Goose Point. "I'll stay at the town house."

"New York in summer?"

She couldn't judge if he was amused or merely indifferent. "I intend to ask Uncle Win for a summer position at La Tourraine, Durant and Von Marron."

"Why on earth would you do that?"

"It's what I want." Eagerness animated her voice as she told him about her portfolio, her fascination and her desire to learn more.

During the silence that opened across the phone lines, Gloria realized her palms were damp. Closing her eyes, she leaned her forehead in her hand. Tell me you need me, she thought. It was the only thing that would alter her decision. Just once, tell me you're proud of me.

"You understand I wouldn't feel comfortable attempting to influence Win's decision?"

"Then you disapprove?" She touched her fingers to her temples.

"I see no reason for you to take a job."

He saw no reason because he expected nothing from her. But she expected much of herself. It wasn't a matter of trying to prove something, not anymore. She knew she was bright and capable. It was a need to employ her intelligence and capabilities for something greater than a crowded social life. The motivation behind her decision was not something she could explain to her father.

"Is Bee Bee with you?" she asked, changing the subject.

"She's in Venice with Prince Raculoski." He sounded indifferent. "There's a possibility Lulu may spend July in Paris." For the first time since he had answered the phone, his voice assumed a note of cautious enthusiasm. "I'm sure she'll expect you to be here."

Gloria doubted it. At spring break, she had flown to Geneva and visited Les Eaux. Her mother had ignored her. Lulu had insisted Gloria could not be her daughter as her daughter was much younger.

"I'm sorry about Georges," she said after pushing aside the

depressing memories of Les Eaux. "How is Thérèse bearing up? I sent flowers and a note."

Pain touched her father's voice. "It's best that Georges died. He suffered a great deal toward the end."

"There's really no reason for you to remain in Paris. Come home. We'll open Goose Point—"

"There is every reason to remain in Paris. Now that Georges is gone, I've assumed full responsibility for the Paris office. Moreover, I wish to remain near your mother."

There was nothing more to say. Somewhere throughout the drama and turbulence of recent years, Gloria had lost the ability to read her father's moods. As a result, they had little to say to each other. Silence spun over the wires and she could hear the distant click of the overseas relays.

"You can't stay alone," he said finally.

"I'm almost twenty-one."

"You'll have to stay with Win and Chissie."

She had foreseen this objection. "I've spoken to Margaret. Do you remember Margaret Porter? She's married now. I've invited Margaret and Edmund to spend the summer with me in New York. Margaret has agreed."

"Then your decision is final."

Listening closely, she tried to read disappointment into his tone. Wished he would say he missed her and wanted her with him.

"Yes."

After hanging up, she poured a glass of brandy and drank it standing in the small kitchen of her apartment. Then, having discovered the solace of work, she devoted the afternoon to her portfolio.

In the beginning, she had assumed numbers lacked emotion. At the time she had sought emotional serenity, and she had taken comfort from the flat immutability of figures and columns. Now she understood her original assumption was in error. The columns in her ledgers were charged with emotion and excitement. Stocks were living entities. The knowledge thrilled and amazed her.

Durant assigned her the drudge jobs in the hope of discouraging her. Pausing at the door to the trading room, he glanced inside, spotting Gloria immediately. She was staring, rapt, at one of the Quotrons instead of delivering the messages bunched

in her hand. She looked so much like Lulu at the same age that
he got a hard-on looking at her.

Irritated, he turned toward the elevators and consulted his
watch. He was due in arbitrage to discuss the Purita buy-out.
Purita was mounting a vigorous defense against Deltron, the
firm's client. What he didn't need right now was the image of a
silver-haired girl, with magnificent tits and a gold-plated ass,
who was taking the spot his son should have filled. It pissed the
hell out of him.

He knew what she was doing. She was buying a little excitement, spending the summer playing on Wall Street instead of
flitting around Europe attending the tony parties. She was dab-
bling in business, obviously the debutante thing to do this year.
Using the firm as a goddamn babysitting service. Not for an
instant did he believe Gloria exhibited a genuine interest in La
Tourraine, Durant and Von Marron. It was all show—a role she
was trying on like a new pair of panty hose. Next summer she
would drift toward another role, maybe interior decorating, or
whatever else was in vogue for next season's crop of bored,
wealthy debutantes.

"Aren't you being a little hard on her?" Chissie asked as they
dressed for dinner at Gracie Square. She leaned to the mirror
and clipped on a pair of emerald earrings. "I recall you mentioned Gloria nearly tripled her portfolio."

"Oh for Christ's sake. A baboon could triple his fortune in
this market. She's just amusing herself for the summer. Treating
the firm like a toy she's just discovered."

"Win." She placed her hand on his arm. "Are you being
fair? Is it possible you're transferring your disappointment about
Gardner into resentment toward Gloria?"

"That's bullshit."

But Chissie was correct in one respect; having Gloria at the
firm affected him more than he had anticipated. He wished to
Christ he had never agreed to it. At odd moments throughout
the day, he discovered he was thinking about her—wondering
where she was, what she was doing. To his irritation, he found
himself inventing excuses to move about the floors more frequently than was his habit. And when he located her, he observed her cool patrician superiority and resented her confidence
and quick mind even as he was drawn by the same qualities. If
she had been a man, if she had been Gardner, he would have

welcomed her as his protégé and would have boasted of her progress and her successes. Because she was damn good. Whatever task he assigned her, she accepted without complaint and mastered quickly. She was a natural. He wasn't the only person who noticed.

"What's this I hear about your new apprentice? Von Marron's girl. The word is, she's damn good."

For once Durant wished the Metropolitan Club forbade business discussion like the Union or the Knickerbocker. He glanced at Charles Houghton then leaned back into his wing chair and drew on his cigar. "Where'd you hear about her?"

Houghton laughed. "The word was on the Street before noon of her first day. You didn't think you could put Bobby's girl on the floor and keep it a secret did you? I hear *Forbes* is planning a spread on her. Heiress following in Daddy's footsteps, the new woman on Wall Street. That kind of thing."

He hadn't known. Dark color infused his face. *Forbes* would make it sound like Von Marron was the driving genius behind the firm's success and Gloria was following a family tradition. Because the story would work better that way, the reporter would find it convenient to forget Durant. He was merely the Von Marron lackey, first for Bobby, now for Bobby's daughter. He had been a fool to believe the deaths of Whitehall and La Tourraine would focus recognition on himself. He had supposed someone might notice that the firm did not miss them at all, but so far it hadn't happened.

"She's just screwing off a summer," he said irritably. "I'll squash the story."

But she returned for the summer between her junior and senior years. Now she had the act down pat. No one watching her would have spotted anything frivolous in her attitude or her performance. Durant assigned her to the trading desk and worked her gorgeous tail off. Richard Bellweather happily reported she was either the luckiest or the best rookie trader he had ever worked with.

Frowning, Durant stood at the door to the trading room and watched her. She ate a slice of cold luncheon pizza without taking her eyes from the screens in front of her. If she realized half the men in the room found reasons to pass by her, she gave no indication. She gave the impression of being totally absorbed in the columns flowing across the screens.

It was then he recognized the handwriting on the wall.

That night he took a room at the Plaza and ordered a thousand-dollar call girl. He got very drunk and did something he had never done before. He struck a woman.

Learning that Lulu would be permitted to attend her graduation services completed the joy of the occasion. Everyone she loved would be there. Margaret and Edmund, the Durants, Gardner, both her parents.

"I'm so glad you could come," she said, hugging her mother, as proud of Lulu as she was proud of her cap and gown.

New lines marked the corners of her mother's mouth and eyes, but Lulu Von Marron looked marvelous, better than Gloria had seen her look in years. Infused with new hope, she embraced her mother and didn't want to let go. Throughout the lengthy ceremony, she continually looked at Lulu's Valium-maintained serenity and Bobby's beaming smile. And she felt as if the pieces of her life were finally coming together.

"My parents look happier than they have in years, don't you think?" she asked Gardner after the festivities. "Mother looks wonderful."

"So do you."

His smile warmed her. The day had been perfect, everything she had hoped for from the breakfast with her parents, to the graduation ceremony, to the dinner and dance afterward. And now Gardner, tanned and handsome, was sitting in her tiny living room, watching her with the smile she had loved since they were children.

"What are you thinking?" Deciding her sherry days were over, she had poured them each a brandy.

"I was admiring your apartment. The contrasts are interesting."

The comment surprised her until she inspected her living room, attempting to see it through his eyes. The furnishings had come from Goose Point or the New York town house or from bargain basements she had rummaged through. Chippendale sat next to dilapidated wicker; family photographs were framed in both silver and plastic; first editions and paperbacks lined the bookshelves; crystal glasses and gas-station giveaways sat on the kitchen counter; Queen Anne and art deco were overlaid by a spill of books, plants, and stained glass. The apartment wasn't what she wanted for the future, but it had been right for her Harvard years. She felt a twinge of regret to leave it behind.

"Mason jars?" Gardner asked, laughing as she placed a silver tray on the lacquered trunk that served as her coffee table.

"Would you rather have a crystal snifter?" She grinned at him, wishing it was this easy with all men. If she were still seeing Jack she would have remained dressed. Instead, she had changed into a loose, silk shirt and her favorite jeans minutes after she and Gardner had entered the door. "Mason jars are in. Where have you been?"

"Recently? Argentina. And no, I don't want a crystal snifter. I'm crazy about mason jars." Smiling, he patted the sofa beside him. "You always manage to surprise me. So what happens next? Marriage? Travel? A job?"

Excitement sparkled in her eyes as she curled into the corner of the sofa and propped her bare feet on his lap. "I'll close this apartment, move the things I want to keep to the town house in New York. I plan to stay with your parents while I'm having the bedroom redone at the town house."

"Ah, a lady with her own establishment. Very wicked."

"Finally my father thinks I'm old enough, thank God."

"Then what?"

"Then I'll talk to Uncle Win about a permanent position at La Tourraine, Durant and Von Marron."

"That should please Dad." He tasted his brandy. "Finally someone from one of the families goes into the firm." His eyebrow lifted when he noticed her expression. "You don't agree?"

"I'm not sure."

Uncle Win's attitude had puzzled her from the beginning. Like Gardner, she had expected Uncle Win to be pleased, but she wasn't certain that he was. She hadn't wanted special favors, and he hadn't offered any, but she had expected more positive feedback, more obvious support. Maybe more warmth. Instead, he treated her with cool indifference. Occasionally, she had sensed hostility. Perhaps hostility was too harsh a word; resentment might be a better choice. But neither made sense.

"I'm sure you're imagining things," Gardner said after she had explained her uncertainty. "Dad's dream is to install one of the offspring of the original partners as the future managing partner of La Tourraine, Durant and Von Marron."

"If the offspring is you, maybe." She turned the mason jar between her palms. "I'll know soon enough. I have an appointment with your father next week." They sipped their brandy and listened to Mozart, and Gloria began to relax as she always did with Gardner. "Has Uncle Win ever accepted your choice to take a position with Home Limited?" The subject was a sore one, and she put the question gently.

"Not really."

"Not even knowing how well you've done?" She recalled Remy claiming every man wanted to be a hero in his father's eyes. "You're heading the South American division, aren't you?"

"I'm flattered that you're keeping track."

"I receive copies of Home's quarterly reports."

He smiled at her, raising his eyes from her open collar. "I didn't know. Does that mean you're interested in becoming active in Home at some later date?"

"Someday I'll have to, like it or not." Her gaze lingered on his mouth before she looked away. "But that's a long time in the future. Meanwhile, what I enjoy most is La Tourraine, Durant and Von Marron. You don't know what it's like to pull everything together, guess right, and win. I love it."

He dropped his hand to her ankle and adjusted her foot against his thigh. "Tell me about it."

When she finished talking it was nearly three in the morning. Giving him a guilty smile, she opened the door and looked up at him. "I'm sorry, the time got away from me. I monopolized the conversation, didn't I?"

"We'll talk about me next time."

"When will that be?"

"I'm leaving in—" He glanced at his watch. "—two hours for Costa Rica. Let's say—Christmas?" Lifting a hand, he touched her cheek. His thumb brushed across her lips. "I won't let you say a word."

They were standing close enough that Gloria felt the electric heat of his body. His fingers on her cheek burned against her skin. Helplessly, her gaze dropped to his mouth and she wondered why they had never kissed, wondered if his kiss would taste of brandy.

When she looked up, he was staring at her and she caught a quick breath as she recognized the desire darkening his eyes. "Oh God," she whispered, her knees suddenly weak.

"Gloria."

In that one whispered word, she heard what she had longed for. When she opened her eyes, she was in his arms, his mouth hard on hers, his hands cupping her buttocks and holding her against the heat of his erection.

She pressed against him, feeling her breasts swell and harden against his chest; her mouth opened beneath his. "Don't go," she murmured, sensing his urgency and a need as great as her own. "Stay."

"Christ, I wish I could." His voice was ragged against her hair. "Why didn't we start this earlier?"

His hand slid to cup her breast and she moaned softly against his neck. "Tell the people in Costa Rica you'll come tomorrow."

"It's an emergency. I have to go." He licked the corner of her lips, slipped his hand inside her blouse and made a hoarse sound as his fingers found her nipple. "God."

Her body ignited under his touch. She pressed against him, her hands flew over his face, his shoulders, and she realized with a shock that she had only imagined she understood passion. She had not. Never before had she wanted a man so badly that her skin burned with longing and her body trembled.

He dropped his forehead against hers and his fingers bruised into her shoulders. "I want you more than I have wanted any woman." Raising his head, he looked into her eyes. "But I don't want the first time with you to be rushed. We've waited too many years to make this a hit and run." This time his kiss was deliberate and gentle, though she felt his erection hard against her body.

The depth of her disappointment left her shaken, but a less turbulent section of her mind agreed with what he was saying. She didn't want her first time with Gardner to be just quick sex. They meant more to each other than that; they deserved better. She wanted to explore his body at leisure, wanted time to offer herself fully.

"I'll wait for you," she whispered. The words emerged with difficulty. She wanted him now. "Christmas seems so far away."

"I'll try to get away sooner." His mouth covered hers, hard and possessive, full of promise. When he finally stepped away from her, he did so with reluctance. "You are so beautiful."

After she closed the door, she returned to the sofa in a blissful daze and wrapped her arms around herself. Gardner. She tested his name on her tongue. It had always been Gardner. There had never been anyone else, not really. Gardner was the only man who understood who she was and why.

Closing her eyes and smiling, she thought about the passion that had exploded between them and knew she would not sleep that night.

* * *

Gloria waited until Uncle Win left the Durant penthouse overlooking Park Avenue, then she dressed carefully for her appointment with him. She selected a tailored Chanel suit in a shade of gray that matched her eyes, a cream-colored silk blouse, and her grandmother's pearl earrings and necklace. She wound her hair into a silvery knot, then presented herself to Chissie.

"The intent is to look businesslike but not too severe," she explained, turning for Chissie's inspection.

"Darling, you look lovely! Like a fashion model. I wouldn't alter a single detail."

"Wish me luck."

Chissie laughed. "As if the outcome is in doubt." Eyes sparkling, she followed Gloria to the door. "I hope the interview isn't too exhausting, I'm hoping you'll attend the Metropolitan Museum costume opening. Win has already begged off. Unfortunately I can't; I'm the chairman."

"Will you be terribly angry if I don't go? I received a packet of reports from Home last week, and I'd planned to read them tonight."

"What is happening to young girls today?" Chissie asked, rolling her eyes. "In my day girls went to balls; they didn't read reports." Leaning forward, she kissed Gloria's cheek and sighed. "Very well. But you're going to the showing at the Herschl & Adler Galleries tomorrow night and that's final. All work and no play . . ."

"Agreed," Gloria answered, smiling. She touched Chissie's cheek. "I love you, Aunt Chissie."

"I love you, too. I hate it that you'll be leaving us next week. Why don't you have the living room painted, too? Then you could stay longer."

Gloria laughed. "At the rate my painters are progressing, I may be here for years."

"There's nothing I'd like better. Now hurry along, you don't want to be late. You look lovely, and I'm confident you'll wrap Win around your little finger."

By the time Chissie's driver dropped her in front of the firm, Gloria had relaxed, believing she had little cause for nervousness or apprehension. Her apprentice period had ended well; she knew Richard Bellweather had recommended her for future hire. Her portfolio performance continued to be impressive. Moreover, she recalled Gardner's prediction. She was family. Of course Uncle Win would welcome her into the firm.

Stepping out of the limousine, she straightened her shoulders, smiled at her reflection in the firm's door, then entered the building.

Durant had been waiting for the call from personnel. He had known it was coming since last summer. Somewhere along the line the decision had ceased to be business-related and had become visceral. His gut instinct was to reject Gloria's application outright. However that would necessitate an explanation to Bobby, and he rejected any obligation to explain or justify.

Not to Bobby Von Marron. Not when the Paris office was limping along as it always had, now with Bobby as the principal screw-off instead of Georges. Georges La Tourraine's death had precipitated no appreciable benefit but had caused a serious depletion of capital necessitated by the buying-in of his partnership interest. It was the Whitehall scenario all over again sans the blackmail.

"Mr. Durant? Miss Von Marron is waiting to see you."

"Send her in."

He stood behind his desk, touched his tie, and watched her enter his office. She walked like a goddamn queen, as confident as if she already owned the firm. She was Lulu Von Marron reincarnated. The cool politeness behind the eyes, the phony smile, the long silky legs. The "look but don't touch" expression this type of woman was born with.

She sat down without being invited to do so and folded her hands in her lap, as composed as if she knew she held the winning aces.

"Personnel directed me to you. I think you know why I'm here, Uncle Win. I want to apply for a permanent position with the firm. I believe my record over the past two summers speaks for itself."

"I know why you're here, and I'm aware of your record."

She smiled, and he recognized Lulu's cool superiority. "I'm hoping my record will persuade you to offer me a position."

He loathed coyness. Gloria Von Marron didn't want "a position," she wanted a vice presidency, closely followed by an invitation to become a full partner in the firm. She expected preferential treatment as her birthright, like her mother before her. She expected him to jump through the hoops because she was a Von Marron.

"Frankly, I have some reservations," he said, maintaining a level tone. Her eyebrows lifted in surprise. "As you may be aware, a new employee represents a substantial investment in training and commitment. It is in the firm's best interest to place that investment in someone willing to return our commitment on a long-term basis.''

"I'm certainly willing to make such a commitment.''

"Are you? I doubt it.'' His gaze flicked over her smooth skin, her shining hair, the slope of breast glimpsed below an opened collar. "Like most women, I suspect you're looking for something to fill the time until you marry. I don't wish to have La Tourraine, Durant and Von Marron used in that manner. We're not a babysitter for debutantes killing time until they find Mr. Right.''

A rush of pink spread over her cheeks. "I'm not killing time, Uncle Win. I'm genuinely interested in investment banking and have been for several years. I made that commitment long ago.''

"Additionally, I'm not convinced women are suited to investment banking.''

"Women are appearing in increasing numbers on Wall Street. Many hold positions of authority and responsibility.''

He nodded with a politeness he didn't feel. "Time will tell if such placements are prudent. Personally, I wonder. There's no place in banking for tears or emotional outbursts.''

The color intensified in her cheeks. "If you will check with Richard Bellweather, you'll discover I am not prone to tears or emotional outbursts. I would have guessed you knew that.''

"You are prone to periods, aren't you?'' he asked drily. The shock in her expression irritated him. They all wanted to be treated equally, but none of them considered or accepted what genuine equality entailed. They wanted equality without sacrifice. "At which time you are likely to make emotional choices instead of reasoned judgments.''

She stared at him. "Surely you don't believe that!''

"Finally, having a partner's daughter in the firm would inevitably create envy and resentment among the other employees.''

"I don't expect favoritism and would reject any show of preference if it were offered. There was no preferential treatment previously, why should there be now?''

"Are you actually so naive as to suppose you didn't receive preferential treatment these past two summers?'' He studied her, annoyed that she didn't simply accept his reasoning and walk away. "Do you genuinely believe Bellweather dances attendance on every ignorant debutante who strolls through this firm's door? Or Dexter? Or James Hadmore or Ames Adderly or any of the others with whom you worked?'' Leaning forward, he laced his fingers on top of the desk. "You should have had your ass reamed for the screw-up on the Singer account last August. Instead you received a mild rebuke. Why? Because your father or I could have fired Dexter's ass if we took it in our minds to do so. And you have access to both of us. You think you didn't get preferential treatment? Bullshit! Men who should have known better were walking on eggs around you. Yes, Miss Von Marron. No, Miss Von Marron. Can I help you, Miss Von Marron? You can't expect these people to forget who you are and who your father is."

In the silence that followed, he tried to guess what she was thinking. But aside from the high color in her cheeks, her face remained impassive. He had an idea she was one hell of a poker player.

"I don't agree the problem is insurmountable," she said eventually. "I believe it can be overcome. I also believe I can make a substantial contribution to La Tourraine, Durant and Von Marron." It seemed to Durant she stressed the last name. Standing, she looked at him across the desk, and he was reminded of Lulu so strongly his stomach tightened. "When may I expect your decision?"

She had beaten him to a standing position, thus placing herself in the position of looking down on him. Moreover, she had asked the controlling question and had taken it upon herself to terminate the interview. Nothing on earth would have convinced him that she did so by accident. Cold with anger, he stood and met her eyes.

"You will be informed."

Lifting her head high, she walked toward the door, then paused to look back at him. For an instant the mask dropped and she looked bewildered, hurt, and very young. Then generations of breeding stiffened her spine and the vulnerability vanished from her expression. She nodded coolly and stepped through the door, beautiful, composed, and as arrogant as a young queen.

Chapter 8

$\mathcal{I}$T HAD BEEN a frustrating and disturbing day. La Tourraine, Durant and Von Marron had been passed over in favor of Lehman Brothers as the manager for the Montrex offering; his secretary had screwed up two appointments; the new arbitrage hotshot hired away from Goldman Sachs was developing into a prima donna; his dinner tonight with the president of Osaki Corporation had gone flat and ultimately proved unproductive. Throughout these events the earlier interview with Gloria had continued to surface in his mind, a distraction he resented.

Durant's irritation increased when he arrived home near midnight and discovered Chissie was still out. Flinging his tie across a living room chair, he shouted for Abrams, then recalled Abrams was in South Carolina attending a family funeral. Swearing, he poured a Scotch and water from the butler's tray near the draperies and drained it in two swallows before he poured another.

Far below, lines of traffic flowed silently along Park Avenue. The only sound in the penthouse living room was the dim hum of the air conditioner and the rattle of ice in his glass. Durant tossed back his drink and waited for the liquor to loosen the tightness in his gut.

"Goddammit."

Every investment banker in town was wooing Osaki. If Von Marron had been in New York instead of screwing off in Paris, the firm would have had a chance to nail down the business. The knowledge ate at him. Instead, Durant had been forced to the social front lines, which was not his forte. His was the cold brilliance that operated behind the lines. He rubbed his forehead. How many lucrative accounts had the firm lost during the last few years because its outside man wasn't in the country?

Brooding, his thoughts returned to Gloria, and he wished to Christ that Chissie was home. Conversely, discussing the situation with Chissie would not have clarified his thinking or resolved a damn thing. Chissie was as blind as the others. Very likely Chissie would see nothing amiss with Gloria's assumption that all she had to do was present herself and La Tourraine, Durant and Von Marron was hers for the taking. Everyone seemed to believe Durant had nothing better to do with his goddamn life than play wet nurse to the Von Marrons. He poured another drink and sat down, grinding his teeth in the darkness.

He had seen Lulu at Gloria's graduation, of course. Astonishingly, seven years in an exclusive looney bin hadn't changed her. She was still wrenchingly beautiful, still beyond reach, still superior. She had given him a coolly polite hand and a distant smile. Not once had she said: Thank you, Win, for managing the firm so Bobby can be near me during this difficult time. Thank you for managing our affairs all these years. Thank you for looking after our daughter. Thank you for being at our beck and call, for kissing the hems of our robes. She hadn't spoken a single word not required by simple etiquette.

Who did she think paid the mountainous bills Les Eaux sent to New York? Who paid for the expensive clothes and her cosmetics? The limousines, the weekends in Monaco with Bobby? Did she think Bobby bothered with such trivialities? That was a laugh. The Von Marrons didn't dirty their aristocratic hands handling bills and invoices. Good old Win Durant did that. Good old Durant made certain the Von Marron bills were paid. He increased the Von Marron fortune, arranged the Von Marron comforts, cleaned up the Von Marron messes. It was he who sweated out the Dow and the deals and the audits and the SEC. Durant dealt with the media and the clients and the behind-the-scenes bloodletting.

For nearly thirty years he had dragged Bobby Von Marron on his coattails and now Bobby's goddamned daughter thought it was her turn for a free ride. Bullshit. Von Marrons were made of the same flesh and bone as other mortals; it was time they learned the world didn't exist solely to serve their whims.

Standing, he drained his Scotch and dropped the empty glass on his chair, feeling the effects of too much liquor, too much stomach acid.

She was here. He had noticed her bedroom light shining beneath the guest room door. The anger that had been mounting all day infused his face with dark color. He clenched his fists.

All the Von Marrons were takers. Bloodsuckers. And the blood they sucked was his.

Knots rose along his jawline. What was the point of waiting? He knew he wasn't going to offer Gloria Von Marron a position at the firm. He would close the doors and walk away before he would hand over what was his. Not to a Von Marron. He would tell her now, though he sensed the decision to do so was unwise; he had been drinking too much. But decades of resentment overwhelmed his judgment. And the anger of remembering her standing and looking down at him.

The guest room door was opened a crack, and he pushed it wider. She was lying on the satin coverlet, reading, her hair a silver halo against the dark headboard. Long golden legs emerged below the tail of a man's shirt. He could tell by the thrust of her nipples against the shirtfront that she wore nothing underneath.

She looked up and smiled. "Aunt Chissie?" When she saw it was him, her smile altered subtly and she lowered her legs, tugging self-consciously at the shirttail. The gesture aroused and irritated him.

"I want to speak to you."

He hadn't intended to sit on the side of the bed, but when he sensed it would make her uncomfortable, he did so. He wanted her to comprehend who was in control, who called the shots in his house and in his firm.

Her eyes widened slightly, and she edged away. The withdrawal enraged him. It was controlling; it was as rejecting as a glance from Lulu. It was the same gesture of contempt, as if contact with Win Durant could somehow contaminate.

He stared at her, not seeing her startled look of surprise and discomfort, seeing instead the curl of Lulu's lip, the arrogance and hauteur that recalled to mind all the slights, real and imagined, dealt by the Von Marrons and others like them.

She wet her lips. "Uncle Win?"

The seductive motion of her tongue sliding across her lips made his groin tighten. He looked at the V of smooth, satiny skin at her collar, the long, silky expanse of tanned legs. This close to her, he could smell the perfumed fragrance of her hair, could feel the warmth radiating from her young body. He recognized her from a thousand fantasies. She was Lulu at this age. She was all the women who had held themselves beyond his reach, all the women who had looked through him as if he were invisible because he lacked a distinguished pedigree, because he had no background.

Raising his hand, he touched her above the knee, his need impulsive and unplanned. All he wanted was to touch a woman like this, young, vibrant, a queen among women. Then he felt her skin shrink and something snapped in his mind. A red film dropped across his vision. Sudden explosive rage burned in his eyes.

"Look but don't touch, is that it? You think I'm not good enough to touch a Von Marron?" The words were raw, almost a snarl. "You think my touch will soil you in some way?" He was on the bed now, shouting down at her. "This is my house, my turf. You don't call the shots here. I'll touch you if I god-damn well want to. I've earned that right."

Shaking with rage, he caught her shirt before she could roll away from him and he ripped it open, catching his breath at the sight of her. Jesus Christ, she was beautiful. Young firm flesh. Nipples as hard and sweet as pink candy. A shiny silver triangle between her legs that beckoned a man to worship. Sun-kissed skin, supple and golden, tinting to pale cream at the bikini strips across her breasts and thighs.

"Oh God." Her gray eyes were wide, filled with shock and fear. "Please, Uncle Win. No."

Her whisper inflamed him. All his life he had waited to hear a Von Marron plead. An erection stiffened his groin, rock hard the instant his hand covered her breast. At the back of his mind he heard a voice telling him to stop. But it was Lulu under him, Lulu Von Marron's hand pushing at his chest and striking him. It was Lulu he dominated, Lulu whose hands he pinned above her silvery, perfumed head as he fumbled with his zipper. He had waited for this for thirty years and now he finally had her.

"Please." She was panting, bucking under him. "Please don't do this."

He forced his knee between those creamy thighs and parted her legs, knowing he was hurting her, beyond caring. Then he thrust into her with a short primitive cry of triumph. It was sex, but it wasn't. He thrust into dry resistance, knowing he wounded her and taking pleasure in the knowledge, feeling himself grow harder, stronger, more powerful than ever before. Each violent stroke exacted a thrill of revenge, fulfilled a deep-seated need. She thrashed under him, fought him, as wildly passionate as he had imagined she would be. But he mastered her, groaning her name, Lulu, Lulu, and he brought her to final submission as he had fantasized for so many years, not finishing with her until he saw tears running into her hair. Not until then did he claim his victory and allow himself to jerk and spill inside her.

When he pulled out of her and stood, zipping his pants, he looked down at her. She lay sprawled as he had left her, face turned away from him, breasts rising and falling with silent sobs, her legs spread wantonly. Sperm mixed with a smear of blood stained her thighs. With surprise, he recognized it was not Lulu on the bed; it was Gloria. It didn't matter. The bitch would think twice before she again looked down her patrician nose at Win Durant. Smiling, he leaned against the wall for a moment. Christ he had had a lot to drink. But goddamn, he felt good.

She didn't move until she was certain he had gone, then she moaned softly and curled into a tight ball, clutching a button in her hand as if it were a talisman possessing the power to obliterate the last few minutes. Eventually, she reached behind and drew the torn edges of the shirt forward to cover her shivering body. She could not stop shaking. She felt cold, colder than the day the ice bridge had collapsed, colder than she had imagined anyone could feel. The part of her mind that had detached from the pain and shock urged her to rise and do something, but her numbed body refused to respond.

She couldn't judge how much time passed before she heard the muted sound of a door closing, but the noise galvanized her and she rolled off the bed onto her feet. Stumbling forward, she snapped off the light and shut the bedroom door. Sagging against the wall, she dropped her head and closed her eyes and waited.

"Gloria?" Chissie spoke softly from the other side of the door. Gloria pressed her fists against her lips and waited until she heard the faintly audible sound of Chissie's heels brushing the carpet, moving down the hallway.

A muffled sob broke against her knuckles and she sank to the floor beside the bed and buried her face in the satin coverlet. Oh God. Uncle Win, he . . . but she couldn't face it, not yet.

She waited until the penthouse was dark and silent, then she pulled to her feet, forcing herself to move, and she turned on the shower as hot as she could stand it. Tears as scalding as the water flowed down her cheeks as she scrubbed her thighs until they were raw and flaming.

What was she going to do? What she longed to do was run to Aunt Chissie for comfort. But that was unthinkable. She couldn't possibly tell Chissie. Who then? Gardner? Tell Gardner that his father had ripped off her clothes and raped her? A shudder of revulsion twisted her mouth. Her father? No, never. Bobby Von Marron would never believe his friend and partner of over thirty years had raped his daughter. And Lulu wasn't even a consideration. Lulu lived in a Valium-tinted world insulated from all unpleasantness.

Weeping quietly, Gloria dropped her head back against the shower tiles, letting the steaming water scour her body. There was no one to tell, no where she could go for comfort. Win Durant had raped her, and there was no one she could tell. No one.

Slowly, she raised her palms and stared at the pink crescents her fingernails had cut into her flesh. She could still taste blood where she had bitten her lip.

A man whom she had loved and trusted since childhood had forced himself on her. Her godfather. He had pushed into her bedroom and forcibly raped her. And she was helpless to do anything about it. Squeezing her eyes shut against the tears, she ran her fingertips over her bruised and aching body before a tidal swell of rage buckled her legs and she fell to the shower floor, supporting herself on her hands and knees.

He knew there was no one she could tell. He knew he would get away with it.

"No," she whispered, choking on the word, watching the water swirl into the drain. "You will pay for this. If it takes the rest of my life." Her teeth opened the wound on her lip.

Winthrop Durant had betrayed her. And he had betrayed her father. She remembered her father telling her Durant's honor and integrity could not be questioned. She remembered him telling her that Win Durant was the best friend the Von Marron family would ever have, that if she ever needed help, she should go to Win Durant. She could count on Win because he loved her like a daughter. Trust Durant, her father had said.

She felt sick.

"I swear it!" she said when the vomit had whirled down the shower drain. Durant would not walk away with impunity.

Feeling stronger, drawing energy from her hatred, she wiped her tears with an angry motion then toweled her hair and dressed quickly in the first slacks and shirt that touched her hand. She had to get out of here, it was imperative. The thought of facing Win and Chissie over breakfast was horrifying, unthinkable. Hurrying, she swept her cosmetics into an oversized handbag, hesitated, then pushed the torn shirt on top of her cosmetics.

Silently, she let herself out of the penthouse and rode the elevator to the lobby. When the doors opened, she ran past the doorman.

Once outside, she placed her hands on her knees and dropped her head, sucking in deep breaths of cool night air, trying to decide where she could go. Her town house was too close; besides, the painters would arrive at eight o'clock. For a time she wandered along Park Avenue, understanding she was still in shock, as ordinarily she experienced no hesitation in making decisions. Finally, she hailed a cab and paid the driver three hundred dollars to drive her to Long Island and Goose Point.

"You sure about this?" the driver asked doubtfully, leaning over the steering wheel to study the house. It looked dark and deserted. "Don't look like nobody's home. You want I should wait while you check it out?"

"No. It's all right." A bitter laugh broke past the silence she had maintained during the drive. Nothing would be all right again.

She paid him and watched the cab pass through the gates before she entered the dark house. Inside, the furniture was covered by white sheets; the antiques and ornaments were stored in the basement vault. For a long moment she stood motionless in the foyer, listening to the silence and welcoming the security and safety of home.

Eventually she roused herself and climbed the staircase. That part of her mind which had remained detached watched as she opened the door to Remy's bedroom instead of continuing forward to her own. The room was exactly as Remy had left it. She ran her fingertips lightly over his cherry wood desk, his books; she looked at the clothing hanging in linen bags inside his closet. Moving through the darkness, she stepped to the window and opened the sash to inhale the scent of the lilacs below. When the rush of memories receded, she inserted a cassette into Remy's recorder and lay down on his bed, hugging his pillow against her breast as Debussy filled the room.

"Chissie?" She pressed the telephone to her ear and looked at the floor.

"Oh, thank God! I've been worried out of my mind. When I came to wake you, your bed was rumpled, but it didn't look as though it had been slept in. I thought . . . where are you?"

"I'm at Goose Point."

"You just vanished! I didn't know if you'd been kidnapped or—"

"I'm sorry. Please believe me when I say the last thing in the world I want to do is worry you."

"When did you leave? I didn't hear a thing."

"Please try to understand, Chissie. I need some time to myself. If you don't hear from me for a while, don't be worried."

Even to herself the words sounded flat and unconvincing, and she ended the conversation as quickly as possible.

During the first week, she ate only when she remembered it was necessary, then she picked at the soup and crackers she found in the staff's pantry. For the most part, she sat on the marble bench beside Remy's grave or she wandered aimlessly along the shore. For the first few days she deliberately blanked her mind, focusing only on small insignificant details.

By the end of the week her mind thawed to the extent that she realized the rape had violated more than her body. Her future had also been brutalized, irrevocably altered in the span of a few violent moments. Her goals, her dreams had shattered the moment Durant ripped open her shirt. La Tourraine, Durant and Von Marron had been taken from her. For years she had looked to the future with tunnel vision, seeing only La Tourraine, Durant and Von Marron. She had focused her entire concentration, her efforts, her intensity on the firm. She had allowed herself no alternative.

Now the future opened on an empty void. Frozen inside, she stood at the edge of the water and stared toward the distant horizon. "What now?" she whispered.

"Win, I'm worried. Gloria has been out there by herself for six weeks. She won't come into town; she won't allow anyone to visit her. When I telephone she sounds as if she can't get off the phone fast enough. Do you think I should phone Bobby?"

Durant laid aside his fork and looked down the length of the table. "She's not a baby, for Christ's sake. If she wants to stay out there and sulk, let her."

"I can't understand it. One minute she's excited to begin a career at the firm; the next minute she's gone. She was so eager, so full of the future. Then," Chissie lifted her hands, "she just vanished. She's isolated herself. It isn't like her."

"For all you know, she's out there with some man having a summer fling. Quit worrying."

Chissie stared. ''You know Gloria wouldn't do anything like that.''

The hell he did. Gloria Von Marron was no blushing virgin. Look how she had seduced him, wearing nothing but a skimpy man's shirt and leaving her bedroom door open so he would be certain to see her. She had sent him an invitation as surely as if she had pasted it on his forehead. Then she had pretended to be surprised. He had seen it before. Wealthy, bored socialites wanting sex without wanting to take responsibility for it. Using sex to get what they wanted.

''Win—I think we should drive up to Goose Point this weekend and make sure Gloria is all right.''

''Let it go, Chissie.''

If Gloria Von Marron was waiting at Goose Point for him to beg her to take a position at La Tourraine, Durant and Von Marron, she was going to wait a very long time. A few minutes in bed hadn't changed his mind. That's what it had been. She thought she could manipulate him by waving a piece of ass under his nose. She thought she could have the firm on a silver platter if she opened her legs for him. It amused him to think she believed he was that stupid, that easily managed. This was one time a Von Marron wasn't going to get what she wanted.

Gloria Von Marron's career disappointments were not his problem or his responsibility. This was one time good old Durant was not going to step in and rush up to Goose Point, wringing his hands because poor little Gloria had a case of the sulks. Screw her.

Dazed and disbelieving, Gloria nodded at the receptionist, counted some bills from a Hermes wallet, then closed the office door behind her. One of the people in the elevator said something to her, but she didn't respond.

Once on the street, she stood still, letting the pedestrian traffic break around her, oblivious to the din of Manhattan's traffic. Horns blared, exhaust pipes rumbled, people muttered as they stepped around her. Someone jostled her forward and she allowed herself to be swept along in the flow. Several minutes later she found herself deposited in front of a corner newsstand. Bright, polished faces smiled from a row of glossy magazine covers, some of them friends. But the cover that caught and held her attention fronted one of the more flamboyant tabloids. She recognized her own face beneath a bold heading: HAVING IT

ALL. The phrase jumped out at her, and she stared at it, struggling to contain the hysterical laughter rising in her throat.

She had it all, all right. She had just learned she was pregnant.

For the same reasons she could confide in no one about the rape, she could tell no one about her pregnancy. As the alternative was repugnant, unthinkable, the decision to have an abortion came automatically. But she didn't make it easily. Her instinct was to fly to Geneva and Lulu, but intellect gradually overrode instinct. She understood the world she had grown up in. Lulu's first thought would be horror at the possibility of a scandal. Lulu would have urged her to have the abortion as quickly and as quietly as was possible. There was no choice.

Surprisingly, the arrangements were easily made. Living with the decision was not, though she desperately wanted the nightmare to end. The night before her appointment in Manhattan, she tossed in her bed at Goose Point, inhaling the heavy fragrance of the last summer roses and feeling utterly alone and bewildered.

Where had everything gone wrong? Why wasn't she living the Cinderella life the newspapers happily imagined? Had there been a crossroads she had failed to recognize?

Having it all. Did the paparazzi really believe that? She had nothing.

As she had done a hundred times before, she stared into the darkness and asked what responsibility she bore for Durant's attack. Had she said something, done something that unwittingly enticed him? Had she in any way indicated she might welcome a sexual advance? Was the rape her fault? As always, the answer was no. And as always, anger and choking hatred followed the questions, providing a concrete focus to relieve the anguish of introspection.

The clinic was located in the upper forties, discreetly identified by a small brass plaque beside the door. It was a pleasant, quiet street; a row of trees shaded the renovated brownstones; there was little traffic.

As Gloria stood before the door the enormity of what she was about to do engulfed her. She knew women who had chosen abortions—Holly Drake, Michelle De Vries, others—and she understood their reasons. But until this moment she had not understood what it meant on a personal basis. She had not comprehended the sense of violation, of shame, the bewilderment, and the deep sense of loss.

"Don't be stupid," she whispered, looking away from the brass plaque. This pregnancy was not the result of a lover's passion. Her life would be destroyed unless she opened the door. The scandal would devastate her parents, herself. A trickle of perspiration dampened her temple as she stared at the door and commanded herself to press the latch.

A car backfired on Fifth Avenue and her skin jumped. Time spiraled backward, and she was no longer standing on the steps of a smartly renovated brownstone, she was transported to Goose Point, turning toward the staircase, hearing the shocked silence that followed the blast, thinking: Remy. Not Remy.

Spinning, she ran down the steps and fled toward Fifth Avenue and the flow of noisy people and honking traffic. Running away was stupid, reprehensible. But she could not go through with it. She could not kill another Von Marron.

Her flight from the clinic marked a turning point in her mind. The inertia she had been experiencing, the sense of drifting aimlessly, evaporated in the necessity of making immediate decisions.

If she was going to have this baby, this baby she resented and did not want, arrangements had to be made.

And she had to tell her father.

The thought of confronting her father crippled her. For two days she paced the rooms at Goose Point, shaking with hatred for Winthrop Durant. She dreaded telling her father that she would be the cause of media ridicule and family scandal. But there was no choice, none. She understood that just as she understood she had to tell her father before he read it in the newspapers. And she had to find the courage to stand firm on her decision not to reveal the name of her baby's father. She could not wreak that final destruction upon Bobby Von Marron.

The day she was scheduled to fly to Paris, she rose early and followed the path down to the beach, sitting with her back pressed to the sea wall, her knees tucked up beneath her chin.

She tried to rehearse the scene with her father, tried to locate the right words to tell him what he would not want to hear. How could she bear his disappointment? A tear collected on her lashes and she dashed it away with an angry motion. This was her choice; she would accept the consequences.

But oh God, it was hard. All she had ever wanted was to look in her father's eyes and see the approval and the pride he had lavished on Remy.

*   *   *

It startled Bobby Von Marron to discover how grown-up she was, how self-assured. Had Lulu been that self-possessed at Gloria's age? He didn't think so. A pocket of quiet existed within his daughter, a calm strength that was different from the strengths of his wife.

"I'm glad to see you," he said over dinner, meaning it. The years had trickled through his fingers like sand, dribbling away without his realizing it until very recently.

All the things he had intended to do, the achievements he had meant to realize, the mountains he had dreamed of scaling—these goals, if such nebulous dreams could be termed goals, had receded with the years. He would never accomplish these things. Would never drape his life over a purpose he could claim as important or admirable.

Such thoughts had occupied him more of late as he watched the inexorable advance of time march across his mirror. What he saw was a man aging better than his father had, but showing an inevitable softening of flesh and character. The strength in his daughter's eyes was not reflected by his own. Loneliness and self-pity had settled over him, and boredom—an ennui that deepened as he understood Lulu would never return to him, not on a permanent basis.

Seeking consolation, he looked at his daughter across the silver and china and told himself he had done one good thing in his life. He had produced this shining, radiant creature. In his daughter, his beautiful daughter, reposed the genes of his father and his father's father. The Von Marron name would die, but the Von Marron spirit, which had jumped over his generation, would live on in Gloria and in her children.

"So tell me," he said, smiling at her. "Is there a lucky young man in your life?" Once she had confided everything, all her little secrets. Had it been so long ago?

A look of pain tightened her mouth and she lowered her head. "No."

Suddenly, surprisingly, he felt almost desperate to know the details of her life. He wanted to know who she was, what she thought, who peopled her world. The young woman sitting before him was a stranger, and the realization stunned him. How could he have allowed this to happen? This was his daughter, the last of the Von Marrons.

Leaning forward, he touched her hand. "No one?" he asked, not believing. She was breathtakingly beautiful. "You aren't seeing Gardner Durant?"

To his astonishment she reacted to the question as if he had struck her. Her face went as pale as cream, and her eyes turned liquid.

"There's something I have to tell you," she said in a whisper.

"Tell me," he said, feeling bewildered.

"I spent the summer at Goose Point." She bit her lip and raised her eyes, looking at him with an expression he couldn't decipher.

"Yes?" Something was wanted, he read it in her pleading eyes, sensed it in her expression. She needed something from him, wanted a specific response. He pressed her hand and wished he could turn back the clock to a time when they had been able to speak easily to one another. "If you wish to explain why you didn't take a position with the firm, there's no need. I understand," he said, floundering, taking a stab in the dark. "Frankly, I was relieved to hear you didn't follow through. I never understood why you thought you needed a career."

"I thought you knew. I wanted you to be proud of me."

His eyebrows lifted. Was that what this was about? How could she glance into a mirror and doubt that he was proud of her?

"Darling, I *am* proud of you. You're bright; you're beautiful; you've never given your mother and me a single moment's worry. You have always conducted yourself as we would hope you would." Tears filled her eyes, and he stared at her with helpless astonishment. He had the distinct impression he was bungling this conversation, but he had no notion what he had said to distress her.

"You've never said it before."

Hadn't he? He must have. "But surely you know we're proud of you. Of course we are." Hoping to reassure her, he sought for examples. "You graduated summa cum laude. You created a sensation at the firm. Durant told me you performed miracles with your portfolio." Her mouth constricted, and she looked away from him. "Darling, I don't know what you're looking for. Short of creating a worldwide scandal, there's nothing you could do to make us feel anything but proud of you."

Instead of returning his smile, she closed her eyes and swayed in her chair. Her face was the color of snow. The sense of bungling something important increased and he spread his hands in frustration. "Gloria . . ."

"I've waited years to hear you say that. And now I've ruined everything."

"I'm sorry, I thought of course you knew." To his great discomfort, tears filled her eyes and she suddenly looked exhausted as if a great weight had fallen on her shoulders. He didn't begin to understand what he was seeing, but it occurred to him that he and Lulu had a great deal to answer for. Not knowing what else to do, he took her hand again and stroked her cold fingers. "Gloria, darling, I'm glad you're in Paris. We've let too much time go by. It will be wonderful to get reacquainted." He tried again when she didn't respond. "You must know that you don't have to have a career or any of that nonsense for your mother and me to be proud of you."

"As long as I don't create a scandal." She looked at him with such misery that he wondered if she were ill.

"I can't imagine you ever would." He wished to Christ Lulu were here and feeling well. He didn't know how to handle this. Silence opened between them, and for the life of him, he could not think of a single thing to say.

"How is mother?" she asked finally, looking down at her untouched plate.

Immediately he brightened with relief. "Better. Lulu was here for a week last month, and she's allowed a pass every weekend." Three years ago the doctors at Les Eaux had agreed Lulu could be released. But Lulu refused to reenter the world. She didn't want to leave Les Eaux. Les Eaux was safe, insulated, and she punished him by remaining there. But, as she had recently agreed to spend longer periods with him, he could deceive himself with hope.

"I'm glad. Bee Bee's gone then?"

"Last year." Had it been that long since they talked? "With you here, I can repay my social obligations with style." Her sober expression worried him. He didn't understand why she didn't return his smiles. "I'm desperately in need of a hostess."

"I won't be staying."

"But I thought—"

"Didn't I tell you? I'm only stopping in Paris for a week." Now she gave him a brilliant smile so dazzling he was completely disarmed. "I thought I'd travel a little, shop. . . ."

This he understood. "The yacht is in Monte Carlo if you want to use it. I understand the Greek Islands are fashionable this year."

She shrugged, the gesture unconsciously elegant. "Perhaps. Don't be concerned if you don't hear from me regularly. I'm not sure what I'll be doing for the next few months. Maybe I'll take

the *Dahinda* through the Greek Islands, maybe I'll visit China
or climb Katmandu.''

He laughed, finally feeling himself on firm ground. ''Finding
yourself? I understand that's the 'in thing.' Have you heard
about Count Orbach's son?'' Trying to make her laugh, he re-
counted the latest gossip making the rounds about Orbach's son
and his infamous efforts to find himself. If there was one thing
at which Bobby Von Marron excelled, it was relating amusing
gossip.

She couldn't tell him.

She had intended to; she had steeled herself for his reaction,
had rehearsed what she would say and her determination not to
reveal Durant's name. She had genuinely believed she had anticipated every possible direction the confrontation might take.
But she had not anticipated that her father would say the words
she had longed to hear for so many, many years. Finally hearing
them had devastated her.

After that, she could not tell him she was about to create an
international scandal. Not after she had finally read approval in
his eyes. Not when she had finally seen the pride. Not after
learning he could forgive anything but a scandal.

That a scandal would erupt, there was absolutely no doubt.
The Von Marron heiress revealed as an unwed mother was too
sensational a story for the press to ignore. There would be pho-
tographs of her wearing maternity clothes, endless speculation
regarding the baby's father. Photographers would swarm on Les
Eaux and the Paris town house. They would dredge up Bee Bee
Halston and Remy's death and the more eccentric gossip about
Lulu.

Gloria shifted uncomfortably and stared out of the airplane
window, her eyes dull with pain. She had to tell him and soon.

But not yet. She couldn't bring herself to destroy the approval
she had needed so badly, not just yet.

Not surprisingly the photographers spotted her in the London
airport despite her dark glasses and the fur halo covering her
silver hair. Ignoring them, she proceeded to the limousine waiting outside, relieved to notice the windows were tinted dark.
Once inside, she leaned her head against the upholstery and
abandoned all hope that the voracious paparazzi might overlook
her. It would not happen.

Lewes was no longer the simple town Margaret had described years ago, but it was not yet fully urbanized. Gloria had

visited here as a child, had been enchanted then as now with the narrow streets and ancient houses.

"Stop here," she instructed the driver.

Margaret and Edmund Tilbury's cottage was outside the town, enclosed within tidy box hedges and shaded by an ancient autumnal oak. When the limousine stopped before the gate, Gloria regarded the modest ivy-draped house and bit her lip, suddenly uncertain.

"Shall I ring, Miss?"

"No. No, thank you, I'll do it myself." A man on a bicycle stopped in the lane to inspect the limousine. Gloria nodded to him, then lifted her head and opened the gate. She stepped up to a small, neat porch.

"Gloria!" Margaret's beloved face, older now and displaying wrinkles at the eyes and mouth, opened in a smile of delight. Hastily, she dusted the flour on her hands across her apron, then opened her arms. "Edmund? Edmund, come see who's here!"

"Oh Margaret." Pressing her face against Margaret's graying hair, she let her arms fall to her sides and her shoulders drop.

The passage of years had not lessened Margaret's ability to hear with her heart. Easing back, she peered into Gloria's face. "What's wrong, darling? What's happened?"

"Oh Margaret." Helpless tears spilled down her face. "I need help. And there's no one else."

Chapter 9

HATRED SUSTAINED HER. Through the weeks and months of waiting, Gloria concentrated on her hatred for the necessary deceptions, hatred for the pregnancy misshaping her body, her growing, scalding hatred for the man who had altered the course of her life. When the fury and blackness built to uncontainable levels, Gloria laced on sturdy walking shoes and explored the lanes and the autumn countryside surrounding Lewes, walking briskly, furiously, her head down, her eyes fixed on the ground. Winthrop Durant's name clanged like a tocsin in her mind, there when she glanced at her swollen body, there when she thought of her uncertain future, there as she tried to prepare herself for the scandal that would tarnish the Von Marron name.

She thought about Durant continually, as she walked, when she cycled into the village to shop for Margaret, during the long nights when sleep didn't come. His face rose before her as she arranged the convoluted machinations that would conceal her whereabouts but allow her to receive mail, the reports from Home Limited, *The Wall Street Journal* and her trade magazines. Durant was with her always, and never more so than when Ian Lacklin, her doctor, examined her. Durant was there beneath the pale, satiny skin swelling over her abdomen.

Revenge consumed her thoughts. Durant had to pay for her loneliness and isolation, for her altered future. She wanted him to pay and pay dearly for the betrayal that would inevitably result in international ridicule and speculation. Someday, she promised herself through clenched teeth, the thought taking her through another day—someday.

Margaret and Edmund Tilbury opened the attic room for her, and Gloria would have spent her term in isolation, brooding beneath the eaves, but for Margaret and Edmund's insistence that she join them downstairs.

"You're supposed to be my widowed niece, not a reclusive lodger," Margaret pointed out, moving about her cheerful, ancient kitchen. Bending, she lifted a bushel basket of apples to a chipped countertop, then pushed a bowl and knife into Gloria's hands. "Peel. It will give your hands something to do." Smiling, she glanced around the kitchen and smoothed her palms over her apron. "Tilbury cottage isn't much like Goose Point, is it?"

The cottage was a hundred and sixty years old, small, and inconvenient by American standards. But it was also snug and homey, and Margaret accepted the cranky plumbing and damp walls with her usual aplomb.

"I like the house," Gloria said. Tilbury cottage offered solidity and a sense of continuity. And the quiet affection between Margaret and Edmund created an ambiance of warmth and serenity. "And I like Edmund, Margaret. Very much."

As usual, Margaret was right. It was good to have something useful to occupy her hands and thoughts. Relaxing, Gloria applied herself to filling the bowl with curling apple skins.

"Odd how things work out. As a young woman I believed Edmund and I would marry one day. But there were problems. I wanted to see the world beyond Lewes; Edmund wasn't interested in travel. I'm ashamed to admit this, but I thought I needed more from life than a carpenter could provide. Silly, isn't it?" A smile accompanied Margaret's shrug. "I went to America, and Edmund married Mabel Claridge."

"Is Edmund the reason you returned to Lewes?"

"When your father released the staff after it was decided your mother should go to Les Eaux, I knew it was time to come home. Mabel had died, and Edmund was alone."

"Do you regret the years apart?" Looking at Margaret now, wearing a wool skirt and warm sweater beneath her ever-present apron, it was difficult to remember her in silk dresses and stiffly coiffed hair. Gloria decided the new image suited her.

"I don't regret the years I spent with the Von Marrons, but I regret that Edmund and I didn't have children. I had you and Remy," she added quickly, "And I'm grateful for you both. If I couldn't have children of my own, I'm glad I had you for a time."

The kitchen sounds and smells permeated the small house, pleasant and comforting. The hiss of gas under the tea kettle, the cidery tang of sliced apples, the rhythmical slap of pie dough against the wooden cutting board.

Margaret dusted flour across her rolling pin. "Do you want to talk about it?" She asked gently, not looking at Gloria. "Or are you going to keep it inside?"

Gloria had known this moment would come; she had dreaded it. Margaret and Edmund had accepted her without question, but she had known the questions would come. The apple in her hands dropped into the bowl and she felt her stomach constrict.

"I've thought about it," Margaret said, rolling a lump of pie dough into a circle. "And I've concluded it wasn't Gardner."

"Gardner?" The name emerged in a whisper. She couldn't bear to think about Gardner.

"If it was Gardner, I don't think you would be here. You and Gardner . . . but the man who's responsible is married, isn't he?"

"I . . . yes."

Margaret's rolling pin flattened the pie dough with a quick, forceful movement. "I was afraid of that. Is there any chance . . . ?"

"No!" An involuntary shudder pulled her lips back from her teeth, and Gloria raised a hand to her forehead. "I loathe him. If I could reveal his name, Margaret, I would. But I can't. I can't tell anyone."

"I swore I wasn't going to preach, but . . . I think you should tell your parents, Gloria. It isn't right for you to go through this alone."

"I'll have to tell them eventually, but not yet." She lifted her eyes, silently begging for understanding. "I can't. Not yet."

Margaret nodded, then sighed. After she pushed the pie into the oven, she poured coffee and sat across from Gloria. "Have you thought any more about placing the baby up for adoption?"

She thought about it constantly. Ian Lacklin had spoken to her about a young couple in the village who could not have children, who would be delighted to take Durant's bastard. Adoption, of course, provided the perfect solution. If her luck held, Gloria was beginning to believe it might be possible to get through this without anyone ever knowing. There would be no scandal. She could return to that moment in Paris with her father, and this time it would lead to the intimacy she sensed they both sought. She had decided to instruct Ian Lacklin to approach the Lewes couple and begin arranging the adoption.

"Margaret!" Her apple knife clattered to the linoleum, and

she pressed a hand to her stomach. "He moved! The baby moved!"

Smiling, Margaret knelt beside her and placed a floury hand against Gloria's smock. "My, he's a strong lad, isn't he? He's saying hello," she said, laughing.

Gloria stared at her rounded stomach and her eyes widened. "My God."

It changed everything.

For months the pregnancy had been an abstract, not a reality. If Gloria thought about the baby she carried, she thought of it only as Durant's bastard. It had nothing to do with her. Until now. A tiny heel or fist pushed against her hand and moisture sprang to her eyes. This was her child too, flesh of her flesh. The abrupt realization filled her with wonder and awe.

Cupping her hands protectively around her stomach, she held her breath and waited for the next movement. A radiant smile lit her features. "Oh Margaret."

From that moment on there was no question of adoption. The hatred that had nourished her through the early months of the pregnancy temporarily vanished. Like all first-time mothers, Gloria's thoughts turned inward and she developed a fascination for the changes occurring in her body. Books arrived at the cottage in bulky packages, and she pored over them before ordering more. She walked religiously, through fog and rain and snow. She ate every scrap Margaret placed before her. The *Journals* and her reports from Home Limited piled up beside her attic bed, forgotten in favor of the tiny caps and booties she was learning to knit. She ordered mounds of baby clothing from the White House in London, and hung over Edmund's shoulder as he cut and sanded lengths of oak for the cradle he was making "our baby."

The euphoria lasted until Christmas and reappeared after the holidays, but as Christmas approached, Gloria's spirits sagged toward depression.

"I've always hated the holidays," she murmured. Moody and feeling out of sorts, she stood at the cottage window watching ice crystals form fernlike patterns across the panes.

"Nonsense." Margaret glanced up from the ironing board. "You used to love Christmas. Don't you remember? All the people and the parties. Do you remember the year your mother opened Goose Point for Christmas? I never saw a taller tree. The Durants came and the La Tourraines. That year there were more titles at Goose Point than in Europe."

The Christmases as a child weren't the Christmases that depressed her. It was recalling the Christmases since Remy's death. This Christmas would be the worst since that terrible year in Paris before she entered Aigmont.

A week ago she had telephoned her father, inventing an excuse to explain why she couldn't meet him in New York for the holidays. His disappointment had seemed genuine, and she had suddenly wondered if Bobby Von Marron was lonely.

There were traditional calls to make, additional lies to be told. Margaret and Edmund discreetly withdrew so she could use the parlor phone in privacy. She telephoned Paris and Rome, Rio de Janeiro and Tokyo, wishing friends a happy holiday and leaving the impression she would most likely be spending Christmas aboard the *Dahinda* in Monte Carlo.

Finally, she had completed all the calls on her list but one. Her finger trembled as she dialed the Durant residence in New York, praying Abrams would answer. When he did, her feeling of relief was intense. At least she would be spared hearing Win Durant's voice. "May I speak to Gardner Durant, please. This is Miss Von Marron."

"Gloria!" His voice was deep and warm, vibrant. "Where are you? I seem to recall we have a date. I talk and you listen, among other things—remember?"

"I remember." Lowering her head, she drew a breath and made her voice emerge sounding unconcerned and cheerful. "I'm afraid I'll have to cancel. I won't be in town for the holidays. But I wanted to wish you a merry Christmas and ask you to give Aunt Chissie a kiss from me."

"Wait a minute. That sounds like you're saying good-bye before we've really said hello." The sound of his laughter reminded her of happier occasions. She closed her eyes. "I have a hundred questions for you, Miss Von Marron. Starting with: why haven't you answered my letters? And: Where the hell are you? Michelle says she heard you were spending the holidays in Monaco; Charles insists you're somewhere in the Greek Islands. One of the Henderson twins swears you were seen recently in Nassau, someone else thinks you're in Switzerland. So—where are you? And why aren't you here? You and I have some unfinished business."

"Oh Gardner." She stared into the fire Edmund had built for her in the parlor grate, then she covered her eyes.

"This must be a poor connection, you sound strange. Gloria, talk to me. What happened? When I saw you in Cambridge, you were a week from bringing Wall Street to its knees. Then mother says you ran off to Goose Point, stopped seeing anyone and now you've apparently vanished. What's going on with you?''

The question was expected; she had prepared an answer. "It's not as mysterious as you're making it sound. I got sidetracked. Wall Street doesn't seem as important anymore."

"Is this the same woman I spoke to in Cambridge?" She heard his surprise. "Wall Street was the culmination of a dream, of years of preparation. What do you mean you got sidetracked?"

Of all the people she was deceiving, she feared Gardner the most. He was her weakest point because she cared so much; he was the most likely to recognize a lie. Eventually he would read about her baby in the tabloids, but he could never learn the entire truth. She could not do that to him. Whatever they had begun together had to end.

"I met someone," she said softly.

"I see." The following silence sliced across the wire like a knife. When he finally spoke again, his voice had gone flat. "I saw your photograph in *Le Monde*, in September, I think, taken in Paris. You were wearing a dress by Anita Pagliaro."

"I didn't know you were interested in fashion." She struggled to keep her voice light.

"You were cheek to cheek with Count Somebody. Esterhazy?"

"It isn't Esterhazy. It's no one you know, Gardner. But . . . I'm very happy." The lie made her physically sick. Bending forward over her swollen stomach, she clutched the phone and closed her eyes against another painful silence.

"I'm happy for you," he said at length.

"So. Tell me about Home Limited. I understand you gave a speech in Rome last month addressing environmental responsibility among the major industrial firms."

"Actually, Gloria, I was about to go out. Perhaps we could save the shop talk for another time."

Pressing her hand to her stomach, she drew a long unsteady breath. "Merry Christmas, Gardner."

She sat in front of the fire, holding the telephone to her breast long after he had hung up. When she could bring herself to sever this final connection, she replaced the receiver then bent forward and wept into her hands.

"Damn Win Durant to hell," she whispered. "Damn him to bloody hell!"

Gardner Durant poured a drink and moved to stand before the penthouse windows. Light snow fluttered past the glass, obscuring the city's holiday decorations. If he had known Gloria would not be in New York for the holidays, he would have remained in Australia and wrapped up the negotiations for the buy-out of the Prolax Bauxite holdings. Obviously he had erred by making assumptions based on a few minutes that had clearly meant more to him than to Gloria. The mood had been warm and teasing that night; he had placed too much importance on a few kisses and a few words whispered after too many brandies.

The depth of his disappointment surprised him. While he had anticipated seeing her to such a degree that he had placed Prolax on such hold, he hadn't recognized any urgency. In what he now saw as arrogance, he had simply assumed she would be waiting for him. Obviously, he was wrong. It disturbed him that he could have misjudged the situation so badly. Aside from finding another man, he had believed she was committed to a career on Wall Street.

On the other hand, he too had veered from Wall Street at her age. He had chosen to accept the Home Limited fellowship rather than proceed in the more natural direction toward La Tourraine, Durant and Von Marron. At the time, he had viewed his decision as an act of rebellion, as an interim solution until he decided what he wanted to do with his life.

In retrospect, his rebellion had been mild. Even then he had understood that his father voted the Von Marron block which, in consequence, meant Gardner remained under his father's influence. In the early years of his association with Home Limited, Winthrop Durant's influence had been a negative, certainly not a benefit. In more recent years Gardner had sensed indifference. His father no longer actively worked against him, but neither did his father support his efforts.

Gardner tasted his drink and turned away from the windows. As he was one or two years away from being offered a vice presidency with Home, he believed his father had finally, albeit reluctantly, accepted his career decision. But the defection had never been forgiven. Time had not softened the strain between them.

It wasn't until the following day that he realized Gloria had not mentioned where she was staying or the name of the man who had altered her dreams. As he had never considered her secretive, these omissions more than anything else signified the change between them. It was a change he deeply regretted.

Gloria's labor began on a blustery March Thursday. Ian Lacklin mounted the attic stairs, examined her, then returned to the kitchen and the tea kettle to share a pipe with Edmund. "Nature won't be rushed," he cheerfully assured Margaret. "The bairn will be along in good time."

"Men," Margaret muttered sourly. She leaned over Gloria's bed to blot the perspiration rising on her forehead. "They don't take this seriously enough!" Anxiously, she peered into Gloria's face. "Is there anything I can do? Someone I should telephone?"

"No." Gasping, Gloria pressed Margaret's hand.

"Perhaps I should call your father. Don't you think?"

"Please, Margaret. Don't."

It would only compound her disgrace to have her father learn of it from someone else. After swallowing some ice water, she dropped back onto the attic bed and stifled a groan. When it was over, she would tell her father. She had planned what she would say and how she would say it. In the best of her rehearsed scenarios, her parents understood and they forgave her. In the best of the scenarios, they didn't demand the name of her baby's father and no hint of scandal appeared in the newspapers. Gloria knew it wouldn't happen that way, but she took comfort in thinking it might.

Margaret adjusted a ball of yarn in her lap and examined her knitting needles. "Have you thought about what you'll do afterward?"

"I'm not sure." The baby had occupied her thoughts exclusively, interrupted only by the worry of what and when she would tell her parents. Maintaining the fiction of her whereabouts had also required attention and energy. The reality of picking up her life and going on had presented a problem she delayed considering, as she had not yet reconciled the image of herself and a baby with the goals which had been the focus of her life for so many years.

"Edmund and I would like you to stay with us," Margaret suggested, touching her hand. "Not forever, we know that isn't possible, but for as long as you like. We feel part of this. We'd enjoy having a little one in the house."

"Thank you. I haven't decided yet what . . ." A hard pain

crushed the breath from her lungs and she panted heavily when it was over. "Margaret? I think you should call Ian. Now!"

Her son was born at two in the afternoon. That evening, when she was allowed to sit up and take him into her arms, she gazed at him with love and awe and named him Robert Winthrop Von Marron. Robert, after her father; Winthrop, so she would never forget.

"He's beautiful," she murmured softly, leaning over the polished oak cradle Edmund had carved. A tiny pink hand curled around her forefinger. "Isn't he the most beautiful, the most perfect baby you have ever seen?"

Edmund Tilbury laughed. "Absolutely." His smile curved around the stem of his pipe. Gruffly, he cleared his throat. "Margaret says you'll be leaving us soon."

Inhaling the good smells of English tobacco and wood shavings, Gloria embraced him. "You've been a good friend, Edmund, but I've imposed long enough."

"It's been no imposition, lass." His voice deepened. "The cottage will seem empty without you and wee Robby. Margaret is grieving already."

"How can I ever thank you?"

"By coming back to visit. Often."

They tiptoed from the attic room and descended arm in arm to the parlor where Margaret waited with a pot of breakfast tea and a plate of biscuits. Standing, she brushed her hands over a tweed skirt and exchanged a look with Edmund who pressed Gloria's arm then turned into the kitchen.

"It's time, isn't it?" Margaret asked gently.

"Yes. I dread it."

Margaret nodded. After embracing Gloria, she quietly closed the parlor door behind her.

The call to the Hotel de Paris in Monaco went through more swiftly than Gloria had anticipated and she experienced a nervous breathlessness as she waited for the desk to ring her parents' suite.

Bobby thought his daughter sounded more self-possessed and mature than he remembered. Holding the telephone tightly, he pictured her as she had been when he had seen her last in Paris. The same sense of loss overtook him now as it had then. He regretted the passage of years that could not be retrieved.

After inquiring about Lulu and their vacation in Monaco, she drew a breath and said, "I'd like you and mother to come to London. There's someone I want you to meet. I need to tell you something, and I'd prefer to do it in person."

Her request wasn't entirely unexpected. For several years he had anticipated a call asking him to meet a young man. The problem was Lulu. Behind him, he heard her moving about the suite, picking up items then letting them fall, the movements listless and indifferent.

He answered carefully, not wanting to alarm her. "Our stay has been wonderful, but exhausting. I think your mother would prefer to return directly to Les Eaux and save a London excursion for another time. Of course I'll discuss it with her."

"Will you come? I need you, Daddy."

She hadn't called him Daddy in years. He found the term oddly touching. "I need you, too," he said, surprised to realize it was true. "After seeing you in Paris last year, I realized we've grown apart. I want to rectify that, Gloria." Watching Lulu, he thought for a moment. "Let's do this, shall we? Lulu and I will drive to Nice tomorrow morning and fly from there to Geneva. I'll go to London the following day. Are you staying at the Connaught?"

"I'll make reservations."

Lulu had taken a seat in front of the balcony door. Ignoring the doctor's instructions, she was drinking again, clasping a glass of vodka against the lap of a Balenciaga negligee.

"We haven't turned out well, have we?" he said after a moment, speaking softly. "Except for you, Gloria. In the end, you'll be the only Von Marron who's worth a damn, the Von Marron to make us all proud." Instead of sounding pleased, her voice sounded strangled as if she were weeping. "Gloria? Is something wrong?"

"I'll tell you when I see you. I have to run, Daddy. I'll meet you at the Connaught the day after tomorrow."

Although he didn't really want a drink this early in the morning, he poured a splash of gin over ice so Lulu would not be drinking alone. "That was Gloria."

"Oh."

When she didn't ask about their daughter, he stifled a sigh and continued speaking, more to make conversation than because he sensed she was interested. "Gloria wants me to meet her in London. It sounds like she's met a young man."

"Is she sleeping with him?"

He stared at her then looked into his drink. "I'm sorry things didn't work last night. It happens, Lulu. We'd both been drinking, we were tired, and it was late. . . ." A flush of embarrassment rose beneath his tanned skin. Dammit. He didn't know what the hell had gone wrong. This had never happened to him before.

"Do you have any trouble getting it up for Bee Bee? Or just me?" One penciled eyebrow rose.

"What?"

"Bee Bee Halston, that slut. Did you think I didn't know? It's a small world, Bobby. I hear things even at Les Eaux."

"Is that why you've been so restless and upset?"

When she pushed back her hair and stared at him, he was startled by the naked hatred in her eyes. "When did it start? At Goose Point? In Paris? How long have you been screwing her?"

"Lulu, darling." Without an idea of what he would say, he knelt beside her chair and tried to take her hand, but she snatched it away. "You've been ill a very long time. I know," he raised a hand, "that doesn't excuse anything." Christ. He hated lying to her. "People talk in circumstances like these. But you have to understand that Bee Bee and I are only friends. She was kind enough to act as hostess for a few parties, that's all there was to it. I know there's been some gossip—that was inevitable, but none of it is true."

Lulu's timing was uncanny as Bee Bee had turned up in his life again, repeating her demands that he obtain a divorce and marry her. The idea of a divorce was ludicrous, out of the question. Lulu was the only woman he had ever genuinely loved. The others, Bee Bee and Baroness Von Edelmann, with whom he had indulged in a brief fling, had been nothing but idle diversions brought about by loneliness and physical need. From the beginning he had known he would wait for Lulu no matter how long it took.

"Do you really expect me to believe that?"

"I hope you do," he said, looking into her eyes. "Because it's true. I love you, Lulu."

Later he tried again to make love to her, feeling a rush of panic when his body didn't respond. Humiliated, desperate to reassure Lulu and himself, he ran his hands over her slim body, licked her still youthful breasts, placed her fingers around his limp penis. Nothing happened. He couldn't get an erection. Sweat rose on his brow as he attempted to remember Lulu in the early years, as he made himself think about every beautiful woman he had known or desired. He buried his face between her golden thighs, stroked himself, tried to recall the last pornographic film he might have seen.

Finally, she shoved him away and rolled onto her side, presenting her back to him. Her body was rigid with anger and offense.

"Lulu . . . Christ! I don't know what to say. This has never happened before." He would see a doctor immediately after he returned from Les Eaux. Most likely this was nothing to be concerned about. After all, he was no longer a kid; these things happened. He hadn't been with a woman in months; possibly that was part of the problem.

Rising from the bed, he tied on a silk robe and stepped into the suite's living room, turning toward the bar. In the darkness, he filled a crystal tumbler with gin and gulped it, then poured another that he carried outside to the wrought iron balcony.

Despite having ended so badly, their holiday had begun in gaiety and high expectations. They had spent the first two days entertaining a small party of friends on the *Dahinda*. Things hadn't started to disintegrate until the third day. That morning they sailed the *Dahinda* to Cannes, intending to swim and then do a little casino hopping after dinner.

Shortly after lunch, Lulu had suddenly burst into tears. One moment she had been smiling and laughing, and Bobby had felt on top of the world, believing everything was going well, believing she was on her way back to him. The next moment she was sobbing hysterically and babbling about Remy. How old Remy would have been now, how talented he was, how handsome and intelligent and engaging. Their guests had risen silently from their deck chairs and had melted away minutes before Lulu's crying jag erupted into rage. She screamed and raked her nails across her breasts; she hurled the luncheon dishes at him; she accused him of killing their son.

He still felt bewildered by how swiftly she had changed. She had proceeded to smash everything smashable on the yacht's deck. Then, when the violence wore itself out, she stood amid the wreckage and screamed accusations that he was fucking Corinne de Plessis, one of their guests.

The only thing he could think to do was remove her after he forced three Valium tables between her lips. He had borrowed Thérèse La Tourraine's Mercedes and had driven Lulu back to Monte Carlo where he checked her into the Hotel de Paris, hoping her favorite hotel would exert a calming influence.

She had not referred to the incident or indicated she expected him to do so. Nor had she mentioned Corinne again. Foolishly, he had believed the storm had passed until she mentioned Bee Bee. Her doctors would have to be informed, of course, and he loathed telling them. But he thanked heaven the holiday was over. What had begun with such hope had ended in disaster.

He sat on the balcony, drinking steadily and berating himself for failing to achieve an erection, trying to conceive an explanation that would put things right again.

In the morning they ordered breakfast in the suite and ate without speaking while the maid packed their luggage.

"I told Thérèse I'd leave her Mercedes at the Marina," he said while they dressed. "Enrico will meet us there and drive us to Nice." She didn't respond, didn't acknowledge he was in the room. "Have you taken your Valium this morning?" He might as well have addressed the wall. Ignoring him, Lulu leaned to the vanity mirror and applied her lipstick, then rearranged a strand of hair. He didn't merit her notice.

They didn't speak while they waited for the car to be brought around, didn't speak as the Mercedes swept along the curves of the Corniche. Once he commented on the spectacular scenery, attempting to draw her attention to the rocky beauty of the cliffs dropping steeply from the road to the Mediterranean. When she still refused to speak, he abandoned further attempts at conversation.

Narrowing his focus to the road, Bobby gave himself to the pleasure of driving. He drove fast, enjoying the soft spring air rushing past the windows, the exhilaration of control as the Mercedes swept the curves twisting along the cliffs. It was a brilliant day. Far below, the sea glistened like rolling silver; an azure canopy arched above. He had a beautiful woman beside him. What more could a man ask? With little effort he could pretend that he and Lulu were young again and life was still filled with sparkle and promise.

"You bastard!"

The hissed invective startled him and shattered his reverie. The car swerved sharply before he brought it back into the lane and glanced at her.

Lulu had shifted in the seat to stare at him. "Did you really think I'd swallow that crap about you going to London to see Gloria? When did you ever care about seeing Gloria? You're meeting Bee Bee, aren't you? Or is it Corinne?"

"I told you the truth. Is it so difficult to believe I'd like to feel closer to our daughter? Lulu, did you take your Valium? You didn't take it, did you?''

"Why should you care? You don't care anything about me. All you want to do is dump me in Geneva so you can run off to London with one of your whores!''

A headache throbbed behind his eyes as his pleasure in the day began to fade. He couldn't turn back the clock. They were not young again. Years ago, Bobby and Lulu Von Marron had ceased to be the perfect golden couple. He had only been fooling himself, living on hope. The days of youth and carefree innocence insulated by the Von Marron name and the Von Marron wealth had vanished forever.

Saddened, he turned his attention from the road and looked at his wife, seeing a beautiful, pampered shell filled to overflowing with hatred, resentment, self-pity. But who was he to judge her? There had been months, years, when he had almost hated Lulu for disrupting his life. He had resented his enforced loneliness, his state of social and marital limbo, the wasted years while she clung to Les Eaux. Self-pity? He had elevated the state to an art, then devoted himself to mastering it.

"What happened to us?" he wondered softly, the words lost in the rush of warm air flowing past the window. Could they have done something differently to save themselves? Anything?

"You wish I was dead, don't you?"

Shock cut across his thoughts and he jerked toward her. "For God's sake, Lulu. Don't be ridiculous!"

"If I was dead you could have your precious Bee Bee or that whore, Corinne." Her lip pulled back, leaving a smear of lipstick across her teeth. "If I was dead, you wouldn't have to worry about the scandal of a divorce."

"Lulu, stop this. Take your Valium."

"You're always urging me to take more Valium. Are you hoping for an overdose?" Her laughter shocked him, scraped across his nerve endings. "You always were a coward, Bobby. I used to wonder how in the world you managed to save Georges's life during the war. Now here you are, absolutely in character, hoping for an overdose or for something else equally as subtle as the tactics you used on Remy."

"Dammit, Lulu. I thought we were past that." Something gave way inside. Years of patience melted under the heat blazing in her eyes. "You and I both had a finger on that trigger. If I was partly responsible for Remy—so were you."

Circles of rouge jumped forward on her cheeks as her face went white. "Bastard. Bastard!"

The Mercedes swerved across the lane then veered back toward the guard wall as Lulu struck wildly at his shoulder. Bright red fingernails lunged for his face and clawed a bloody trail down his cheek.

"Lulu! Jesus!" He fought the hands flailing at him, fought the swerving Mercedes. Screams rang in his ears as he struggled to slap her hands away from the steering wheel.

"You want to kill me? It's easy, you coward!" The heel of her shoe spiked down hard on his ankle, and the gas pedal shot to the floor.

"Christ!" The pain in his cheek and ankle screamed at him. Fear motivated the fist he brought down on her thigh. He thought he heard a bone snap and the sound sickened him, but there was no time to think about it. Pulling on the wheel, fighting it, he tried to establish control as the car swerved across the lanes and scraped the rock face banking the curve. The impact of metal against rock bounced them back onto the road, sent the Mercedes careening toward the guard wall.

"If I die, you son of a bitch—so do you!" Teeth bared, Lulu fell against him, fighting with elbows and hands for control of the wheel. Her weight on his thigh kept his foot pressed against the gas pedal.

They struck the guard wall at a speed exceeding ninety kilometers per hour. There was time for astonishment, time to witness Lulu's exaltation as the Mercedes broke through the stones and sailed out over the cliff face. Sunlight glittered on the tears filling his eyes. He heard her cry Remy's name. There was time in the last seconds to wrap his arms around her before the grill of the Mercedes smashed against the first rock outcropping.

The car crashed end over end down the cliff before it dropped into the sea and slowly sank.

Chapter 10

$\mathscr{B}$Y THE TIME Gloria arrived in New York, stunned and disbelieving, unable to think beyond the next moment, Win Durant
had completed the funeral arrangements. To protest Durant's
involvement would have raised questions and speculation Gloria
lacked the emotional energy to deal with. It distressed her
enough to discover the Von Marron name emblazoned across
the headlines.

The Times devoted a full page to the accident and her parents'
obituaries; *The Washington Post* traced the family's ascendency
from the eighteen hundreds; the tabloids insisted Lulu had been
wearing the Von Marron diamond at the time of the accident
and claimed the diamond was cursed. *The Wall Street Journal*
profiled the original partners who had formed La Tourraine,
Durant and Von Marron. *Manhattan* featured Gloria as the city's
latest poor little rich girl.

At some point each article contrived to exaggerate Lulu's in-
stability, and most portrayed Bobby as a millionaire playboy.
Scandal mongers and gossip columnists crawled over the Von
Marron history and added creative embellishments. According
to the columnists, Lulu hadn't wandered, confused and disori-
ented, through Bergdorf Goodman in her lingerie—she had
skipped through the store stark naked. The gossips hinted in
print that Bobby had bedded dozens of Europe's most beautiful
women. Speculations as to the cause of Remy's death ranged
from absurd to disgusting. Gloria, who attracted the largest portion of the media interest, was pictured with a dozen different
men, the implication being that Manhattan's latest poor little
rich girl sought Daddy in a series of sexual liaisons. Sickened,
Gloria threw the newspapers aside.

She moved through the days like an automaton; the smallest

decisions were overwhelming, complicated, and draining. It had been Margaret who first heard the news on the radio, then rushed to the Connaught to find her, stunned and shaking, standing helpless in the lobby as flashbulbs exploded in her eyes. Margaret who verified the radio report, then dialed Chissie Durant and placed the telephone in Gloria's shaking hands. Margaret who managed to keep Robby away from the press. Margaret who telephoned William in New York and instructed him to prepare the town house for Gloria's arrival. Margaret who insisted this was not the time to make a decision about Robby, who assured her Robby would be well taken care of in Lewes. And it was Margaret who drove her to London and assisted her aboard Home Limited's jet.

Now she sat in the first pew at Saint James Church and watched Win Durant mount the steps between the flower-draped caskets to deliver the eulogy. Her clasped hands trembled on top of her purse, and her face was as pale as the silvery hair coiled on her neck. But her eyes remained dry beneath her dark veil. Hatred absorbed her tears.

Because of Winthrop Durant she had not seen her parents in nearly a year. She had not touched them or embraced them, had not spoken the words they needed to hear. Now the words would never be said.

If it had not been for Durant and what he had done to her, she would have affected a reconciliation with her father. She would not have disgraced herself and her family's name. That was the bitter worst of it. Now she would never know if her parents could have forgiven her for Robby. She would never know if they had loved her enough to forgive the scandal. A single tear slipped beneath her veil and dropped to her gloved hands.

Society names from all parts of the world packed the church, listening to Durant regret the loss of Bobby and Lulu Von Marron. With Chissie's guidance, Gloria had invited a select few to a private reception at the Hotel Carlyle following the service. She had chosen the Carlyle deliberately because she couldn't endure the thought of Winthrop Durant moving about her town house, touching her things. She wanted no memory of Durant in her home. The number of guests had been chosen with equal deliberation. She desired a group small enough that she would not feel overwhelmed, but large enough that few would notice she did not speak to her father's partner and lifelong friend.

Gripping her hands, she stared at him through the dark netting of her veil, and she wished with all her soul that it had been Winthrop Durant inside that crushed lump the officials had dragged from the Mediterranean.

The funerals and the interment became a contest of endurance. The reception at the Hotel Carlyle and the endless murmur of condolences were events to be borne before she could escape to solitude. Briefly closing her eyes, Gloria leaned against the doorway to the buffet, shutting out the crush of beautifully clad mourners. A hum of low-pitched voices buzzed in her ears, and she wished for an aspirin.

"I still can't believe it." Red-eyed and weeping, Chissie Durant gripped Gloria's elbow. The accident had aged her. Above the standing collar of a silk Valentino, Chissie's complexion appeared sallow and lifeless. Dark purplish smudges bruised the skin beneath her eyes. "Lulu's gone." Bewilderment and pain brought fresh tears to her eyes.

When Gardner stepped forward, Chissie leaned into his shoulder as he slipped an arm around her waist, then she shook her head in a helpless gesture and allowed someone to lead her to the powder room.

"She's taking it very hard." Gardner studied Gloria's pale face and frowned. "How are you—honestly?"

"It doesn't seem real." Feeling the exhaustion of the last few days, she gazed at the clusters of people, at the somber colors. "None of this seems real. I know it happened, but I can't make myself accept it."

If she let herself believe and feel, she sensed she would fall apart. The part of her mind that accepted her parents' death wanted to smash and destroy everything at hand, wanted to tear her hair and howl her grief. But that wasn't the Von Marron way.

She glanced up at Gardner, catching a moment of unguarded tenderness in his gaze, and she longed to lean into his strength and accept whatever comfort he could offer. She badly needed someone to hold her and love her. And it would have been so easy to step forward. But she held herself apart, her shoulders stiffly squared, her eyes painfully dry.

"Let's get out of here," he said, touching her sleeve. "We'll go somewhere quiet for dinner and talk. It might help. Someone who looked a lot like you once said I was a good listener."

It sounded wonderful, exactly what she needed. "Thank you, Gardner, but I don't think so." To soften the rejection, she tried to smile. "I'm not good company right now."

"I'm not looking for good company. I'd like to help a friend."

"I appreciate it." Tears moistened her eyes, and she dropped her head. "But no one can help. This is something I have to work through alone."

Because her head was lowered, she didn't realize Win Durant had joined them until he spoke. "I hope you were pleased with the eulogy."

Immediately her head snapped up and a rush of adrenaline stiffened her spine. Hatred darkened the color of her eyes to granite, but she welcomed the emotion. Hatred was easier to bear than pain and grief.

When she didn't reply, Durant cleared his throat and glanced at Gardner. "I believe you're aware I'm the executor of your parents' estate. There are no major surprises in the wills. There are several secondary bequests, but you're the primary beneficiary. When you feel up to it, we'll get together and review the details."

"I'll make an appointment next week."

"I'm sure you know how sorry I am that Bobby and Lulu are gone. If there is anything I can do . . ."

Hysteria rose at the back of her throat and strangled her. She wanted to laugh, wanted to spit in his face. His expression of sadness was as hypocritical as the sentiment he had expressed in the eulogy. Win Durant was no friend of her father's. And she would never forget he had called her mother's name the night he raped her. Win Durant didn't regret her parents' death; why should he? With her father gone, Durant had what he wanted. La Tourraine, Durant and Von Marron.

When Win stepped forward, his arms lifted to embrace her, Gloria's face went ashen and her lip twisted over her teeth. A tremor of revulsion convulsed her shoulders and she jerked backward. For an instant Durant's features froze, then the hands he reached toward her continued upward to adjust his tie as if that had been his intention. He murmured something to Gardner, and then withdrew in the direction of the bar.

Gardner lifted an eyebrow. "What was that all about?"

This time when she looked at him, she recognized Win Durant's dark eyes, Win Durant's powerful physique, Win Durant's sensual mouth. Repelled, she stared at him with an expression of distaste. And suddenly she needed to escape, to get away from him. This, too, she blamed on Win Durant. She and Gardner might have had a future together; now it was impossible.

"I'm very tired," she whispered, looking away from him. "Do you suppose anyone will notice if I leave?"

"I'll drive you home."

"No!" Pressing a hand to her throat, she drew a breath and made herself speak more softly. "Thank you, but William is waiting downstairs." It was too abrupt. There had to be something more to say. "Did I hear you telling someone you're leaving for Yugoslavia tomorrow?"

She pretended to listen as he explained the Yugoslavian project, but she concentrated on his face, seeking Chissie in his expression and trying to block any reminders of Win Durant. Then, with a shock that took her breath away, she recognized her son's chin and brow. Robby had the same warm dark eyes, the same smiling mouth. Robby was Gardner's half brother.

"Gloria?"

She hadn't thought of it before.

"Gloria?" His hand shot forward to steady her. "Are you all right?"

The relationship was obvious. It had always been there, but she had not allowed herself to recognize it. Not once. God. She pressed a hand to her waist, feeling sick.

"I have to leave," she whispered, staring at him and seeing Robby.

"Gloria, I'm worried about . . ." But she was gone.

La Tourraine, Durant and Von Marron was his now.

Durant strode briskly across the marble-tiled lobby and rode his private elevator up to the twenty-sixth floor. The elevator opened onto a sweep of plush carpeting and softly gleaming antique furnishings. The muted tones of mauve, cream, and teal were intended as soothing, but Durant had always considered the blend stimulating. Not stimulating in the same manner as the small, second office he maintained on the firm's trading floor, but stimulating as a reflection of power and position.

Years ago the twenty-sixth floor had been dubbed the golden square, referring to the four partner's suites that occupied each window-wrapped corner of the floor. Though furnished individually, each suite contained an identical office, a smaller secretary's office, a fully stocked bar, a private conference room, a full bath and small kitchen, and a sleeping room. Each suite had a private entrance as well as the formal double doors that opened onto a central reception area.

The receptionist, beautiful enough to be mistaken for a model, gave him a provocative smile which he acknowledged with a brief nod. She had great tits and an ass that gave him the sweats to contemplate. But long ago he had learned not to dip his pen in the company ink.

Before entering his office, Durant paused to allow himself a moment of triumph. The gold plaques on the four sets of double doors ringing the reception area read: Georges La Tourraine, Edison Whitehall, Robert Von Marron II, Winthrop Durant.

Except for his own, the offices were unoccupied. He had outlived the bastards. Justice had won; La Tourraine, Durant and Von Marron was now his. Or would be as soon as he completed the buy-back of the Von Marron partnership. Christ, it felt good. It felt goddamn wonderful. Wearing a smile, he opened the heavy doors to his office.

For the past thirty years he had begun his working day by setting aside fifteen minutes to consult with his secretary, Lucille Ivory. She served his morning coffee in the firm's paper-thin china which had once graced Louis XVI's table, then she seated herself to the side of his desk and opened a leather-bound note pad across her lap. Unlike the receptionist, there was nothing about Lucille Ivory to tempt his thoughts from business.

"Swords are being drawn in the pits," she announced. "Another vacant office . . ." Her bony shoulders rose in a shrug.

"Any blood drawn?"

"Not yet. But soon."

"Those offices have been vacant for a long time." Edison had been dead for years; Georges had never used his office, and Bobby had appeared only rarely since taking up residence in Paris.

"The point is, the vacancies are expensive. No one expects them to continue, especially now that Mr. Von Marron is gone. They expect you to invite three new people to invest in a full partnership. Hence the swords. Everyone is jockeying for position. If that's your intention, I'd suggest you extend the invitations soon before ambition and greed kills someone down there."

He returned Lucille's grin. She knew he preferred to keep his department heads at each other's throats. Competition and a vacant executive office encouraged peak performance. But Lucille had a point. At Bobby's death, the infighting had reached a new crescendo. If he let it continue too long, he could end by losing some of his stellar performers.

"So, what are they saying?"

"The bankers are certain you won't invite any traders to become partners. The traders secretly agree so they're furious, and they're waging war on the bankers."

"Who's winning?"

Lucille laughed, showing a row of small capped teeth. "At the moment it's a standoff. But the situation's heating up. The bankers are screaming that the traders are delaying their orders; the traders are screaming that the bankers are banging their stocks. They're both right. Halverson says Lehman stole the Rockefellar deal, but a better bet is the Rockefellar people saw what's going on and took a walk. You should also know that Lefkowicz claims Whitney cost the firm half a million dollars by delaying fund authorization on a house trade that was over Lefkowicz's limit."

"I'll think about it."

He already knew he would not invite anyone to become a full partner. The vacant offices would be converted into a small auditorium and two formal conference rooms. He intended to enlarge the number of limited partnerships to appease ambitions and calm the blood lust raging below. The limited partners would continue to share in the firm's profits, but the second tier would be restructured in such a manner that the combined votes of the limited partners could not override his own vote. The present partners would scream when they learned the numbers he had in mind. More limited partners meant smaller bonuses. They would also scream when they learned the mix of bankers versus traders would be roughly equal. Fuck 'em. They could take it or look elsewhere.

Before he could undertake any significant changes, he had to complete the buy-back of Bobby's shares. "What time is Miss Von Marron's appointment?" he asked Lucille.

"Two o'clock. Louis Galbain of Galbain, Drexel and Anderson will be present as you requested, plus Gabriel Dickerson from in-house. Miss Von Marron did not mention if she will be accompanied by counsel or accountants."

He thought a moment. "We'll play this one by ear. If she has counsel, fine, we'll proceed as planned. But if she comes alone, we won't bring in Galbain and Dickerson. Not yet." Lucille Ivory's thin eyebrows arched, but she noted the direction without comment.

After Lucille returned to her office, Durant sipped his second cup of coffee and considered Gloria Von Marron. She was going to be very, very wealthy. The newspapers were playing it up big, speculating on the extent of the Von Marron fortune. So far, only *Forbes* had estimated a figure actually in the ballpark. The others were at least twenty million too low.

There had not been a day during the last two weeks when he had not seen Gloria's photograph smiling out at him from one of the major newspapers. For the most part the photographs were standard file stuff, showing her cheek to cheek with some European playboy cavorting in one of the world's exotic playpens. But there was one haunting photograph he could not forget. The photographer had caught her standing on the steps of Saint James Church immediately after the funeral, looking tragically beautiful and fragile. Vulnerable and alone.

That anyone could regard Gloria Von Marron as fragile or vulnerable made him smile. The frosty bitch had sat through the funerals like an ice maiden. As far as he knew, she had not shed a single tear for the dearly departed. She had watched him deliver the eulogy with eyes as hard as gray stones. The media professed to admire her dignity and courage, but he knew that behind her public facade was a calculating mind no doubt tallying the assets before the caskets were in the ground. He knew for a fact she had not bothered to visit Bobby and Lulu in nearly a year. There was no love lost there. No grief stricken orphan.

His mouth thinned as he recalled the reception at the Hotel Carlyle. He had tried to let bygones by bygones, had tried to do the decent thing and offer his condolences. But she had jerked away from him and shuddered. She had embarrassed him in front of his son. For that, he did not forgive her. And he resented the hell out of being forced to further enrich her by paying her millions of dollars to buy back Bobby's partnership shares.

When Durant understood Gloria had come alone, he nodded a signal to Lucille, then escorted Gloria into his office instead of leading her to the conference room where Galbain and Dickerson waited. Instead of seating herself on the pale leather sofa in the conversation area as he indicated, she chose a chair facing his desk. Disguising his annoyance, he collected the portfolio from the glass table in front of the sofa and placed it before him on the desk.

"You're looking well," he commented pleasantly, running a slow glance over her blue silk suit. The tint of the soft cream-colored drape at her throat matched her skin. He recognized Lulu's pearls. What he didn't comprehend was the flat chill hardening her eyes. What the hell did she have to be pissed off about?

He was about to hand her a goddamn fortune that she had earned merely by an accident of birth.

"My attorneys have reviewed my parents' wills. As you suggested, there were no surprises."

He frowned. "I was prepared to review the wills with you today." She met his stare and didn't look away. "Very well. I assume you met with Wellsley and Halberd, and I further assume they explained the estate should be settled within a year."

"Everything seems straightforward. The only item in question is the partnership buy-back."

"I foresee no problem." His shoulders lifted in a shrug. "The agreement is clear. I'll buy in Bobby's partnership interest as I bought in the shares of the other partners. Independent accountants will determine the share value. Unless you have an objection, I'll engage Louis Galbain of Galbain, Drexel and Anderson. The firm is first rate and performed a similar evaluation after Whitehall and La Tourraine died."

"Finally, it's all yours," she said softly, watching him. He couldn't read her expression. "That's what you've always wanted, isn't it? That's why you ignored the partnership provisions and haven't replaced the original partners."

He stared at her, and then allowed a tight smile. If she wanted to play hard ball, he had no objection. She was out of her league. "I built this firm. I nurtured it with my sweat and my ulcers. I earned it."

"And someday you will destroy it. My father was this firm's conscience. Without him, there's nothing to restrain you, is there?"

"What the hell are you trying to say?"

She must have sensed she had gone too far because she looked toward the windows and bit her lip. Her obvious struggle for control disappointed him as he hadn't expected her to be silenced so easily. When she spoke again, her voice emerged cool and clipped.

"As I understand the agreement, I have no choice regarding my father's partnership. They must return to the firm. But some flexibility exists on the timing of the buy-back. I would prefer to wait until after the firm has gone public. Obviously, a public offering will affect the share valuation."

His voice was sharp. "Where did you hear about a public offering?" Goddamn Bobby Von Marron. They had agreed the decision was to be kept confidential until the preliminary research and paperwork had been completed.

"From my father, of course."

"At various times throughout the years, the partners have discussed taking the firm public, but at no time was it considered an immediate possibility. I can't think why Bobby would have given you the impression the most recent discussion was any different."

She hesitated. "Then you're not planning to file with the SEC?"

"Absolutely not. La Tourraine, Durant and Von Marron has always been privately held and will continue to remain so."

"I see." The look she gave him made him wonder if she did indeed see. "Are you willing to swear to that?"

"If swearing will reassure you," he answered stiffly. "You won't receive the windfall a public offering would have provided, but you have my personal assurance that you will receive a fair price for the Von Marron shares."

Knots rose along his jawline. He expected her to apologize when she understood she had given offense. When she did not, his gaze chilled.

"I think, however, you should be prepared for a lower figure than the media is hyping. The media has no access to the firm's internal accounting. I'm afraid they have inflated the value of the firm and your interests." Before she could comment, he opened the portfolio and launched a detailed explanation of Home Limited's current position. "I'm willing to retain my seat on Home's board and will continue to vote the Von Marron stock until such time as you may decide on other arrangements."

She stared at him. After what seemed a lengthy hesitation, she nodded. "You may continue for the present."

For the first time since his son's twenty-first birthday, he was speechless and his mouth fell open.

"There is something you need to understand, Miss." Anger thinned his lips. "You do me no great favor by retaining my services on Home's board. I am doing *you* a favor by discharging the Von Marron responsibilities, as I have always done. I do this out of loyalty to your father and your family."

"I don't think so." Her expression was as tight and cold as his own. "You don't understand loyalty. What you do, Win, you do solely for yourself. Before you remind me of all the services you've performed for my family, you should know I recognize your motivation as being solely that of self-interest. I loved my father, but I had no illusions about him. In many ways Bobby Von Marron was a weak man, and you exploited his weakness.

By handling those items my father found upsetting or inconvenient, you made him dependent. And subsequently, easy to manipulate.'' Standing, she stared down at him. "You won't find me that easy to manage.''

"Who the hell do you think you're talking to?'' Furious, he rose behind his desk. "After that little speech, give me one good reason why I should continue to cover your ass at Home Limited.''

"Because Home Limited runs millions of dollars through La Tourraine, Durant and Von Marron. How much in fees did you bill Home Limited last year? One million? Two? You're not on Home's board as any favor to me or my family. You're there to make goddamn certain Home's business continues to flow through this firm.''

Suddenly he realized this was no air-brained debutante or some bimbo lacking the sense to come in off the streets. Gloria Von Marron was smart, damned smart. She had it figured. Now he understood her earlier withdrawal. She hadn't wanted a confrontation until she learned what she could regarding any plans for a public offering. All right, he had underestimated her because she was a woman, because she was young and beautiful. He wouldn't make that mistake again.

Instantly, any suggestion of anger dropped from his features. What she had just told him was that she understood Home Limited's importance to La Tourraine, Durant and Von Marron. And she had warned him the account could be vulnerable.

"Dear Gloria, I regret this meeting seems to have taken a harsh turn,'' he said smoothly. When had she last called him Uncle Win? He couldn't recall. Raising an engaging smile, he spread his hands in a gesture of conciliation. "We've been friends, almost family, too long to end on a sour note. Please sit down and let's—''

Turning at the door, she stared back at him with such hatred that his eyes narrowed. "We are not friends; we are not family. You *raped* me, you bastard! Maybe you can pretend it never happened, but I won't.''

"*Raped* you?'' He was genuinely astonished. Then outraged. "Don't give me that shit. You wanted it.''

"You son of a bitch.'' Her face was as white as paper; her hands clenched into fists.

"That was no rape, far from it. Did you jump up and run out of the room? Did you scream or shout for help? Hell no.''

"I trusted you!''

"And if it was rape, why didn't you call the police or tell someone?" Placing his palms on the desk top, he leaned forward. "No way. Maybe it makes you feel superior to pretend it was rape—but it sure as shit was not!"

The corner of her mouth twisted. "What if I told you your attack resulted in a pregnancy? What if—"

His laugh was ugly. "Forget it. Do you think you're the first to try that number? You were no virgin, sweetheart. You'd been fucked before. Who knows how many sampled the wares before I did? Enough that you aren't going to lay that shit at my door." His eyes ran over her breasts and slim hips. "Your abortion bills are yours, not mine." Now he was enjoying this. "All these years I've carried the Von Marrons. I've lined your pockets, kept your names out of the newspapers, cleaned up after you. But this is one mess that is all yours. There was no rape."

"I was right," she whispered, staring at him with burning eyes. "All those years—you hated us." In the silence, she straightened her shoulders and raised her chin. Her gray eyes shifted from fire to ice. "You betrayed my father's trust and you betrayed mine. We trusted you and cared for you. If it takes the rest of my life, you are going to pay for what you did to me."

He laughed out loud. "Better men than you have tried to bring down Win Durant." A threat came into his eyes and he let her see it. "They all failed."

"I will succeed," she promised. "You'll pay. If it takes the rest of my life."

She closed the door quietly behind her.

That Gloria Von Marron had accused him of rape and had threatened him provided additional justification for what he had intended from the beginning. The difference now was a heightened sense of pleasure.

He stood behind his desk and smiled with anticipation as Lucille Ivory ushered Louis Galbain into his office. After Lucille had poured sherry and had withdrawn, he folded his hands over a large envelope, the only item on his desk top. "It's time to call in a marker, Louis."

Louis Galbain smiled. "Why do I sense I'm not going to like this?"

Louis Galbain reminded Durant of Bobby Von Marron. Both came from celebrated backgrounds; both moved easily in society; both possessed that polished boredom which screamed wealth and breeding. Galbain frequented the best clubs, attended the best parties, boasted the best clients. Durant imagined he could see a silver spoon implanted between Galbain's handsome lips.

He went directly to the point. "I want you to cook the books on the Von Marron buy-back."

Sherry spilled over Galbain's exquisitely tailored slacks. "Win, are you crazy? It can't be done. No. Forget it."

"You're supposed to be the best there is. Find a way."

"Win—for Christ's sake. Listen to me. We're dealing with multimillions here. With this much at stake, Miss Von Marron's attorneys and accountants are going to go over the figures with a microscope. I'm telling you it can't be done." Galbain touched a linen handkerchief to his brow. "Even if it could—and it can't— the risk is appalling. Galbain, Drexel and Anderson has worked years to achieve our reputation. To risk it on something like this would be insane. No. Absolutely not."

"It's because of your reputation that I want you." A smile brushed Durant's mouth. "I haven't heard a whisper of scandal attached to your name. Never. Not a hint, not an innuendo. Your professional integrity is an accepted given; your personal life hasn't a single blemish. You are a respected elder in your church, you have a lovely wife and three beautiful children. You have an exemplary life. Everyone in town respects your abilities and swears by Galbain, Drexel and Anderson."

"Exactly," Galbain said. "That's why I must decline."

"No, my friend, that is why you will do precisely as I ask."

Lifting the envelope, he let the photographs inside spill over his desk top. The one that slid nearest Louis Galbain showed Galbain sitting naked on a wooden chair. Standing beside him was a child, perhaps eight, maybe as old as ten, dressed in a miniature bride's gown. Galbain held her hand around his erect penis. Her dulled eyes stared at the camera in mute appeal. In the photo nearest Durant, the child, now naked except for the bridal veil, sat on Galbain's lap. His penis thrust up between her opened legs. Sweat stood on his upper lip; lust glazed his eyes.

"Oh my God!" Galbain whispered. "I'm going to be sick."

Durant touched one of the photographs with his fingertip. "Do you see what I mean, Louis? I think you'll agree to what I'm asking, and gladly. I think you'll manage to deflate the value of Miss Von Marron's shares, and you'll do it in a way that can't and won't be detected." He smiled. "I think you'll shave the evaluation by . . . shall we say, fifteen million dollars?"

"Who else has seen these photographs?"

''No one. Yet.'' Durant held a particularly fascinating photograph to the light. ''Yes, my friend, I think you'll save me fifteen million dollars.'' He smiled at the photograph. The child resembled Galbain's youngest daughter. ''You're motivated.''

Irresistible instinct pulled Gloria back to Lewes. To have struggled against it would have proven as futile as resisting a riptide. She needed Robby. She needed to bend her head to his sweet-smelling hair and hold him and love him. She needed what family she had left, needed the reality of Robby's tiny solidity.

Not until she sat in Margaret and Edmund's ancient, cheerful kitchen did the tensions of the past weeks begin to ebb. Here, with Robby cuddled on her lap, she finally relaxed and the knots stiffening her shoulders began to loosen.

''I love you,'' she murmured to her son. The rocking chair creaked rhythmically on the kitchen linoleum. ''You're the best thing in my life.''

Smiling, Margaret looked up from the stove. ''He's a treasure.'' Tilting her head, she studied Gloria, and a frown replaced her smile. ''When did you last have a good night's sleep?''

She couldn't remember. ''I've had a lot to think about.'' Leaning back in the rocking chair, she held Robby close and shut her eyes. ''I've been in constant meetings with lawyers and accountants . . . trying to catch up with what's happening at Home Limited . . . dodging reporters . . . missing Robby, thinking about him.''

''And?''

''I can't take Robby back to New York, Margaret.'' She kept her eyes closed, feeling the pain constrict her chest. Unconsciously, her arms tightened around Robby's blankets. ''The headlines are finally starting to die down. Revealing Robby now would only raise a fresh scandal. They'd rake it all up again. Remy, the innuendos about my parents. Speculation about Robby's father. Plus,'' she drew a breath and opened hard eyes, ''there is something I have to do. To succeed, I'll need time and no distractions.''

''You know you can leave Robby with us for as long as you need to.''

''I know. I . . .'' Tears appeared on her lashes. ''Oh Margaret, I hate this. I love him so much. But the time isn't right. There's someone . . . something I have to do. Do you understand?''

"No," Margaret answered slowly. "But I know whatever it is, it's burning you up."

"Yes," Gloria whispered. "I have to do this for my father, for myself, and for Robby."

"Gloria—"

"I wish I could tell you, but I can't. I can't tell anyone." Lifting a hand, she covered her eyes. "Please try to understand. I have to take care of this or I won't be able to live with myself. I wish I could say it will be over quickly, but, Margaret, it may take some time."

"That doesn't matter. We love Robby."

Bending, Gloria held Robby to her breast and inhaled the baby sweetness of his skin and hair. "Our time will come," she murmured against his warm neck. "Give Mummy a little time." After a moment she wiped her eyes on the hem of his blanket and managed a smile. "There's something else I've been thinking about. This kitchen. I want to install a new stove and refrigerator. New cabinets. Tile or carpeting."

"Gloria, you don't owe us anything. You know we're happy to keep Robby and help however we can."

"I'm not doing it for you," Gloria said, smiling. "I'm doing it for Robby. He spends a lot of time in this kitchen. He needs a new stove."

Margaret laughed. But later, when she told Edmund about the plans for the new kitchen she wasn't smiling. "It means we'll have Robby for a long time, and I'm glad for our sake." As she and Edmund were approaching fifty, it was too late to begin a family of their own. Robby would be their only experience of having a baby in the house, and she planned to love every minute. "But I'm very worried about Gloria. I wish I understood what this was all about."

Edmund lifted an eyebrow and shifted his pipe. "Don't you know, lass? It's about revenge."

Chapter 11

 𝓣HIS TIME there was no need to concoct fabrications to explain her absence because friends expected her to seek temporary seclusion. During the weeks at Lewes, while Gloria let the healing process begin, and while she waited for the attorneys and accountants to arrange the partnership buy-back, she delighted in the time with her son. Each day brought a fascinating new change. The hint of an emerging dimple, a new sound, a smile especially for her.

Occasionally she drove into London for dinner; she attended a wedding in Paris; she spent a weekend in Capri at the Countess Corbina's villa; she sailed to Corfu with a party of friends. The time away from Robby was deeply regretted, but she was determined no unnecessary mystery should be attached to her name. She arranged enough public appearances to prevent excessive media curiosity as to her whereabouts. Her worst nightmare was imagining a reporter tailing her back to Lewes and discovering her secret.

The days passed quietly and happily. Observing Robby's development, taking part in it, provided a consuming fascination. Nothing Robby did was too small or too insignificant for notice and praise.

"There was a time—when you were climbing trees and making mischief—that I couldn't have imagined you changing a diaper," Margaret observed, laughing.

Smiling around the pins in her mouth, Gloria nodded. "And actually enjoying it." Finishing the job, she lifted Robby and kissed his nose, laughing when he gurgled. "Down you go, big fella. We'll see you in the morning."

"Will you join us for coffee in the parlor?"

"Thank you, but I have a stack of Home Limited reports I

need to review.'' Because Gardner's name appeared on so many of the reports, she had procrastinated.

After closing the attic door behind Margaret, Gloria assured herself that Robby's blanket was snug around his small shoulders, then she sat on the edge of her bed and dropped her head into her hands.

In two days she would return to New York. Two more days, then she would have to leave Robby. She dreaded the thought. How had her parents managed? How had they found the emotional strength to leave Remy and herself and go dancing off to Europe for the season? Hadn't it felt like leaving one's heart behind? Or had they cared? Did having each other make all the difference?

She had no one but Robby. And sometimes he frightened her. It would be so easy to target a lifetime of love on his tiny form. It would be appallingly easy to smother him with care and affection. But she sensed that loving too much could be as crippling as loving too little. When the time was right, when she had settled the score with Durant, she would find a balance in her feelings for her son.

Rising, Gloria moved to stand beside Robby's cradle and she placed her hand gently on his back. She wanted so much for him. She didn't want him ever to wonder if he was loved. She wanted him to know his mother and know she loved him.

''When this is over, I'll never leave you again,'' she whispered.

Returning to the attic bed, she lay down and folded her hands behind her hair, staring at the ceiling. This, too, Durant would pay for, separating her from her son.

Closing her eyes, she clenched her teeth and thought about Durant as she did nearly every waking moment.

The game would have to be played on his turf and that meant Wall Street. The only thing Win Durant prized was position and power. That was how she would take him down. What the method would be, she didn't know yet, but an outline had appeared. She knew where to begin.

Sometime before dawn, she brought Robby into her bed. ''My little love,'' she murmured, smoothing back his silky hair.

She understood that Robby was an explosive secret. And she knew secrets had a way of becoming known. For an instant her resolve wavered. Perhaps the wisest thing to do was to put Durant out of her mind and get on with her life. The fire storm of scandal would scald her and her son, but they would survive. They had each other.

Then her thoughts returned to Win Durant and she remembered him denying he had raped her.

"Just grant me a little time, darling. I have to do this."

Yugoslavia wasn't the end of the world, it only seemed that way, Gardner decided. He stood at the window of the Belgrade hotel suite Home had engaged for his use and looked out at a row of drab concrete buildings. From this vantage he could glimpse the sunset reflecting across the Sava River in a series of rippling slivers seen between the buildings.

There was no hot water in the suite's bathroom and the cold water performed on a schedule no rational being could comprehend. The furnishings, like the staff, had doubtless been fresh and sturdy once, but now both showed the effects of age and neglect. Ordinarily, Gardner adapted well to the inconvenience of travel, but tonight he felt irritated by the city's depressed facade, by the scarred and sagging furniture, by a telephone that functioned only intermittently.

For several days he had been attempting to locate Gloria Von Marron. For a time it had appeared he was nearing the end of a long and frustrating trail. An attendant at Dominique Le Clerc's wedding had been certain Gloria planned to spend a weekend with Adrianne Corbina in Capri. Each evening for the past week he had placed a call to Adrianne's villa. None of his calls had gone through. Grinding his teeth, he frowned at his warm drink, wondering what one had to do to obtain ice in this place.

Adrianne Corbina made it her business to know all there was to know about European society. If anyone knew where Gloria was hiding, it would be Adrianne. Deliberately, Gardner looked away from the telephone and seated himself before a desk of World War II vintage, then he opened his briefcase and removed a sheaf of papers. But he couldn't concentrate on lignite and antimony.

Pushing the chair from the desk, he swiveled to face the dying sunset. Where was she?

He didn't doubt that her vanishing act was intentional. Moreover, he no longer believed the explanation of another man. No concerned lover had been at her side helping her through the ordeal of Bobby and Lulu's funerals. If she had been telling the truth, there should have been. Possibly she had had a relationship that didn't last, but he didn't buy that argument. No one had seen her with a man who seemed special to her, and she made no mention of a relationship during the time she had been in New York.

He swallowed his warm drink and thought how easy it was for a young woman of Gloria's wealth and social connections to conceal her whereabouts. With the world as a playground, the people he and Gloria knew were continually on the move, rushing from the beaches of Cap d'Antibes to a shoot outside Dublin to skiing at Gstaad to a party in New York, Palm Beach, or Rome. If Gloria wasn't seen for a time, it could be assumed she was ahead of one group or following another.

The acknowledgment that someone could easily vanish answered one question, but it didn't explain why. Or where Gloria went when she disappeared or what she did there.

That she refused to confide in him stung. He had hoped she understood he cared about her and would be there for her in the event of trouble. What type of trouble she might be encountering, he couldn't begin to guess. But something was wrong. It wasn't like her to vanish and ignore his letters.

He caught the telephone on the second ring, but it wasn't Adrianne. After listening a moment, he informed his limousine driver he would be downstairs shortly. The call reminded him that he was late for dinner with Baroness Frederica Dubrovna.

The moment he stepped into the corridor and locked the door behind him, he heard the shrill jangle of the telephone inside the suite. This time it had to be Adrianne because he expected no other call. He looked at the key in his hand, hesitated, then turned toward the staircase.

Pride or something very like it altered his decision to trace her. She had made it clear his attentions were not wanted. If she wished him to know where she was, she would tell him; his whereabouts were no mystery. She knew where to find him.

"Gardner, darling," Frederica murmured later. They were lying across her circular, silk-dressed bed, smiling at their naked bodies reflected in the mirror mounted on the ceiling.

"It occurs to me that not all the buildings are as drab inside as they appear from the street," he said, watching her in the mirror.

Frederica drew one red fingernail down his chest. "It makes me very sad, darling, but I think this is the last time we will be together." Bending her dark head, she teased her tongue around his nipples.

"Why is that?" In the mirror above, her smooth skin absorbed the candlelight and glowed like ivory satin. Her dark hair slid over his groin.

"No woman wishes to compete with the shadow of another." Groaning softly, she caught his nipple between her teeth and licked it. "I will miss you." The warm ripple of a sigh flowed against his skin. "How I shall miss you!"

"I'm not committed to anyone, Freddy. You know that."

"Not here," she said gently, looking up as she touched her hand to his erection. "But here." Her fingertips brushed his chest and his forehead. "I cannot compete with a memory or a dream, darling. I do not wish to diminish myself in that way."

He stared down at her, then swore.

"Yes," she said, sadly. "It is that obvious. Such a pity." Trailing her hand down his torso, she walked her fingers along the inside of his thigh and released another sigh. "I envy this phantom of yours, my beautiful Gardner."

He swore again, cursing Gloria Von Marron wherever the hell she was.

Gloria glanced up once, then read through the documents again. The only sound in the conference room was the ticking of a massive grandfather clock and the occasional click of cup against saucer. One of the five men who watched her cleared his throat and coughed into a handkerchief. He made an apologetic sound but did not speak.

"These figures cannot possibly be correct," she said finally, dropping the documents on the table.

"The best people in the firm have been over the numbers with a magnifying glass," Howard Wellsley said. He looked uncomfortable. "On your instructions, we hired the accounting firm of Oak, Adderly, and Tomlinson. They've crawled over the figures as well."

"And?" She shifted her stare to Wilkie Tomlinson.

"You want the truth?" he asked bluntly, regarding her from beneath heavy white eyebrows.

"Yes, of course."

Tomlinson glanced at the documents on the tabletop and his lips pulled up in a snort of derision. "I'll go to my grave believing you've gotten a royal screw. I've been around long enough to know when something stinks, and this stinks. But," Tomlinson silenced her with a raised hand, "proving it is something else. These books are certified by Galbain, Drexel and Anderson. They're Clorox clean. Clean firm, clean reputation. You aren't going to find whiter white. That's what makes this so dirty. If Galbain cooked these books, it means someone got to him. Someone leaned on him hard."

"Win Durant."

Oliver Halberd broke into the silence. "Let's not make hasty accusations we may later regret. It's possible we grossly over-estimated the value of La Tourraine, Durant and Von Marron. Mistakes happen; until now we haven't had access to hard figures." No one spoke. "I believe we're agreed a firm of Galbain, Drexel and Anderson's reputation would not offer a misrepresentation. Additionally, neither our law firm nor your accounting firm," he nodded to Tomlinson, "has been able to uncover a single error."

"Horseshit. This stinks, Halberd." Wilkie Tomlinson tapped his finger on the stack of documents. "Whoever cooked these books did it brilliantly. The evidence is buried so deep we'll never find it. God knows, we've tried. I've got more man hours in this project than I want to think about and so do you. But just because we can't find the fraud doesn't mean it doesn't exist. It's there; I can smell it. I can see it on the bottom line. And you aren't going to convince me that some asshole over at Galbain, Drexel and Anderson dreamed this up by himself. So who did? Who stands to gain? You know goddamn well who. Your tennis pal, Winthrop Durant."

Gloria turned cold eyes on Oliver Halberd. "You are fired, Oliver."

"Gloria . . . Miss Von Marron!"

Ignoring Oliver Halberd's distress, she addressed her comments to Howard Wellsley and Wilkie Tomlinson. "As nearly as I can estimate, the final buy-out figure is about forty percent below what I anticipated. So, what do you suggest, gentlemen? What's my next step?"

"You suck it up and thank God they didn't get you for more." Tomlinson shrugged.

"Do you agree?" she asked Howard Wellsley, her face expressionless.

He touched his tie. "We could file an objection."

"Come on Howard, an objection based on what?" Tomlinson spread his hands. "Show me some evidence. Show me one error, one single provable example you can use as a basis for a filing. It's not here, not where we're going to find it." He turned to Gloria. "This was no surface fraud. This goes deep. To find the truth, we'd have to peel this bastard back like an onion. But to do that, we'd need all the records from La Tourraine, Durant and Von Marron. And I mean the genuine records, not the phony crap this shit is based on. And I'll tell you something. We'll never get it. What we'll get—what we've gotten—is thirty pounds of supporting documents, all adjusted to prove we're getting the straight numbers. You can forget filing an objection, Wellsley. It'll only be a waste of your time and a waste of the lady's money.''

Gloria lowered shaking hands to her lap. Goddamn Win Durant. He was making her pay for the scene in his office. But it wasn't solely her inheritance he had stolen, he had also stolen Robby's legacy.

"I can't believe what I'm hearing." Oliver Halberd stared at the faces around the table. "These insinuations are utterly unfounded. You have convinced yourself criminal fraud must be involved based on absolutely nothing but disappointed expectations. There is no evidence whatsoever to support an allegation of wrongdoing."

When she was certain she was in control, Gloria stood and placed the documents inside a slim Bottega briefcase. "If I hadn't just fired you, Oliver, I would ask you to explain how the firm could afford to pay multimillion-dollar bonuses last year but now seems barely able to cover overhead. As you seem to feel there is no discrepancy, I would ask how you justify La Tourraine, Durant and Von Marron paying for the conversion of the twenty-sixth floor when, according to these figures, they are on the verge of laying off key personnel. If I hadn't fired you, I might be interested in hearing your explanation of why everything except these documents indicates La Tourraine, Durant and Von Marron is having a banner year."

"There's no evidence—"

"Let it go, Oliver," Howard Wellsley said hastily.

"Very well, then." Face expressionless, she addressed Howard Wellsley and Wilkie Tomlinson. "Unless one of you can come up with something, I'll sign these papers on Monday of next week." After snapping shut the briefcase, she raised her head and met Wilkie Tomlinson's eyes across the table. "In your opinion, is there any possibility Oliver could be correct? Is there any possibility however remote that we overestimated the stock's value and these documents are clean?"

"In my opinion? No possibility at all. You got hosed."

"You believe that even though there is not a single digit of hard evidence?"

"The point of cooking a set of books is to do it so well no fraud can be detected. They knew going in these figures would be subjected to intense scrutiny." He shrugged. "The other side had all the chips. All we've got is what they chose to provide."

"One last thing, Mr. Tomlinson. How much money do you estimate was stolen from me?"

"There's no way to tell. But your friends over at La Tourraine, Durant and Von Marron and those at Galbain, Drexel and Anderson didn't go to all this trouble for peanuts." He closed his briefcase, then held the door of the conference room for her.

"I figure between ten and fifteen million."

"Could be," he said. "Anyway you look at it, you got raped."

Startled, she stared up at him. "Yes," she said, quietly. "I got raped." Again.

"I shouldn't think the salary would matter all that much," Ryerson Forbes said smoothly. At Princeton, her father had known Ryerson as Chubbs Forbes. Gloria could see why.

"What matters, Ryerson, is getting shortchanged. That's not going to happen to me again. I'm worth more than twenty-five thousand, particularly as we both know seventy-five is scale." Because she was a Von Marron, personnel had sent her directly to the firm's senior partner. Personnel had not done her a favor. She glanced up at the framed row of Forbes ancestors then looked again at Ryerson.

"We at Black Brothers believe in leaving our people room to grow. Other firms may offer a larger entry salary, but—"

Gloria stood. "Thank you for your time. Please give my best to Barbara."

"Gloria, I urge you to reconsider. You must realize women are a relatively new entity on the Street. Even with your name and contacts, I doubt you'll be deluged by a multitude of offers. We at Black Brothers consider ourselves a progressive firm. We hire the brightest and the best. I think you'll be interested to learn we have two black department heads and several women holding positions of responsibility."

"Good for you." Realizing the sarcasm was lost on him, Gloria glanced at her watch. "If you'll excuse me, I have another appointment."

Once outside, she drew a breath of cool autumn air and turned her face toward 45 Wall Street. For a moment she stared at the La Tourraine, Durant and Von Marron building, her mouth tight, then she squared her shoulders and walked toward Hanover Square. This was only the beginning; she hadn't expected the path to be strewn with roses.

Harry's, where she ended up for no particular reason, was a popular watering hole for bond traders, crowded even at this early hour. The food was undistinguished, the noise level catastrophic, and the ticker tape positioned over the bar reminded one of time and dollars. In balance, there was Harry, a sturdy beaming Greek who dispensed cheer during bull markets and credit during bear markets.

He waved at Gloria from behind the bar and beckoned her forward before frowning at a Brooks Brothers suit occupying the nearest stool. "Where are your manners? The lady needs a seat, so give her your seat!"

Laughing, Gloria protested. "No, please. I'll find a place in a minute." She blew Harry a kiss. "You haven't changed a bit." He grinned and gave her a thumbs-up sign.

The man in the Brooks Brothers suit slipped from the stool and insisted Gloria take it. "I wouldn't think of disobeying Harry," he said, smiling. "But there's a price."

"Isn't there always?" He was a trader, of course. She recognized the quick movements, the intense eye contact. Bond traders were more frenzied than stock traders, but both had a look of hunger about them, a look of being continually rushed, as if they were late for a crucially important appointment.

"I have to know your name. You are absolutely the most gorgeous woman I've seen outside a film theater."

"Who's asking?" She raised an eyebrow and smiled at his rumpled hair.

"Ah, a careful type. I like that. You have the dubious pleasure of addressing Franklin T. Nemiro, acclaimed trader of bonds—quality, junk, whatever else is hot. Now why, you ask, is Franklin T. Nemiro, acclaimed trader of bonds, sitting in Harry's at two in the afternoon, tipping down his third Scotch? Because he has just taken the beating of his life, and before you floated in here on a cloud of—Calèche isn't it—he was contemplating where to drown himself." He smiled. "Harry can vouch for me. I'm thirty-one, divorced, have a house in East Hampton, a co-op in town, and I made over three hundred thousand last year. My father, who is a physician and one of the Philadelphia Nemiros, was initially astounded but is now of the opinion that I am grossly overpaid. I assure you I am not. Now that you know everything about me, will you marry me and save me from the East River?"

Gloria laughed. "I'm pleased to meet you, Franklin T. Nemiro."

"In that case, let me buy you a drink. Can I spread the cheese on your crackers? Do anything at all for you? Bar keep! Bring my future bride a drink, for heaven's sake, and we need more cheese down here." He smiled into her eyes. "Have you noticed I'm trying very hard not to be rude? I am exerting more will-power than I ever exerted before in an effort not to stare at your legs. I know you have fabulous legs, I can see them from the bottom of my eyes. Are you ever going to tell me your name?"

"Gloria Von Marron."

"Jesus, you're kidding! Not *the* Gloria Von Marron!" Slapping a hand over his heart, Franklin T. Nemiro staggered backward a step and Gloria smiled. "I can't believe it. All that," he waved a hand to indicate her silvery hair, her slim elegance, the long expanse of silky legs, "and you're rich, too. What are you doing here?"

"I'm looking for a job."

"Good God. I guess fifty million isn't what it used to be." Leaning past her, he shouted down the bar. "Make those drinks doubles. Seriously, you can't be looking for a job."

"I am."

"Banking or trading?"

"At this point, I'm not particular."

"Banking, definitely." He tugged a hand through his hair and considered her with a thoughtful expression. "Have you tried The Bear?"

"Bear Stearns? They're a good block house, but not what I'm looking for."

"You're right, of course. My mistake. The Bear wouldn't appreciate you anyway. The obvious question is—"

"Off limits." She didn't want to discuss La Tourraine, Durant and Von Marron.

"Fair enough," he said easily. "Okay, let's see. How about Salomon Brothers?"

"I'm looking for a job, not a case of ulcers. Their tough-guy image isn't my style."

"Goldman Sachs?"

"Too nice." She was enjoying this. "Word is they won't do a hostile takeover."

"Ah ha, the lady has claws. How about First Boston?"

"Let's wait and see what the new chief does. They're in transition."

"You're making this tough. All right, have you thought about Nestor Brothers?"

Nestor Brothers. She tilted her head. "They're in midtown, aren't they? On Sixth?"

"The new Wall Street. The more I think about it, the more I think Nestor Brothers might be just the ticket. The word is they're looking for brains and contacts. And they're good. They're giving the big kids a run for the smart money. There are a lot of bright people up there."

Gloria had met Charles Nestor and recalled his daughter from Chapin. The firm was solid, well established and, as Franklin T. had suggested, Nestor Brothers was aggressive and eager.

"Thank you," she said, slipping from the bar stool. "I may give them a try."

"Wait a minute. You aren't leaving are you? I mean, we have to discuss the wedding, the honeymoon, how many children we'll have. We haven't discussed the important things. Let's have dinner and talk about where we'll live."

Laughing, she shook her head. "It's only three o'clock."

"Okay, we'll wait an hour."

"I'm sorry."

"We'll wait two hours. We'll wait until tomorrow. Next week? How about two weeks from today? Okay, what are you doing in November?"

It had been so long since she had laughed, so long since she had seen that particular look in a man's eyes and felt a stirring of response. Looking toward the door, she caught Harry's eye and tilted her head slightly toward Franklin T. Nemiro. Harry winked and nodded.

"All right, Franklin T. Nemiro, dinner. A week from tomorrow."

"And to think," Franklin T. sighed, pressing her fingertips to his lips. "An hour ago I was thinking about drowning myself. Ain't life grand?"

"Honestly? It hasn't seemed so lately."

"That is going to change."

"Oh yes," she agreed, gently disengaging her hand. "That is going to change."

Charles Nestor appeared younger, leaner, and more energetic than when Gloria had seen him last. He wore a crisply tailored

Saville Row wool in a shade of gray to complement the silver at his temples. The tie was Hermès, the cologne English, the vitality was his own.

He opened the door to his office and led her back inside after instructing his secretary to serve coffee.

"Well, what do you think?" he asked when they were settled before windows that offered a sweeping view of lower Manhattan. "You've seen everything."

"Very impressive."

She meant it. In contrast to La Tourraine, Durant and Von Marron's old-world elegance, Nestor Brothers boasted a sleek, contemporary style that subtly underscored the firm's aggressive philosophy. Edward Hopper canvases added to the statement, as did the David Hockney drawings featured in the private dining room. The only painting Gloria had noticed that dated prior to the turn of the century was a Mary Cassatt hanging in the reception area leading to the offices of the senior partners. Everything else was twentieth-century, now, poised on the leading edge of the future.

It wasn't necessary for Charles Nestor to explain the firm's minority-hiring policy. During the tour Nestor had given her, Gloria had observed the balance for herself. And she had seen enough to be convinced tokenism played no role here. Ability and results were what counted at Nestor Brothers.

"I'm pleased you think so. We pride ourselves on the newest technology, the latest methodology. We have the best information network in town. And the best people." He looked at her. "I'd like you to be one of them."

Gloria's brow rose. "Just like that? You haven't asked my qualifications."

Nestor's smile told her the statement was naive. "Everybody in town knows you're looking for a home, Gloria. Your background is a given. We know you graduated Harvard summa cum laude, that you apprenticed for several summers at La Tourraine, Durant and Von Marron, and that you were considered brilliant there. We're aware of your personal history, of course. We know you're fluent in French and Italian." He shrugged. "I believe you'll make a significant contribution to Nestor Brothers."

She studied his expression, then nodded. "I think so, too. I want to learn everything there is to learn about investment banking."

"The way I hear it, you have a substantial head start."

During the next hour they discussed the terms of Gloria's

employment contract, her salary, and which department she preferred. At the finish of the discussion, Charles Nestor toasted her with his coffee cup.

"Welcome to Nestor Brothers. I couldn't be more pleased." Leaning forward, he placed the cup and saucer on a glass table. "There's one final point we need to discuss. It's inevitable that I'm going to hear questions—and so are you—as to why you didn't accept a position with La Tourraine, Durant and Von Marron. It's natural to assume LTDVM would be your first choice."

"I'd rather not discuss it."

"Frankly, so would I. But the question is certain to arise, and we should agree on a response. I'll have a better grasp of what our response should be if I understand your reasoning. I assure you this discussion shall remain in confidence."

The question was reasonable, but she hesitated. Finally, she directed her gaze to the view of lower Manhattan and decided to trust him—on a business level. "I have cause to believe Winthrop Durant misrepresented the value of La Tourraine, Durant and Von Marron in order to buy back my father's partnership at a deflated cost. If this is true, and I believe it is, Durant stole millions from me."

Nestor stared at her. "That is a very serious accusation."

"I can't prove it. But I have reasons for believing it's true. There are . . . other things as well, of a personal nature. For the purpose of this conversation, it's fair to say a high level of hostility exists between Durant and myself. To accept a position with La Tourraine, Durant and Von Marron while Durant is there would be impossible. Unthinkable."

"How extraordinary," Nestor mused, watching her. "I always believed Bobby and Win were friends as well as partners."

"My father thought so, too."

"I see." Nestor laced his fingers together. "Your frankness is commendable and appreciated. Therefore, I will be equally frank." Pausing, he watched her expression. "Certain assumptions can be made based on what you've said." Shrewd experience flickered at the back of his eyes. "Revenge can be a powerful motivator."

Gloria's expression did not alter. "I said nothing of revenge."

Nestor continued as if he had not been interrupted. "Vast amounts of money have been made as a by-product of revenge. Appalling lapses of judgment have occurred for the same reason. However, I'm willing to gamble on your intelligence and judgment. But, if your private war with Win Durant gets in the way of either of those qualities, Gloria, we will have to reassess the situation."

"I understand."

"I hope you also understand what you're up against. Novices assume there is one Wall Street. There are four. Two actual sites: the Street itself and here, in midtown. And two mental states: the old guard and the new wave. The old guard—Durant—has an advantage you don't have. A network of old-boy contacts maintained through clubs and favors owed and favors earned. The old guard is firmly entrenched, and they see things through a different morality."

"I understand that."

"I'm not suggesting the new wave is more moral or more ethically correct than the old guard. They are not. When money, power, and ambition are at stake, abuses occur. There is as much blood on the floor now as there ever was. You know that. But new wave abuses are less flagrant, more private. The old guard still uses a broad sword—the new wave is more likely to use a rapier. Do you understand what I'm telling you?"

"Durant can strike at me, but I'm powerless to hit back. I don't believe that."

"There's no question you can hit back. It's done all the time. But I'm cautioning you that Durant's arsenal is larger than yours. He has resources you lack and won't develop for years to come. Certainly you can strike, but don't expect to deal a fatal blow. It's unlikely."

But not impossible. She would find a way.

"I believe I'll enjoy corporate finance," she said, changing the subject.

The essential first part of her plan was now in place.

Durant and Gardner emerged from lunch at the Downtown Association and walked toward Water Street instead of turning back toward Wall Street and La Tourraine, Durant and Von Marron.

A cold breeze blew off the East River, turning Pine Street into a wind tunnel. They turned up their collars and lowered their heads.

"If you were in town more often, we could do this more frequently," Win Durant commented. "Home's board is willing to offer a vice presidency and give you a corner office. McPherson said he had Cornish feel you out, but you declined."

"I'm not ready to make that commitment."

"Does that mean you're considering—"

"No." For years La Tourraine, Durant and Von Marron had been a dead issue, but his father continued to raise the subject. "I'm not ready to settle into a desk job. I will one day, but not yet. When I accept that corner office, it will be because I want Tobler's job."

"Tobler is aware of that. He's comfortable with it. It's time he began to groom a successor."

Gardner thrust his hands into his coat pockets. "Walt is ten years away from retirement. Plus, selecting Home's next president isn't entirely his decision. I imagine the board will insist on having the final word."

"The board will do as I suggest."

Gardner glanced at his father. "Frankly, I'm a little surprised you're still representing the Von Marron interests." His father's mouth thinned. "Gloria has been interested in Home Limited for years. I assumed she would take an active role." He hesitated, then decided to proceed. "Mother indicated there's some kind of problem between you and Gloria."

"The problem is dealing with a spoiled bitch who thinks the world should be presented to her on a goddamned silver platter. As to actively participating in Home Limited—I thought you were smarter than that." Durant's tone sharpened. "Surely you can see what she's doing. Yes, she has volumes of material sent to wherever the debutantes are frolicking this season. She may even glance through some of it. But I haven't seen a Von Marron yet who knows shit about business or wants to. Not when someone else is willing to shoulder the responsibilities for them."

They walked in silence, turning right onto Wall street. The bitterness in his father's voice had always been there when he spoke about the Von Marrons, but Gardner had failed to recognize it. Possibly because he hadn't wanted to.

Of all the people he knew, he most admired his father. Without background, money, or any obvious advantage, Winthrop Durant had risen to occupy a seat at the top of the world's pyramid. It was an astonishing accomplishment. What puzzled him was why his father didn't seem to enjoy his achievements. His influence was felt by world leaders, he moved in rarified circles. Yet Win Durant appeared to despise the very people he had spent a lifetime emulating.

His father's comments about Gloria Von Marron were equally surprising, particularly the emotion with which they were voiced.

Regardless, Gardner couldn't bring himself to consider the estrangement more than temporary. The families had been too tightly interwoven for too many years, too much a part of each other's history for a permanent breach to develop.

They shook hands in front of the La Tourraine, Durant and Von Marron building. "Do you know what Gloria is doing now?" he asked his father. "I thought I'd try to see her while I'm in town."

"I've heard she's been nosing around the Street looking for a job. As no one is interested in hiring her, I imagine she'll take herself off to Europe and do what she does best. Play and screw. I can't think why you would want to see her."

Anger tightened Gardner's mouth. "Whatever is going on between you and Gloria is your business. But she's not a spoiled bitch and she isn't the type to screw around. She's not looking for a free ride. Whatever you may think about her right now, don't assume I agree because I don't. Understand?" To soften the words, he smiled. "After all, the lady is my boss."

Durant's face twisted into something ugly. "Don't ever say that again where I can hear it." Without a backward glance, he turned and entered the building. The heavy doors hissed shut behind him.

Chapter 12

$\mathcal{A}$FTER SIX MONTHS of waiting, working, and learning, Gloria judged the moment right for her first strike. Restless with anticipation, she telephoned Margaret in Lewes, though she knew Robby would be asleep. "Tell him, 'soon.' " Closing her eyes, she remembered her son as he had been a month ago, birthday cake smeared around his small mouth, his arms lifted to her. It seemed impossible he could be a year old. "Soon."

She dressed carefully for the board meeting, choosing a soft leather skirt, muted green jacket and brushed silver accessories. She wore her hair short, swept behind one ear. The result was smart and businesslike.

Several blocks from the Home Limited building, Gloria instructed her driver to pull to the curb. The early spring day beckoned, and despite a sleepless night she felt an excess of nervous energy that she hoped a walk would discharge. Additionally, she wanted this moment to last. After weeks of planning and preparation, she wanted to savor every detail of this particular day.

Not hurrying, she walked along the crowded pavement, confident in her plans and in what she was about to do.

She had deliberately waited before making any move until she felt secure and firmly in place at Nestor Brothers. To achieve that goal, she had worked harder and longer than ever before, being the first person to arrive each morning and the last to depart at night. The hours not at her desk or in meetings she spent sitting in the firm's library, reading and learning. Piles of documents went home with her each night. The successes had begun to come.

Immersing herself in work to the exclusion of nearly everything else was a deliberate choice calculated to leave her too weary to worry about Robby or to dwell on the less satisfying areas in her life. Firmly, she focused her energy on mastering the intricacies of corporate finance and kept the knowledge of Robby, her pain and guilt at being apart from him, in a secluded corner of her mind.

Today the weariness that formed such a large part of her life did not show, but it was there. Long hours and months of intensely focused concentration had taken a toll in lost sleep and missed meals. But she revived herself now as always by thinking about Win Durant. And she drew strength from the resultant energizing burst of hatred. Hatred was the fuel that propelled her in the mornings and sustained her through the long night.

As she stepped through the heavy doors of the Home Limited building, Gloria paused to indulge a private moment of pride. A John Singer Sargent portrait of her great-grandfather dominated the lobby. It amused her to recall that his distinguished features had awed her as a child. They no longer did.

The physical layout of the Home building had changed little since Bobby's father had commissioned the design, but the interior had grown far afield from the original decor. Over the years Home had collected pieces from the countries in which the firm did business, and Home Limited now owned one of the finest collections of African art to be found anywhere in the world. European acquisitions, Alaskan carvings, Scottish woolens, oriental porcelain, and the South American collection were displayed on various floors of the building. The result was an eclectic excitement one felt immediately upon stepping through the doors.

Someday this would belong to Robby. What she did, she did for her son as well as for herself.

Stepping out of the elevator on the sixth floor, Gloria paused a moment, then pushed through the doors leading into the boardroom which she hadn't seen since she was a child. Little had changed since the days of her grandfather, whose portrait hung on the east wall. He had not intended Home's boardroom to be luxurious or impressive. This was a working room; the utilitarian furnishings reflected that philosophy. Gloria glanced at his portrait, smiled, then turned to greet the men who governed Home Limited, many of whom she was meeting today for the first time. They said the right things and smiled pleasantly, but she sensed a definite undercurrent of curiosity and resistance.

"It will require time," Walter Tobler suggested, in apology

for the lukewarm reception. He led Gloria to one side as the directors served themselves coffee from the table against the back wall. They carried their coffee to the board table, arranged their note pads and pens. Durant had not yet arrived.

"I have time," Gloria said lightly. She was aware the directors watched her while pretending not to, wondering what her presence meant.

"Miss Von Marron—"

"Gloria, please."

"Gloria, then. Ah, have you discussed today's agenda with Win?"

"No, I have not. The only people who have seen a copy of the agenda are you and I."

"I see." Tobler looked uncomfortable. "I think I should mention Win has several friends of long standing sitting on this board. I doubt they will support a vote calling for Win's resignation. The issue will fail for lack of board backing."

The objection was not unexpected. "Naturally I would welcome the board's support, Walter. But I don't require it." The smile she gave him did not warm her eyes. "Perhaps the Home board has been governed by numerical majority in the past, but henceforth we shall vote stock as required by the bylaws. Unless I've miscounted, my stock constitutes a comfortable majority."

"That's correct," he said slowly, looking at her. "However, the board has always believed it best benefited the company to govern by majority of opinion without placing extraordinary weight on one person's number of shares."

"In violation of company bylaws."

After touching his tie, Tobler cleared his throat. "A share vote would mean the Von Marron block controls the company."

"Yes," Gloria agreed pleasantly. "I believe that was my great-grandfather's intent when he founded the company, and it was also the intent of my grandfather who developed it. It is also my intent. The board exists only to advise and suggest."

Walter Tobler stared at her. As clearly as if he had spoken, Gloria understood Tobler was balancing her words against her age and her sex. He looked appalled.

"At present, I wish only to replace Win Durant; I will take his seat on the board. However, if you believe there are directors who will object to Win's resignation or to my active involvement, you may inform them I will accept their resignations immediately. You and I will arrange a meeting to discuss suitable replacements." A thin smile curved her lips. "We have a few minutes before the meeting begins, Walter. I suggest you use this time to speak privately with those whom you feel will wish to support Durant. You may mention how we shall conduct business in the future, and you may solicit resignations from anyone who objects.''

Walter Tobler blinked and assessed his own position, then he nodded without speaking and moved away from her. She watched which directors he approached and made a mental note for later consideration. Enough board members had taken their places at the table that the seating arrangement had become obvious. Tobler sat at one end of the table; Durant at the other. She approached the west end and seated herself facing the portrait of her grandfather. An abrupt silence occurred as she opened her briefcase and arranged her papers before her.

Home's directors exchanged glances with each other before William Asterly coughed into his hand and then addressed her. ''Excuse me, Miss Von Marron, but I believe you've taken Win's seat.''

She smiled. ''Indeed I have, Mr. Asterly.'' The silence deepened and grew heavy.

Without glancing up from her notes, Gloria knew when Durant entered the room. She felt the tension become electric. Still without looking up, she felt his stare, sensed his contained fury as he turned from his usual seat and took the vacant chair at the center of the table.

''Now that everyone is present,'' Gloria said, making a point of looking at her watch, ''we may begin. Walter?''

Walter Tobler rose at the end of the table. ''It is my honor to welcome Miss Von Marron.'' Without once looking at Durant, Tobler ran through a brief history of Home Limited and the Von Marrons who had sat at this table. Bobby Von Marron's two visits were glossed over quickly. ''You will be pleased to learn Miss Von Marron intends to follow in the steps of her illustrious family. She will be taking a permanent seat on this board.''

''Thank you, Walter.''

Walt Tobler glanced at his notes. ''Miss Von Marron has asked to present the first two items on today's agenda. Unless there is an objection . . . ?''

Durant spoke for the first time since entering the room. ''There was no copy of an agenda accompanying my meeting notice.''

''I don't seem to have one either,'' Asterly said. The others made a show of searching their papers and heads nodded.

"An oversight, I'm sure," Gloria said smoothly. "Mrs. Stavely, please pass the board a copy of today's agenda." Feeling the adrenaline pumping through her system, she rose to her feet.

"Thank you for your welcome, gentlemen. I assure you I will endeavor to uphold my responsibility to this company in the same spirit as my family has always done." From the corner of her eyes, she watched Mrs. Stavely place copies of the agenda on the table in front of the directors. Win Durant started forward as he read the first two items. When he lifted his head, his eyes were black with hatred.

"As you are aware, Home's board seats nine directors. In the past, one of those seats has been filled by Winthrop Durant at the Von Marron family's request. As I will now take that seat, Durant's services are no longer required." Her eyes met his and the moment was sweet. "You may offer your resignation now, or you may protest the decision, in which case I will ask the board to vote for your dismissal." There was no choice. She knew it; he knew it.

"My resignation will be on Tobler's desk by noon tomorrow."

"I've taken the liberty of instructing Mrs. Stavely to prepare a resignation statement for your signature. If you will sign it on your way out, the matter can be retired immediately." She offered no word of thanks or gratitude. The omission was intentional.

Nine faces stared at her. The condescending smiles she had noticed earlier had vanished.

"Unless I hear an objection," Gloria continued, "we shall invite Mr. Durant to remain through the next item on the agenda as it concerns La Tourraine, Durant and Von Marron." Her chill gaze did not warm as she addressed the following remarks to the entire table. "Gentlemen, Home Limited has placed its investment banking business with La Tourraine, Durant and Von Marron for the past thirty years. Acquisitions have been arranged through La Tourraine, Durant and Von Marron, as have divestitures, stock offerings, financings. Last year alone, Home Limited paid over six million dollars in banking fees to La Tourraine, Durant and Von Marron. In the past, with the Von Marrons holding a substantial interest in both firms, the arrangement was profitable. At present there is no advantage in continuing to place Home's banking business through La Tourraine, Durant and Von Marron. It is time for a change, gentlemen. I suggest we consider a proposal from another investment bank."

No one at the table looked at Win Durant. His face had turned a dark plum color, and knots rose along his jawline.

"In a moment Mrs. Stavely will invite Richard Nestor, Jr., to step inside and explain the benefits of placing our investment banking business through Nestor Brothers." She paused. "That is, of course, if you agree with me that a change is not only advisable but desirable. While I do not require your consent to make this change, naturally I would prefer to do so knowing I have your full support."

Gloria let her gaze travel slowly around the board table, pausing for a moment on each man. Her cool, steady eyes reminded each director he could be replaced as easily as Win Durant. The power had shifted in this room, and the vote she requested called for an acknowledgment of that shift. It was merely a formality, a tool to humiliate Durant.

"Walter? You will call the vote, please."

"Christ," someone muttered.

"Shit!"

As she had anticipated, the vote was unanimous with one abstention. Durant. Cold fire blazed in her eyes as she watched him silently rise to his feet. He stared at her, still without speaking, and the moment was the sweetest she had experienced in years. She felt light-headed with it, giddy with it, as she watched him walk away from the table.

Then he stopped at the door and turned and smiled at her. Damn him to hell; he smiled. And she understood she had drawn blood, but she had not dealt a fatal blow. In his smile, she saw her naiveté and inexperience. The joy drained from her triumph.

Still, she thought as Richard Nestor, Jr., delivered his presentation, she had removed a viper from the heart of her company. She had sliced six million dollars out of La Tourraine, Durant and Von Marron's top line. When the news of Home Limited's change in investment banks hit the papers, and she had already released statements, gossip would fly like confetti. The unanswered speculation would cost La Tourraine, Durant and Von Marron clients. She held on to that thought and the memory of Durant's rage.

But it wasn't enough.

Having decided to send the supporting actress roses and a dinner invitation, Durant leaned back in his theater seat and forgot the play, freeing himself to think about business.

The Von Marron bitch was like a persistent mosquito diving

in for a nip here, a bite there. None of it hurt, not really, but the continual annoyance enraged him. She was like a goddamn walking publicity department for Nestor Brothers, one who specialized in seducing business away from La Tourraine, Durant and Von Marron. When she was successful, it sent him reaching for his indigestion tablets. And she had enjoyed a number of significant successes, starting with the Home Limited account.

That one had hurt. The fees from Home Limited had carried La Tourraine, Durant and Von Marron through the lean times and had contributed significantly to profits during the fat years. Even after Gloria had hinted the firm could lose Home's account, he hadn't believed it. He had allowed himself to become complacent, and even though he had warned himself not to underestimate her, he had. Not for an instant had he believed she would take an active seat on Home's board. Not once had he imagined she could force the board to vote out La Tourraine, Durant and Von Marron. But she had. And it had been so goddamn simple that he felt like flogging himself for stupidity.

She had used the bylaws like a bludgeon. He had done the same on occasion, but judiciously, saving that particular hammer for times when it was the only way to get what he wanted. In the normal course of events, he had allowed Home's board of directors to believe they had an equal vote in governing the company.

Gloria Von Marron had come through the boardroom door swinging a club. Exactly as he had done thirty years ago. He would have sworn that if she really wanted a seat on the board, and if she found the courage to follow through, that she would sit there like a mouse and not make a squeak. He sure as hell hadn't guessed she would think to pull out the bylaws and recognize the power they gave her. He certainly had not anticipated how fast she could move when she was ready. But she had. She had indeed. And that business about the agenda being "overlooked" had been a clever touch. If he hadn't loathed her so completely, he might have admired her. The truth in that thought caused his stomach to cramp.

At this point, the furor over Home's switch in banking firms had long since died down. Home had made its statement; La Tourraine, Durant and Von Marron had made its statement. Walt Tobler had been interviewed; Durant had been interviewed. The lies and half-truths had marched forth, trailing excited speculation in their wake. He had lost a few clients; Nestor had gained a few. In the end it was business as usual.

And it was business as usual now, except the loss of a client here and of a deal there infuriated him when he traced those losses to Gloria Von Marron. Christ, she was everywhere. The opening of a new exhibition at the Met, the opera, the ballet, a gallery showing, a charity ball, the latest tony restaurants. And always she had some client of Durant's backed into a corner talking, talking, talking. As an outside man, she made her father, who was the best Durant had known, seem like a tongue-tied bumpkin. There didn't appear to be anyone she couldn't charm out of his portfolio. And she was a team player. She didn't just hustle Nestor's corporate finance division, she pitched clients for portfolio management, stock issues, acquisitions, mergers, you name it. Charles Nestor was a damned fool if he didn't fall on his knees and kiss her feet every morning when she swept through the firm's doors. She was a consummate rainmaker. Gloria Von Marron was taking Nestor Brothers from a submajor to a bulge firm and was earning Nestor a bundle in the process.

Durant would have wagered his club memberships that she was lording it over everyone at NB, playing queen to the peasants. A tight smile curved his mouth. Right now she was thinking she was hot shit, but that was going to change. Her majesty was going to receive a lesson in humility. She was going to learn just how green and ignorant she was. He only wished he could be there to enjoy the expression on her face when she heard the news.

"The final round of bidding will take place on the fourteenth," Gloria said into the telephone. "Yes, in our offices. As we want to guarantee our client a completed deal, we're asking each bidder to bring his investment banker to the auction in case there are questions regarding financial capability." Through the glass wall of her office, she could see her associate, Mark Denton, speaking to the group from Research. Research would check out the prospects and financials of each final bidder. "I'm sorry, I can't tell you the number of finalists, but I can say there are more than two bidders and less than twelve."

The phone rang on her desk as soon as she replaced the receiver. She reached for it absently, not lifting her head from the auction list until she heard Franklin T's excited voice.

"Have you heard? Jesus, Gloria, nobody down here can talk about anything else! It's going through the Street like shit through a goose!"

"About Texaco? Old stuff, Franklin T., we had it this morning."

"No, about La Tourraine, Durant and Von Marron."

Her back stiffened. For a minute she couldn't think what he was talking about. Then she knew. Her pencil snapped between her fingers. There was only one thing that could cause this stir. "Tell me," she whispered, knowing what he would say.

"Durant is taking the firm public. Morgan and The Bear will comanage; they'll get top billing on the Tombstone. Rumor has it this has been in the offing since last summer; only Durant's been sitting on it, delaying. The rumor mill doesn't say why. Can you believe this? I suppose the private houses will all go eventually, but—La Tourraine, Durant and Von Marron? Shit. Half the Street claims they knew it all along; the other half is stunned."

She felt sick. Tears of rage scalded her eyes, and she swiveled her chair to face the wall. The bastard. The immoral criminal bastard. In some dark corner of her mind, she had expected this. Unconsciously, she had been waiting for the other shoe to drop. That she had known it was coming made it no easier to bear.

"Are you still there? Look, I've got to run. I'll pick you up about eight for the benefit. I thought we'd—"

The moment she hung up the telephone it rang again, and she stared at it as if it were a cobra.

She couldn't remain at her desk as if this were a normal day like any other, as if she hadn't just learned she had been cheated of approximately fifty million dollars. She ran a rapid calculation on the machine at her elbow. Fifty million minimum.

Enraged and sickened, feeling certain that everyone knew and watched her, she put on her jacket and hat, then lifted her head high and walked to the elevators and then out of the building.

Once outside, she hesitated, uncertain what to do next. At least she knew where she would go. There was only one place when the fury and pain became overwhelming.

"I heard," Charles Nestor said. His secretary had put Gloria's call through immediately upon hearing her name.

"I'm going to Goose Point for a few days."

"Take as long as you need. Mark Denton can handle the Bentrex auction. We'll move Marlys Mill in on the Pantron merger."

Her shoulders dropped with relief when it became apparent Charles would not ask for details and didn't ask if she wanted to talk. Franklin T. and the traders hadn't learned the full story yet—that Gloria Von Marron had been screwed over. But the bankers knew. Investment banking was a small, incestuous community. There were few secrets. Charles Nestor knew the terms of the partnership buy-back agreement at La Tourraine, Durant and Von Marron just as the people at La Tourraine, Durant and Von Marron could guess to the penny the amount of the Nestor bonuses. Everyone knew everyone else's business. Charles Nestor knew when Gloria had sold her father's partnership and probably knew the approximate buy-back figure. He would know when Durant had first started investigating a public offering. By this time tomorrow, everyone on the Street would have it put together.

She pressed a hand to her stomach and swallowed the nausea threatening to choke her.

By the time Gloria turned her Mercedes onto the gravel drive leading into the estate, William had arrived and had opened the house. He carried her bags up the steps of the veranda and opened the door for her.

"Mrs. Orrin is coming in to cook and I've arranged for two local women to manage the cleaning. May I inquire how long we'll be staying?"

"I'm sorry, but I don't know yet." One of the first things William had done was throw open the windows to the summer breezes. Beneath the scent of the sea and the summer roses, the house smelled of dust and disuse. The musty odor saddened her. Goose Point was meant to be lived in, Gloria thought. It was meant for laughter and bright sun-washed days. It was meant for sailing boys and tomboy girls, for lawn parties and hunts and glittering summer receptions. Goose Point had never been intended to sit silent and shrouded.

"It's good to be back, Miss," William said, pulling a sheet from the foyer setee.

At first she agreed. But as the days passed Gloria decided she wasn't so certain. The restorative power of Goose Point failed to relieve or diminish the rage and hatred that consumed her, that burned and charred and twisted her thoughts.

The need for revenge gnawed at her like a ravenous parasite. It wouldn't let her alone. She boiled with hatred the moment she pulled herself out of bed after a restless, sleepless night. She couldn't eat. She couldn't think of anything but Winthrop Durant and what he had done to her. She took each offense and drew it through the furnace of her mind, polishing her injuries in the fire of hatred until they glowed and pulsed and consumed her.

When her mind rebelled and sought respite, she tried to think about Robby, but not even memories of her son could cool the heated tangle of her thoughts.

She kicked a stone into the waters of the Sound, then padded across the hot sand to sit with her back against the sea wall. Dropping her silvery head, she pressed her forehead against her knees. No, there was no peace to be found thinking about her son. There was guilt and fear of exposure. Love and remorse, yearning and shame, but no sense of peace.

Robby should have been with her at Goose Point. This was his home; this was where he belonged. He should have been paddling in the bubbles rolling up the beach as she had done at his age, as her father had done. If Robby were here, she could watch him grow and be part of his life. She could share his delight when he discovered the secret path to the beach and the hidden space behind the lilacs. In time she would fill the stables for him and open the music room.

None of these things would happen until she had avenged herself. The hatred overwhelmed her. Winthrop Durant, may he burn in hell, had to pay for raping her body, her mind, her emotions, and her legacy. He had to pay.

"But how?" Scorching handfuls of sand filled her fists. "I swear to God I will find a way to take the bastard down!"

If it meant working harder, she would work harder. If it meant abandoning any semblance of a social life, she would willingly abandon her social life. If smashing Win Durant could be accomplished only by sacrificing her time with Robby for a few more years, she would make that sacrifice and endure it somehow. Whatever price was required, she would pay it and gladly.

Now she understood that crushing Durant could take years. She had been naive to hope she could do in a year or two what others had failed to accomplish in a decade or more. Regardless of how hard she drove herself or how much she learned, Durant would always be years ahead of her in knowledge and experience. As she could never hope to catch up, she could never aspire to beat him as an equal.

But she could beat him. That, she didn't doubt. And she would. The method was there; she sensed it, knew its presence like that of an unseen lover seducing her forward. At present she was too inexperienced to see the way clearly, but one day the veil would drop and she would know what to do. She lived for that day.

Gardner Durant studied his mother in the shade cast by the umbrella protecting the sidewalk table from the midday sun. She had stopped coloring her hair after Lulu Von Marron's death, and he decided he like the gray. Her soft white curls suggested her age but did not detract from her appearance. Chissie Durant was still a handsome woman.

"It's good to see you," he said, reaching across the checkered cloth to press her hand. "I'm sorry Dad didn't come with you."

"You know your father, he's convinced Wall Street would fold without him there to look after everything. I can hardly get him away for a weekend. I didn't attempt to persuade him to accompany me to Paris."

Gardner smiled and nodded. "I've been wondering if he'll consider retirement now that the firm's gone public." If he hadn't been watching her, he would have mistaken his mother's laughter for that of a much younger woman.

"Good heavens, no. I can't imagine Win retired, can you? Admittedly, I don't know much about business, but as I understand it, your father retained enough shares in your trust and mine that, combined with the shares he owns outright, he still holds a majority interest. Does that make sense? Anyway, Win is guaranteed a seat on the board and as far as I can tell, he still runs the show."

"He wouldn't have it any other way," Gardner agreed.

"So tell me what's next for you."

"Rio de Janeiro." When he had learned his mother was coming to Paris to attend the showings of the spring collections, he had cleared his calendar to spend time with her. This was the first leisure day he had allowed himself in far too long a period, and he decided he was enjoying it immensely. After ordering a Kir for her and Cinzano for himself, he adjusted the table umbrella, then talked about closing his Paris apartment and shipping to Rio the items he had collected over the years.

"I've leased a villa overlooking the harbor. If it's half as lavish as the agency's brochure indicates, I'm going to hate leaving for work in the mornings."

"Liar." Chissie Durant smiled at her son. "You're happiest when you're tramping around a logging camp or hacking through some jungle. I've never known you to care about any apartment or house except Goose Point. Goose Point is the only house you've ever mentioned with anything approaching affection or attachment.''

Laughing, he acknowledged she was correct before he shifted in his seat to face the pedestrian traffic flowing past the velvet ropes separating their table from the pavement. ''Have you heard from Gloria?'' he asked casually. ''I hear from her at Christmas—a few lines across the bottom of a card—and I see her name on company directives and memos, but I haven't actually seen her in a couple of years.''

Sudden tears filled his mother's eyes, and she offered a tiny sound of apology. ''I'm sorry. I get so upset when I think that Lulu's daughter . . . I always expected . . . there's an ongoing estrangement. We don't see her anymore. Win's intractable about it. For a while I met Gloria for lunch occasionally, but it was a strain. I don't know why. I tried to ask her about it, but she was evasive. Eventually we stopped scheduling the luncheons. It just . . . seemed easier.'' Opening her purse, she found her handkerchief and pressed it to her eyes. ''I can hardly bear to think of it. You must know Lulu and I used to dream that you and Gloria . . . well, this is a fine thing, isn't it? You stay in Paris an extra day just to see me, and I go weepy on you.''

While she composed herself, Gardner thought about the board meeting held two weeks ago in New York. Tobler had requested his presence and he had flown in for the meeting expecting to see Gloria. She hadn't been there; she had been in Washington D.C., but he had recognized her influence behind the board's offer of the South American vice presidency. For the first time in Home's history, the board had created a vice presidency not tied to the New York office. With that restriction lifted, he had felt comfortable accepting the promotion. As Gloria would have known.

After ordering lunch, he sipped his wine and leaned back, enjoying the warm September sunshine and his mother's innocent gossip. After a time his thoughts drifted.

Gloria Von Marron was avoiding him. He supposed he had known it for a couple of years, and he accepted her decision. But avoiding him wouldn't be as easily accomplished now that she sat on Home's board of directors. Eventually they would encounter one another. He was a patient man; he would wait.

Chapter 13

*T*HE PUBLIC OFFERING made Win Durant a very wealthy man. More importantly, the infusion of fresh capital catapulted La Tourraine, Durant and Von Marron from a medium-sized old-line house into the coveted position of major player. Durant gloried in the media interviews, the attention, the broader capital to play with and to build on. He looked and felt younger than he had in years. Everything was going his way.

For a time it had seemed touch and go. Internal tensions had reached flash point throughout the restructuring following Bobby Von Marron's death, then again as an equally sweeping reorganization became inevitable as a result of the public offering. In retrospect, Durant recognized it would have been wiser to delay major changes until the public offering. Because he had not, the firm had suffered cataclysmic internal strife. He had lost a dozen young stars who had taken themselves off in a huff of greed and ruffled ambitions to seek new pedestals at one of the private houses where partnership and instant wealth were still accessible.

Before the doors closed behind them, Durant's phone had lit up with calls from headhunters offering him a hundred brilliant young men and women eager to train under the legend of Wall Street.

Standing at the door to the cavernous trading room, he clasped his hands behind him and watched as the room filled. The news from the Tokyo and London markets blared over the squawk box and several of the traders hunched forward, listening intently. Others gleaned the morning newspapers. Three waiters from the firm's private kitchen moved through the room taking breakfast orders and pouring coffee.

Pleased, he turned toward the elevators, the scent of freshly brewed coffee following him into the corridor. He had it licked. He was sitting on top of the pile, untouchable. He had more money than he or his heirs could spend in two lifetimes; his board was stacked with friends who didn't dare cross him; he felt youthful and challenged again. His only regret was that his mother was not alive to witness his success.

The thought was rare enough to startle him. He hadn't thought about Ada Mae Durant in thirty years, hadn't thought about Ripley, Oklahoma, since the day he returned there to bury Ada Mae. He had been a junior at Princeton, puffed with a sense of his own importance and destiny. Wearing a newly purchased three-piece suit, he had stood in the red dirt beside Ada Mae's grave and despised her for dying before he could prove how wrong she had been.

For as long as he could remember, his mother had insisted he was destined for the rigs like his no-good father. She had lifted his hands and inspected the dirt and grease under his nails and then told him to accept what he was. People didn't change. She had warned him against dreams because dreams could corrupt. He saw her in his memory, smoothing her calloused hands over a faded print dress and staring at the dust grinding down the linoleum floor of the tiny rented house. "Don't you go dreaming, Win. Don't let dreams eat you up. Don't go trying to be something you're not."

Standing before the corner windows of his twenty-sixth-floor office suite, he looked north toward Manhattan's skyline. This was his town; he owned it. He was a long, long way from Ripley, Oklahoma, and Ada Mae Durant. Although he had enjoyed a few breaks along the way, he had pulled himself to the top of the heap by his own efforts. He had done it alone.

Today, no one cared if a man came from linoleum floors and tarpaper walls as long as he could do a deal. Things had changed. In Durant's day, brilliance had counted for shit unless it came wrapped in the right background and the right connections. If he could start over today, he would have made it to the top without Bobby Von Marron, or Whitehall and La Tourraine. Today, he wouldn't need a Mayflower connection or a dance card.

"Good morning." Lucille Ivory walked into his office carrying her note pad and his morning coffee. "Full schedule today. You have the executive committee in half an hour, an appointment with Mrs. Kennedy and her attorneys at ten, then a phone conference with the deputy secretary of the Treasury and the chairman of the New York Stock Exchange, and lunch with Ivan Boesky and Andrew Colquist.''

''Cancel lunch.'' When Lucille looked up at him with a lifted eyebrow, he leaned back from his desk and pursed his mouth. ''Boesky and Colquist have made us a lot of money over the years, but we're open to public scrutiny now.'' Colquist, that egotistical fucker, played it too close to the line. There were only so many times a man could spit into the wind without getting his face wet. The time had arrived to ease back or risk getting splattered.

Lucille smiled. ''Is this an example of, and I quote, 'Winthrop Durant's justly celebrated intuition'?''

''*The Wall Street Journal*, right?'' He laughed.

''*Newsweek.*''

''Let's say it's an example of knowing when to buy and when to sell.''

He didn't need Ivan Boesky or Andrew Colquist. He didn't need Home Limited. He didn't need anyone. That's what made him invulnerable. He called the shots; he was in control.

A few flakes of snow danced past the bare trees and drifted toward the ground, slowly covering the frozen lane.

''Lovely,'' commented Robby's nanny. Her wide cheeks were pink with cold, bunched into a smile. ''Perhaps we'll have a white Christmas after all.''

Robby lifted his face to the floating snow and his arms waved in delight. Laughing, Gloria turned the stroller back toward Tilbury House. The new wing for the nursery and nanny's room was almost finished. Due to the design and Edmund's genius, the new rooms did not disturb the integrity of the house. The exterior had been carefully aged to give the appearance of being an integral part of the original design.

Once inside, Gloria pulled her scarf from her hair and shook the snow from her coat before placing it on the hall peg. The smell of wood shavings and hot tea and the fresh green scent of the Christmas tree made her smile as she bent to peel away Robby's snowsuit.

''What a wiggle worm you are,'' she said, laughing and pulling a sleeve over his closed fist. ''What are you holding?''

''Sno','' he said, pleased with himself. ''See sno', Mummy.'' Running forward, he opened his hand proudly, then blinked at his tiny, empty palm in astonishment.

But he had spoken to Margaret. He had run to Margaret and had called Margaret "Mummy."

Pain spread a mist over Gloria's eyes, knifed through her stomach. She rose to her feet with difficulty and met Margaret's stricken gaze above Robby's head. In the silence, the nanny looked from one to the other before catching Robby in her arms.

"Come along, young sir. It's time for your nap." Hastily, she bore him out of the room and up the attic stairs.

"I'm sorry," Margaret apologized quietly. "He just started that recently."

White-faced, Gloria moved to the chair in front of the parlor fire and dropped into it, leaning forward to hold her hands to the flames. The heat warmed her palms but didn't penetrate to the cold lump forming inside her stomach.

"I should have anticipated this," she whispered, speaking more to herself than to Margaret. "But I didn't. And I didn't know it would hurt this much."

Margaret's hand pressed her shoulder. "He needs you, Gloria."

She heard concern in Margaret's voice, but no reproach and no hint of judgment. The reproach lay in her own thoughts.

"When I'm here," she said finally, "my other life seems distant and unimportant. I look at my son, and I wonder how I can bear to leave him. I tell myself this time will be different. This time I won't leave without him." She lifted her face, a plea in her eyes. "But I have to."

"They grow up so fast."

"Margaret, if I quit now, then the last year and a half of separation will have gone for nothing. I can't quit."

There was no longer a choice. Her hatred and her obsession for revenge swept her forward on a course she could not alter. If she let Durant do what he had done and walk away free, she would never forgive herself. He had to suffer as she had suffered. He had to feel the same pain she felt when she looked at her beloved son and heard him call another woman Mummy. Durant had to pay for the pain he had caused.

Kneeling, Margaret stroked Gloria's cheek. "Is there no way you can put aside whatever is driving you? No way you can take Robby home to Goose Point?"

"No." The hoarse whisper scraped her throat. The moisture in Margaret's eyes made her own eyes tear.

Later, when everyone was in bed and the house was silent, Gloria returned to the parlor and wrapped herself in one of

Margaret's shawls, sitting before the embers in the grate. The only light in the room came from the dying fire and the lights twinkling on the Christmas tree.

Win Durant had stolen more from her than he would ever guess.

He had stolen the weeks and months before her parents' deaths; he had stolen these precious years with her son. He had stolen her money and her legacy, and he had poisoned her memories.

For she saw now that the wonderful Christmases she remembered at Goose Point were blackened in her memory by Durant's presence. When she thought of them, she recalled his dark eyes judging the mountain of expensive gifts, his gaze following her mother. She remembered his envy and resentment and recognized betrayal awaiting opportunity.

Remembering, she burned as hot as the embers in the grate. No, she could not turn aside from what she had sworn to do. Durant had shattered the trust and honor of her parents, herself, and her son. She could not walk away and hope to forget. Not as long as either of them lived.

She lowered her head and wept in the snowy silence.

Franklin T. Nemiro sat up in bed and refilled his wine glass. Leaning back against the pillows, he watched Gloria emerge from the bathroom, elegant in a creamy silk dressing gown, her glorious hair still wet from the shower.

"It isn't working, is it?"

"What isn't working?" she asked, pulling a comb through her hair before the dressing table mirror.

"Us. You and me."

She met his eyes in the mirror, then came to sit on the side of the bed. "We agreed to keep it light, remember?"

"I love you."

A look of pain constricted her expression. "Don't, Franklin. Please."

"You don't love me, do you?" He knew he was committing a fatal error, but he was powerless to stop himself.

"I enjoy your company. I'm not seeing anyone else. Can't we leave it at that?"

"You don't have time to see anyone else." The attempt at a joke was lame, but the best he could manage.

Her smile pierced his heart. "Isn't this a classic example of the pot calling the kettle black? You work as many hours as I do.''

''No one works as many hours as you do.'' A few months of seeing her two and three times a week had elapsed before he had noticed the obvious. She was always working; she never quit. Their relationship had developed in the midst of large social affairs peopled by potential clients. He could count on the fingers of one hand the rare instances when she had agreed to dinner for two. Those few occasions sparkled in his memory like briefly held jewels, as precious as they were rare.

He looked at her and promised himself he would let it go; he would say nothing more. Instead he stroked her wet hair and blundered on, taking the conversation from awkward to disastrous. ''I love you. I want to know everything about you.'' Her face closed; he watched it happen. ''We've been seeing each other for months, but I don't really know you.''

This, too, had taken weeks to realize. On the surface she was open and comfortable to be with, quick to laugh at the world's foibles, at him, at herself. Only with time had he learned to recognize the curtain she drew around her privacy, shielding large areas of her life and herself. He had believed the curtain would drop as their relationship deepened from curiosity to affection and finally to something more. But she continued to keep parts of herself locked away, inaccessible.

He was a man who dealt with hard figures, he wasn't comfortable with mystery or elusiveness. With another woman he would have lost patience months ago and would have walked away. But Gloria Von Marron was like no other woman. For one thing, she listened. When he spoke, she looked directly into his eyes and he felt himself connected, truly connected in a way he had never before experienced. She listened and she heard what was said and what was left unsaid. Because she listened and because she cared, he found himself revealing bits and pieces of himself that he previously wouldn't have dreamed of confiding to anyone. He wanted to know her in the same way she knew him. Wholly, with nothing held in reserve.

''You know everything about me,'' she said finally. ''The media has made my life an open book.''

''They know and I know only what you choose to tell,'' he said, recognizing the evasiveness in her answer. He smoothed the line between her eyes with his fingertip, hoping to salvage the conversation with tenderness. Then, helpless to stop, he stumbled on, saying what he had sworn he would not. ''What drives you, Gloria? Where do you go when you disappear? Why do you look so sad when you think no one is watching? Who is the child in the photograph you keep hidden in the top drawer?''

Instantly her eyes chilled and a chasm opened between them. Although she didn't move he felt the chasm widen, and he understood he had gone too far. Regretting his questions, he attempted to reassure her. "Don't you know you can trust me? I love you."

Was it too much to ask? That she trust him with the details of her life? If someone had told him six months ago that he could find fierce independence existing side by side with an aching vulnerability, and could find them in the same woman, he would have dismissed the duality as ludicrous. But he had seen her put together a couple of the largest deals in town. And he had seen her expression when they passed a mother and child in the park. There were details to reconcile the two images. There were reasons, and he wanted to share them. He wanted the trust she could demonstrate by lifting the curtain.

"You searched my bureau?" Her tone was as frozen as her expression.

"I was looking for some extra deodorant a few weeks ago. I wasn't spying on you, if that's what you mean. Finding the photograph made me realize how little I really know about you. Gloria, intimacy is more than sharing a bed and shop talk." He wanted more than the use of her body, he wanted—hell, he didn't know how to phrase it—he wanted *her*. "I want to share your life. The good and the bad. I want to know what you think about when you're alone. How you feel about things other than work. What was your childhood like? Do you miss your parents? I want to share all of it."

Her face was carefully expressionless, but he knew her well enough to understand her hesitation signaled a decision. When he tried to speak, she placed a finger across his lips then touched his cheek with greater tenderness than she had before. He was elated until he read the sadness in her eyes. They made love again, slowly, tenderly. And he felt like weeping because he recognized she was saying good-bye. And there was nothing he could do or say to change her mind.

The next day he telephoned her office and her secretary paused briefly then explained she was out. He hung up the phone, buttoned his vest and pulled on his jacket. Then he went to Harry's where he had first met her and he disgraced himself by getting stinking, falling-down drunk. Weepy drunk; nasty drunk. Drunk enough that he could not recall the candlelight shining in her silvery eyes and hair, or the provocative scent of her perfume, or his happiness when he made her laugh.

Nineteen hundred and eighty-four was a strange year. Many firms were taking a beating; young brokers had their books burned and departed the Street for less perilous careers back home; the bears reaped a harvest; the bulls swallowed their losses and grimly predicted better days were coming.

Gloria stared at her Quotron until her eyes ached and burned, and eyedrops ceased to help. In June she played a calculated hunch and put her clients and herself heavily into Carnation at fifty-three dollars a share.

"Why Carnation?" Mark Denton asked. They were at Gloria's desk, snatching a hasty lunch out of soggy cartons. "Nothing indicates it's in play." Lifting a carton, he peered inside, made a face, and then took another bite.

"I don't know. Intuition, just a feeling . . ." When he laughed, she grinned. She was willing to share the tip, but not her research sources. "What is this stuff we're eating? Lord." Wrinkling her nose, she pushed the cartons away.

Denton nodded, watching her. "Think I should put my people in?"

"That's up to you." Shrugging, she brushed back a wave of hair. "I don't have anything concrete. I'm not wired on this. But you might take a look at the 10-K. The multiple seems to be at a discount both relatively and absolutely."

At the end of summer Nestle announced its intention to buy Carnation, and Gloria sold at eighty-three a share. Her clients, one of whom profited six hundred thousand dollars, were ecstatic.

Her reputation was made.

From the beginning, Gloria had understood that accepting an active role in Home Limited's management meant she would inevitably encounter Gardner Durant. The surprise was not seeing him again, but that it hadn't occurred sooner. That it had not was due more to coincidence than to design. During Gardner's previous board presentations, she had been out of town on Nestor business, arranging details for mergers, scouting acquisitions for clients, working with corporate finance departments.

Knowing he would be present today, she arrived early for the board meeting and irritated herself by ducking into the powder room to check her hair and makeup. An emerald silk blouse highlighted the green flecks in her eyes; her hair, twisted into a coil at the crown, gleamed like silver. Studying her reflection in the mirror, she wondered what changes Gardner would see.

She examined her image for a long moment, then turned aside with a sound of annoyance. What did it matter? Her life and Gardner's had turned down separate paths. There was no more room in her life for Gardner Durant—especially Gardner Durant—than there was room for Robby. Not now. Every minute was consumed; she had no time and no desire for unnecessary complications.

Still, she drew a small, involuntary breath when he came into the boardroom midway through the meeting. And she dropped her hands to her lap to conceal a tremor when he looked at her and smiled. Dismayed by her reaction, she frowned and deliberately returned her hands to the tabletop, nodding at Walt Tobler to proceed.

Gardner spoke for an hour, detailing the devastating environmental impact of the lumber industry in the South American countries. He argued persuasively for expanding reforestation, for stepping up the company's reclamation projects.

Gloria watched him as he spoke and discovered her thoughts drifting from his presentation and focusing on the man. Gardner had changed, not in large ways, but more subtly. His expression was more controlled than she remembered. He moved and spoke with confidence and self-assurance that suggested he was comfortable with himself and his place in the world. The tropical sun had bronzed his skin, and there were lines at the corners of his eyes and framing his mouth that she didn't recall. He had grown into the maturity she had always sensed in him.

A feeling of possession overwhelmed her, followed by a quick, deep bite of jealousy. Biting her lip, she shook off the feeling with difficulty. She had no right to feel possessive of Gardner. It was she who had made the decision to walk away. Because she had no choice, she thought bitterly. Gardner's father had seen to that.

Immediately after the meeting adjourned, she rose to her feet and thrust her papers into her briefcase, hoping to escape with a cursory nod. But Gardner caught up to her at the door and walked with her toward the elevator.

"Am I imagining things, Boss Lady, or are you avoiding me?" He grinned down at her, tall, tanned and impossibly handsome.

"I don't see you for years, and the first thing out of your mouth is an accusation." She intended to keep the conversation light and easy. A few insignificant words, then they would say good-bye.

"I'd like to talk to you. Will you have dinner with me?"

"Dinner?" She should have expected this, but she had not.

"Someplace neutral, where we aren't likely to run into anyone either of us knows."

She made a show of consulting her watch, then shook her head and glanced at the floor indicator above the elevator doors. "I'm sorry, Gardner. I have an appointment tonight. I'm putting together a complicated merger." They stepped into the elevator, and Gardner pressed the button to close the doors before anyone could join them.

"Gloria, I think it's important we discuss the rupture between the Durants and the Von Marrons." Instantly her eyes narrowed. "I understand Home Limited moved its investment banking business out of La Tourraine, Durant and Von Marron."

"A long time ago."

"I learned about it only recently. Until then, I didn't realize how serious the breach was."

"I appreciate your concern," she said with cool politeness, "but there is nothing to discuss. This is between your father and me." The elevator seemed to descend in slow motion. The topic and standing this near him made her acutely uncomfortable.

"I'm not going to believe the situation can't be resolved until I've learned what happened." Catching her lightly by the shoulders, he looked into her eyes and Gloria felt her chest constrict. "That's not the only reason I want to see you."

"I'm sorry, Gardner, no. Dinner isn't a good idea."

The elevator doors opened and she stepped into the lobby with a feeling of relief.

"I'm sorry to rush, but I have a meeting and I'm already late," she said as he opened the outside door for her. He followed her to the curb and stood on the pavement as her driver opened the car door.

"I'll be in Manhattan for six weeks, squirt." Her head jerked up and she looked at him, tempted to smile. "I'll call you every day—that's a promise. I'll wear you down. You'll beg to have dinner with me just to end the harassment."

She laughed as the car pulled from the curb. Then she leaned her head back and tried to recall the last time her laughter had been genuine.

As promised, Gardner telephoned her office at least once every day. Chewing the end of a pencil, Gloria watched through the glass wall as her secretary laughed into the telephone, then leaned forward and doodled little hearts across a scratch pad.

"Was it Gardner?" she asked when Helen Markley entered her office.

Helen nodded and raised a curious eyebrow. "I don't know why you won't talk to him. If this guy looks half as good as he sounds . . ." She ended on a sigh. "The guys I meet are married, gay, or ready for the rubber room. I'll bet those are for you," she added, watching through the glass wall as a young man wearing a Rhinelander delivery uniform wound through the desks toward Gloria's office. "More roses."

Gloria tipped the boy, who folded the bill into his pocket. "I'm getting rich on you, Miss Von Marron," he commented cheerfully.

She waited until he had gone before she opened the box. Today the roses were white, the petals creamy beneath her fingertips. Like the others, the card read: Dinner at eight?

"We sent yesterday's dozen down to Research," Helen reminded her. "The day before we sent them to M & A. Where do you want these to go?"

"I'll keep them," Gloria decided. "The pinks have started to droop. Throw them out and use the vase for these." She examined the vases of roses overwhelming her office, lifted the stack of cards growing beside her keyboard. A sigh of resignation dropped her shoulders. "Get him on the phone."

"I surrender," she said when he answered.

"Excellent."

"There are conditions."

"You are speaking to a man who has negotiated with jungle guerrillas. I understand conditions. Shoot."

She drew a breath. "The problems between your father and me are not a topic for discussion. That's off limits. Agreed?"

"For the moment." He conceded with reluctance.

"And it has to be an early night. I'm snowed under with work. Agreed?"

"I'll skip salad and dessert."

She smiled at the roses. "In that case—I'd love to have dinner with an old friend."

An hour later, she threw down her pencil and shoved a hand through her hair. Annoyed with herself, she slapped shut the file folder she was working on and carried it to Mark Denton's office.

"I need a favor. Do you have time to run these figures for a double check?"

"Are you kidding?" Mark accepted the folder and tossed it on the pile on his desk. "After what you did for me on Carnation? For you, I would walk across hot lava."

"You're committing to about three hours work," she warned.

"No problem. Consider it done. What's up?"

"I hate to tell you."

"I've already agreed—so tell."

Bright pink blossomed on her cheeks. "I need a manicure, and I need to buy a sensational dress."

Mark Denton grinned and wiggled his fingers. "It's worth three hours of work just to learn you're human. So who's the lucky guy?"

"No one special."

"Right."

"Just an old friend."

The old friend stood back and examined her with a low whistle. "I apologize for calling you squirt the other day. You have definitely grown up. You look beautiful!" She handed him her fur, and the haunting scent of Calèche enveloped him as he dropped the sable over her shoulders.

Abruptly he remembered her sitting beside him on the Goose Point beach. He couldn't remember the occasion, but he recalled her nose, sunburned and peeling, and a scab on her knee.

"Why are you looking at me so strangely?"

"I'm sorry, I was thinking what a swan you grew up to be."

"I'd offer you a drink, but—"

"But we're rushed. I understand perfectly—an early night."

"Yes." She raised an eyebrow at his smile, then stepped past him into the corridor.

He took her to Le Refuse, very expensive, very exclusive. There were six tables, each situated to afford the diners absolute privacy.

"How did you find this place?" Gloria exclaimed, delighted. "It reminds me of Au Pactole in Paris. My father used to take me there before he put me on the train to Aigmont." A shadow crossed her expression, gone before he could identify the emotion behind it.

"I think about your father on occasion," he mentioned over drinks. "I miss him."

"Really?" She looked surprised. "Did you like him?"

"Of course I liked him. I think I spent more time with your father than with my own when I was growing up. Dad never seemed to have time to play. Bobby taught Remy and me to shoot, to sail, to hunt. I learned to ride on the horses in the Goose Point stable. When I decided to accept the Home Limited fellowship instead of pursuing a career with La Tourraine, Durant and Von Marron, Bobby was very supportive. It was a difficult period. He was there if I wanted to talk and, from some of the things he said, I think he did much toward helping my father accept my decision."

"I don't believe your father has ever accepted your decision, Gardner. Surely you know that."

"I think he's finally coming around." It mattered less with the passing years, but he hoped this was true. "If Dad believed there was any possibility that I might end up with La Tourraine, Durant and Von Marron, I doubt he would have taken the firm public. He would have kept it as a private dynasty."

"I don't wish to discuss this," Gloria said sharply.

He studied her in the candlelight, thinking how astonishingly lovely she was. Moreover, time had strengthened her. There was less compromise now than he remembered. "We never had taboo areas before, Gloria, are they really necessary now?"

"Gardner, there are things you don't know, and it's better that you don't."

"I don't like secrets. I never have. If there's something going on here that I don't know, then tell me." When she looked away from him and refused to speak, he continued. "Our families have been close friends since before you and I were born. Do you think it's reasonable to allow that relationship to disintegrate without discussing it? Aren't those years worth some attempt at salvage?"

She stared at him. "I mean it, Gardner. I won't pursue this line of conversation. If you persist, I'll leave."

Reluctantly, he set the mystery aside for the moment. That she had agreed to see him was a beginning; the rest would come in time.

"Very well. So, what would you like to discuss instead?" He remembered when her gaze had been direct and open. Now it was not. At some point she had learned to keep people at a distance to protect her thoughts and her secrets. He decided there was something sad in that. He regretted the loss of her innocence, for he guessed loss of innocence lay behind the caution in her eyes. Watching her, he wondered who had taught her not to trust, who had hurt her that much.

"Let's talk about you," she suggested, gradually relaxing. "You're doing wonderful things in Brazil and Argentina. Profits have increased forty percent since you took over the Rio office." They talked shop through the first course. "Now," she said, her gray eyes teasing, "tell me about Elena Braganza. The recent article in *Town and Country* mentioned you as La Braganza's premier escort."

"La Braganza and I are just good friends," he said, smiling. "How about you? Is there anyone special?"

"Not at the moment."

"Why not?"

"I beg your pardon?"

"Why isn't there someone special? You've done what you set out to do. You've triumphed on Wall Street; you've been lauded in *Barrons*, in *Manhattan Inc.*, and in all the other major periodicals. You've established a name for yourself. Isn't it time to think about the personal side of your life?"

"The personal side of my life is fine, thank you."

"Is it, Gloria? From what I hear, you don't have much of a personal life, just business." Reaching across the table, he clasped her cold fingers. "You don't have to prove anything. That ended when Bobby and Lulu died."

"Is that what you think I'm doing? Trying to prove something?" She withdrew her fingers from his hand.

"Isn't it?"

"Maybe that's part of it," she conceded after a moment. "But not all. I haven't accomplished what I have to do." She met his eyes across the table. "When I've met my goal, then I'll take time for me."

"What goal could possibly be more important than you?"

"Please, Gardner. Let's not get into this."

Talking to her was like tiptoeing through a mine field, trying to avoid explosive subjects. "Another taboo area?"

"I'm sorry."

"So am I."

In the taxi, he turned to look at her, not satisfied by the direction of the evening. She had turned up the collar of her fur and dropped her chin so he couldn't observe her expression. "Gloria, you and I have known each other a very long time. We grew up together; we're part of each other's history. That's important to me. Somewhere along the years, we lost the ability to trust each other. I'd like to change that."

"Oh Gardner." The genuine hopelessness in her voice surprised and troubled him. "So much has happened."

"Tell me about it. Talk to me, Gloria. Tell me what's happened that is so terrible you and I can't be friends because of it."

"We'll always be friends. It's just . . ." But she wouldn't finish the thought or explain further.

At the door to her town house, he touched her shoulders and turned her to face him. "I'm going to put this friendship to the test. Will you have dinner with me again tomorrow night?"

"That isn't fair. I have work to finish, meetings, appointments—"

"Will you have dinner with me tomorrow? As proof of friendship?"

"Gardner!"

"Will you?" He smiled, watching a struggle ensue behind her eyes. "How can I believe your protests of friendship if you won't see me?"

"Dammit. All right." Finally, she gave him a smile of resignation. "But these are unfair tactics. No wonder you've beaten our South American companies into submission. You're relentless."

"Absolutely."

He wanted to kiss her but he understood their relationship balanced on a fragile edge. Instead, he touched his lips to her forehead and made himself walk away.

Immediately Gloria understood she had been outmaneuvered. Having capitulated once, she couldn't reasonably refuse to see Gardner again. And there was no acceptable reason short of the truth that he would accept. The truth was out of the question. She told herself she had no choice, not really; she told herself she continued to see him only with reluctance. But she was aware of being happier than she had been in longer than she could remember.

Was that so wrong? She turned the thought in her mind, wondering if she was indulging in self-pity or if she sought to rationalize an act of folly. Still—didn't she deserve to be happy even if for a brief period? Other women her age were married and building homes and families. They had time for lunches with friends, for vacations with their husbands. Whereas all Gloria did was work. Even when she attended social events she used them as an opportunity to solicit new clients. Her life centered fully on business, either on behalf of Home Limited or Nestor Brothers.

Surely, she had earned a few weeks with Gardner. When he returned to South America, she would return to the frantic schedule she considered normal.

Turning from the ballet on stage, Gardner whispered in her ear. "What are you thinking?"

"I'm trying to justify being here with you instead of at the office working on the Connecticut Public Service offering."

"All work and no play . . . did you remember that in your list of justifications?"

"It was first on the list."

She pressed his arm and smiled, liking him, liking being here with him. And knowing it was sheer madness. To be with her, Gardner acted against his father's wishes. Gloria didn't need to be told Win Durant would object strenuously to Gardner seeing her. Gardner was not the type of man to seek parental approval, and he was not the type to allow anyone to dictate his life in any case, but she knew it wasn't a pleasant situation. Twice their photographs had been featured in *W*, and they had been mentioned in Suzy's column. Win Durant would have seen the photographs and he would have responded with a barrage of sarcasm.

In her case, she knew she was playing with fire. She was attempting to balance her attraction to Gardner against her knowledge that a continuing relationship was impossible. Too many secrets lay between them—her secrets. Secrets that could tear apart the fabric of Gardner's life.

But she couldn't stop seeing him, not yet. Something inside, empty for too long, hungered for Gardner Durant's strength and durability, for his quick intelligence and quiet humor. There was comfort in being with someone who knew her history, to whom she did not have to explain herself, someone who accepted her without expectations or judgment. When she was with Gardner, she was less conscious of being a Von Marron and more aware of being a woman. The difference made her blossom.

Outside the theater, he cupped her elbow in his palm and

smiled down at her. She drew a quick breath at the desire darkening his eyes. "Will you join me for a nightcap in my suite?"

"You're at the Plaza Athénée, aren't you?" It was a stalling question. She understood what he was asking, and had known this moment would come. Whenever she thought ahead to the inevitability, her mind had shied from a decision. But she wanted to go with him. God, she wanted to lie in his arms and love him. Recently, it was all she thought about, every time he looked at her, whenever they accidentally touched.

"I'll be returning to Rio next week, Gloria."

Next week? Dismay shortened her breath. Their time together had sped past. When she was with him it seemed as if they had forever, as if this golden autumn was endless and magical and given to them to share and enjoy for as long as they wished. Until the tensions building between them erupted in a preordained explosion.

Like adolescents in the grip of an irresistible force, they had stolen moments from work to share a hasty lunch, or a quick trip to the Museum of Modern Art or to the Frick, taking guilty pleasure in the escape to each other's company. At Gardner's suggestion, they had played at being tourists in their city. They visited Lady Liberty, explored Chinatown, toured the Met. They did things they had not done since childhood, as awed now as they had been then. And for the first time in years, Gloria had felt at peace with herself. All the dark emotions, all the memories that drove her, that obsessed her, slipped to a far recess in her mind, and for a few weeks she became the young woman she might have been. At ease with herself, almost carefree, shining in the light she saw reflected in Gardner's eyes.

She loved him. She had always loved him.

Wetting her lips, she stared at his mouth and felt dizzy with wanting him. "Yes," she whispered. "Oh yes."

Theatergoers broke around them as he examined her expression. When he saw what he needed to see, Gardner embraced her tightly and murmured against her hair. "I've wanted you for so damned long."

The warm length of his body pressed to hers sent a tremble through her and she suddenly felt as weak-kneed as a teenager. "Find our driver," she whispered against his collar.

They didn't speak in the car, there was no necessity. They sat facing each other, their hands loosely intertwined on the seat between them. She studied the curve of his lips, the intensity in his eyes, and she felt the sexuality crackling between them.

The moment he closed the door to his suite, he drew her into his arms, his mouth hard and hungry on hers. She felt his urgency and responded with her own urgent touches and whispers.

"Do you want a drink?" he asked, his voice thick with desire.

"Brandy." Her response was automatic, unthinking, a flashback to her small apartment at Cambridge where this unfinished business had begun. A drink was the last thing she wanted.

Watching her as she removed her fur, he dialed room service. "This is Gardner Durant in suite 1077. Please send up a bottle of your best brandy." He covered the mouthpiece. "Are you hungry?"

"Very," she said, teasing him. She kissed his ear, ran her fingertip over his lips.

"Just brandy," he said into the phone, watching her. "And make that a rush order."

The moment he hung up the phone, she stepped into his arms, running her hand inside his jacket. "It seems like we've waited a lifetime." Shaking fingers traced his jawline, his temples, his eyelids.

The heel of his palm pressed the soft slope of her breast, and a sound of longing sighed in her ear. "Where the hell is that waiter?"

Wrapping her hands around his neck, she laughed up at him. "Forget the drinks."

"Darling, I'd love to. But the moment I carry you into my bedroom, the waiter will appear at the door." He kissed her deeply. "I don't want any interruptions." After glancing at his watch, he returned to the phone and dialed the concierge. "This is Gardner Durant in suite 1077. I wish to report a missing person. This is a matter of extreme urgency."

Gloria burst into delighted laughter as he grinned at her.

"Yes, my friend and I are very concerned. One of your room service waiters left the kitchen for our room some time ago and hasn't been seen since. Yes, thank you. I appreciate it. Please let us know if you locate him."

"You're very special, do you know that?" Gloria asked, pressing her forehead to his shoulder. He could have telephoned the kitchen and complained; instead he had made his point with humor rather than anger. Before she could lift her mouth to his, a knock sounded at the door.

The concierge carried a tray inside. Murmuring apologies, he placed the brandy on the table before the sofa and backed out of the room. "We're so sorry for any inconvenience, Mr. Durant. Please accept this with the hotel's compliments."

"Did you locate our missing waiter?"

"I'm certain he'll turn up." The concierge bobbed his head at Gloria and murmured another apology. "Usually we—"

"We understand. Thank you and good night."

Gardner closed the door then turned to stare at her. "You are simply the most beautiful woman I have ever known." His voice deepened. "If you knew how many times I have imagined this moment . . ."

Crossing the room, he caught her up in his arms and kissed her thoroughly, then carried her into the suite's bedroom and placed her tenderly on the bed. His fingers fumbled with the buttons covering her breast.

"I love you. You know that, don't you? I think I've loved you since we were toddlers, maybe from the first moment I saw you in your crib." Laughing softly, he bent to kiss the swelling curve of her breast.

Gloria's breath thickened in her throat. Toddlers. Cribs.

"Oh my God," she whispered. Her throat closed against a dark, bitter taste.

What in the hell was she doing? She was minutes away from going to bed with her son's half brother. With the son of her rapist. Her eyes widened. This was wrong. She could not do this.

Pushing him away, she sat up abruptly and swung her legs over the side of the bed. Tears rose in her eyes.

"I'm sorry, Gardner. I can't . . . I'm sorry." Jumping to her feet, she turned her face from his startled expression and pushed at the buttons on her blouse. She couldn't force the damned things through the loops, her fingers shook so badly.

"Gloria, what—"

"I can't do this."

She heard his bewilderment. "Did I say something to offend you? Do something?"

"No." When she forced herself to face him, she saw his hurt and his lack of comprehension. "I can't explain, please don't ask it of me. I just . . . this is wrong." Spreading her hands, she appealed to his understanding even as she knew it was impossible. "I know we both . . . but I can't."

She despised herself and what she was doing. The look on his face wounded her with guilt.

"I thought—"

"I know what you thought," she interrupted quickly. "I'm to blame. I believed I could handle seeing you. I thought I could keep everything safe and in perspective. But I can't. Please don't call me again." Almost running, she returned to the suite's living room and dragged her fur from the foyer closet.

"Gloria, for God's sake. Wait!"

She could not bear to look at his rumpled hair, his bare feet, his opened collar. She loved him. And he didn't understand; he didn't deserve this. She felt like screaming her frustration and hatred. Life was so goddamn unfair.

The only thing she had ever wanted was to be loved. That was the thrust and focus of her life. Just to love and be loved in return. Gardner Durant knew her and still loved her. If Robby had been fathered by any man except Win Durant, she could have told Gardner everything and know he would accept her without judgment. She knew this because she knew him. But Robby's father was Win Durant. Damn him to hell.

"Let me go."

"Not until you tell me what this is all about."

Anguish widened her eyes. "I can't."

Jerking away from him, she pulled open the door and ran toward the elevator. Blinking rapidly, she managed to hold back the tears until she reached her town house. Then she sat in the darkness, still wearing her fur coat and gloves, and she bent her head and listened to the phone ring and ring.

"You look like shit," Mark Denton observed cheerfully, slapping a file on her desk. "When's the last time you had a good night's sleep."

"Go away."

After pushing aside a pile of papers, he sat on the edge of her desk. "Rumor has it the ice princess has tumbled. And the 'old friend' is phoning every few hours and burying Nestor Plaza in roses."

"I mean it, Mark. Get lost."

"The guy's crazy about you, and it looks like you're not too happy about saying good-bye, so what's the trouble? Do you want to go somewhere and talk?"

"Look. Thanks for your concern, but this is my problem, and I'll deal with it. Okay?"

"I get the message; you're saying it's none of my business. But Gloria, for a while you came floating in here every day looking like a million and glowing like a neon sign. Now you're working until midnight every night; you're exhausted and evil tempered; you look like a refugee from the workhouse. That's love, sweetie. Tell Uncle Mark all about it, and maybe he can help. I've been there once or twice myself.''

"I wish I had never told you about Carnation or mentioned the Pentico deal.'' She shoved back a wave of hair. "Stop hovering, Mark, you don't owe me anything. I'm fine. I like to work; I thrive on work. It's therapeutic.''

His steady gaze drew attention to the bluish circles beneath her eyes, the tiny lines of weariness disturbing her forehead. "I used to believe that tough-guy crap, Von Marron. In fact, ninety percent of the people around here think you're the toughest broad in town. But I know better. Give it up, babe. Call the guy and go live a normal life. You don't need this. At the rate you're going, you'll burn out before you're thirty. You know I'm right; you've seen it happen. This is no life for someone who—''

"Get out of my office, Mark. Right now. I don't need or want any instant analysis.''

He lifted his hands and slid off her desk, backed toward the door. "I'm only trying to help.''

"If you mean that, get me the spread sheet on the Clicko merger. I'm not leaving tonight until I have it worked out.''

It was after midnight when Gloria's driver delivered her to the door of her town house. Her mind was numb and she was stumbling with fatigue. Good. That meant she might sleep tonight. She desperately needed to sleep and obliterate thoughts of Robby and Gardner and Win Durant. Life seemed to have become a dark coil spiraling into nowhere. The file on her lap felt heavy and overwhelming, but work was preferable to pills. It was better to work until dawn than to weaken toward artificial relief. Tonight, she might have been tempted.

Stepping to the pavement, she nodded to the driver, then waited beside the car, seeking the energy to walk into the building. Cold night air flowed across her cheeks and she turned up her collar thinking it would be an early winter this year. The magical autumn had ended.

She saw him then. Gardner Durant was leaning against the side of the building, hands thrust deep in the pockets of his overcoat, watching her. For a brief instant, she closed her eyes. She lacked the energy for this. Finally, not wanting him to know how deeply the sight of him affected her, she lifted her head and walked briskly forward.

"How long have you been here?"

"My plane leaves in a few hours, Gloria." He looked as exhausted and angry as she was. "I didn't want to leave without learning what went wrong."

They stood close enough that the cold, misty plume of his breath mingled with hers, but he didn't attempt to touch her, and for that she was grateful. But he looked at her with eyes so like her son's that she felt a dart of pain beneath her ribcage.

"We made a mistake," she said, speaking in a voice so low he had to lean forward to hear. Reaching for strength, she raised her head and met his eyes. "We mistook friendship for something more."

"I don't believe that." He stared at her. "I love you, Gloria, and I think you love me. Or were beginning to."

"I'm sorry, but you're wrong. There's no point discussing this."

"The hell there isn't! I've thought about it. I've gone over every day we spent together, every conversation. Whatever sent you running out of my bed has nothing to do with you or me." Anger drained the warmth from his eyes. "This has to do with whatever is going on between you and my father. You're allowing some kind of crazy hatred or vendetta to influence our relationship."

The blood drained from her cheeks then returned in a rush. "We have no relationship, Gardner. Not the way you mean. We're old family friends. That's all."

"Is that really how you want it?"

"That's how it is."

"I see. Then I owe you an apology." Pride stiffened his expression. "I'm sorry to have troubled you, Boss Lady. It won't happen again."

She watched him turn on his heel and stride to the curb, favoring the leg that had been wounded in Uganda. A taxi appeared and he stepped into it without a backward glance, for which Gloria thanked God. If he had looked back, he would have seen her shatter into a million pieces.

Emotionally exhausted, she begged a few days off and flew to London, then drove to Lewes, driving too fast and not caring. She needed Robby, needed to feel her son's face pressed to her throat and his arms around her.

She stopped at Tilbury House to pick up Margaret, then drove to Robby's day school and parked beside the playground fence.

The children were bundled in bright shapeless snowsuits though the sky was a clear ice blue and no snow was immediately expected. She spotted Robby at once and smiled at his bright pink cheeks and laughing eyes. A familiar ache tightened her chest.

"I love him," she said quietly, not certain if she referred to her son or to the man he would grow up to resemble. She saw Gardner in Robby's dark eyes and firm, smiling mouth. The Von Marrons were there, too, in Robby's profile, in his slender body. But today as she watched her son she saw his half brother.

"He'll be four in March," Margaret said, watching as Robby tossed a large red ball to a giggling bundle wearing a blue snowsuit. "He asks about you, but I don't think you're entirely real to him, Gloria. It worries us."

Pushing her gloved fingers through the fence, she leaned her forehead against the cold chain link. The more successful she became, the more explosive her secret became. The scandal, when it broke, would no longer be that of a socialite heiress who had erred. The disgrace would be professional as well, a Wall Street scandal. She had enemies who would play the scandal to the limit and do what they could to capitalize on salacious headlines. No one played on the Street without making enemies among the other players. She had stolen her share of deals, had come in on other firms. Win Durant was not the only Wall Street force who would take pleasure in her downfall.

"I wish it was over." She closed her eyes, feeling the exhaustion. "Sometimes it feels as if I'm this close. Other times I know I'm not even in the ballpark."

"It will be very difficult for Edmund and me when Robby leaves us. We love him like our own." Gently, Margaret touched her sleeve. "But Robby needs you. And I think you need him, Gloria. You frighten me sometimes. You're so driven, so consumed with . . ." she let a shrug finish the sentence. "My dearest, can't you let it go?"

"No." Heat closed her throat. "I can't."

Win Durant had taken everything from her. She thought of Gardner and her eyes burned with dry pain. She thought of her father and wondered if her successes on Wall Street would have made up somehow for Remy. If her successes would have been enough to balance the disgrace of bearing a fatherless child. She thought of the mammoth trust funds Win Durant had set up for Chissie and Gardner, with money belonging in part to herself and her son. She remembered Durant denying what he had done to her.

"I can't quit."

That night Robby was allowed to have dinner with the adults in honor of Gloria's visit. Shy at first, then showing off with greater confidence, he enchanted her.

After dinner, he climbed onto her lap in front of the fire. "You smell good, Mummy Gloria."

"So do you." Four months ago he had started calling her Mummy Gloria. Margaret had become Aunt Margaret.

He waited until his dark eyes started to droop and his nanny had come to fetch him to bed, then Robby pressed his face against her hair and whispered loudly, "Can I go to your house?"

She held him so tightly he protested. "Not this time," she answered in an unsteady voice. "But someday soon."

It had to be soon; it simply had to be. The scandal no longer mattered; she had come to terms with the inevitable. If she knew Durant was crushed, she would sail through the scandal without turning a hair. It wouldn't be important. But she had to destroy Durant first. Depressed, she regarded the fire with a steady gaze. Tonight was one of the nights when her goal seemed so far away as to be almost unattainable.

"Things aren't working the way we anticipated, are they?" Margaret asked, bending over her knitting. "Occasionally I think back and wonder if we made the right decision keeping Robby a secret. Poor little fatherless lad."

"He has a father," she said bitterly, staring into the fireplace and listening to the click of Margaret's needles. Suddenly it seemed wrong to have concealed Durant's identity from Margaret. Dear Margaret, who had welcomed Robby and the disruption to her household and who did so without asking awkward questions.

She had carried the full weight of the secret for so long. Perhaps if she shared the pain, some of it would ease and she could find peace with herself.

"Robby's father is Winthrop Durant."

"Oh my God!" The yarn spilled from Margaret's lap and the needle jerked, scratching a pink line across her wrist. She stared at Gloria first in disbelief, then with profound shock. "Win Durant? But he was your parent's friend. Your godfather. He was always . . . oh dear God. Not Win Durant."

"He raped me."

Speaking in a halting voice, she told Margaret all of it, looking into the fire so she did not have to see the tears in Margaret's eyes. Revealing the full story was not a bid for pity or sympathy. She was simply too weary to carry it alone anymore.

But she had erred. Telling the story did not blunt the sharp edge of her hatred or her compulsion toward revenge. If anything, reliving Durant's crimes strengthened her energy and resolve.

Book Three

1987

Chapter 14

$\mathscr{G}$OOSE POINT WAS LOVELY in May. Scarlet roses climbed the south side of the veranda, and the lawns resembled freshly trimmed velvet. Afternoon sun glowed against the house front, warming the traditional spring coat of cream-colored paint.

Gloria tied the boat at the pier, stretched, and climbed the steps to the gardens and walked toward the stable, empty now as it had been for a decade. She walked leisurely, taking pleasure in the warm breeze on her bare legs and the rich earthy scents of summer. Further up the beach someone was barbecuing and she could smell the sweet drift of woodsmoke. What she missed was the tangy, sharp odor of horses that had formed so large a part of her childhood.

Stepping up to the lower rung of the corral fence, she folded her arms along the top rail and examined the raked ground, undisturbed by hooves or groomers for several years. Most of her summers had been spent here, riding around and around, sitting tall and straight in her dark habit, daydreaming about blue ribbons and first kisses.

Smiling, she stepped down from the fence and faced the water rolling in the Sound. From here she could see the monument marking Remy's grave and the stone bench beside it.

Sadly, she could no longer remember Remy with any clarity. What she remembered were scenes, frozen into memory's unreality, where emotions seemed deceptively genuine but time and distance had blurred the faces. She remembered the turmoil of emotion during that long ago summer of Debussy, but when she tried to summon Remy's smile or the sound of his voice, her mind shifted to the Wyeth portrait hanging in the music room. The portrait had become her memory. It depicted Remy standing beside the grand piano dressed in white-tie, his expression youthful and solemn. It seemed so long ago.

Crossing the lawn, she approached the stone bench beside the marble slab and sat down, wondering if she had really known Remy, wondering if anyone really knew anyone else. In the end, Holly Drake had been right. Each person was alone.

With some surprise, she realized she felt lonely today. The moment she identified the source of her restlessness, she realized that she had been lonely for a long time.

Frowning, she looked toward the house as if Goose Point could dispel the sudden empty feeling. But the house was silent. No music floated from the windows of the music room. No sound came from her father's den or from her mother's upstairs bedroom. The stable was deserted and the beach empty. Biting her lip, Gloria dropped her head. So often in the past she had found Goose Point's solitude regenerative, but today she wished she could spread the lawns with one of Lulu Von Marron's noisy garden parties or hear Bobby's horses cantering up the gravel path, home from the hunt. Goose Point had been intended for noise and laughter and gaiety. So had she.

"It didn't work out for us, did it?" she murmured, looking at the slab covering Remy's grave. "The Von Marrons didn't turn out well. Mummy and Daddy withdrew from life, each in his own way, you gave up . . . and me? I've spent five years running in place." Tilting her head back, she offered her face to the sun. "I wanted the last of the Von Marrons to be the best of the Von Marrons. But success doesn't mean much if there's no one to notice and no one to share it with."

They called her a variety of names on the Street. The Ice Princess, the Von Marron bitch, the Whiz Kid. Whatever they called her, they said it with grudging respect; she supposed that counted for something. It hadn't taken long for word to get out that her bonus this year had been one of the largest in the industry. She had earned it through long hours, missed sleep, and by sacrificing any semblance of a personal life. She had earned it by bringing megafees to Nestor Brothers through her untiring efforts to beg, barter, or steal business from La Tourraine, Durant and Von Marron.

When all was said and done, had she wounded Durant?
No.
La Tourraine, Durant and Von Marron continued to thrive. If she had dented the firm's bottom line, it was a small dent. A fender bender. Insignificant.

So, what did that leave her to show for five years of fourteen-hour days and meals eaten on the run? Five years of concealing her son and seeing him only two or three times a year. What did she have to compensate for the loneliness? A huge bonus? She didn't need money. A row of tombstones embedded in lucite to commemorate her more spectacular successes? They reminded her of the blue ribbons she had once collected. As there could never be enough, the ones she had lost meaning.

Most important, had she moved closer to making Durant suffer? No. She had frustrated herself to near desperation; she had played every angle she knew, but Durant still sat undisturbed at the top of the pile. She had infuriated him, enraged him, maybe she had even drawn a pinprick of blood. But she had not toppled him. Despair clouded her expression. How long could she continue to batter herself when it had begun to appear Durant was as invulnerable as his legend?

The question was as insubstantial as the breeze blowing through her hair. She would continue forever. All she had to do to revive the inner fire was to feel the pain of loneliness. Or think of Robby. Or remember her father advising her to trust Win Durant. Then it was all there again as fresh as if the betrayals had occurred yesterday.

Closing her eyes, she clenched her hands against the marble bench. Occasionally she comprehended that her compulsion for revenge was consuming her life and slowly digesting the years. When she allowed herself to understand, she felt sickened. But she was powerless to put paid to Durant's account. She could not. Her hatred and her need had become an integral part of whoever she was, whatever she had become. She could not set aside her obsession any more than she could alter her history. It was.

William appeared on the veranda steps and cupped his hands around his mouth. "There's a telephone call, Miss."

Standing, she put her hands to the headache behind her temples, then she shook out her hair and moved toward the house with long strides.

The phone call was expected. This time, she hoped Oakbridge and Saunders brought good news.

Win Durant studied the man walking beside him. At first glance Alf Cowper could be mistaken for a Wall Street regular from one of the old-line white-shoe firms. The three-piece pinstripe suit screamed conservatism as did the fashionably scuffed shoe tips. He wore glasses, which Durant suspected he did not require, and he carried a monogrammed briefcase featuring a prominently displayed designer stamp. Alf Cowper could move through any firm on the Street without drawing a second look. That was what made him good.

"So. What have you got?"

Cowper waited near a park bench until a woman pushing a baby stroller had passed them. Caution and discretion were also what made him good.

"Fear is the word. No one knows who Levine and Boesky are going to name next. Instead of yelling fire, you can empty a building this quick by whispering SEC." Cowper snapped his fingers. "The way I read it, Drexel is practically out of the picture. They're so busy issuing statements swearing they didn't know what Levine was doing that business has almost stopped over there. Truth is, they're scared shitless that the SEC is going to turn over another connection to the firm."

"What are the chances of that happening?"

"Slim to nil. Everything I'm turning up indicates Drexel is clean, and the purge is about finished. Unless the SEC is sitting on something that hasn't leaked, everyone can start to relax. The big fish are already in the net." Cupping his hands around a match, he lit a cigarette and exhaled slowly. "One more thing. Are you aware someone is doing a number on you?"

Durant looked at him. "What are you talking about?"

"Oakbridge and Saunders is running an investigation on you. They're very expensive, very exclusive, and very good. Whoever wants to know about you is wealthy, has clout, and knows where to look."

Durant shifted position and frowned. "I want the name. Have it on my desk the day after tomorrow."

"Breaking and entering pays triple time."

"Get me the name."

There was little point attempting to anticipate who might be investigating him. Durant hadn't gotten where he was without making enemies. A dozen people sprang to mind who hated him enough to hand him to the SEC. Only one thing was certain: it wasn't the government. The SEC didn't employ private firms to do their legwork. Plus, he had already given a deposition regarding the trades currently under SEC investigation. He had come up clean, of course.

The entire insider-trading scandal was a fucking joke. Ninety-eight percent of the Street were pissing in their collective pants because ninety-eight percent of the Street operated on the thin edge of the regulations. Most traders would be hard pressed to explain how inside information differed from a legitimate tip or an exchange of information over a drink with a friend. There was no clean-cut black-and-white, only large gray areas. Violations occurred almost as a matter of course, and before the recent scandal, no one had given it much thought. Most of what the SEC and the newsmagazines labeled as a violation was business as usual.

Of course there were exceptions. At the top of the scale were men who knew damn well what constituted standard operating procedure and what added up to flagrant violation. You didn't pay a man to break the law without knowing it was a fucking violation. Now Boesky and Colquist were cooling their asses in jail. Colquist was cheerfully handing his associates over to the Feds and cutting a hell of a deal for himself.

Durant applauded his foresight in cutting loose. For the past couple of years Boesky and Colquist hadn't had a clue they were exchanging tips with Durant, and neither did the men who formed Durant's network. He was safe.

Years ago, he had put together six holding companies, each of which owned four other companies, and those dummy firms each owned another three companies. When Durant wished to act on an inside tip, he pulled up a random buy pattern on his personal computer and washed the buy through half a dozen companies which could not be traced to him. The orders went through three world markets, using a dozen different brokers.

Interestingly, several of his trades involved those currently under investigation. But because he had been smart enough to vary the purchaser and the site of purchase, no pattern emerged to flag his buys and sells as anything but coincidence. Moreover, he had filtered his orders through a maze of holding companies and thirteen different brokers, spreading the number of shares so no one buy was large enough to elicit unwanted attention.

The tip system was set up with similar care. The information passed through several informants before going to an answer phone connected to a number registered in an assumed name. Payment flowed back down the line in the form of a receipt showing an amount deposited in a Bahamian account. None of it could be tracked to him.

But someone was trying. And according to Cowper they were

sniffing in the right places. Whoever it was would pay with his balls.

Two days later he had a name. Gloria Von Marron.

Gloria accompanied her client to the elevator, then returned to the firm's private dining room and signaled the waiter for another cup of coffee. When Mark Denton dropped into the upholstered chair across from her, she lifted her head from the documents she was reviewing.

"You look terrible," she said, studying him.

"I'm trying to save the McClintock account and it isn't looking promising. I'll have a martini," he said to the waiter then shrugged at Gloria's raised eyebrow. "McClintock is a teetotaler, and if ever I needed a drink, this is the time. We're talking about six hundred thousand in annual fees."

"Do you want to talk about it?"

"I don't even want to think about it. Tell me about the great investigation instead. Has our government's little helper turned up anything interesting?"

"Interesting, yes. Useful, no." Durant's dirty little personal secrets disgusted her, but using them against him would hurt no one but Chissie. What she needed was a business connection. As she might have predicted, Durant had covered his tracks so thoroughly she couldn't prove a damned thing. Frustration pinched her mouth and she pushed her coffee away. "There's a lot of smoke, but no fire."

"Maybe Durant's clean," he said, teasing her.

"You know as well as I do that Durant is dirty."

"The stories are legend. But catching him is another thing. The old bastard hasn't been around this long without learning where to hide the bodies. If the SEC can't find them, you aren't going to either. Do you want the olive?"

"Thanks." Nibbling Mark's olive, she examined the David Hockney drawing above his head. "I really thought Oakbridge and Saunders would turn up something. I'd bet everything I own that Durant is in this up to his lying mouth. But even the most promising trails turn into smoke and blow away."

Street talk had it that Durant had been questioned at length about the Carnation trade. But that meant nothing; so had she. All she knew was that Durant was heavily involved in insider trading. Gut instinct told her so. "Oakbridge and Saunders keeps drawing a blank." She thought of the telephone call she had taken at Goose Point and how bitterly disappointed she had been. For weeks she had hoped she was nearing the end. She had fantasized about Durant in disgrace, in jail, and eventually barred from the Street. Dropping her head, she covered her eyes and swallowed the coppery taste of defeat.

"So what happens next in the great Durant–Von Marron vendetta?" Mark grinned, finished his martini, and followed her into the corridor toward the elevators. "Why don't you just arrange a shoot-out and be done with it? You start in front of Trinity Church because you're the good guy, and Durant starts at Water Street. Can't you just see it? High Noon on Wall Street. You'd look great wearing a pair of sable-trimmed six-shooters. By Valentino, of course."

Gloria laughed and took his arm. "Thanks, Denton. It helps to have someone to talk to. Not much, but a little."

"Liar."

"I'll have to come at Durant from a different angle. But not today. I'm due at a Home Limited board meeting in fifteen minutes."

The frustration rested in sensing the answer was there and had always been there. But she couldn't see it. Someday she would. The problem was, her somedays were melting into years. Feeling a sense of depression settle around her shoulders, she glanced at her watch with an unsettling sensation of watching time slip away.

Gloria Von Marron.

The name followed him like a goddamn plague. He heard her name lauded over lunch; she was talked about in his clubs; he tripped over her at openings, benefits, and private parties. Some limp dick in personnel—who no longer worked for La Tourraine, Durant and Von Marron—had even suggested the firm should attempt to hire her away from Nestor Brothers. Now the bitch dared to probe into his life. She had the effrontery to hire a team of private investigators to spy on *him*.

He knew what Oakbridge and Saunders would find. They would discover the blond interior designer he kept at the co-op on East Fifty-Third Street. Undoubtedly, they would learn about the client "parties" at East Hampton. None of this concerned him. Von Marron wouldn't take his sexual peccadillos public because of Chissie. And blackmailing him to prevent Chissie from learning of his extracurricular activities wasn't part of the picture. Gloria Von Marron didn't want money. She wanted him begging and pleading at her feet. She wanted him bleeding on

the carpet. She wanted him out of La Tourraine, Durant and
Von Marron.

That was not going to happen. Never.

Leaning back from his desk, Durant tented his fingers beneath
his chin and reviewed his activities very carefully. An hour later,
he smiled. Oakbridge and Saunders would find innuendos and
sidelong implications. But they would find absolutely nothing
concrete. Any trail they sniffed out would lead into the maze
and finally to a blank wall. If the SEC couldn't nail him, neither
could Gloria Von Marron.

Reaching for the telephone, he dialed Alf Cowper. "I want
to know everything there is to know about Gloria Von Marron.
I want to know who her clients are, how much money she makes,
who she's fucking, where she eats lunch, and what she ate. You
get the picture, Cowper? Every time she shits, I want to know
it. I want everything. I'll decide if it's important, you just get
the details."

Six weeks later, he tossed aside Alf Cowper's latest report
and decided Gloria Von Marron was the most boring, the most
frustratingly predictable woman alive. He didn't need Cowper
to tell him what she was doing right now. All he had to do was
glance at his calendar. Tuesday? Tuesday she worked out in
Nestor's private gymnasium from six in the morning until seven.
Then she showered, dressed, ate a light breakfast at her desk
and worked through until dinner. Dinner would be with a client.
This week the client would be someone from IBM or from Texas
Instruments. After dinner she would return to her office and
work until midnight, then it was directly home and into bed
alone.

At first it had astonished him to discover she didn't have a
string of playboy millionaires panting after her. After two weeks,
he understood it. The jet-setters were panting around her all
right, but she didn't give them a second glance. Christ, she
didn't have time. Occasionally on a weekend, she gave one of
the poor bastards a break and let him buy her dinner or escort
her to the theater or a party. But more often when she didn't
work through the weekend, she drove up to Goose Point. Sometimes she invited a man along, more often she didn't. She took
along a stack of files to keep her company.

The woman was a work machine. No wonder she was becoming a goddamn legend. Normal people with families and outside
interests could not compete with this type of single-mindedness.

He thought about that. Why would a healthy, beautiful young woman prefer business to pleasure?

Even on vacation, when she might be expected to cut loose a little, she played it on the dull side. In July when everyone fled New York City, she had flown to London and then driven south to a nowhere place called Lewes. Instead of meeting a married lover, which might have been interesting, she had stayed with a couple old enough to be her parents and had entertained herself by playing nanny to their five-year-old. Jesus. Her life wasn't even close to the glamorous image portrayed in the magazine layouts.

She worked like a drone, lived like a nun, and of all the exotic places in the world she might choose to play in, she picked Lewes for her holiday. It was the goddamnedest thing. There wasn't a whiff of anything useful in any of Cowper's reports.

He came within a tick of missing what was right under his nose. He wouldn't have noticed the discrepancy if Chissie hadn't received a letter from Gardner while Cowper's most recent report was fresh in his mind.

Chissie read him the letter after dinner. "When do you suppose Gardner will marry?" A wistful expression softened her eyes as she folded the letter back into the envelope. "I'm beginning to think we'll never have grandchildren."

"Grandchildren." Something stirred at the back of his mind.

"Sometimes I wish we'd been able to have more of our own. That's silly, isn't it? Wishing for children at my age. I'm too set in my ways to cope with diapers again. And tricycles and all the rest. Still . . . it will be nice to have grandchildren."

"At your age." He stared at her.

She continued speaking, but he didn't listen. He was thinking about a couple in Lewes old enough to be Gloria Von Marron's parents. A couple presumably in his and Chissie's age group. But who had a five-year-old child. He excused himself, put on his jacket, called his driver, and returned to the office.

This time he didn't skim Cowper's report. And this time he didn't find it dull. In fact, the report was an intriguing puzzle leading to some interesting speculation.

Immediately he focused on an item he had inexcusably overlooked at his initial reading. The car she leased in London was rented in a phony name. Smiling broadly, he released a sigh of satisfaction. The fictitious name indicated she didn't want anyone tracing her to Lewes. That indicated there was something in Lewes she wanted to conceal, and that meant he had her. Now it became merely a matter of unraveling the threads.

Reading slowly and meticulously, he looked for an outside meeting or for someone who came to the house in Lewes. Nothing. He found no hint of a deal coming together, no suggestion that her stay at Tilbury House was a blind to cover a business meet.

He started again. An hour later, he leaned away from the desk and rubbed his eyes. What had Chissie said that triggered a need to have another look at the report? The older couple and the kid.

Once again, he began at the beginning of the report and read through the pages. This time he didn't skim the accounts of Gloria buying the boy a puppy, or of Gloria romping with the kid in the garden, or Gloria pedaling beside him on his tricycle. Surprisingly, she spent a hell of a lot of time with that kid. Durant decided she was one fucking high-priced babysitter.

But there it was. Apparently she was crazy about that boy. Immediately upon arriving at Tilbury House, she picked up the woman, then drove straight to the kid's nursery school. Which impressed him as overdoing the case, as the kid would arrive home in an hour or so, and she would have seen him then. It seemed more logical to assume Gloria and Mrs. Tilbury would use the time before the kid arrived to gossip and exchange personal news instead of driving off to see a kid they were going to see in an hour anyway.

Bingo. He stared at the page in his hand.

She hadn't traveled to Lewes to visit the older couple.

She had gone there to visit the kid. Ruffling through the pages of the report, he highlighted each section dealing with the child. Yellow streaks jumped off the pages, forming about eighty percent of the report. Leaning forward, Durant studied the information and frowned. It was definitely the boy.

A moment later his mind flashed back. He remembered her saying, ''What if I told you a pregnancy resulted?'' Concentrating, he stared at the pages in front of him, trying to pinpoint the date she had seduced him, matching it against the boy's age.

Jesus Christ. He had assumed she was attempting to hold him up for the cost of a pricey abortion. But what if she really had gotten herself pregnant, and what if she had *not* arranged for an abortion as he had assumed? What if . . . ?

Swiveling his chair toward the lights winking on across the city, he reached for the bottle of Glenlivet on his desk and tipped it over a crystal tumbler.

It wasn't his nature to rush to premature conclusions, but he savored the possibility. Wouldn't the sleazy tabloids love it? Von Marron Heiress Reveals Illegitimate Child. Wall Street Princess Declares a Dividend. Jesus. He laughed out loud.

In the morning he telephoned Alf Cowper.

"I want you to return to Lewes and find out everything you can about the old couple and the kid. I believe I know the woman's maiden name, but I want confirmation. I want photographs of the boy. Anything and everything."

When this assignment had been completed, he would shift Cowper onto something else. Cowper should have picked up on the child, but he hadn't. On final reading, Cowper's report read like a testimonial to Miss Gloria Von Marron. Durant suspected the poor bastard was half in love with her.

He didn't have long to wait. Cowper's report arrived on his desk a week later. Robby Tilbury's birth certificate read Robert Winthrop Von Marron.

Closing his eyes, Durant rubbed the bridge of his nose. It was definitely her child. He had her in his palm; he could make a fist and crush her whenever he wished.

Some of the Tilbury's neighbors believed Robby Von Marron was the orphaned child of Margaret's deceased niece. Others thought the child was adopted. The grocer's wife believed the child was somehow connected to the pretty young American who visited regularly. Everyone agreed Margaret and Edmund Tilbury's fortunes had improved miraculously since Robby's arrival.

Margaret Tilbury's maiden name was Margaret Porter. As in Margaret Porter who had been Gloria's nanny for fourteen years. Everything fit.

Except the child's name. Why had she chosen Winthrop as her son's middle name? Concentrating, Durant attempted to place the sequence of events. At the time her son was born, if he recalled correctly, Gloria Von Marron would not have felt inclined to honor him.

Jerking upright, he blinked at the page in his hand. The cunt. She meant to pin this on him. He saw it now. The minute he died, she would announce her son, smile at the press, and claim she had named the boy after his father, Winthrop Durant. Two seconds later she would be in his attorney's office claiming part of his estate. Jesus. That was the plan; he felt it in his gut.

She'd trot out her bastard kid, swear Durant was the father, and contest his will. That was how she planned to reclaim the money from the partnership buy-back and the public offering. Through the kid.

He telephoned Alf Cowper. "I want to know who Von Marron was fucking six years ago."

"That will require some digging."

"I want the name of that kid's father. At least a list of who's possible."

It wasn't until he hung up from Cowper that he withdrew the photographs from the padded envelope accompanying the report. Shock narrowed his stare. For an instant he thought he was looking at photographs of Gardner as a child. Arrange the hair a bit differently, widen the nose a fraction, give the kid a couple more pounds, and . . . He shook his head. When he looked again he saw the Von Marron profile. Lulu's aristocratic nose. Bobby's smile.

This was not his child. No coincidence of coloring or vague facial resemblance could make it his child. If this was his kid, he would have known. If this was really his kid, Gloria Von Marron would have been sitting on his desk years ago screaming for a large portion of his fortune. She would have used the kid before now.

But she had named him Robert Winthrop.

No. It wasn't possible. He had only been with her once, for Christ's sake.

Gradually he relaxed, having convinced himself the impossible was indeed impossible. Once his thoughts settled, he concentrated on how best to use the information. After considering all the ramifications, he concluded the fact of Robert Winthrop Von Marron was too explosive, too marvelous to waste on impulse. Robert Von Marron was not going to vanish. He would still be there when the moment was right.

And who could tell? Maybe the bitch would get lucky. Maybe she would discover something she could use against him. If she did . . . He smiled.

He almost hoped she would find something just to give him an immediate reason to expose her secret. The headlines would be sweet.

Meanwhile, to cover all bases, he phoned his attorneys and instructed them to make absolutely certain that Chissie and Gardner's trusts were airtight and administered by trustees who could not be influenced or bought. He wanted men utterly above reproach, incorruptible, who would exercise their fiduciary obligations regardless of temptation or outside pressure. He listened to the roster of current trustees and nodded grimly. Tomorrow he would put Cowper to work on them. If there was anything—anything at all—in anyone's background to indicate that he could be levered, even in a minor way, that man was gone.

He wanted his legacy administered by men even he could not get to. If Gloria Von Marron attempted to break the trusts or come in on them in any way, she would hit a brick wall.

She was tacking close to the shore when William raised the blue flag to signal she was needed. Either she had an urgent telephone call or a visitor. As Gloria wasn't expecting any calls, it was most likely someone from the city. Swearing softly, she angled toward the pier. It was a glorious day for sailing and she hated to cut the outing short. The long Labor Day weekend had given her time to prepare her presentation for the meeting in Houston and still have a little time for herself, a rarity.

After securing the boat, she tied a short terry robe over her swimming suit and climbed the steps toward the veranda.

"It's Lewes, Miss. You're to call back when it's convenient. I thought you'd want to know immediately."

Her eyebrows shot upward in alarm and she rushed toward the phone in her father's study.

"Margaret—that is, Mrs. Tilbury—said the boy is fine and you aren't to worry. She said it isn't anything urgent."

"Thank you, William." Her shoulders loosened. An unexpected call from Lewes was always cause for anxiety. "Oh, I almost forgot. That photographer, the one who's made a career of stalking me—I saw him hovering near the hedges again. Call Sheriff Billington to run him off."

"The usual way, Miss?"

She sighed. "Yes, dammit. Take him some sandwiches and a beer while you're waiting for the Sheriff to arrive. The man must think we're crazy, feeding him before we run him off. Didn't you tell me he requested we stock Coors beer?"

William smiled. "Yes, Miss."

She shook her head and called over her shoulder. "Do we have Coors for him?"

"Two cases. As you ordered, Miss."

Laughing, she continued into Bobby's study and placed the call to Lewes. It was a nutty world.

"This probably isn't anything important," Margaret said

when she came on the line. Gloria's smile vanished and she leaned forward over the desk. Margaret wasn't the type of woman to imagine shadows where none existed. "A man was in the neighborhood last week asking questions about Robby. I learned of it today. Apparently, he said he was with an insurance firm, but that doesn't make sense."

Immediately Gardner came to mind, and Gloria's stomach cramped. Would Gardner investigate her life? "Can you describe the man?" As she listened, one hand covering her eyes, the knot in her stomach released. It wasn't Gardner.

"Do you think he could be a reporter?" Margaret asked.

"Possibly." Biting her lip, Gloria thought it through. There was no point sending William out to buy a pile of newspapers. If the story had broken, she would have known by now. Her phone would have lit up like a fireworks display with calls from people eager to gloat over the scandal under the guise of sympathy.

"There's nothing in the papers over here," Margaret volunteered.

"And nothing here." It didn't make sense. If a reporter had discovered her secret, no force on earth could have prevented the story from hitting the headlines.

"Lewes isn't the small town it used to be," Margaret said after a minute. "It's certainly possible the man is someone local whom I haven't met. There could be an innocent explanation."

"I suppose that's possible, still . . . Margaret, let's take Robby out of nursery school for a while. I know he loves school and his friends, but I'd feel better if we exercise a bit of caution."

"A small break might be welcomed. Regular school begins in three weeks."

"I don't want to overreact to something that is probably nothing. But . . ."

"I agree."

They chatted about the new puppy and Gloria's last visit and firmed her plans for the holidays. After she hung up, she sat for a moment looking out the window, trying to figure it out.

Someone could have followed her from London, it was possible. She had been living on borrowed time from the beginning. And once someone knew about Lewes, the rest would be easy. What puzzled her was the resulting silence. Silence didn't square with her knowledge of the press.

But if the man wasn't a reporter, who was he? Did Win Durant have something to do with this? She turned the possibility in her mind before concluding Durant couldn't be behind the interest in Robby. If Durant had learned about Robby, he would use the information to destroy her. He would have no reason to delay. Again, she would have known by now.

As one day after another passed without anything appearing in the newspapers, she began to relax. By the end of the week, Gloria felt a little sheepish about withdrawing Robby from school. Though she had assured herself she was not being an alarmist, clearly she was. She and Margaret had taken a handful of idle questions and built them into something menacing. Feeling foolish, she telephoned Lewes and asked Margaret to return Robby to school and his friends.

"I'm feeling a bit sheepish, too," Margaret admitted laughing. "Edmund has teased me unmercifully. Even Nanny is giving me sly looks. What's that saying about old fools?"

"Whatever it is, it certainly doesn't apply to you." Gloria smiled. Margaret was the most sensible woman she knew. "Better an ounce of prevention—if we're quoting old sayings."

Mark Denton passed her glass wall, and she gave him a dazzling smile. He stopped and raised an eyebrow.

"Good news?" he asked, leaning in her door after she had completed the call and hung up the telephone.

"No news. Which in this case—"

"—is good news. Look, Von Marron, we need to discuss the Charton team and the Houston trip. I'd love to trot along and watch you strut your stuff . . ."

"But?"

"But I've got a wife who's starting to look at me like I'm the Connecticut rapist. Someone who jumps in her bed late at night but is never seen during daylight hours. She spends more time with Phil Donahue than with yours truly. If it's all the same to you . . ."

"Sounds like you're calling in a chit," Gloria said, smiling.

"Smart girl. No wonder everyone around here genuflects when you sashay down the hall."

"If you can square it with Nestor, it's okay with me if you'd rather spend a weekend chasing Merrilee around the house than spend it working in Houston."

"I thank you. Merrilee thanks you. Our future firstborn thanks you. You are a prince among men."

"Go away, Denton," Gloria said, grinning. "Some of us have work to do."

"You're not nearly as tough as you pretend, Von Marron.

Beneath that bitchy power look beats the heart of a marshmal-
low.'' He gave her a thumbs-up sign.

''Denton? If you were thinking about getting into U.S. West,
this might be a good time.''

''U.S. West? I'll punch it up and have a look. You might want
to take a look at Purina.''

Smiling, she watched him go. She liked Mark Denton, liked
it that he didn't make sexual innuendos and had never hit on
her. Friends were harder to come by than lovers. For a moment
she thought about Mark's weekend in contrast to the weekend
she expected, and she sighed without realizing she did.

At the end of the day, she leaned away from her desk and
rubbed her temples. Then, after making certain everyone had
gone and feeling foolishly adolescent, she opened a heavy security law book. Two white rose petals lay pressed between the
pages. She touched the petals with her fingertip. Then, suddenly
irritated, she closed the book with a snap and pushed it back on
the shelf.

Chapter 15

$\mathcal{A}$CROSS THE STREET and several stories below, the digital sign on the Houston First National building flashed the time of day then blinked a temperature reading of seventy-nine degrees. The people flowing in and out of the building wore light cottons and summer linen. Briefly Gloria thought about the tweeds and wools appearing on Manhattan's Fifth Avenue then she turned away from the window and addressed the men in the conference room.

"Yes, we're seeing some anxiety. Shareholders are concerned their shares will be diluted by the new offering. Undoubtedly this accounts for the recent spate of selling and the subsequent down tick in price." She indicated the figures scrawled across the blackboard. "But we're talking only a point and a percentage. By all indications we can be confident the price will bounce back. Charton is a sound company with solid management and a history of strong performance. Our surveys indicate Charton's market is expanding and its future is bright."

"From what I hear, the Charton board is nervous. They're jumpy about dumping another million and a half shares in the midst of a sloppy market."

The speaker, Don Kubiac, sat at the far end of the table, arms crossed over his vest, watching from half-lidded eyes. This was not the first time he had interrupted with a challenge. From the moment the team from First Sequoia had entered the room, Gloria had sensed Don Kubiac viewed Nestor Brothers as an adversary. The resistance inherent in his flat tone and crossed arms confirmed what she had picked up during last week's telephone conversations.

"It may be to Charton's benefit to pare the number of shares offered at this time," she agreed, giving him one. "That's why we're here. To obtain a sense of Charton's current thinking and

239

to develop a game plan for all eventualities. Before we adjourn this morning, I hope to reach a consensus regarding what advice we'll offer if our advice is solicited."

Don Kubiac exchanged a glance with a member of the Sequoia team, then returned to Gloria. "Before we consider Charton's alternatives, there's another problem that needs to be settled. We're not pleased with the number of shares Nestor is off-loading on us. Plus, we want the first road show with the Charton people and the participating firms to be held on the West Coast."

"We can certainly discuss share allotments," Gloria responded. Her tone remained pleasant but cool. "I can be flexible on that issue. To a degree. But the major road show will be held in Boston. That point is not negotiable."

"I'm afraid it will have to be." Arms still crossed, Kubiac leaned back in his chair and gave her a lazy smile. Although he didn't look at his team, Gloria had the impression he was mounting a performance for their benefit. Flexing in front of the troops. "We believe the West Coast offers better weather and more convenient travel facilities. We feel the syndicate partners would rather meet in San Francisco than in Boston."

From the beginning, she had anticipated a clash. The only question had been where and when it would occur.

"We are not conducting the underwriting presentation for the convenience of the participating houses." She met his stare down the length of the table, aware that her team and his had fallen silent. "May I remind you that Nestor is managing this offering. Nestor will decide the site and the content of the meeting. Nestor will host it. It's our show."

"We disagree. Sequoia has agreed to accept nearly the same issue risk as Nestor. We believe we should have equal voice in where and how the presentation is made." His smile focused on her breasts, then dipped to her hips. The smile suggested he viewed this contest as a man/woman issue as well as business. "I'm afraid we're firm on this one, honey. We insist on hosting the road show."

What she did now would determine the course of the deal. Either she retained control or she allowed Kubiac to wrest it away. A tiny smile touched her lips.

"If you are intractable on this point, then we're deadlocked, Mr. Kubiac. Because I'm intractable, also. The road show opens in Boston. Period. If you can't accept that decision, we will excuse Sequoia from the deal." In the ensuing silence, she heard someone swallow. The Charton deal would bill over a million in fees, and she was taking a calculated risk that Kubiac would not pull his team out. If he did, the resulting delay would be damaging. Kubiac knew it; that was his lever.

His smile edged toward a grin. "As I said, I'm afraid we're dug in on this. If you don't bend, we'll just have to say adios. Now, that's not what you want, is it?"

"Withdrawing is your prerogative." Her gaze didn't waver, but her eyes narrowed. "However—if you do decide to pull out at this late date, I will see to it that Sequoia does not participate in another Nestor Brothers offering."

"Is that a threat?"

"Finally we agree on something. Of course it's a threat. I will not allow you to screw around with this deal or to delay it. If you do, there will be unpleasant consequences."

"You can't back that up." His smile shifted. "You don't have that kind of clout."

Letting him see her irritation, she pushed back her sleeve and consulted a slim gold watch. "We'll take a fifteen minute recess. During that time, Mr. Kubiac, I suggest you make a few phone calls and discover just how much clout I have."

"I'll do that, honey. I'll do just that. Then we'll see where we stand."

The Sequoia team rose and silently filed from the conference room. They did not speak until they reached the hallway, then Gloria heard her name mentioned followed by a burst of laughter.

P.G. Goad joined her at the coffee cart. "Don't worry about it. The guy's a prick." After pouring coffee, he leaned against the cart and toasted her with his cup. "So. Who's going to win this shoot-out? Have you really got the clout to give Sequoia the boot?"

She smiled and shrugged. "We'll know when they return."

"What do you think, Blume? Think Charlie Nestor will back our lady gun-slinger?"

Tilting his chair backward, Topper Blume crossed his ankles on the tabletop. "I don't know. We're sharing the books with Sequoia on three other deals that I'm aware of. They'll be royally pissed if we screw them over on this one."

"They're trying to screw us over. They're trying to grab control." P.G. studied Gloria. "Okay, Blume, I got five bucks that says Nestor gives Gloria carte blanche."

"I'll see your five and raise you five."

While they waited for the Sequoia team to return, Gloria rehearsed the next day's presentation to the Charton executives. "You've got the boards and the presentation booklets?"

Blume nodded. "In my room."

By this time tomorrow, the bulk of the work would be finished. There were still the road shows and the presentation to the Nestor traders, but the in-depth material would be complete.

When the door opened, the Nestor group turned. P.G. Goad examined the sullen faces of the Sequoia team, then grinned broadly and held out his hand to Blume. Blume peeled two fives from his wallet and slapped them into P.G.'s palm. They grinned triumphantly at Don Kubiac.

"Fuckers." He took his seat and scowled at Gloria. "All right. What time do we meet with the Charton board?"

No mention of the road show. No mention of the share allocation. "Eight o'clock in the morning." Her smile was cold. "My name is Miss Von Marron, Mr. Kubiac. Not honey. I suggest you remember that." She stared at him until he shrugged and looked away. "Now, if you'll open the file Mr. Blume is placing in front of you, we'll review tomorrow's presentation."

She had won. Winning was as instinctive a need now as it ever had been, but the taste of winning was not as sweet. That evening, as she stood to one side of a party at a posh River Oaks address, she wondered how she would have responded if Kubiac had won. Was winning really that important?

That she could think such a thing indicated she was more exhausted than she had realized. Winning was the only thing that counted. The only thing. What else did she have?

Don Kubiac walked out of the Charton boardroom and into the corridor, standing to one side of the chairman of Charton's board, waiting to speak to Gloria. When the chairman turned aside, Gloria nodded to Kubiac and raised an eyebrow.

"Yes?"

"What you did in there was . . . flawless. For a moment I thought the deal was going to go down. I thought we'd lost it. You turned it around." He gave her a lopsided smile. "I'm not very good at apologizing, but . . ."

Now her smile was genuine. "Your part of the presentation was seamless. Brilliant. But I guess you know that."

Kubiac groaned and rolled his eyes. "Gracious in victory? You make it hard to hate you, Miss Von Marron."

Lifted by the euphoria that followed a successful presentation, she nearly invited him to call her Gloria. Then she noticed his gaze flick to her breasts. That was a complication she didn't want. "Excuse me, I'm having lunch with Peter McAbee." Charton's chairman of the board caught her attention and lifted an eyebrow toward the elevators. She nodded.

"Until Boston, then," Kubiac said, watching her walk away.

Still experiencing an adrenaline high, Gloria moved toward the elevator and chatted with McAbee until the doors opened onto Charton's marble and glass lobby. She stepped out of the elevator, turned toward the doors and felt her smile freeze.

Peter McAbee strode forward, smiling broadly, extending his hand to the man crossing the marble tiles. "Where you been, boy? We haven't seen you in a coon's age. Step over here and let me introduce you to the prettiest little filly you ever feasted those tired old eyes on. And smart, too. This here is . . ."

Gardner Durant grinned. "Hello, Boss Lady."

"Gardner . . . what a surprise. What are you doing here?" Color rushed into her cheeks and she swore under her breath for suddenly feeling as flustered and off balance as a teenager. Seeing him unexpectedly cut the ground from beneath her feet, leaving her uncomfortably defenseless.

"Working, what else? Doing my best to keep you Von Marrons in panty hose and sable. How are you, Gloria?"

"You two know each other?" Peter McAbee thumbed back his Stetson and beamed at them.

"Somewhat." The warmth of Gardner's smile paralyzed her. "Actually, Boss Lady, running into you is a stroke of luck. I have some items I need to discuss with you before Home's next board meeting. Are you free for dinner?"

"My plane leaves at five." She didn't want this. Moreover, she had arranged for a few days of vacation and intended to drive up to Goose Point later tonight. Aware that Peter McAbee watched and listened, she made herself respond as she would have if her relationship with Gardner had been solely business. "Is this urgent?"

"I think so, yes."

"I believe there's another flight at seven-thirty," she said finally. Reluctantly. It meant delaying her drive to Goose Point until morning. It meant seeing Gardner alone. "If we meet early . . ."

"I'll send my driver for you at, say, four-thirty?"

An instinct she had learned to trust warned her to decline. Being alone with Gardner Durant was as sensible as leaning over a powder keg with a lighted match. Frowning, she gave him the name of her hotel and agreed to the time, regretting every word.

They had encountered each other infrequently since that final, painful night in front of her town house. Gardner had attended four Home Limited board meetings; they had run into one another at parties during the holiday seasons. A cool politeness marked their exchange of greetings. They each maintained a carefully neutral posture. When social necessity required a moment of conversation, they held the topic to business or indulged in small talk as forgettable as it was tedious. Afterward, she felt moody and depressed.

Promising herself this meeting would resemble the others, impersonal and brief, Gloria returned from her lunch with McAbee in time to shower, change clothing, pack, and check out of the hotel before Gardner's driver appeared in the lobby. She followed the driver and her luggage outside to an ice-blue Jaguar.

Following an uncharacteristic bout with indecision, she had chosen to appear neutral and businesslike. Her hair was twisted into a severe chignon. She wore a slim black suit with a boxy jacket, and she carried a narrow leather briefcase. It was what Mark Denton teasingly referred to as her power look, intended as asexual, distancing, and subtly intimidating.

When she realized the Jaguar was speeding in the direction of the airport, she felt tempted to instruct the driver to deliver her directly to American Airline's gate. Whatever problem Gardner wished to discuss could be handled by phone. Only when she considered that he would know she had sought the coward's way out did she clench her teeth and lean back against the seat.

"Driver, where are you going?" Leaning forward again, she frowned as the car swept onto the airport grounds. Either the driver didn't hear or chose not to answer. He passed a row of hangars and turned onto the tarmac, easing to a stop a hundred feet from one of Home Limited's jets.

Immediately, she saw Gardner standing near the ramp, talking to one of Home's pilots. When the Jaguar halted, he walked toward her, wearing summer khakis and a navy jacket with an open-collared shirt. She looked at his bronzed skin and smiling mouth and felt her chest constrict. This was a mistake. A terrible mistake. She lacked the strength to be alone with him.

Instead of joining her inside the car as she expected, he opened her door and waited as she stepped out with a puzzled expression. The driver closed the trunk of the Jaguar and carried her luggage aboard the plane. "Gardner? I don't understand."

"You agreed to have dinner with me." Smiling, he took her arm and walked toward the ramp. "I know a great little place in Cancún."

She stared. "Cancún?"

"I'm kidnapping you."

Angry color flared in her cheeks. "I'm afraid you've wasted your time and mine. I told you—my flight leaves at seven-thirty. I've made plans—"

"I phoned William. By now he's already canceled your flight and your driver. McAbee said everything is squared away on the Charton deal. Surely your other work will keep for a few hours."

"Your presumptuousness is absolutely breathtaking. This is simply not possible."

"The place I'm taking you, La Habituala, has the biggest lobsters you'll ever see." Still holding her arm, he led her up the ramp and into the plane. Resisting would have created a scene. After pausing to order drinks from the attendant, Gardner dropped into an arm chair and grinned up at her. "This is only a temporary kidnapping. After dinner Max will fly you to New York." Behind him, the flight engineer closed the cockpit door. Through the window she could see the ramp moving away from the plane.

"I can't believe you're doing this!"

Max Reinhart's deep voice rumbled over the speaker. "Nice to have you aboard, Miss Von Marron. If you folks will fasten your seat belts, we'll be on our way. We're estimating two hours and fifteen minutes flight time. Should have you there in time to enjoy a remarkable sunset."

"Better do as the man says and fasten your seat belt." Leaning back, Gardner smiled at her.

"Dammit!"

Recognizing defeat, Gloria threw her briefcase on the sofa, then shook her head and sat down. After the attendant brought her drink, she took two long swallows, then watched the tarmac rushing past the windows. In a moment she was looking down at Houston's treetops.

"This is outrageous." She glared at him, deeply resenting his assumption that she could be maneuvered so easily. Then she noticed the twinkle in his dark eyes and abruptly felt the weight of their shared history. This was exactly the sort of thing he and Remy had done to her throughout the years of growing up. A series of pranks with her as the victim.

Her mouth twitched, and suddenly she was laughing. Great

gusts of laughter that swept away the tensions of the last few days. When she could speak, she wiped her eyes and smiled, more relaxed than she had felt in a week.

"Gardner Durant, you are an impossible, infuriating man. You always have been." And one of the few men she had never been able to manipulate. So much for Mark Denton's theory about her power look. It hadn't intimidated Gardner or prevented him from wisking her off to Cancún. "Are you certain you couldn't find a great lobster house in Houston?"

"If you're not in the mood for lobster, I know a marvelous steak house in Rio. . . ."

She spread her hands and laughed. "No, thank you. Lobster is fine." For a moment their eyes met and held, then Gloria closed her fingers around her drink and looked away from him. Unaccountably her mouth suddenly felt dry, and her fingers trembled slightly.

Her powerful physical reaction to him amused and dismayed her. She wondered what Peter McAbee or Don Kubiac would make of this, Wall Street's whiz kid turning shaky inside because a man looked at her. A smile touched her lips. They wouldn't believe it.

Striving for control, she glanced at her briefcase, then at Gardner. "I believe there were some items you wanted to discuss?"

By the time they finished reviewing and discussing the material Gardner wanted to put before the board, Max was bringing the plane down over a thick carpet of tropical growth.

Leaning away from the papers spread across the table, Gloria crossed her legs and arched an elegant eyebrow. "None of that was urgent, my friend. I've been had."

"I wanted to see you."

She closed her eyes briefly, hearing in his voice what she both feared and wanted. "Dinner," she said quietly. Turning to the window, she watched the tangled undergrowth sliding past below. "That's all. Then Max takes me home to New York."

"Agreed. From this point, we'll play it however you like. With one exception."

"Which is?"

Each time she looked into his eyes a tiny shock electrified her system. She had not allowed herself to remember his physical impact, had not had enough time to strengthen her resistance.

"No more shop talk."

Business was a safe, painless topic, one that insulated her

from intimacy. Business was the focus of her life. He didn't understand that he was insisting she strip away her strongest defense. Or maybe he did.

"What on earth will we talk about?" she asked lightly. When he laughed, she added, "That's not a rhetorical question."

"Yes it is."

Gardner's driver let them out a block from La Habituala and they walked to the restaurant along a broad avenue. The peninsula air was soft and warm, humid and scented with flowers Gloria couldn't identify. Closing her eyes, she inhaled and smelled the sea.

"This is the first time I've been to Cancún." It was an inane statement, but one that didn't refer to business.

"Cancún is one of Mexico's newest cities. It doesn't attract the carriage trade, but it's building a solid tourist base." When Gardner took her arm, she stiffened, then made herself relax. "We're not likely to run into many society types."

Watching the people who passed them, a mixture of locals and tourists, she noticed loose cotton dresses, sandals, light jackets similar to the one Gardner wore. It amused her to realize she was overdressed for the first time in her life. Because she had to say something, she said, "Obviously you've been here before."

"Often enough that I bought a suite at the Fiesta Americana."

"I didn't realize Home—"

"Home doesn't. I'm funding a dig a few miles outside Tulum." When her eyebrows lifted, he pressed her arm to his side and smiled. "Surprised? I've been interested in archaeology for years."

"I didn't know."

He told her about it over dinner. But first she ducked into the ladies room and brushed out her hair, removed her boxy suit jacket, and opened her collar.

When Gardner stood to hold her chair, he noted the change and winked. Absurdly, his approval pleased her.

"The margaritas are wonderful." They dined in a garden setting, surrounded by candlelight and baskets of tropical roses. Bougainvillea dripped from overhanging tree limbs, the delicate fragrance of hibiscus lingered beneath competing scents. "Tell me about your dig."

Thirty minutes later, she understood she had made a mistake. There was nothing as provocative or as seductive as genuine enthusiasm. Gardner communicated his excitement for archaeology with intensity and conviction, and Gloria found it impossible to decide if her response was intellectual or something more physical. The occasional brush of his fingertips, the curve of his lips, the sound of his voice—with a mounting sense of helplessness, Gloria felt herself succumbing to the romantic setting, the warm night, and Gardner Durant.

Gradually she realized neither of them had spoken for several minutes. His intent gaze made her aware of the night fragrances and the warm tropical air soft against her skin.

"I tell myself you can't be as beautiful as I remember," Gardner said quietly. "Then I see you again and you are."

"Oh, Gardner." She closed her eyes, then opened them. "I've missed you." His large hand covered hers, and an electric current raced through her body. She knew she should stop this now while she still could. But she looked into his eyes, and her protest died in a soft gasp. The intensity of desire darkening his eyes, and the heat of his hand against her skin drew her nerves taut. She looked into his eyes and wet her lips, wanting him. Needing him.

"This time it has to come from you," he said quietly.

"Yes. I know." She looked at his mouth, met his gaze, and knew there was no turning away. "Take me home," she whispered.

There could be no histrionics at the last moment, no running away. But she didn't want to run away, she wanted the selfishness of lying in his arms and feeling him inside her, and she closed her mind to the recriminations that would come later. Later, she would deal with the consequences. At this moment she was caught in a trembling force that had been building for years. She couldn't and didn't want to stop it.

They did not speak again until they stood inside Gardner's suite at the Fiesta Americana. Pale moonlight washed through the balcony windows illuminating a simple Spanish colonial decor.

Gardner tilted her face up to his and searched her expression. "Are you very sure?"

In answer she lifted on tiptoes and kissed him. His tongue parted her lips, and his hands tightened on her waist. Later she sensed there would be regrets, but right now she wanted him. When he lifted her in his arms and carried her into his bedroom, she made a small sound against his throat.

Trembling with urgency, they made themselves go slowly, tormenting each other with the exquisite torture of delay. Eyes locked, they undressed each other with shaking hands. Gardner groaned softly when her silk blouse whispered from her shoulders and her breasts appeared, hard and swollen, ivory in the moonlight. His erection pressed against her naked hip as he lay beside her on the bed and gently cupped her breast in his palm.

"I want to memorize every inch of your body," he murmured, circling his tongue around her aching nipples. His hand moved from the valley between her breasts to trace the contour of her hips and stomach.

Gloria arched to meet the heat of his hands, but when he parted her legs to stroke the feathery silver, her urgency could no longer be contained. "Now," she moaned, the whisper a plea. "Oh Gardner, now."

She cried his name when he entered her, and her body lifted to his thrust. Yes. She felt him inside her, filling her, felt her body clasp and pull him deeper. "Oh, yes." They moved together gently, then with escalating passion until she heard the rush and roar of breath and blood pounding in her throat and in her ears, until her body trembled on the edge of a precipice, and tears of joy blinded her. When she came, his name on her lips, the explosion was shattering, stunning . . . and left her drained and shaken.

They lay in each other's arms, recovering, until Gardner eased away to open the draperies to the soft night breezes. A thin patina of perspiration covered his body, a beautiful athletic body that moved with unconscious elegance and economy of motion. Tousled hair fell forward in damp curls on his forehead. His skin was sun-darkened almost to mahogany.

"I love looking at you," Gloria said softly from the pillow.

Returning to the bed, Gardner stretched beside her and placed his lips on her stomach, her breast, her mouth. "I love you."

She closed her eyes, feeling her nipples harden and rise as he brushed his palm across the tips. "Please. Don't complicate things."

He stopped her words with a deep kiss, then placed his fingertip across her lips. "You don't have to say anything, I'm not asking anything from you. Just listen. I love you. I have always loved you. Nothing that has happened between us has changed that." His fingers moved along the inside of her thigh, and she bit back a groan. "Lie still and let me love you."

He began by kissing the instep of her foot, then licking a path to the back of her knee. When his mouth reached the tender inside of her thighs where his fingers had been, she moaned and arched to him and felt the fire of his skin against hers. A tiny scream choked her when his mouth covered her. When he finally entered her, her body was damp and trembling, and she reached for him blindly, gripped by a passion she had only guessed at before.

There was no further discussion of Gloria returning to New York. In the morning, she bought shorts and slacks from the hotel shops, a pair of leather and silver sandals, and a light dinner dress. Gardner insisted on buying her silver earrings and a silver looped necklace.

"I want to give you something. Plus, I doubt pearls go with this dress," he said, laughing when she protested.

She made no attempt to analyze what she was doing. The justifications and rationalizations would come later. Until then the weekend belonged to her and Gardner, forming an island in the middle of her life.

"You look rested and relaxed this morning. Wonderful."

Lush jungle growth encroached on the road. The highway reminded her of a gray tunnel opening through green waves.

"Are you suggesting I looked haggard before? Fickle man. Last night you said I was beautiful."

"You're always beautiful. Today you also look relaxed." Looking away from the road, Gardner glanced at her and lifted an eyebrow. "Where are you going?"

"To Tulum. To inspect your Mayan ruins."

"You know that's not what I meant."

She lifted a finger to the frown between her eyes. "We agreed—no business talk." Surprisingly, they had managed to abide by the agreement.

"I'm not talking business necessarily. I'm talking about you. What makes Gloria Von Marron run?"

Letting her hair blow in the breeze rushing past the car window, Gloria shrugged, tried to keep her voice light. "You know as well as anyone."

"I thought so once, but I'm not sure anymore. What do you want? What are you looking for?"

"Right now? A cold drink."

"Coward." They grinned at each other and let the moment pass. "We haven't finished with this."

"I know."

Everything had changed, and they both knew it. There were questions that now would have to be answered.

"But not yet," she said, looking out the window.

* * *

Max Reinholt would fly her to Manhattan in the morning. Gardner would return to Rio. They walked along the beach fronting the hotel, hands intertwined, watching silvery ribbons of moonlight ripple across the water.

"When will I see you again?" Gardner asked.

Gloria stopped at the edge of the water, letting the foam rushing up the beach wash across her bare toes. "I don't know."

Gently, he cupped her shoulders and turned her to face him. He studied her expression in the pale light. "A better question might be: Will I see you again?"

She drew a deep breath, held it, and exhaled slowly. The moment for truth had arrived. As much as she could reveal. "I'm sorry, Gardner. I don't think so. Not like this." Immediately, she felt the pain.

He stared at her in silence. "So what do we do? Return to seeing each other two or three times a year across a board table? Is that what you really want?"

"What I want isn't a consideration. I think you know that."

"It should be." He looked into her eyes until she dropped her gaze. "It's time, Gloria. Talk to me."

Stepping away from him, she moved down the beach toward the darkness and away from the lights flickering on the hotel terrace. Pushing her hands into the back pockets of her shorts, she faced the water and lifted her chin.

"I am going to ruin your father." She spoke quietly and with conviction. "If it takes ten years, twenty, I am going to destroy Win Durant." When Gardner said nothing, she glanced at him then turned back toward the dark waves rolling up the sand. The world, her world, came with the tide, rushing in on her. Her throat tightened with familiar hatred. "First, your father cooked the books when he bought back Daddy's partnership. I estimate he stole ten to fifteen million dollars from me. Second, before I agreed to the buy-back date, I asked if your father had any plans to take La Tourraine, Durant and Von Marron public. If a public offering was imminent, as my father had indicated, obviously it would have been to my advantage to wait. Your father assured me there was absolutely no possibility of the firm going public. I suspected he was lying, but there was nothing I could do." Her voice roughened. "You know what happened. He cheated me out of another thirty or forty million."

In the ensuing silence, she heard her pulse beat rising above the rush and hiss of the waves.

"Those are serious allegations," Gardner said finally. "Can you prove any of this?"

"No. If I could, Win Durant would be in jail."

"Isn't it possible this could be a misunderstanding?"

"Gardner, don't." Turning her head, she stared at him through the darkness. "This is between your father and me. I don't want you caught in the middle."

"Is that why you've never told me any of this?"

"That's part of it. There's nothing you can say or do. I don't want you drawn into it."

"If you sat down with him, talked to him . . ."

There was no humor in her smile. "Do you think he'd write me a check for sixty million?"

"Gloria—"

"No." The smiled dropped from her lips and she raised a hand. "Don't. I mean it, Gardner. Please stay out of this. If you think this is merely an unfortunate misunderstanding because I have no proof—you're wrong. It happened. It's a betrayal that cuts deep, and nothing is going to change that." For one terrible second she longed to tell him the whole truth. The words jumped to her lips—the rape and Robby. Swallowing hard, she jerked away from him and back toward the water, clasping her fists against her sides. "Leave it alone."

She heard him step up behind her. His hands ran up her arms and framed her shoulders. "I can't believe my father would do anything to harm you. Whatever led you to believe the stock buy-back was fraudulent can surely be explained. If you'll just give it a chance."

"You're wrong. I'm going to destroy him, Gardner. You need to understand that nothing will stop me. That's why I can't see you again." Lifting a hand, she covered her eyes. After a moment she made herself speak, striving for a calm tone. "I know you care about your father. You believe Win Durant is a paragon—"

"Wait a minute, Gloria. Don't tell me what I think. I've known for a long time that my father can be ruthless. I've heard the street talk. But I can't believe he could be Bobby's friend and partner for thirty years and your godfather, and then deliberately cheat you."

"Are you suggesting that I'm lying?"

"I'm suggesting there has to be an explanation."

Looking up at him, loving him, Gloria experienced a rush of hopelessness. "I know you feel compelled to defend him. I understand that. But I don't want to hear it.'' Feeling chilled despite the warm breezes, she pulled away from him and clasped her arms over her breasts. ''I shouldn't have told you any of this. I should have trusted my instincts.''

''You should have told me years ago. Then we could have straightened this out, and we'd be done with it.''

Tears of frustration glittered on her lashes. ''What do I have to say to make you understand? There is nothing to explain. Win Durant betrayed me; he stole millions. He has to pay for that. Destroying him is the only thing I care about or think about. It's the center of my life!''

''Darling—''

''Gardner, please. Don't patronize me. Don't tell me your father's crimes can be excused by a few pretty words. You wanted to know what drives me? I've told you. You wanted to know why I won't see you again. I've explained. That's how it is. I beg you to stay out of it.''

''I can't do that.''

Gloria felt the tension and weariness return as she met his stare across the dark sand. ''If you confront your father, he will only deny everything. He'll believe I'm trying to turn you against him. In the end, all you will accomplish is to create a breach between your father and yourself.''

''I don't believe that.''

''Then you don't know your father.''

''Now who's being patronizing, Gloria?''

They returned to Gardner's suite, undressed silently and lay in bed without touching, waiting for morning.

Sometime near dawn, as the sky began to lighten from indigo toward pale pink, Gardner spoke. ''I have a feeling you haven't told me everything. There's more, isn't there? I want to know, Gloria. Let's be done with all of it.''

''There's nothing more,'' she whispered, turning her face into the pillow.

She couldn't tell him. Even now she protected Durant from his son's knowledge. She had never hated him more.

Chapter 16

GARDNER WATCHED as she crossed the tarmac and mounted the steps leading into the plane. At the top of the ramp she paused to look back before she stepped inside. He waited until the plane turned at the end of the runway, raced past him, and lifted into the sky. Only then did he finally believe she would let the lie stand.

The plane banked to the north then curved out of sight. He swallowed the last bitter drops of coffee, then crumpled the paper cup and tossed it toward a trash bin he passed on his way to the parking lot.

Driving too fast, he turned the car out of the lot toward the archaeological dig northeast of Tulum. Eyes fixed on the road ahead, he recalled his conversation with her on the beach, seeking something in Gloria's feud with his father to explain her ongoing disappearances throughout the years. He could find no discernable link. Reluctantly, he concluded she had revealed one layer of herself, but not all. And in protecting or concealing the remaining layers, she had lied to him.

A mixture of resentment and angry pride formed his first reaction. Because he loved her and was willing to share with her all areas of his life, he had assumed a similar willingness from her. Although she hadn't spoken of love, he had seen it in her eyes, had felt it in their lovemaking. He decided he didn't understand Gloria Von Marron's concept of love; he could not comprehend love without trust.

This thought led to his father. The misunderstandings between Gloria and Win Durant were the key. Once that problem was resolved, he sensed the rest would fall into place. While he respected Gloria's desire not to place him in the middle of an unpleasant situation, he was in fact in the middle of it. He loved

254

them both. He didn't see his role as neutral, he saw it as an obligation to resolve the difficulties.

The dirt road that cut off the highway was little more than a rutted trail slashed through encroaching underbrush. Two miles of bone-jarring road led Gardner to the clearing where he parked near a line of dust-powdered rental cars leased by Colorado University. Beyond the roped-off area to his right, Professor Addleman reconstructed Mayan methods of island farming. To his left, a crew of students labored in the heat to clear a small crumbling temple from centuries of decay and jungle growth.

Professor William Greene removed his hat and wiped a kerchief across his balding head. He smiled and extended a hand. "Come to help?"

"For a few hours. I'm returning to Rio later this evening. How's it progressing?"

"Slowly."

Some of the ruins among the multitude dotting the Yucatan peninsula were archaeologically important; some were not. At this point in the dig there was no valid method to determine if the emerging temple would add a significant piece of information to the overall puzzle.

After a brief hesitation, Gardner turned away from the students painstakingly plying their brushes to a tumble of fallen stones and instead chose a machete, then joined a group of laborers enlarging the perimeters of the clearing. The work was strenuous and demanding, exactly the sort of exertion he needed. Raising his arm, he swung the knife and stepped forward, establishing a rhythm.

There was a possibility Gloria would never fully confide in him. He had to accept that. But could he accept a relationship where one of the partners withheld parts of herself? How long would he continue to love her, knowing she didn't trust him? Straightening, Gardner placed a hand against the middle of his back and looked toward the temple appearing layer by layer from the thick tangle of earth and undergrowth. He stared at it for a long moment, then stepped forward and angrily hacked at the roots and scrub until one of the students rang the midmorning bell.

"Who can say?" Bill Greene shrugged and added canned milk to a thermos of fragrant chicory coffee. "We peel history back one pebble at a time and hope we'll learn something new. Maybe we will; maybe we won't." He spoke around a thin cigar clamped between his teeth. "Maybe we'll never learn why the Mayans abandoned the Yucatan."

Gardner tipped the thermos over his cup. "Or maybe there's a city out there buried under centuries of scrub and pine and dirt that holds all the answers."

They had repeated the conversation a dozen times during the past three years. Gardner tasted his coffee, winced at its strength, then stretched his neck against his hand. He thought about the hidden cities, slumbering beneath the debris of centuries. "Secrets. Mysteries. It drives a person crazy."

"We have to accept that we may never discover all the answers. Still . . . look at it." Shifting the cigar to the corner of his mouth, Bill Greene waved a sun-blackened hand toward the temple. "The magnificence outweighs the questions. Doesn't it? You and I are the same, Gardner. Even if we knew for a certainty the questions would never be answered, we'd still be here. Because of the sheer beauty and magnificence. Because this is part of mankind's history and you and I stand in awe of history. Our history must be preserved and protected." He laughed. "Plus, you and I hate secrets. If there is a chance, even a small chance, that this temple might solve one of the mysteries, expose one of the secrets, I'll keep breaking my back and you'll keep pouring money into the project."

Smiling, Gardner propped his elbows on his knees and cradled his cup between his hands.

He gazed up at the emerging temple stones and understood he would not be returning to Rio tonight.

The weather in New York City was mild and pleasant, resembling late summer more than autumn. Having slept on the plane, Gardner walked across the tarmac to the waiting limousine feeling refreshed and confident in the decisions he had made. Before entering the car, he paused to glance toward Manhattan's skyline and relish being home. In spite of the traffic congestion, the crime, the sense of living life on fast forward, New York City was the pulse beat of the world and the place he loved best. He felt the excitement the moment he stepped off a plane.

He had known always that he would return. Since Walt Tobler's heart attack in May, Walt had been talking seriously about retirement. Home's board had asked Gardner to accept the presidency upon Walt's retirement. It was time.

His internal clock signaled the moment had arrived to return home. It was time to accept the office with the wrap-around windows, time to settle his personal affairs. It was time to reach an understanding with Gloria and plan their future, or put the relationship to rest.

The limousine delivered him to the door of La Tourraine, Durant and Von Marron.

"Gardner!" Lucille Ivory's penciled eyebrows soared, then came together with her broad smile. "Is your father expecting you? He didn't say a word, and I have him scheduled for—"

"This is strictly spur of the moment. If he's tied up, I can return later."

"We'll see. Guess who's here," Lucille called, opening Durant's office door and leaning inside. She waved Gardner forward. "I imagine you'll want lunch canceled. John Peterson can fill in with the Shearson people." She studied Durant's expression. "Or Will Summit."

"Get Summit," Durant said.

Gardner gripped his father's hand. During the past year Win Durant's hair had turned almost entirely white. His face was deeply seamed beneath a sun-lamp tan. Photographs did not do him justice. In a recent spread in the *Times Sunday Magazine*, Durant's blunt features gazed out at the reader with a deceptively bland expression. One had to meet Win Durant personally to feel the electric vitality in his dark eyes or the impact of authority and power that were as much a part of him as the lavish office and the figures scrolling across the screens of his desk terminal.

"Am I catching you at a bad time?"

"As a matter of fact . . ." Durant glanced at the papers spread across his desk. "But I can manage lunch if we do it here and if Lucille can shift the Shearson people." He smiled. "You know Wall Street. If you're not running from one meeting to the next, you're malingering. What brings you to town?"

"Let's save that for lunch." Pushing back his cuff, Gardner consulted his watch. "I have an appointment with Walt Tobler in his office. Then I'll meet you here about twelve-thirty. Is that agreeable?"

They chatted a moment longer, speaking of inconsequential matters, then Gardner left and Durant frowned at the papers scattered across his desk top. He made a sound of disgust and pushed back in his chair. Christ. He wished Gardner were in the office next to his own. At this moment Gardner's defection seemed as fresh as yesterday.

Swiveling his chair, he faced toward the skyline and scowled. If Bobby Von Marron, damn him, had not seduced Gardner to

Home Limited, Durant would never have taken La Tourraine, Durant and Von Marron public. The firm would have remained privately held and he would not now be fighting an internal insurrection. If the firm were still private, the board would not be split and that goddamn John Peterson would not be politicking for Durant's seat and title. Going public had made him a target in his own fucking firm.

In the end, he would win, of course. John Peterson would find his ass on the street, and those who supported him would follow. The point was who had the power and who lost it. The point was winning. After a certain amount, money was no longer an issue. Money was only an indication of the player's status. It wasn't how many chips one had, it was what and whom one bought with them.

He passed a hand over his eyes. Gardner should have been here. It should have been Gardner, not John Peterson vying for managing director. Then he would not have entire departments frozen, waiting to see which way the wind blew. He would not have secondary shoot-outs occurring in the corridors. Or men staking career ambitions on himself or John Peterson, and consequently so paralyzed with anxiety they couldn't manage a whorehouse in Nevada if the deed was handed to them.

What infuriated him most was knowing that while he and John Peterson battled for the throne, the king's soldiers sat around the trading room playing with themselves instead of staying on top of business. Internal rumors ruled the day. In every department the hotshot superstars were too busy exchanging gossip to bother with business. He was astonished the press hadn't picked up on the internal strife, particularly as La Tourraine, Durant and Von Marron had taken a brutal beating in the bond market during the last few months. At last count the firm's losses were approaching forty million.

He scrubbed his eyes. Peterson had him so wrapped and tangled in political horseshit that he didn't have a minute to spare for anything else.

Briefly, Durant considered canceling the lunch with Gardner. He was in no mood for light chitchat. Before he had firmed the decision, Lucille buzzed to announce Gardner was waiting in her office.

He pinched the bridge of his nose. So, why the hell not? Like everyone else, he was too distracted to accomplish anything constructive.

They ordered drinks in the firm's private dining room, discussed the mild weather, today's headlines, and Gardner inquired about business. Durant refrained from glancing at his wristwatch. "It's a bull market. Business is good."

"From what I'm hearing, it might be time to batten down the hatches. The dollar is soft; foreign investors are grabbing U.S. assets. There's some uneasiness regarding the West Germans—whether they'll abide by the Louvre Accord."

Durant's impulse was to laugh out loud. What did Gardner know about financial accords? Granted, Gardner's position with Home Limited provided him enviable access to government heads, state departments, and industry's high rollers. But Durant hardly imagined the resultant conversations centered on the world's capital markets.

If a turnaround was in the making as Gardner suggested, Durant would have known long before his son, and he would have clamped a lid on every department. Peterson didn't have him so disconcerted that he would overlook the obvious. But Gardner was wrong.

"I think we have things well in hand," Durant commented dryly. If he sounded superior and a bit pompous, he had earned that right. "So, how long will you be in town?"

"I'm leaving tonight, but I'll return in about a week." Gardner paused. "I've decided to accept the offer of Home's presidency. I'll need a week to clean up a few items in Rio, then I'll take the office next to Walt's. Walt intends to retire next fall. Until then, I'll serve under his direction."

"Congratulations," Durant said finally. The words tasted like ashes. "Have you told your mother you'll be coming home?"

"I'll see her before I leave tonight."

Durant pressed his fingertips to his temple. Years ago he had glimpsed this moment on the horizon. His son sitting in the president's seat at Home Limited, devoting his life to enriching the Von Marron coffers, to running the Von Marron company and cleaning up the Von Marron messes. Even though he had seen it coming, the reality sickened him.

"I spent some time with Gloria recently. I'd like to talk to you about it."

"Like father, like son," he said softly, staring at his son. "First I carried the Von Marron robes, now it's your turn. Jesus Christ."

"I think we should discuss the misunderstandings between you and Gloria."

"What?" His thoughts came down hard on what his son was

saying. At once he grasped this was the purpose for today's lunch. "What did she tell you?"

"Enough that it's apparent a series of serious miscommunications have occurred, probably on both sides."

Leaning forward, Gardner spoke quietly and earnestly, recalling years of shared history, friendships, and partnerships. He spoke of families as interwoven as rope, of the tragedy of watching a lifelong relationship unravel. Durant endured it as long as he could before he exploded.

"That's enough! What you have overlooked in this touching saga is the degree of inequality. What did Bobby Von Marron ever contribute to this holy friendship? This sacred partnership you speak of? Nothing." His brow lowered, and his eyes narrowed to slits. "I built La Tourraine, Durant and Von Marron. I took this firm from a hole-in-the-wall, shit outfit and built it into a powerhouse. When Kennedy or Johnson or Reagan wanted to speak to an investment banker, did they telephone Bobby Von Marron? Christ, no! It was Win Durant on the other end of the line. Bobby Von Marron attended the White House parties, but he didn't do the deals. He couldn't even manage his own screwed-up life. Who cleaned up the mess after Whitehall's death? Who smoothed it over when Remy blew his brains across a wall? Who made the arrangements for Lulu to enter the world's most exclusive nuthouse? Who created a spot for Miss Debutante when she wanted to play at daddy's firm?

"I did. Win Durant. It was me paying off the newspapers to keep Lulu's shoplifting sprees off the front pages. Or her half-naked romps through Bergdorf's. I was the one who sat on the Home board of directors all those years so the almighty Von Marrons could jet set around the globe. I quadrupled the Von Marron fortune. Me." His dark eyes glittered and burned. "And what did I get in return? Did I ever hear: 'Thank you, Win'? Did I ever receive a single token of gratitude?"

Gardner stared.

"Don't speak to me about sharing history with the Von Marrons. They wanted a lackey, and they got one. That's the history you want to preserve. Because of the time and the circumstances, I took the job, and I took their shit. It was a trade-off. I was the buffer between Von Marron and life's unpleasant realities, and in return I used his capital and his connections to build an empire that has become a legend."

A silence opened between them, then Gardner said, "Gloria

believes you shaved the numbers on the buy-back of Bobby's partnership.''

Durant's laugh was explosive and ugly. "She can't prove a goddamn thing.''

"You know about it?''

"I know what the Von Marrons owe me. Bobby didn't build this firm. I did. It was my neck on the line, my blood on the floor.''

"Christ.'' Gardner's face paled and his voice emerged in a whisper. "You're saying she's right. You did shave the numbers.''

"Don't look at me like that. Don't you dare pass judgment on me! You weren't there. You don't know what it was like to stand in the background and watch Bobby Von Marron bow to the press and accept accolades that were rightfully mine. You didn't have Lulu Von Marron look at you like you still had dirt and grease under your fingernails. I took what was yours and mine and your mother's. That's all.''

Gardner lifted a hand to his forehead and covered his eyes. "And the public offering?''

Durant shrugged. "It was always a possibility. From the firm's beginning. She knew that.''

"You would have profited equally if you had taken the firm public earlier. By deliberately delaying, you cost Gloria millions.''

"That's business. I'm not cleaning up after the Von Marrons anymore. I don't owe them anything. They owe me.''

Gardner opened his eyes and looked across the table before he slowly rose to his feet. "You did this to Gloria because Bobby and Lulu didn't say 'thank you'?'' Incredulity roughened his voice.

"The Von Marrons take what they want as if by divine right. Did any of them ever want something they couldn't have? Did they ever do without a goddamn thing? Have they ever expressed a single word of gratitude to those who serve them?''

"Stop. Don't say any more.'' Gardner looked physically ill.

"Come back here, goddammit!''

Without a backward glance, Gardner left the dining room. Through the doorway, Durant watched him approach the elevator, then step inside. He eased down into his chair and swept aside his untouched salad. Goddammit it to hell. Heat scalded his stomach, and bile poured into his throat. The look in Gardner's eyes, his expression—it was betrayal. Gardner sided with the Von Marrons.

And he knew whose fault it was. Gloria Von Marron.

Leaving the dining room, he returned directly to his office, striding past Lucille Ivory without a word, slamming the door shut behind him. Using his private line, he telephoned Alf Cowper.

"Get me an hour-by-hour schedule for Von Marron's bastard. I want it on my desk by this time next week." He wanted the information ready, in a file he could touch and see and contemplate.

Lucille rapped at his door, then leaned inside and gave him a look of caution. "The arbitrageurs and the head of trading want a meeting. They claim they're picking up some strange signals in the market."

"Fuck 'em. They say that every week. Tell them to stop jerking off in the halls and get some work done."

Gloria Von Marron had completed the work Bobby Von Marron had begun. She had turned his son against him. And for that she would pay.

She should have spotted it. She didn't know why she had not. Icahn and Sir James Goldsmith were stalking the streets in search of rich prey; she had come up against them before. Yet not once had she linked them or any of the other notorious raiders to Home Limited. Exhaustion, a crowded schedule, a simplistic assumption that hostile raids happened to other companies, not to Home Limited—whatever the reason, the possibility of raiders putting Home Limited into play had simply not crossed her mind.

"Stop beating yourself," Wilkie Tomlinson advised briskly. "It hasn't happened yet. I'm just cautioning you that it will."

"It's a miracle they haven't moved in on us."

"Home is cash-swollen and ripe. The firm ranks second in the primary mineral markets, and there's too much cash on the balance sheet. That, coupled with the understated values of oil and gas reserves makes Home a rich target. It's only a matter of time."

Walt Tobler passed a hand over his eyes. "The world has gone crazy. I've spent most of my life believing a profitable company was the mark of a man's success. Now, instead of being a point of pride, excess profit draws down the bloodsuckers and could result in losing the company. And what can we do? Hand it over and watch helplessly as the labor of a lifetime is dismantled and the pieces spun off like bits of lucrative garbage."

Gloria studied the financial statements and graphs spread

across the conference table, then raised her eyes to Wilkie Tomlinson. "All right. We're in danger. I'm not willing to hand over my company, so what can we do to protect ourselves? Can we install a poison pill?"

"That's one possibility," Tomlinson said.

"But you'd rather see us spin off the reserves?"

"Not rather than—in addition to. Home will be less attractive if there's less cash." His heavy white eyebrows met above a smile. "I'm suggesting a corporate spending spree. Diversify. Buy some shoe stores or some grocery stores. Acquire something in the high tech lines. I'm advising you to spend money."

Gloria laughed. "Shoe stores?"

"Whatever. Maybe a nice little Latin American country."

Walt Tobler groaned, then managed a smile. "We've got the money to pay for it."

"Better you spend the reserves than sit on your innocence and wait until someone like Boone Pickens moves in with a siphon to spend it for you. Whose pockets do you want to line?"

"Point taken." After collecting the papers on the table, Gloria folded them into her briefcase. "I'll put Mark Denton on this if Charles Nestor agrees. I imagine he will. There'll be several million dollars in fees before we're finished. Denton has a nose for bargains."

Leaning away from the table, Walt Tobler rolled a glass of ice water across his forehead. "It's hot in here."

"Are you feeling well, Walt?"

He ignored the question. "Gardner Durant was in my office this morning."

"Gardner?" Her eyebrows rose. "He's in New York?"

"He accepted our offer of the presidency."

Gloria bent over her briefcase so Tobler couldn't observe her expression. "I'm glad," she said.

"After he cleans up his desk in Rio, he'll take the office next to mine. I believe he'll be ready for the position by this time next year."

Glancing up, Gloria studied Walt Tobler's color and posture as he moved to stand before the window. He had aged considerably since his heart attack. She had heard rumors he was no longer as dynamic or as diplomatic as he had been just eight months ago.

She placed her fingertips on his sleeve and spoke with affection. "Walt, no job is worth sacrificing your health for. Do you genuinely believe it's a wise decision to wait another year before you retire? You and I both know Gardner doesn't require a year of preparation.''

"I'm a year shy of full retirement benefits." He stated it simply, continuing to look out the window. "I know it sounds foolish—I have a fortune in investments—but the heart attack frightened Susan. She, well . . ." He shrugged.

"Dear Walter. Do you think I'd allow you to lose any benefits if you wished to retire early? After all the years, after all you have done and all you have given to this company?'' Gently, she turned him away from the window. "Tell Susan not to worry. You'll retire with full benefits and a generous bonus whenever you feel you're ready. Whether it's today, tomorrow, or six months from now.''

He closed his eyes briefly then smiled. "Gardner could be ready in three to six months.''

"I agree. And the south of France is lovely that time of year. You and Susan could take the *Dahinda* and sail for a month or two, relax, and take your time about planning the future.''

Pink rushed into his cheeks, momentarily submerging the pale shadows. "Your grandfather would have been very proud of you. Your father, too, of course.''

"Thank you." She wondered if he was right.

Her desk phone rang at seven o'clock. She put aside her sandwich and drew a breath. It had to be Gardner. She had been waiting for his call since she had learned he was in town.

"I'm not sure I'm glad you're still at your desk, or if I hoped I wouldn't be able to reach you," he said. His voice sounded flat and tired.

"Walt told me you accepted the presidency. I know the board will be as pleased as I am. Congratulations.'' She dropped her forehead into her hand, loving him, hurting inside. As he could have telephoned his acceptance, the Home presidency was not why he had flown to Manhattan. "You spoke to your father, didn't you?''

"When you said you believed my father was guilty of fraud regarding the partnership share buy-back, I rejected the accusation as impossible. I genuinely believed this could be nothing but an unfortunate and unpleasant misunderstanding. I was angry that you could imagine anything else.''

"Gardner—''

"Let me say this. I believed you were wrong, absolutely. I also believed a solution was relatively simple. Once my father learned of your suspicions, he would be astonished, then angry, then finally anxious to respond to the items in question. In retrospect, this sounds embarrassingly adolescent and simplistic. But I believed if I brought things into the open and could effect a dialogue between the two of you, a forthright discussion would dissolve the misunderstandings.''

Gloria closed her eyes. ''I didn't want you caught up in it.''

''This is the most difficult thing I have ever had to say.'' After a moment of silence, he continued. ''You were right. I believe my father deliberately defrauded you of several million dollars on the partnership buy-back. I also believe he delayed the firm's public offering primarily for the purpose of denying you larger profits.''

''I'm so sorry you had to know any of this.''

She didn't have to ask if Gardner and his father were estranged. She knew them both; it could not have been otherwise. For one searing moment she felt a dark burst of exultation. It was Durant who kept her from her son; there was a primitive justice in knowing she had driven a wedge between Durant and his son. Imagining his pain made her dizzy with pleasure.

As Gardner spoke, her pleasure turned to dismay. She had never intended Gardner as a weapon. That had never been part of her plan. Whatever satisfaction came from relishing Durant's wound, it was not worth the pain she heard in Gardner's voice.

''I shouldn't have told you.''

''I pushed you to it. I insisted.''

''I didn't want you hurt by this, Gardner.''

''I'll be in town again next week,'' he said in a dulled tone. ''There are things we need to discuss.''

''It's too late,'' she said, guessing what he meant. It was years too late.

''I don't accept that. I have some things to work out, and so do you. Then we'll decide where we go from here.''

After they hung up, Gloria leaned forward and pressed the heels of her hands against her eyes. Gardner believed he had all the pieces of the puzzle, but he didn't. The center piece, Robby, was missing. They had no place to go from here.

When the phone rang again, she picked it up hoping Gardner had called back. But it was a voice she knew only by code.

''Who is this?''

''Gloria Von Marron.''

''This is D.C. I don't have much time, so listen. There's a bill now in committee which is going to the Hill next week. The bill will limit the deductibility of interest generated by the financing of a leveraged buy-out. Do you understand? The committee is also proposing a fifty percent nondeductible tax on green-mail profits.''

"Good Lord." Her breath expelled in a soft rush. "Are you certain? Is this firm?''

"If the committee accepts the proposal, an official announcement could appear as early as next week.''

The phone went dead, and Gloria fell back in her chair. For a moment she stared at the receiver in disbelief, then she tilted her head back and thought it through. The market had spent the summer climbing a wall of worry. And the level of merger and arbitrage activity had given new meaning to the term speculation. In Gloria's opinion, the arbs were solely responsible for the last two hundred point run-up on the Dow. If legislation limited the amount of deductible interest on a leveraged buy-out, merger and acquisition activity would plummet overnight. The market would react violently. She swore softly, then dialed the telephone.

"Denton? What are you doing right now?''

"At the moment I'm playing host to thirty guests. Friends whom I have neglected to the extent that I am astonished anyone accepted our invitation. We're about to sit down to dinner.'' She could hear laughter and party chatter in the background. "I don't mean to rush you off the phone, Von Marron, or to be rude, but—what's on your mind?''

She relayed D.C.'s information and briefly sketched her conclusions.

"Holy shit. Who else has this?''

"At the moment, just you and me. But you can bet the news is going to get out, and it will spread like fleas on a dog, friend.''

"Good God. Do you realize what's going to happen?''

Speaking in a dry voice, Gloria admitted the thought had occurred.

"Order in some coffee and some Chinese, Von Marron. I'll be on the next train into town.''

By the time Mark Denton arrived at the firm, Gloria had begun to pull her clients up on the screen, and she was running vital signs checks, examining cash versus stock components, studying her trading positions. Selecting two of her largest portfolios, she ran various percentage scenarios on the numbers, checking bottom-line figures in the event of a one hundred point drop, a hundred and fifty point drop, and a two hundred point drop.

She saw immediately that Nestor Brothers should dump its

entire inventory of Over-The-Counter stocks. She would speak to Charles Nestor first thing tomorrow morning to work out the timing. First the clients, then the firm—liquidity was the major concern.

"Do you honestly think the market could drop two hundred points?" Eating Chinese out of a sagging carton, Denton stood behind her and stared at the screens over her shoulder.

"I don't know. But when you consider everything—it could get rough. Very rough."

She didn't see Denton again until four-thirty in the morning. By then they had both compiled lists of clients they would begin calling at eight o'clock. Gloria's desk had vanished beneath two inches of printouts, notes, and files.

"How many do you think we can get out in time?" Mark dropped into a chair and let his head fall backward. Hours ago he had discarded his tie. His collar was open, his dinner slacks displayed a grid of wrinkles.

"No way to guess. But we've got a week to try. Maybe."

"Some clients are going to ignore our advice. They've had a hell of a bull ride—they aren't going to want to believe the market is going to turn south."

"Maybe it won't, Mark. That's the risk. Maybe we're reading it wrong." A headache spread behind her eyes. Admitting to a wrong guess was not a Wall Street hallmark. "It's possible we're about to advise our clients to take profits now and to get out, then the market will soar another two hundred points before the end of the month."

"You don't believe that."

"No, I don't. But those who rely on a crystal ball can end up eating a lot of ground glass."

"Not this time. It's time to harvest some of the gains." Denton yawned. "Well, I've done all I can do tonight. I'm going home and try to talk Merrilee out of divorcing me and then take a shower. I'll be back here for breakfast. Are you ready to call it quits?"

"I'm right behind you."

The fatigue hit her the moment she stood. But she welcomed it. Maybe she would be too tired to stay awake thinking about Gardner. And Robby. Or about the future.

Chapter 17

THE FIRST CHARTON ROAD SHOW was held in Boston on the
third Friday of October. Gloria and the Nestor team welcomed
the Charton executives, the comanagers participating in the offerings, and the potential investors. Then her team alternated
with the Charton executives and Don Kubiac's Sequoia group
for the remainer of the presentation.

As the Charton management finished responding to questions
from potential investors, a member of the hotel staff approached
the head table and gave Gloria three messages, each from Mark
Denton asking her to phone immediately. Unfortunately, the
messages arrived just as the luncheon plates were being replaced
with desserts and coffee. Hesitating, Gloria glanced toward a
bank of public phones situated outside the doors before she
checked her watch. She didn't have enough time. Following
P.G. and Topper to the head table, she stepped to the podium
and arranged her notes. The next fifteen minutes were hers.

Throughout the opening of her presentation, the meeting room
doors opened and shut with annoying frequency. She made a
mental note to speak to the hotel staff, who had been instructed
not to interrupt the presentation. Gradually her annoyance deepened to unease as the number of arriving messages increased as
did the number of departing bankers. When a messenger approached the podium, expressly against her instructions, Gloria
understood something had happened. The messenger murmured a word of apology then placed another note from Denton
on the podium before her. Pausing midsentence, she scanned
the message.

Disregard previous instructions. Interrupt Ms. Von Marron.
Large block letters followed. GLORIA. CLOSE THE MEETING AT
ONCE AND PHONE ME. URGENT. MARK.

Lifting her head, she cast a quick glance toward Don Kubiac. He sat to the right of the Charton management, staring at the message he had just received, a frown between his eyes. The investment bankers had begun a mass exodus.

There was no decision to make. Mark would not have advised drastic measures without reason. For one brief instant Gloria met Don Kubiac's gaze, then she leaned to the microphone. "This concludes our presentation, ladies and gentlemen." From the corner of her eye she observed Kubiac's expression, hoping she had read him correctly as she had just canceled his remarks addressing the timing and pricing of the Charton offering. He made no gesture of protest. "If further questions occur, please contact your Nestor Brothers representative or Charton's management. Thank you."

Generally the underwriters and potential investors would have lingered to speak to the Charton executives or to Gloria and Don Kubiac. Today, a unified rush erupted toward the doors before Gloria had finished speaking. The Charton executives blinked and watched the exodus with expressions of dismay and bewilderment.

In different circumstances, Gloria would have hastened to reassure her clients. But whatever was happening was widespread and urgent. Nodding an apology to the Charton people, she sprinted up the aisle. The nearest bank of public phones was occupied. Frustrated, her sense of alarm building, she followed Kubiac up the fire stairs to the next floor. Not surprisingly, the phones there were also in use. Without speaking, they turned back to the fire stairs and climbed to the next floor. Three phones were unoccupied. Leaving a space between herself and Kubiac, Gloria dialed Nestor Brothers in New York.

"Gloria? Thank God! The fucking idiots on the desk wouldn't interrupt the meeting until—"

"What's happened?"

"The Hill announced the proposed tax legislation. At last count, the market had dropped one hundred points!"

"What?" Needles of ice shot through her body. Her knees buckled and she gripped the shelf beneath the phone. Her pulse throbbed in her neck. "Oh my God," she whispered.

"The telephones are ringing off the wall. It's chaos here. TV crews are everywhere, here and downtown. Get back here. Nestor is calling a meeting of the investment policy group and the executive committees. He'll wait for you."

"A hundred points . . . my God!"

"Phelan's talking to Chicago. They're trying to get the futures in line with the cash market, but the DOT system is down due to the heavy volume, and the tape is running an hour late. The programs are hitting the floor like an avalanche and breaking all the limits on the downside."

"The tape is an hour late," she whispered, parroting it back. It was the worst thing a trader could hear. "My God."

"I've taken the liberty of asking Walt Tobler to send Home's plane so you don't have to wait for a commercial flight. Get yourself out to the airport, Von Marron, and get back here."

She hung up the phone and stared at it. When she turned around, Don Kubiac was looking at her with a glazed expression. "Jesus Christ!"

"A hundred points," she said, staring at him.

"That's not a correction—that's a fucking crash."

The man behind Kubiac dropped the telephone and stood staring stupidly at the receiver as it twisted on the cord. When he lifted his head, his skin had turned a sickly yellow shade. "I just lost five million dollars," he said in a dazed tone. "Just like that. It's gone."

Gloria recognized him from the meeting. He had been verbal throughout the luncheon presentation. Confident, cocky, almost arrogant. Clapping a hand over his mouth, he stumbled forward and pushed into the men's room.

"The party's over," Kubiac muttered, watching the door swing shut.

He couldn't believe it. He could not fucking believe it. Holding a tumbler of Glenlivet so tightly his fingers turned white against the crystal, Durant stood in front of his Quotron, mesmerized by the numbers and the size of the blocks being sold. The numbers rolled soundlessly across the screens. The buttons on his phone flashed crazily.

One hundred points. He had been through down cycles before, but not like this. No one working the Street today had experienced this kind of fall. IBM; down. Texas Instruments; down. General Electric; down. The advance/decline ratio was heavily weighted by the number of declining issues. The ticks were minus 1113. He waited for La Tourraine, Durant and Von Marron to flash on the screen. Down.

Looking away from the screens, he rubbed his eyes and ran a rapid calculation in his mind. Yesterday a share of LTDVM had sold at thirty-five; today it had fallen to twenty-nine. In less than twenty-four hours, his personal fortune had shrunk by millions. Jesus.

He drained his drink, noticing his hand was unsteady, then he poured another straight Scotch.

The problem was not today, he knew that. The problem would come on Monday. What the fuck was going to happen on Monday? Would the market rally, or would the collapse continue?

Goddamn the program traders and the smart ass MBAs who pedaled portfolio insurance. In trying to abort risk, they had created a marketplace which was superconductive. And from the time of inception, the Chicago option and futures exchanges had been nothing more than a form of off-track betting. Not surprisingly, this kind of wild-assed investing was going to finally bring down the market.

Behind him the door opened and he heard Lucille walk directly to the bar, drop ice into a glass, cover it with vodka, then fall into a chair.

"We're getting killed," Lucille said finally. "The desk has already absorbed twenty to twenty-five million in trading losses. That was the estimate at three o'clock. Will Summit is trying to get a final readout. It will probably take most of the weekend to sort out the carnage. What's going to happen?"

Hot white rage pounded the base of his neck. "We're going to get savaged. And there's not a goddamn thing we can do to stop it. I told Peterson we should buy a seat on the Tokyo Exchange. I told the board it would be the most important four million this firm ever spent. But the fucker persuaded the directors to put the money into art work for the dining rooms." A harsh sound scraped the back of his throat. "I hope the cocksucker is standing in there now, looking at his goddamn paintings!"

"At least there'll be a market for the paintings after today."

He passed a hand over his eyes. If La Tourraine, Durant and Von Marron had purchased a seat on the Tokyo Exchange as he had advised, they would have had a chance to come out of the fire storm alive. They could have dumped the house accounts through Tokyo and been out of the market before the New York Exchange opened Monday morning. Then, no matter what happened on Monday, the loss would have been contained. As it was, he could dump some stock through London, but there wasn't enough lead time to come out of it clean.

"What's going on downstairs?"

"Chaos." Lucille pressed the vodka glass to her throat and closed her eyes. "Peterson fired Norwood, the senior analyst."

"For once Peterson and I agree. Norwood should have seen this coming. That's why we paid his ass."

"Al Norwood did see it. His report has been on every director's desk for two weeks. He predicted Washington D.C. would interfere in the capital markets; he detailed the problems with the budget. He had the limited interest deductions two weeks ago and only missed the date of the announcement by three days." As an afterthought, she added, "Peterson apologized and asked Norwood to stay on, but he walked."

Durant swore softly and steadily. The market collapse was occurring in the middle of a corporate war and consequently the firm was taking a substantial hit. Acid flooded his stomach at Lucille's revelation that they had had the information on their goddamn desks, but neither he nor John Peterson nor anyone else had been taking care of business enough to read the damn thing. Peterson was a Harvard asshole, but even Peterson would have taken some cautionary steps to avert wholesale disaster if he had read Al Norwood's report. As for himself, he had been distracted by the boardroom bloodletting and by thoughts of Gloria Von Marron poisoning his son against him. The lapse had cost him several million and had also buried his pride underfoot. When the press learned La Tourraine, Durant and Von Marron had been caught with its pants down, there would be no more talk about Winthrop Durant as a living legend.

Breaking through the inertia of shock and resentment, he instructed Lucille to call a meeting of the executive committee. Maybe one of the hot shots would have some inspiration as to what they could do to prepare for Monday, something he had not already thought of. He doubted it, but nothing was impossible.

The instant he looked down the conference table at the faces confronting him, he understood calling the meeting had been a mistake. He hadn't spoken two words before John Peterson interrupted with accusations that Durant had dropped the ball by not reading and acting on Norwood's analysis. Anything Durant said in defense would sound like a lame excuse. Infuriated at being one-upped, he reminded Peterson that his division was taking the heaviest hit. The meeting exploded into accusations and recriminations.

When Durant was utterly certain no one present had any constructive solutions to suggest beyond what the firm was already doing, he did something he had never done before. He threw up his hands in disgust and walked out of the meeting. There was nothing to do but wait for Monday.

Nestor's kitchen provided silver urns of coffee and tea, rows of Diet Coke, and platters of pastries for the meeting, but no one approached the table. They sat in anxious silence, waiting for Charles Nestor. Gloria brushed back a silvery wave of hair and ran a fingernail down the column of figures she held in her lap.

"You self-righteous bitch!"

Surprised, Gloria looked up into Marlys Mill's narrowed eyes and twisted mouth.

"You got your clients out, didn't you? You're just too god-damn lucky to live. You're always right, aren't you?"

"That's enough." Charles Nestor's voice cut across the room like sharp-edged glass. "Von Marron shared her information the morning after D.C.'s call. Some of you chose to act on it; some of you did not. It was a judgment call. We're not going to rehash today's events or what led up to them. We're here to plan what happens next."

He consulted a file, then handed a sheaf of papers to his secretary to be passed among them. "I want each of you to obtain a list from everyone in your department of any orders that were not transacted before the Exchange closed. I want the stocks and amounts no later than Sunday noon. Arbitrage activity is temporarily suspended. For those of you who are wondering—yes, the firm took a hit. We'll know how bad by Sunday morning." He gave them a humorless smile.

"Our floor partners, Gladstone and McCaulley, will assess the firm's position and what has to be done to get us out. Naturally, we'll trade through Tokyo and London. To effect a smooth exit, I've sent some of our people from the Geneva and Paris offices to help handle the order flow in London. Denton, you'll be our point man with that group. If we oversell, I'm not concerned about being short against the box in this market. Between Tokyo and London, we should be nearly out by the time the New York Exchange opens on Monday. Gloria, you will work with Campbell on the firm's trading account. As our O-T-C inventory is fortunately near zero, that desk will work with the listed people to make certain our clients are getting timely executions. My son, Richard, will remain on the floor to back up our floor partners.

"No one knows what's going to happen Monday. But the press seems to think we do, and a few are getting nasty as they believe we're withholding information." There were a few smiles. "Until further notice, this firm's policy shall be that no one—and I mean no one—talks to a press representative except my son or myself. Richard and I will prepare a statement regarding the firm's position, and we will deal with the press. Make absolutely certain your staff and your departments understand that anyone who gives a statement to the press will be terminated immediately."

"What is the firm's position?" someone asked.

"Optimistic. If the market falls through the floor on Monday, we shall continue to be optimistic. When the market crashed in twenty-nine, many people were ruined. But many made money, among them my father and grandfather. Let's all keep in mind what Nestor Brothers is about. We do not traffic in rumor or innuendo. Whatever happens, Nestor Brothers will survive. Because this firm views change as a prescription for opportunity. Your job is to find the opportunity in your area of expertise and to capitalize on it."

Buoyed by Nestor's speech, the group relaxed enough to sample the coffee, Diet Coke, and pastries.

"Lord, this has been a day," Gloria said to Denton.

"And this is just the beginning; there's going to be a string of them. But, do you know what, Von Marron? There were a couple of good moments, too. Old Victoria Beauvier phoned this afternoon to thank me for taking her out of the market earlier in the week. She was crying. I didn't know you blue bloods knew how to cry."

"Oh, yes. We cry," she said softly. Turning, she straightened her shoulders and placed her empty coffee cup on the table. "I hope you brought a toothbrush and a sleeping bag, Denton. We're going to be here for a while."

"I figure if we work straight through, we'll have a handle on it by midnight Saturday. We sleep most of Sunday, then meet back here about six o'clock. The Tokyo Exchange opens at seven our time."

Gloria nodded. "Sounds good to me. It appears we signed on for the package tour."

They looked at each other and laughed.

Although there was absolutely nothing he could do, Durant went to his office Saturday morning, drawn there by the same dark instinct that draws people to crash sites. There were nearly as many people in the building today as would have been present during the workweek. They gathered in small groups, shifted, then re-formed, speaking in hushed voices. Others sat at their desks, staring at nothing, surrounded by stacks of newspapers, crushed coffee cups, food cartons, boxes of stale, dry pizza, and overflowing ashtrays. Someone had brought in a portable TV, and a group collected before it, watching CNN reporters interview a multitude of analysts and experts. The consensus, loudly expressed, concluded none of the so-called analysts and experts knew shit about anything. After an hour, Durant threw down the firm's monthlies, swallowed another antacid tablet, and left the building. When he discovered it was standing room only at his club and all his favorite bars, he returned to the penthouse.

"Win, you're wearing a track in our carpet," Chissie said, looking up from the sofa and the novel she had been reading before he arrived.

"It's going to fall again on Monday," he said, continuing to pace. "Most of them are sitting around talking like it's over. Talking about writing an obituary or their memoirs: I was there and lost twenty million dollars for the accounts I managed, but we all survived. It's become a goddamn can-you-top-this contest. People are standing around in groups saying things like, 'Sure, you lost twenty million, but some guy over at Salomon took a hit for over forty.' Or, 'Did you hear about this options player? He went down for four million of his own money.' " He raked a hand through his hair. "They think a hundred points is as bad as it's going to get. And they came out battered but alive. Monday will leave bodies in the aisles."

"You could be wrong," Chissie suggested mildly.

"No." He had been on the Street too long not to trust his gut. "Monday the program trading is going to kick in with a frenzy, and there's no way to stop it. The futures are going to go crazy. And the market is going to topple like one domino kicking down the next. And there isn't a goddamn thing I can do!"

Standing, Chissie smoothed her hand over a tan cashmere skirt, then touched his sleeve. "As long as you're going to pace anyway, let's go for a walk. It's a lovely fall day and we haven't walked together in years." Warming to the idea, she removed her sable from the foyer closet and smiled. "Maybe we'll buy a hotdog from one of the street carts—we used to do that occasionally when we were younger, remember? They have croissant carts now, did you know?''

He didn't want to walk, didn't give a rat's ass what kind of day it was outside. But he was wound too tight to remain in the penthouse. Watching Chissie read a novel as if this were a weekend like any other weekend set his teeth on edge. Getting out would solve that problem.

They walked several blocks before either spoke. ''We should do this more often.'' Chissie took his arm, slowing the pace he had set. ''I'd almost forgotten what autumn smells like. Remember when William used to burn the leaves at Goose Point and how good it smelled?''

Gradually relaxing, he slowed and pressed her arm to his side. ''I hate to admit this, but you were right. Walking was a good idea.'' Ahead was a coffeehouse, and they turned inside without discussion. An aroma of freshly ground beans mixed with the crisp air followed them to their table.

''Win, can we talk a minute?''

''I haven't changed my mind, Chissie. I'm not going to the Groton's dinner party tonight.''

''It's been canceled. Every event in town has been canceled.'' Almost shyly, she touched the back of his hand. ''Win, it worries me to see you so upset. Isn't it time you thought about retirement?''

He stared at her, watched her draw a long breath before she hurried on.

''Would it really be so terrible if John Peterson assumed responsibility for the firm? Things have changed so much—it isn't like it was when Bobby and Edison and Georges were alive. Those were great days, wonderful exciting days, but they're gone. And we're not getting younger.''

Still he said nothing, but he felt the dark color rising in his face.

''I know leaving the firm would create a vacancy in your life.'' She smiled down at her cup. ''That's an understatement, isn't it? But we can fill that vacancy with travel and with each other. Couldn't we? Maybe spend some time in Paris and get reacquainted?''

What she suggested was not worth discussing. Listening, watching her, he experienced an uncharacteristic moment of tenderness. ''I haven't been much of a husband to you, have I?'' The question appeared out of nowhere, a sentimental embarrassment.

"Oh, Win, that isn't true." Reaching across the table, she clasped his hands. "I was never pretty or exciting like Lulu, but even so I had my share of proposals. I've never regretted choosing you. Every marriage has it's ups and downs, and we've had our share of both. But you and I have always been solid."

"I've always admired you, Chissie." He could not believe the maudlin words falling out of his mouth.

"I've never doubted it, Win. Not for a moment."

"You've been a better wife than I've been a husband." Jesus. And in a Madison Avenue coffeehouse. He didn't know where this was coming from.

"That's not true. I could have had a husband who drank too much or who made life unpleasant in a hundred other ways."

"Chissie, I think you realize retirement is not an option." Seeing her disappointment, he returned the pressure of her hands. "I've given too much to the firm, made too many sacrifices. I can't walk away. I can't hand that asshole, Peterson, everything I've built and value. It's mine."

"Yes," she said softly, watching him. "I knew you would say that."

She looked away from him then, and he thought how fine her profile was, only lightly touched by age. When she faced him again, her chin was firm.

"Very well. Then what's to be done about Peterson?"

The answer came to him in a flash. Chaos was opportunity for the man with eyes to recognize it.

"An emergency board meeting. There will never be a better time," he said, thinking out loud. His thoughts raced ahead, planning, checking for hidden mine fields.

"I guess you're thinking about kicking some ass."

Jolted, Durant stared at her then laughed for the first time in weeks. "Leigh Chisholm Durant! I have never heard you talk like that. Not in—how many years?"

She smiled, pleased by his reaction. "Times are changing, and people have to change with them. That's what Gardner says." She stood when he did, waited for him to drop some bills on the table. "Win—what's wrong between you and Gardner?"

Instantly, his expression tightened. "I don't want to discuss it."

"It's serious, isn't it?"

"Not now, Chissie."

"We'll have to discuss it eventually."

"Not now."

The mention of Gardner's name brought an accompanying rush of pain and anger. He transferred his fury to John Peterson and allowed the hatred to build until he felt his mind sharpen and begin to throw off sparks. Now was the perfect time to chop off Peterson's balls, put them in his mouth, and sew his lips shut. It was so simple he almost laughed, merely a matter of seizing the opportunity.

On Sunday afternoon Marlys Mills tapped on Gloria's glass wall, then entered her office carrying two cups of coffee. "I've come to apologize," she said, setting one of the cups on the papers in front of Gloria.

"No need. We were all upset."

"Look, I was jealous because you were here to take D.C.'s call, and because you had the brains to act on it, and I didn't." Marlys leaned against the doorway and looked at Gloria. "I've never liked you. It's never seemed fair that you can look like that, be rich, and be smart, too. I've seen your photo in the newspapers, wearing a designer gown, dancing with some celebrity or a wealthy social type, then watched you breeze in here the next day as fresh as if you'd had twelve hours sleep, then pull off some brilliant coup. I didn't like you because you have a fabulous life, and I don't."

"You have a husband who loves you and two beautiful children."

"I know. I figured that out this weekend." When she smiled, Marlys was pretty. "When I woke up this afternoon, my husband wanted to make love. But I was too tired and my ulcer was acting up. I started thinking about that. I'm thirty-two years old and I have an ulcer for God's sake. I'm tired and scared all the time. I wake up worrying about my accounts, and I go to sleep worrying about my accounts. I worry about my bonus, and I worry if someone is going to get a bigger amount and what that means. I don't know a single person in this business who has a decent sex life. The last time I had time to read a novel I was in the hospital having labor pains."

"You're going to quit, aren't you?"

"As soon as this crisis is over. Anyway, I wanted to apologize for dumping my frustrations on you. And I guess I wanted to hear myself say I wouldn't trade lives with you even if I had the chance."

After Marlys had gone, Gloria leaned forward and closed her eyes. After a moment, she opened her middle desk drawer and touched Robby's photograph. He would be seven years old in March. It had been seven years.

She closed the drawer and tried to smile when Mark Denton came into her office.

"Twenty minutes to show time, Von Marron." Dropping to the edge of her desk, he placed a file in front of her. "You look as bad as I do. Didn't sleep either?"

"Too tired to sleep. I kept worrying we might have overlooked something. Does Charles want us to get a fix on the direction of Tokyo's market before we start unloading?"

"Nope. We're to liquidate all securities listed in the Orient. The Tokyo Exchange closes at one A.M. our time; then we've got three hours to figure out where we are and reorganize before the London Exchange opens at four-thirty A.M. our time. We unload the leftovers through London."

"What's this file?"

"In all the hullabaloo, I haven't had a chance to update you on Home Limited. I've put a hold on the file until we know what's going to happen tomorrow and later this week. Chances are, there'll be some bargains when the dust finally settles. We can file some 13-Ds by the end of the week which are going to look like steals this time next year."

Standing, Gloria pressed her hands against the small of her back, then bent and touched her toes. "It's going to be a long, long night."

Mark drained his coffee, looked at his watch. "Let's do it. I'll meet you for breakfast in the trading room in time to discover if we rode in on our white horses and saved the firm, or if all this was a waste of time."

The next time she saw Denton it was eight in the morning, thirteen hours later. Denton fell against her office door and stared at her with bloodshot eyes. "I'm whipped."

Holding up a hand, Gloria spread her fingers, signaling she needed five more minutes. When she hung up the telephone, she fell back in her chair and rubbed her eyes. "We're out." Her ear ached from the pressure of the telephone, and her back felt as if the muscles were on fire.

"Marlys says they've set up big-screen TVs in the trading room for anyone who wants to watch CNN's Tokyo and London coverage over breakfast. Can you stand it? We've got an hour and a half until New York opens."

They joined a large group of traders standing in front of the

TV screen. Immediately, Gloria decided watching the debacle was worse than hearing it over the telephone.

"Oh Jesus," one of the traders moaned. His face was white. "London went like a rock. Today is going to be a bloodbath!"

The television camera moved in tight on a man sitting at his desk staring up at the London and Tokyo markets. He sat perfectly motionless, clutching a pencil with both hands.

The Nestor group watched in silence, then someone murmured, "The guys who watched Hiroshima go up in a cloud must have looked like that guy. That's how their faces looked."

Gloria turned away. Already the phones were starting to go crazy in the trading room. Very few people were eating the breakfasts being served. Without speaking to anyone, she rode the elevator upstairs to the gymnasium and stood under a hot shower for twenty minutes, hoping the steam and hot water would wash away her fatigue. But she kept thinking about the traders in London and Tokyo staring up at the board.

Durant felt good. He felt great in fact.

Step by step, he laid it out to the board of directors. He showed them how John Peterson had disrupted the smooth functioning of vital departments that had been profitable for decades. He provided details of a "star system" within the firm and showed the board how Peterson's cronyism had sliced into the firm's profits. As the grand finale, he explained with devastating effect how a seat on the Tokyo Exchange would have contained the hit the firm had taken on Friday.

Turning slowly, he gazed pointedly at the exquisitely lit Van Gogh hanging behind him, then he again faced the board. "If this board had taken my advice, the firm would be out of the market clean. Right now. Instead, we face further brutalizing. When that happens—not if, gentlemen, but when—this firm will require strong, experienced leadership to effect a comeback. Someone will have to clean up the debris Peterson's appalling lack of foresight has created. Do you wish to entrust that responsibility to the same man whose incompetence has cost this firm millions? I can't think that you do.

"Peterson's greed and uncontrolled ambition have damaged and come near to destroying La Tourraine, Durant and Von Marron. The internal tensions within this firm must end and must end today if we are to fully cope with the crisis at hand. Therefore, before you leave this room, I ask your unanimous vote of support and confidence. And I want John Peterson out of this firm.''

Once again Lucille opened the door and gestured frantically. He scowled at her, and she gave him a despairing look, then closed the door.

He looked at each man sitting at the table. "Should you decide to retain Peterson in any capacity whatsoever, I shall wage a proxy fight like no one here has ever witnessed.''

All eyes shifted to Peterson as Durant sat down and clasped his hands on the table in front of him. Peterson had turned apoplectic with rage.

"Friday's crash was a one-time fluke." Peterson shouted. "No one could have anticipated this. Durant, having the advantage of hindsight, has suggested—''

"I call a vote." James Whitney Richardson, who sat on nine boards, lifted his pocket watch and made a display of consulting it. "I don't have time to listen to a string of mewling excuses. I have two other meetings to attend; it's going to be a bitch of a day. Let's get on with this.''

Peterson slapped his palms on the table. "I demand the same time Durant was given!''

"You're in no position to demand anything. If you crawl out of here with your hide and your balls intact, you can count it a lucky day.''

"For Christ's sake, Durant, call the fucking vote, will you?'' Durant called the vote.

When he strutted out of the boardroom fifteen minutes later, his firm was his again. Peterson had been stripped of all power. Persona non grata. Five minutes from now, Peterson would be cleaning out his desk.

Lucille waited in the corridor, pacing in a frenzy of impatience. Before he could reprimand her for trying to interrupt the board meeting, she rushed toward him, babbling.

"It's bad. Oh God, it's bad. There was some up and down activity at first, then just down. The Dow has dropped three hundred points since the market opened." She looked at Durant with a dazed expression. "In August the Dow hit twenty-seven hundred. Ten minutes ago it stood at twenty-three hundred. They're saying it will crash into the nineteen hundreds before the day's over.''

There was nothing he could do to stop the market from going through the floor. But he had built La Tourraine, Durant and

Von Marron from nothing once. If it was necessary, he could do it again. What mattered was this was his company and no one, absolutely no one, could take it from him.

Chapter 18

$\mathcal{O}$NE LOOK at the screens on his desk terminal entirely obliterated Durant's optimism. "Good Christ!" Stunned and disbelieving he sank into his chair and watched the unfolding devastation. Twenty-nine was beginning to look like a picnic. Almost immediately he understood the market would not rally. The historical three hundred point drop was not going to turn around; it would get worse. The market was falling through the floor, dropping further as he watched. The institutions were dumping massive volumes of shares. The GM Pension was dumping one hundred million dollars worth of stock each hour. Programmed trading had kicked in and was like a Frankenstein rampaging out of control. Chicago was aiding and abetting. It was a slaughterhouse.

A dizzying tide of rage and impotence blurred his vision. He had regained control of his firm only to see it savaged. Almost running, he hastened to the elevators and rode them downstairs. The doors opened on a scene of chaos beyond anything he had witnessed. His initial impression was frenzied activity, people running in the aisles, shouting into telephones. Then he saw others, many others, standing in shocked silence contemplating a point in space or staring blankly into the depths of a coffee cup. Some wandered aimlessly from aisle to aisle. The noise level had reached gargantuan proportions. People shouted, screamed; phones shrilled on every desk. Garbled announcements blared over the speaker system.

Stomach churning, he ran from desk to desk yelling orders, shouting instructions. "All limit orders are stopped! No limit orders!"

At the OTC desk, he spun a trader away from his desk and phone. "Don't answer the goddamn phone, you fucking idiot!"

283

The man gaped at him. "If you don't answer you don't have to make a market. Do I have to spell it out for you? There is no one home at this firm! Get it?" He screamed at them, pointing out the obvious, fighting to save what he could.

The phones in the trading room screamed frantically for attention, but Gloria's floor remained eerily silent following a burst of morning activity.

"Spooky, isn't it?" Marlys Mill asked no one in particular. "I suppose no one's calling because they're already out or they think they can't get through or they're frozen and unable to act."

"I have an idea this lull is only momentary," Gloria said. "Five minutes ago I heard the Exchange may close early."

Marlys's face went white. "That means . . ." A shudder thinned her lips. "I won't say it; I won't even think it."

But they were all thinking it: if the Exchange closed early today, would it reopen tomorrow?

Marlys shook her head and stood up straight. "God, those poor guys in the trading room. They're buried. Bill Koontz told me one of the big institutions lost nine million dollars before he could phone in the order."

"The tape is still running late," Mark Denton said, coming out of his office. "Jesus, I've never seen anything like this. Do you think they'll really close the Exchange early?"

Tripp Campbell expressed the fear sweeping brokerage firms across the nation. "What if it doesn't reopen?"

They looked at each other. Then the phones started to ring; the eerie silence had ended. Toward midafternoon a platoon of secretaries and messengers moved through the Nestor building distributing memos stating that Charles Nestor had received a commitment from Phelan and the other governors of the Exchange that the market would remain open. Nestor moved past Gloria's office looking visibly relieved.

"Charles!" Gloria covered the mouthpiece of her phone. Her client's panicked voice continued shouting in her ear. "Do you want to position IBM?"

She was asking Charles Nestor if he wanted to buy out her client's shares with the firm's dollars and hope like hell that Nestor could sell the shares tomorrow at a profit.

Charles Nestor stood in the door to her office, staring at her. She knew his mind was racing on fast forward, weighing rumors against hard information, trying to guess if the Exchange would open tomorrow, if there would be a rally, trying to balance his anxiety about committing the firm's capital to a possible loss.

"How much?"

"In this account—ten thousand shares." She peered at her screen. "Bid one hundred offered one-oh-five, five by five hundred." The row of buttons along the bottom of her phone flashed insistently. "There's stock ahead and more to come if the market stabilizes."

Knots lifted along Nestor's clenched jaw. He hesitated briefly then gave her a firm nod. "Bid them ninety-five."

Gloria returned to the phone. "Nestor will bid ninety-five on a clean-up or we'll start you at one hundred on the first one thousand and work the balance. We are not accepting limits at this point. Is that agreeable?"

"Yes. Oh God, yes. Just get me out of this!"

Mark Denton shouted from his office. "Charles—do you want to position twenty-five thousand shares of P&G?"

"Do it."

Reaching, Gloria punched a button and took the next call. She listened a moment, then called, "We're in touch with a large-scale seller of GE. Do you want to position them?"

"Go ahead."

She stared at Charles Nestor through the glass wall over her desk, knowing he was hanging the firm on the line. If the Exchange didn't open tomorrow, or if the collapse continued, Nestor Brothers would be out of business. She heard the squawk box announce: The firm is now long GE in size. Charles smiled and gave her a thumbs-up sign.

Thirty minutes later a Rhinelander delivery boy staggered through the lanes of desks carrying an immense flower horseshoe toward Gloria's office. Cradling the phone between her ear and her shoulder, Gloria opened her purse and handed the boy five dollars, then continued the call. An hour passed before she found a minute to extract the card and read it.

Good luck, squirt. Win big. The world is watching.

She was still smiling when Denton appeared to inspect the horseshoe. "Gardner Durant?" he asked. She nodded. "You know, Von Marron, you ought to marry that guy. I like his style."

"That's not a good idea."

"Why not?"

"I'll tell you about it someday," she lied.

They returned to the telephones.

An hour later the Exchange closed on schedule and a silence

spread throughout the firm as profound as the shock that caused it. Numb, Gloria stared at her screen in disbelief. At the closing bell, the Dow had dropped a total of five hundred and eight points. If the crash continued tomorrow, Nestor Brothers—along with many other old-line houses—would be destroyed.

Others were struggling with the same realization. There were no gatherings in the corridors, very little interchange. Each person stared at his screen, stunned, and tried to understand what he was seeing, tried to comprehend the unthinkable.

When Gloria realized she had been sitting immobile staring at her screen in exhausted silence for at least twenty minutes, she stood and reached for her coat. No one spoke as she moved toward the elevators, and she spoke to no one until she reached the ground floor and stepped outside into the cold night air.

A half-dozen TV camera crews rushed toward her. Lights flared in her face; questions flew like bullets.

"What will happen tomorrow, Miss Von Marron?"

"What's happening upstairs?"

"How much has Nestor lost?"

Ducking her head, she murmured, "No comment," and pushed through them. Once on the next block she slowed her pace, hoping the walk would ease the cramps in her stomach. Everything depended upon tomorrow. Like everyone else in the financial industry, she felt almost sick with anxiety. Would the market reopen? Would the collapse continue?

She walked until the tension loosened in her back muscles and along her shoulders, until she was calm enough to comprehend and enjoy the solitude and relative quiet. Eventually, she made herself displace Nestor Brothers from her thoughts long enough to remember the rose horseshoe leaning against the back wall of her office. A fleeting smile touched her lips.

Gardner. Tonight she missed him with an ache that was physical. He was savvy enough to tell her to win big; he knew what today had been like. It would have been marvelous to meet him now, knowing he understood.

She waited for a walk light, then pushed her hands into the pockets of her coat, lifted her head and crossed the street. She and Gardner were approaching a crisis point in their relationship; she understood that. Very soon Gardner would ask her to make a commitment. And if she could not or would not, that would be the end.

For years she had believed there could be no future for them; that was the premise on which she had proceeded. But Gardner's confrontation with Durant had altered the balance. That Gardner had chosen to believe her had opened a door.

Because she was exhausted and her defenses not as strong as they usually were, Gloria allowed herself to extrapolate the future as she wished it to be. Beginning with the night in Cancún and thinking forward, she admitted the relationship had held together despite the revelations of that night. She had told Gardner she believed his father guilty of criminal fraud, but Gardner hadn't turned away from her. In tonight's fantasy, neither did he turn away after learning of Robby's existence.

She examined the possibility. Perhaps she had been too inflexible by believing she could not tell Gardner about her son. Perhaps she had underestimated his capacity for acceptance.

Lifting a hand, she rubbed her cheek. If their relationship was to continue, she had to tell Gardner about Robby. There was no choice. She could not reveal the name of Robby's father; on that point she would have to lie. But she had to tell Gardner about Robby.

Then what? How did she explain the years she had concealed Robby's existence, the years spent apart from him? What half-truth could she offer to justify choosing Durant's world instead of her son's world?

The questions whirled through a mind too fatigued to deal with them. As she rounded the corner and saw the TV crews clustered in front of Nestor Plaza, she released a low sigh.

The personal questions would have to be placed on hold, but that was nothing new. Her personal life, such as it was, had been on hold for years. Recognizing the thought as bitter, she put it from her mind and squared her shoulders before she pushed through the TV squads and entered the building.

Marlys Mill and Mark Denton met her at the elevators. "Good news," Denton said. His face was expressionless. Like everyone, he was too exhausted to muster an appropriate reaction. "The Tokyo Exchange opened half an hour ago—it may be a rally. It's too soon to tell for certain, but it's heading in that direction."

"Nestor sent champagne to all the floors the minute the market closed," Marlys added, rubbing red-rimmed eyes.

They joined the group assembled in Charles Nestor's office suite and waited for Charles to speak.

He gave them a weary smile. "This is the quietest celebration I've every attended. I know you're tired—most of you haven't been home since early Sunday morning."

They inspected each other and a few strained smiles appeared. They all looked disheveled. Gloria wore the same Chanel slacks suit she had put on Sunday morning, wrinkled now and the worse for wear. Her hair was limp; her makeup had long since faded. Her eyes were dulled by fatigue and burned from lack of sleep.

"You've done a hell of a job, people," Charles Nestor said. "I know you're worried about tomorrow. So am I. But I have confidence the market will reopen."

"You're still bullish?" someone asked in tones of weary amazement.

Nestor laughed. "Not bullish, but optimistic." He raised his champagne glass to them. "Because we've got the best people on the Street." They managed a cheer. "Now go home and get some rest."

Gloria collapsed across her bed still wearing the Chanel pantsuit. She was asleep in five seconds.

Durant couldn't sleep. The impotence of helplessness ground his stomach like shards of glass. Popping antacid tablets and drinking straight Scotch, he paced the penthouse living room, his mind hopscotching across the carnage. Clients who dated back to the beginnings of the firm had suffered appalling losses. The firm had taken a staggering hit. His department heads reminded him of men he had seen during the war, dazed by shock, unable to function.

Throughout the day, he had watched the bloodbath occurring on his Quotron, had confirmed the firm's trading losses in the stream of memos flowing across his desk. Perversely, he felt exhilarated by the challenge of rebuilding, at other moments he felt as stunned and bewildered as anyone on the Street.

Standing in front of the penthouse windows, he peered down at Park Avenue and prayed the market would open tomorrow. At the end of the day he had permitted his traders to make markets, his mind having finally thawed to the extent he understood making markets was the only way to get back into the order flow and win back some of what had been lost. That is, if the market rallied. He suspected his efforts were too little and had come too late. Regardless, everything depended upon the market reopening.

Turning, he paced to the fireplace, looked into the grate, then returned to the windows. What caused him the most anxiety at the moment was anticipating the newspapers. Fury bit at his stomach. His source at *The Times* had informed him that John Peterson had wasted no time scheduling an interview. He was taking La Tourraine, Durant and Von Marron's internal wars public. By this time tomorrow, certainly by Wednesday, the financial community would learn La Tourraine, Durant and Von Marron had taken a huge hit. Peterson's version of the debacle would place the blame squarely on Durant's shoulders. The firm's stock would drop again, further eroding Durant's personal fortune.

His personal fortune was the least of his worries. He needed capital for the firm. The hit they had taken, the erosion of the stock price—the combination was deadly. This time there was no Bobby Von Marron to turn to, no Home Limited, both with seemingly inexhaustible funds. To maintain the firm's bracket status, he would have to develop capital from some other source.

Somehow he would. La Tourraine, Durant and Von Marron was his firm. He had proven that no person could take it from him, now he would prove that no event could take him down either.

The regular seven o'clock morning meeting was subdued. The usual brisk exchange of risqué jokes didn't occur. Nestor Brother's large trading room remained uncharacteristically hushed. A few people nibbled at the breakfasts on their desks but most of the food was ignored. Waiters picked up the untouched trays. Everyone ordered coffee; almost everyone forgot to drink it.

If the market dropped another five hundred points today, the firm would shut its doors. Everyone at Nestor Brothers would be out looking for a job.

Charles Nestor set aside the usual agenda and delivered a short speech urging optimism and opportunity. The traders listened in silence.

"What do you think?" Mark Denton asked when the meeting adjourned.

Gloria smiled. "I agree with Charles. America is not going out of business."

"I hope you're right, Von Marron. We positioned a lot of stock for the firm's account yesterday—let's hope we can dump the stuff at a profit."

"Fat chance." Marlys Mill chewed her thumbnail. "The market's going to take another dive."

For a time it appeared Marlys would be right. Virtually all

the Dow stocks opened late. Then the market staggered up a few points. Then the MMI index began to move up sharply. Gloria stared at her screen watching as the market danced and swayed and struggled upward. As the quotes began to flash, a sense of euphoric relief tingled down her spine. The major Dow stocks finally opened, reflecting the underlying strength of the MMI.

Scarcely daring to blink, she watched IBM and GE reopen, along with the other stocks she had positioned for the firm. She drank coffee, ran calculations on her computer, and felt the mounting stress bunch her shoulders and knot her lower back. The question swiftly became when to unload. Now, when IBM had climbed back to a hundred? Or should she wait and hope it went higher? Ignoring the headache thudding behind her eyes, she drank cold coffee and stared at the screen.

When IBM reached one hundred and eighteen dollars a share, her nerves collapsed and she reached for the telephone. She sold ninety-five hundred shares at a twenty-three dollar profit for a net gain exceeding two hundred thousand dollars. She looked at the figure without expression, without elation. Then she punched up the market on GE, up six and a half, and chewed the eraser end of a pencil stub as she worked on her next set of calculations. By two o'clock, all the MMI stocks were open and trading. It was widely believed the Feds had begun to force liquidity into the system.

At the end of the day, they gathered in Charles Nestor's office suite.

"I don't know what to say," he began. A waiter moved through the group pouring champagne. "What you did today was brilliant. Mill, you made six million dollars for the firm. Campbell, you made eight." Slowly, he went around the room calling names and raising the ante. Finally he stood before Mark Denton and Gloria Von Marron. "Denton, you netted twenty-eight million dollars for the firm's accounts. Von Marron, you came in at thirty-one million." He raised his glass to the room. "It's been a hell of a day!"

They were too drained to celebrate. The victory party was somber, listless.

"I can't work it out in my mind," Marlys said, leaning against the wall and closing her eyes. "This is the worst market crash in history. Yet we made money today. Close to a hundred million. Some guy down South murdered his broker and killed himself—but we made a hundred million." Several people nodded, as bewildered and dazed as she. "How is that possible?"

After the meeting, Gloria returned to her office and sat at her desk a moment before mustering the energy to go home. She pulled a rose from Gardner's horseshoe and inhaled the fragrance.

Everyone seemed to agree the worst was over. The market had reopened; Nestor Brothers had emerged triumphant. The days ahead would be rocky, but the doors of the firm would remain open.

A stack of newspapers lay piled on the floor beside her desk and briefly she considered reading through them, then decided she lacked the stamina. She possessed enough energy to straighten her desk and get herself home; that was all.

When she came across the Home Limited file, forgotten during the firestorm of the last few days, she leaned back from her desk and rubbed her eyes. As Denton had predicted, there were now a multitude of bargains suitable for acquisition. First thing tomorrow, she would make a shopping list.

The phone rang as she was stepping through the door and she glanced at her watch then looked at the phone before she sighed and moved back to her desk.

"It's Gardner. How are you holding up?"

"I miss you." It wasn't what she had intended to say, probably it wasn't wise. "I've never been this exhausted in my life." She smiled at the horseshoe. "Thank you for the roses. They brightened a dark day."

"Is the worst over?"

"I think so, thank God."

"Things are about wrapped up here, I hope to be in New York for the weekend. I'd like to see you."

Gloria let a silence develop as she struggled with the advisability of agreeing. She was too fatigued to concentrate on the problems complicating her personal life. At the same time, there was nothing she wanted more than to see Gardner and be with him. "I had planned on going to Goose Point for the weekend. Get out of town."

"Would you like some company?"

She hesitated. "Yes. I'd like that."

After she hung up, she leaned forward and dropped her head into her hands. In a moment of weakness she had agreed to something she sensed was unwise. Regardless of fantasies founded in exhaustion, she knew she wouldn't tell Gardner about

Robby. Just as she knew there was nothing Gardner could say that would deflect her from destroying Win Durant. In the end, she would have to walk away from the relationship. She had come too far; she no longer had a choice. The pain accompanying the realization constricted her chest and closed her throat.

But they could have one weekend. She could give herself one perfect weekend to remember.

When she walked into her town house, she gave her coat to the maid and leafed through the mail before deciding there was nothing important enough to warrant immediate attention. After running a hot tub, she positioned Robby's photograph on the dressing table where she could see him.

Relaxing in the tub, she leaned back and stared at Robby's picture, missing him. A sense of depression swept her thoughts. After seven years she was no closer to bringing Durant down than she had been in the beginning.

Thinking about Durant deepened her depression but it also burned the fatigue from her body and replaced it with hatred.

She had sacrificed everything because of Durant—the life she might have had and a large portion of the life she did have. She had given up seven years with her son, had abandoned the hope of a future with Gardner. She had not visited the Paris town house in years; the *Dahinda* remained anchored and unused in Monte Carlo. Goose Point slumbered under dust covers. The things she loved best were vacant and distant.

And for what? Durant continued unpunished.

The thought was too devastating to contain and she looked away from Robby's smiling photograph, forcing her mind back to the safe zone of business. She made herself think about her clients and her accounts; she reviewed the events of the past days. As always she found comfort in the immutability and concrete reality of numbers.

Numbers. Accounts.

She sat up abruptly, splashing water over the side of the tub.

"My God!" Her mind raced, pulling up the numbers that had flowed across her terminal, recapturing fragments of recent headlines. "Oh, my God!"

Standing, she snatched a towel and blotted herself dry with hurried motions, then tied a Porthault robe about her waist. Almost running, she hastened down the hallway to the pile of mail and newspapers she had left on the foyer table. In a moment she had *The Wall Street Journal* spread open across her living room coffee table. She ran a trembling fingertip down the

NASDAC listings until she found LTDVM. The stock had dropped to a stunning fourteen dollars a share.

Gloria closed her eyes and fought a wave of dizziness, then she thumbed quickly through the pages of the paper until she located the interview with John Peterson.

"Yes," she whispered, collapsing backward on the sofa.

The answer had always been there as she had sensed, but the timing had not been right. Not until now.

Excitement hardened her eyes. She felt dizzy with it, drunk with it. And she knew she would not sleep tonight.

Moving to her desk, she seated herself and drew a tablet forward, making lists as she thought it through.

When she finished, she sat in front of the living room windows with Robby's photograph beside her and she watched the sky gradually lighten. And she savored the final sweetness of Durant's ruin.

Less than a mile away, Win Durant paced his living room following another sleepless night. Today the rumor mill had operated at the speed of light. He'd heard that Salomon and some of the other major houses were laying off people by the hundreds. Some of the firms had frantically chopped out whole departments; other firms quietly celebrated the fact they were still in business. Others struggled to assess the damage against the avalanche of paper burying back offices. The velocity of the marketplace had outraced humans and computers.

He pulled a hand through his hair and swallowed his Scotch and water. He needed capital. Bargains glittered like gold across his Quotron. This was the time to buy in shares of La Tourraine, Durant and Von Marron; the price would never be this attractive again. The firm's share price had hit an all time low, but he had no free capital to take advantage of the opportunity. Frustration ate at his nervous system.

He would have walked over his grandmother for the capital to buy in more shares.

Chapter 19

ALTHOUGH GLORIA SLEPT LITTLE, she entered the firm on Wednesday morning with a light step.

"You look rejuvenated," Mark Denton said, staring. "Tell me your secret. I still feel like I've been run over by a truck."

Gloria smiled, waved, and continued directly to her office. Within minutes she confirmed that La Tourraine, Durant and Von Marron had sold at thirty-five dollars a share before the crash and was now at fourteen. Rumors persisted that the firm had taken a crippling hit resulting in heavy losses. John Peterson's *Journal* interview underscored the Street gossip. She had what she needed.

Reaching for the phone, she called Walt Tobler at Home Limited and instructed him to arrange an emergency meeting of the Home Limited board of directors for early afternoon.

Tobler hesitated. "Should we consider delaying the meeting?" he asked after learning the purpose. "Gardner will arrive Monday."

She knew Gardner would be in New York for the weekend. "At this point I'd prefer to avert any possible conflict of interest. Please call the meeting for today." Gardner was an unavoidable part of her plan to destroy Durant, but she could spare him the discomfort of sitting through the opening salvo.

Having arranged the board meeting, she telephoned Charles Nestor in his office. "Charles, I want the firm to go into the box on LTDVM."

"You want us to make a market in LTDVM?"

"Yes. I want to be high bid. Home Limited's board is meeting in a few hours. I believe I can guarantee Home will buy whatever shares Nestor accumulates. If Home doesn't, I will. I will personally guarantee your take-out."

He was silent a moment. "Considering current rumors and the savaging LTDVM's shares took, you can anticipate a large number of shares. You may be looking at hundreds of thousands of shares, Gloria."

"I'm prepared to spend millions."

"I see." Nestor didn't hesitate. "Then Nestor will make the market."

Wilkie Tomlinson explained to Home's board of directors what he had previously explained to Gloria and Walt Tobler. His advice was the same, if phrased more urgently.

"Your choice is to acquire or be acquired. Before the crash, this company was a cash-rich plum waiting to be plucked. Now, in the aftermath, you're a sitting duck, gentlemen. I think I can promise that right now, someone is examining your 10-K and rubbing his hands in glee. The events of the past week coupled with Home's cash reserve have catapulted the company to the list of the top ten companies where book value is nearly three times market."

"Good God!"

"Exactly." Wilkie Tomlinson nodded. "Every moment of delay increases your risk of takeover. My advice is to create a less attractive target by deploying your cash reserves. Immediately. Poison pills and anti-takeover strategies are of little use if the price being offered is high enough."

Walt Tobler rose at the head of the table. He repeated the urgency of Tomlinson's analysis and advice, quickly reviewed the bargain situation created by the market crash, then turned the presentation over to Gloria.

"Although we need to act swiftly and decisively, we need not act rashly. Before acquiring additional firms, we must ask ourselves which companies are compatible with the parent firm's needs and objectives. Collier's department ran an analysis of compatible industries and firms—the analysis is in the file Mrs. Stavely is placing before you. There are at least three possible candidates that look attractive. Of these, I have selected the one I believe dovetails best with our operation. Please take a moment to read through the first proposal."

March Block was first to break the silence. He looked up at her. "La Tourraine, Durant and Von Marron?"

"Yes." She met his eyes, remembering he had served on Home's board during Durant's tenure. "As you can see from the breakdowns, Home Limited spent seven million dollars last year on investment banking fees. If we were to acquire an investment bank, those fees would not be a total loss. They could contribute to overall profits.''

March Block considered the figures on the page before him. ''why La Tourraine, Durant, and Von Marron?''

''The firm's stock is currently at a bargain-basement price. Informed rumor, partially confirmed by the Peterson article in yesterday's *Journal*, insists La Tourraine, Durant and Von Marron suffered a substantial loss during the market crash. This would indicate internal weakness.'' She met March Block's stare. ''Other houses profited during the collapse. La Tourraine, Durant and Von Marron did not. If the losses are as great as suggested, La Tourraine, Durant, and Von Marron will not recover its former position without a massive infusion of capital. We have that capital, gentlemen. With new management and a transfusion of funds, the firm can become a profitable asset.''

Block looked at the others at the table, then returned to Gloria. ''As I understand it, Win Durant owns controlling interest in La Tourraine, Durant and Von Marron. There is no way in hell Win is going to sell out.''

''He won't have a choice. There are three large-block shareholders in the firm: Win Durant, his wife, and his son. The blocks held by Mrs. Durant and by Gardner Durant are in trusts administered by the trustees named in the file before you.''

Block shook his head. ''Durant's wife and son aren't going to sell him out.''

''If Home Limited extends an offer to the trusts with a high enough premium, the trustees will have no choice but to tender.'' Gloria's eyes hardened. ''Their fiduciary obligation will require them to accept our offer regardless of the family's wishes. In light of the market crash, I believe we can show the trustees that our tender meets and exceeds any fiduciary obligation, as the trustees could not conceivably hope to match our offer in the open market. Not now or in the near future.''

''Jesus Christ!''

''Combined with shares purchased through the market, the trust blocks will give Home Limited control of La Tourraine, Durant and Von Marron. Once Home Limited acquires the trust shares, we will hold the majority block.''

''Let me understand this,'' March Block said slowly. ''You aren't planning to approach La Tourraine, Durant and Von Marron with a buy-out offer. You're just going to take them over whether they like it or not?''

Gloria's gaze was cool. "Do you believe Win Durant would consider a purchase offer from this company?"

"Can you assure me that what's going on here is not personal?"

"Certainly there are personal elements. My father helped found La Tourraine, Durant and Von Marron. Quite naturally, I have a family interest. If Home Limited acquires La Tourraine, Durant and Von Marron, I will accept a seat on the board of LTDVM. The SEC will require that I resign my position at Nestor Brothers in favor of taking an active role in the management of La Tourraine, Durant and Von Marron."

In a way, the moment was ironic as she and Denton had both received indications from Charles Nestor suggesting they would be invited to commit capital to Nestor Brothers as full partners. If Home Limited acquired La Tourraine, Durant and Von Marron, she would have to offer Charles her resignation instead.

"What you need to understand, March, is regardless of my personal interest, I would not place Home Limited at risk by urging this board to acquire La Tourraine, Durant and Von Marron if I did not believe the investment was advisable for Home. Placing personal considerations aside, I believe you can see from the figures I've provided that acquiring La Tourraine, Durant and Von Marron makes sense in terms of their needs and ours. It's a sound business combination."

Block threw his pen on the table, looked away from her.

"There's something in all this that bothers me." Jim Whitley addressed the table. "I agree an investment bank is a logical acquisition. And I agree La Tourraine, Durant and Von Marron appears to be an excellent choice." He looked at Gloria. "But to acquire this firm means we have to raid the personal trust of our future president. Has anyone asked Gardner Durant how he feels about this? Not only are we preparing to liquidate what I assume is the primary portion of his trust—but we're going to use those shares to steal his father's firm."

"I have not discussed this with Gardner Durant and do not intend to do so unless the board agrees to proceed with the plan as outlined. Should the board agree, Walt Tobler will inform Gardner of our decision." Gloria drew a breath. "If Gardner's trustees accept our tender offer of twenty-five dollars a share as I propose, that is an eighty-percent premium over what could be realized in the open market. And the offer does not take into account the illiquidity of LTDVM shares. Gardner will profit handsomely." She stared at Jim Whitley. "We are not stealing

Win Durant's firm. La Tourraine, Durant and Von Marron is a publicly held corporation open to a legitimate takeover bid.''

A silence stretched, then Ames Rockefellar shrugged. ''Sounds like a done deal to me. Let's do it. The figures work; everything works. If the press is right, and La Tourraine, Durant and Von Marron suffered the large losses the newspapers think it did, then the firm needs capital and they're going to have a damned difficult time finding it with figures like these. On the other hand, we're top heavy with capital and need to dump it somewhere. This acquisition sounds like a perfect jigsaw fit.''

There were more questions, two hours of discussion, then Gloria nodded toward the end of the table. ''Walter? Will you call the vote, please?''

When the votes had been recorded and the meeting adjourned, Gloria walked directly to the ladies room outside the board room doors. She leaned her hands on the sink and dropped her head.

She breathed deeply, then raised her eyes to the mirror and smiled.

She had won. Finally, after all these years, the end was in sight. It was almost over.

The jolt was worse than what he had felt while watching the market fall five hundred and eight points. Durant reacted as if he had taken a powerful blow to the gut. His knees buckled and he fell backward into his chair. His stomach suddenly felt tight and queasy.

Closing his eyes, he counted to three, then blinked at the Autex again. It was still on the screen, the letters NBRO next to LTDVM. Followed by the letter L.

Jesus H. Christ. Nestor Brothers was making a market in La Tourraine, Durant and Von Marron. It appeared to be the high bidder by three-eighths, and a large buyer which explained the L on the screen.

Sweat collected in his temples and trickled along his jaw. Removing a handkerchief, he blotted his brow and stared briefly at the buttons starting to flash under his phone.

Jesus Christ. Gloria Von Marron was moving in on him; she was raiding his firm. He could not fucking believe it.

Calm, he told himself, stay calm. Think it through. When he believed his knees would support him, he pushed to his feet and poured a shot of straight Scotch from his private office stock.

He drained it in a gulp and poured another, waiting for his hands to steady.

All right, he would fight her. If she wanted a stock war, she would get one. He would buy in the shares himself.

Except that was not possible; he lacked the capital. He couldn't buy in enough shares to make a difference. Acid chewed at his stomach. So, what next? He could halt a landslide sell out. It was a beginning. He could call in some chips, exert some pressure. Buy himself some time.

Reaching for the telephone, he dialed Louis Galbain's office. Dispensing with any opening exchange, he went directly to the point. "Nestor is in the box as a large buyer of LTDVM. The fuckers keep raising the bid to smoke out any sellers."

"I heard about it five minutes ago."

"You are not to sell your blocks of shares. Do you hear me, Galbain? You are not to sell out."

Galbain laughed. "Are you crazy? Of course I'm going to sell. Do you know how much money I've lost on these shares? There's a chance the Exchange will want to audit your books, Win, to determine the adequacy of the firm's accounts. The word is, you don't have the capital for a full recovery. If I can dump this stock at a premium, you can bet your sweet ass I'm going to sell."

Durant lifted a hand and covered the rage and frustration burning his eyes. "I still have certain photographs, Louis . . ."

"They aren't worth half a million dollars." The phone went dead in his hand.

He dialed the next number on his list, went through it again. "You owe me, Dremmel."

"Like hell I do. I've repaid that debt fifty times over," Axel Dremmel said into the phone. "You're through, Win. They're taking bets on the Street as to how long you'll last after Von Marron acquires enough stock to demand a seat on the board."

He hung up on Dremmel's laugh. The bastards smelled blood already. He wondered if the arbs had begun to chew on his carcass yet.

Next he phoned the trustees of Chissie's trust.

"Under no circumstances are you to sell any shares of La Tourraine, Durant and Von Marron."

Judge Ellis MacNammera spoke for all the trustees. "That is not your decision, Win. I've been informed a tender offer may be coming in at a premium of eleven dollars a share. If the offer is made, we'll decide if it is in Mrs. Durant's best interest to liquidate the block.''

Durant felt sick. He had no leverage whatsoever with the trustees; he had made certain of that himself.

"Don't screw me around," he snarled at Willis Everett, the trustee for Gardner's trust. "You know right now what you'll decide. What is it?''

Everett hesitated. "It's true I've received information indicating a tender offer may be forthcoming, but it seems inappropriate to comment until the offer is actually made. However, in light of the recent crash, Win, it's difficult to conceive that La Tourraine, Durant and Von Marron shares will reach twenty-five dollars in the foreseeable future . . .''

He slammed down the phone. His goddamn hands were shaking like loose paper in a breeze. Leaning forward he pressed his fingertips to his eyelids.

All right. He didn't have enough capital to wage a proxy contest. The fucking trustees were behaving as if profit were the sole consideration; he couldn't lever them. His chips weren't worth shit when stacked against the Street's eagerness to gloat over his downfall.

He stared at his screen without blinking and watched the volume in LTDVM explode across the terminal.

What in the name of God was he going to do?

The New York market remained volatile; skittish investors continued to dump shares. Headlines were confusing. Tokyo had fallen a record number of yen, closing at 21,910.08.

By Thursday afternoon, Nestor had purchased 4.5 percent of La Tourraine, Durant and Von Marron's stock. Late in the day, Home Limited filed a 13-D on LTDVM with the Securities and Exchange Commission indicating it had acquired 5.3 percent of the firm's outstanding shares. Walt Tobler authorized Gloria to proceed with a cash tender offer of twenty-five dollars per share for the remaining outstanding stock. The activity generated by Nestor's market had pushed the price to eighteen dollars a share. As Gloria had anticipated, the arbs were now circling the market.

There was no doubt that Chissie and Gardner's trusts would accept the tender offer. But to assure herself, Gloria telephoned each trustee personally. During the course of her conversations, she alluded to the possibility that Mrs. Durant and Gardner Durant might not wish to liquidate their shares of La Tourraine,

Durant and Von Marron. The trustees uniformly admitted this was a troubling aspect. They also confirmed that the family's wishes could not be a consideration in the final decision. The trusts had been established for the purpose of removing emotionally charged decisions from the trust's grantor and beneficiaries.

Gloria's smile was cold. There was satisfaction in using Durant's family against him as he had used her to vent his resentments and grievances against her family. But there was also pain.

He could not eat. He could not sleep.

Antacid tablets had ceased to provide any relief; his stomach felt as if it were on fire.

Chissie looked into the breakfast room, frowned, then returned to her bedroom without speaking.

Gesturing to Abrams to remove his plate, Durant leaned back with his coffee, then, when Abrams had gone, he shook open *The Wall Street Journal*. His hand jerked, and scalding coffee spilled over his jacket and trousers.

He saw it immediately; his worst nightmare realized on the front page center column. HOME LIMITED FILES 13-D ON LA TOURRAINE, DURANT AND VON MARRON. Nestor was representing the buyer of his firm. Shock blanked his eyes. When his chest loosened and his pulse beat slowed, he made himself read the article, his fury and frustration mounting.

The article alluded to recent enormous losses within the firm, briefly traced the history of both Home Limited and La Tourraine, Durant and Von Marron, and noted the two firms would once again be united under the Von Marron banner.

He felt physically sick. He thought for a moment he would vomit.

Gloria Von Marron had put his firm into play; she was making a public move on him. And there was not a single goddamn thing he could do to prevent it from happening.

La Tourraine, Durant and Von Marron was his life. There was nothing else. And all the years, all the sacrifices he had made were about to be swept away. That goddamn fucking cunt was going to take it away from him.

She would throw him out on his ass. He would have no duties, no office, no power. He would have no place to go. He would be out. His firm stolen out from under him. Gloria Von Marron would sit behind his desk in his chair. Bobby Von Marron's daughter.

Everyone in the business would laugh themselves sick that a debutante had toppled a Wall Street legend. Had tossed him off the pinnacle without chipping a fingernail.

Chissie peered inside the breakfast room. "Win?" Alarm narrowed her mouth and she stepped forward. "Are you feeling well? You look . . ."

He walked directly to the guest bath and threw up into the toilet. Afterward, he brushed his teeth and washed his face.

"Win? You're frightening me."

Ignoring her, he went into his study and closed the door. Before he telephoned Alf Cowper, he considered all the angles. Revealing Von Marron's bastard would cause a scandal of international proportions. The headlines would embarrass her, discredit her. But the scandal would not stop her from raiding his firm.

He thought he knew what would.

He reached for the telephone.

It had been one hell of a week. Gloria's mind continued to run on double time, and she could still feel the tension biting into her shoulders. Shifting on the car seat, she stretched her neck against her hand, then turned to face Gardner. She told herself to let go of the past week and think only of the present. This was to be her perfect weekend, perhaps the last weekend she would have with him.

"I'm glad to see you."

Gardner looked away from the road and smiled at her. "I'm glad to see you, too. Now that you're talking, there are things we need to discuss, squirt."

That he called her squirt suggested he intended to be open-minded, that he was willing to at least listen to an explanation.

When she didn't immediately respond, Gardner turned back to the road. "Tobler informed me Home Limited has filed a 13-D on La Tourraine, Durant and Von Marron."

"Yes." She hesitated. "I owe you an explanation, and I intend to give one." As much as she could. "But not right now." Reaching, she touched his sleeve, and let him see the appeal in her expression.

They drove without speaking, enjoying Vivaldi and each other's company, unwinding from the week behind them. Before turning the car down the gravel drive to Goose Point's veranda,

Gardner parked before the heavy iron gates and turned to face her.

"Home can't acquire a controlling interest in La Tourraine, Durant and Von Marron without the trust shares."

Immediately, Gloria felt the tension return. "I'd hoped we could delay this conversation. Please try to understand, Gardner. I'd like this to be a perfect weekend with no business between us. Just you and me."

He touched her cheek. "I wish it could be. But I don't think that's realistic. Too many things are hanging over us."

"We can try."

"When we drive through these gates, we'll do as you ask and try to put this discussion behind us. But there are some things that have to be talked about first." His hand dropped from her hair to the top of the seat. "You must be aware that I can't agree to any plan that will injure my father. You must know that, Gloria, so what is this weekend about? Good-byes?"

"I guess that depends on you."

Hesitating, he glanced toward the autumn sun playing across the front of the house. "I don't know yet how I feel about Home's bid for La Tourraine, Durant and Von Marron. I haven't worked it out. Personal considerations keep getting in the way. Obviously, there are significant advantages to both firms, but I'm having difficulty accepting that you would use mother and me as weapons against my father."

She bit her lip and looked away from him.

"If you proceed, Gloria, you'll have your revenge. You'll destroy my father. But if you use me as part of the process, you will also destroy whatever chance you and I might have had. Is that what you want?"

"Surely you understand the trusts are a point of vulnerability." Speaking in a low voice, she continued to look out of the window. "Anyone seeking to take over La Tourraine, Durant and Von Marron will approach the trusts."

Gently, he turned her face until she was forced to meet his eyes. "This isn't anyone. This is you. Regardless of advantages or benefits to either firm—you and I both understand revenge is the underlying motivation." He studied her expression. "Let it go, Gloria. There are a dozen other firms that meet Home's criteria and mesh with Home's objectives. Destroying my father won't change the past. Walt says you intend to telephone the trustees Monday to discuss the tender offer. Don't make those calls."

"I can't stop now," she whispered. "I've come too far, given up too much. I have to do this."

"I love you, Gloria, you know that. And I think you love me. Are you willing to throw our future away? Does it mean so little? And Home's future presidency—are you willing to alter that, too?"

"The presidency?"

"You're placing me in a situation whereby my shares will help destroy my father, then, as Home's president, you'll expect me ultimately to be responsible for his firm. Outsiders, and possibly my father, may believe I stood to gain considerably from this acquisition. Rumormongers who won't believe I engineered the takeover will certainly be aware I acquiesced to it if I accept the presidency. If you proceed, Gloria, you'll not only destroy my father's career, but mine as well. I can't accept the presidency under the circumstances unfolding now."

Gloria swore softly. "I never wanted you to be part of this."

"If that's true, then back off. Tell me you won't make those phone calls Monday to the family trustees. Tell me we'll find a different target for Home's cash."

Leaning her head back, Gloria closed her eyes. Gardner was right. It had been unrealistic to hope they could delay this discussion until after the weekend.

Finally she looked at him. "I've dreamed of this moment for years. Sometimes it was the only thing that kept me going. I've sacrificed more than you can know, too much to quit now that I'm so close. I'm genuinely sorry you're part of it. I wish that wasn't the case. But I have to acquire your trust shares and Chissie's to make this happen."

"I see."

She knew he thought he understood, but he did not. Seeing the pain in his expression, she longed to tell him about the rape and about Robby. Then he would understand why she could not stop. Clenching her teeth, Gloria turned her face toward the water in the Sound. Telling him about the rape was impossible—not even a consideration. But finally she could tell him about Robby now that it was almost over. She didn't want Gardner to learn about her son through the tabloids. When the right moment and the right circumstance appeared, she would tell him about Robby.

"Gardner," she said, trying again. "You don't understand. You don't know what I've sacrificed to reach this moment. You can't know what it's been like. Every single day for nearly seven years I have thought about your father and what he did to me."

Instantly she recognized her mistake as she watched him attempt to align seven years with the date of the buy-back of her father's partnership. Because this was not the right moment to confess Robby's existence, she hurried past the error, bringing his attention again to the present.

"I'm sorry, I wish this didn't involve you. But Monday morning the trusts will receive an offer from Home Limited."

He stared at her. "The crazy thing is, I believe you. I think you do regret involving mother and me. But not enough to change your mind."

Her voice emerged in a whisper. "I have to do this. Otherwise the last years will have been for nothing."

"I love you. Doesn't that count for something?"

Gloria felt the tears in the back of her throat. Pressing her lips together, she lifted her gaze toward Remy's grave.

"I love you, too, Gardner."

"That's the first time you've said it."

When she looked at him, he was smiling, and for a brief joyful instant she thought it would be all right. Maybe they could get through this. Then she saw that his smile didn't warm his eyes. Whatever they felt for each other, it wouldn't deter her from using him against his father. And he could not forgive her for that.

"It isn't going to work for us, is it?" She stared at his wide mouth and his dark eyes, and she felt a twist of pain. She wished the past could be changed, and they could have the future they should have had.

"I don't know."

"We have this weekend."

The words sounded adolescent and foolish. Abruptly Gloria remembered that devastating Christmas in Paris so long ago. Remy was dead; Lulu was hysterical; her father wandered in a private world of pain and shock. Bewildered and hurting, she had said, "But it's Christmas, we have Christmas," as if somehow Christmas day could create an island in the misery, as if they could push aside the past and everything would be wonderful for that one day.

"I'm beginning to understand this weekend," Gardner said finally. He stroked her hair, and his thumb caressed her cheek. "Make love to me, Gloria. Right now."

She tried to read his expression, seeing a mixture of urgency, desire, regret, farewell. Knowing she was about to lose him made her want him with an urgency that sent a tremor down the length of her body. "Yes," she whispered. "William won't arrive for several hours."

Gardner drove through the gates and parked the car in front of the veranda. Taking her hand, he led her across the emerald lawns and down the steps to the beach. The water rolling up the shore was chilly, but the sand had absorbed the sun's heat and was warm and yielding beneath their feet. Watching her, without speaking, Gardner removed his shirt and spread it over the sand near the sea wall. Then he kissed her, deeply, passionately, holding her against him as they sank to their knees, as his fingers lifted to her silk blouse.

"The night after Remy's funeral—do you remember?"

"I remember," she murmured against his lips. Her hands moved over his hair, his shoulders, seeking to know and remember.

"I wanted you even then."

"You sent me back to the house." Autumn sunlight glowed across her breasts in tones of fire and ivory as Gardner smoothed her blouse over her shoulders. He kissed one trembling nipple, and she gasped and caught her lip between her teeth.

"Then in London," he said against her throat. "And later at your apartment in Cambridge. I've spent my life wanting you."

First she undressed him, then she lay back on his shirt, feeling the heat of the sand through the thin material. She looked at his lean, tanned body, feeling her stomach tighten, then she closed her lashes and opened her arms to him. "I used to imagine making love to you on the beach."

They made love slowly, each wanting the moment to last. Exploring, teasing, they touched each other with stroking fingers and lingering tongues, letting the heat build until their need became too explosive to contain. When he finally entered her, and she felt her body close around him, she called his name and she said the words. "I love you. Oh Gardner, I love you."

Afterward, they lay together in a tangle of limbs and laughed at the sand sticking to their perspiring bodies. When they heard William's car door slam, they brushed off the sand, smiled, then went to the house and changed into shorts before returning to the beach with a tray of martinis and toast and caviar. Sitting with their backs against the sea wall, they watched the afternoon shadows steal across the sand toward twilight.

"Where would you like to go for dinner?"

She sat with her head against his shoulder. "I thought we'd stay here. Barbecue a couple of steaks, throw together a salad . . ."

"Good."

She laughed. "You're being agreeable."

He dropped a kiss on her hair and smiled. "I can't think of anyplace I'd rather be. I always loved Goose Point. The weekends and the holidays. I remember asking mother why we didn't have a place in the country, and she said we'd never find any place as perfect as Goose Point. The answer made sense then and does now. Do you come here often?"

"As often as I can. Not as often as I'd like." She clasped her arms around her knees. "Sometimes the memories are overwhelming."

Gardner stretched his legs in front of him and looked toward the water. "Remember when Remy and I first learned to sail?"

She grinned. "How many times did you capsize Dad's boat?"

"Bobby had more patience than we deserved."

"Remember the time you and Remy let me come along, then one of you thought you saw the Loch Ness monster?"

"So we threw you in as bait," Gardner laughed, remembering. "We thought we'd become famous if we caught a sea monster."

"I still miss him sometimes." She hugged her knees tight and pushed her heels into the sand. "I don't know what Remy and I would have done if we hadn't had each other. Mom and Dad were always going somewhere. They never really had time for us. That changed as Remy grew older and they began the battle over his future. But during the growing up years, it seemed all we had was each other. I used to envy you because Chissie and . . . because your parents were there for you."

"It wasn't like that. When I remember those years, there's a blank spot where my father should be. He was always working. I used to envy you and Remy for having a father who did something besides work, who knew how to enjoy life. It was years before I understood my father didn't accompany us to the polo fields because he had never played polo. He never learned to sail or ski or to ride a horse. The firm was the only thing he cared about." They were silent, then Gardner slipped his arm around her shoulders. "Are you getting cold?"

Firmly, Gloria banished Durant from her mind and wound her arms around Gardner's waist. "What I would like right now is a hot shower for two," she suggested in a throaty voice.

"What will William think?" he teased, smiling against her mouth.

"William will probably think you and I are doing what we should have done years ago."

"Sensible man, William."

Laughing, they ran toward the house. And with each step Gloria felt her anxiety dropping away. The weekend was going to work. When they had talked in front of the estate gates, she had wondered if she had been foolish to hope they could put Home Limited and La Tourraine, Durant and Von Marron and the rest of the world on hold. It was beginning to appear they could.

But later, as they lay in bed together, she looked at Gardner's sleeping face and felt the first sharp ache of a pain she sensed she would carry for a very long time. Possibly because she hadn't wanted to face what destroying his father would do to Gardner, she hadn't allowed herself to consider the consequences to him. Obviously, he was correct; he couldn't accept Home's presidency under these circumstances. She should have realized that from the beginning.

At a time when his career goals and ambitions were within his grasp, she was forcing him to alter his direction. Gloria didn't doubt a dozen firms would leap at the opportunity to acquire Gardner Durant's talents. She knew he had received attractive offers in the past. But that was not the issue. Home Limited was as much Gardner's company as it was hers. Perhaps more so. The firm bore his stamp in every department. His innovations had helped advance the company to the coveted position it now occupied. There was not a person at Home Limited who did not agree that Gardner had earned the top slot.

Was she so selfish, so narrowly focused, that she would sacrifice Gardner to satisfy her obsession to destroy his father? Was she that driven?

God help her, the answer was yes.

The past and the future it pointed toward remained between them despite their efforts to pretend they did not. Gardner felt the tension at odd moments, saw it draw Gloria's expression when she didn't know he watched. Once, when they were making love, he caressed her cheek and discovered it wet with tears. It wasn't necessary to ask the reason. He knew whatever drove her also caused her pain. He also knew her obsessive hatred for his father was greater than her love for him. This, he did not understand.

She was a woman of great pride, yes. And her sense of having been betrayed cut deep. He understood that. Had their positions been reversed, he believed he would have experienced similar shock and hatred. He, too, would have wanted revenge for the betrayal of family trust and loyalty. But he could not believe that he would have sought vengeance at the cost of his own future. He would not have used Gloria as a weapon in his personal war.

Opening an icy can of Coors, Gardner lifted his face to the sun and questioned if he was being honest with himself. When terrorists had abducted Andre Rodriguez, he had not relied on the Brazilian authorities. Without a moment's hesitation, he had ordered Che Arnand's mother and son picked up immediately. If Andre had not been released—would he have made good on his threat to match beating for beating, brutality for brutality? He doubted it, but he didn't know for a certainty. However, he knew he could never have used Arnand's mother and son if he had known them or had loved them.

Lowering his head from the bright sunlight, he watched Gloria moving about the deck of the boat. She was bright, lovely, sexually exciting—and driven. Moreover, he knew there were pieces still missing from the puzzle.

"I'm going in for a minute," she said, smiling at him as she removed a terry cover-up. The swimming suit she wore underneath was a black one-piece, cut high over her thighs, low at the breast.

"The water's too cold."

"Just for a moment."

He watched her dive into the water, then moved to the rail and grinned as she surfaced, gasping at the cold.

He loved her. He wanted to marry her and fill the rooms at Goose Point with beautiful children. He wanted to wake each morning to the excitement of knowing she slept beside him. He wanted their shared history to continue.

But it wasn't going to happen. His chest tightened against the loss. He might have been able to reconcile his love for Gloria and his love for his father and their hatred of each other. But he could not be a willing party to his father's destruction. He could not accept the obsessive quality that allowed Gloria to use him.

When she pulled herself out of the water, laughing and shivering, he wrapped her in the terry cover-up and held her close to him. Her mouth tasted of tears.

"Don't tear us apart," he said softly.

"I don't have a choice." She pressed her face against his shoulder and clung to him.

He held her and felt the laughter run out of her body, felt her tremble in his arms. Over her wet hair he watched as William descended the beach steps and ran a blue flag up the wharf pole.

"We could ignore it," he suggested when Gloria lifted her head and noticed the flag. He spoke lightly, knowing they would not ignore the flag.

"I wish we could."

He kissed her, lingering over her mouth, then he fired the auxiliary engine and steered the boat back toward the pier. One glance at William's anxious face and he knew the matter was urgent and that it involved Gloria.

"There's a call from Lewes, Miss," William said when they were near enough that Gloria could jump to the dock.

William caught her as she landed on the pier. She examined his expression, her face pale, then she spun and sprinted toward the house, choosing a childhood shortcut Gardner had forgotten years ago.

"Lewes?" he asked, easing the boat into the slip.

William's mouth worked as if he wanted to speak, then he made a motion with his hands and hurried forward across the sand to the steps.

There was so much he didn't know, Gardner thought as he tied the boat and secured it. Areas of Gloria's life remained closed to him. Hell, he didn't know if Lewes was a person or a place. Whoever or whatever, the mention of Lewes had caused her face to go white and had sent her running off without a backward glance.

At the top of the beach stairs, he paused to brush the sand from the bottom of his feet and pull on his tennis shoes. When he was certain he had conquered any residue of jealousy, he continued into the house.

The moment he saw her slumped forward, her face twisted with pain, he knew something was terribly wrong.

"Darling?"

"No police," she whispered into the telephone. "I'll take care of it from this end."

"Gloria? What's happened?"

Bright autumn sunlight streamed through the tall windows, washing all the color from her face. Her eyes were a pale lavender gray. She stepped backward when he moved forward and she raised her palms. "Oh, Gardner." Her voice was raw, a hoarse whisper.

He couldn't pin down the changing emotions constricting her expression. Fury, fear, hatred, despair. His stomach contracted.

She passed a hand over her eyes, swayed on her feet. "I wanted to tell you. I was waiting for the right moment. Now even that has been taken from me. Now . . ."

Brushing aside her protests, he caught her shoulders and ran his hands over her chilled skin. She tensed and went rigid beneath his fingertips. "Whatever it is, darling, whatever's happened, it can't be so bad that—"

"My son has been kidnapped."

At first the words did not register. He looked down at her, a smile of reassurance on his lips. Then, as he understood what she had said, his immediate thought was that she was joking. Despite her pallor and the desperation behind her eyes, despite the trembling that shook her body, he thought it had to be a joke.

"Your son?" He repeated the words, not believing them.

"His name is Robby. He's seven years old." She would have collapsed to the carpet if he hadn't caught her and eased her onto the Queen Anne settee. "Goddamn Durant!" Tight fists formed against her lap. "Goddamn him to hell!" Dropping forward, she closed her eyes and pressed both shaking fists hard against her mouth.

"My father?"

He stared at her, unable to conceive that Gloria had a son. And she had concealed the knowledge for—what was the boy's age?—seven years. He shook his head to clear it, staring at her as if he were watching a stranger.

Rage blazed in her eyes when she raised her head. "Your father kidnapped Robby! That bastard took my son!"

It was like wandering into a theater midway through the second act. "Gloria, that can't be true."

"That's the message the kidnappers phoned to Margaret: 'Tell the bitch her son is in his father's care.' Oh, God. God. I didn't think even Durant would go this far!"

Shock dulled his thought processes. She could not be saying what it sounded like she was saying. He dropped to the settee beside her, struggling to understand. When he worked it out, he felt as if someone had kicked him in the groin; the air left his lungs in a rush. Turning, he stared at her in disbelief.

He spoke slowly, trying to breathe. "Are you saying you had an affair with my father? That you have a child by him?"

She spun to face him on the bench. The blood rushed back into her face, and her eyes turned almost black.

"An affair? Never! Win Durant raped me! He came into the guest room and forced himself on me!"

A vise clamped around his chest. "No. That is not possible. There has to be a mistake." Pushing to his feet, he shook his head. The vise tightened around his ribs.

"There's no mistake." Her mouth twisted. She looked up at him, then her face collapsed. "Oh Gardner. Oh my God. I swore I'd never tell you. I didn't want—"

But he could not stay to hear any more. The room had gotten very hot. There was no air. All he could think about was getting out of there. Images of Gloria lying in his father's arms rose in front of his mind. He imagined her body arching upward, the nipples taut and rose-colored, her eyes closed, her lips parted. He saw his father rising over her, pushing into her.

"Jesus Christ." A sour taste flooded his mouth. His stomach rolled.

"Gardner, please."

She stretched a hand to him, but he continued stepping backward, away from her. Tears wet her stranger's face; her unfamiliar eyes were anguished.

At the door he turned and pushed past William without seeing him. For a moment he sat in his car, frozen, his knuckles turning white where his hands gripped the wheel.

It wasn't true. It couldn't be true.

He turned the ignition, stepped hard on the gas and heard a spray of gravel behind him.

His father and Gloria.

Unwanted images played before his eyes. Gloria. And his father. Kissing her magnificent breasts. Stroking the feathery silver between her legs. Thrusting into her. A sharp, bitter taste returned to his mouth, and he spun the car to the verge of the road, opened the door, and vomited into the grass and autumn wildflowers.

When nothing more came up, he pulled himself back inside the car, wiped his mouth, then dropped his forehead against the steering wheel. For the first time since childhood, his eyes filled with tears.

Chapter 20

WHEN THE TELEPHONE RANG, Durant laid aside his newspaper and smiled. The call was expected.

"It's Miss Von Marron, sir," Abrams said from the doorway.

"Gloria?" Looking up from the novel she was reading, Chissie removed her glasses and regarded him with a hopeful expression. "Maybe she's changed her plans about the firm."

"I'll take the call in my study," Durant said to Abrams. He freshened his drink at the butler's tray and pressed Chissie's shoulder as he passed. "You could be right. It wouldn't surprise me if Gloria has changed her mind. Wouldn't surprise me at all."

In no hurry, he entered his study, closed the door, and seated himself behind his desk. Before he picked up the telephone, he selected one of the Havana Coronas Senator Shackley had brought him from Cuba. Shackley insisted each was lovingly rolled between the thighs of nubile young Cuban beauties. He clipped the end with a gold utensil he had received from the club as a token of appreciation for his years as president. Chissie had purchased the gold and malachite lighter at Davidoff's for his birthday.

Leaning back, he puffed, then smiled at the lazy curl of smoke floating toward the bookcase. The fragrance was as rich and sweet as the scent of victory.

After crossing his ankles comfortably on top of his desk, he picked up the telephone.

"You filthy son of a bitch! Where is my son?"

Pleasure widened his smile. The famed Von Marron control had shattered.

"The terms are simple." He exhaled toward the ceiling, absently seeking patterns in the drift of smoke. "You get him back when you call off the raid on La Tourraine, Durant and Von Marron.''

"You'll spend the rest of your life in jail, Durant. I'll see that they hang you!''

"Now, now, Gloria dear. Do calm yourself. Do we really want to bring the police into this?'' He rolled the cigar between his fingers, examined the quality of the ash accumulating at the tip. There were few things more satisfying than a genuine Havana Corona at an appropriate moment. "Police mean reporters. You know that. Are you prepared to break the story about young Robby? And what will you tell the press, I wonder, to explain why you've concealed Robby all these years?''

"I'll tell them you raped me, you slimy bastard!''

"Ah, yes. That old story. And I suppose you'll suggest the child is mine?''

"You know he is!''

"I know you'd like to hang it on me. The press would love that, wouldn't they? A juicy sex scandal to follow young Robby all the rest of his life and yours. No, my dear, I doubt you really want that. So, we'll leave the police out of this, shall we?''

She made a choking sound. Rage, despair, he couldn't put a label on it, but the sound gave him great pleasure. "What do you want?'' she asked finally, her voice low, almost inaudible.

"First, you back off the family trusts. There will be no tender offer. Second, you sell me all the shares of La Tourraine, Durant and Von Marron that you have accumulated to date. My offering price is seven dollars a share.''

"Seven dollars?'' Incredulity followed by rage thinned her voice. "You're offering seven dollars per share?''

She had bought in stock at prices ranging from fourteen to eighteen and had intended to tender for the balance at twenty-five. Durant calculated she would lose millions. It was a just price for the inconvenience and anxiety she had cost him.

The deal he was negotiating was a nice piece of business. In effect, he was taking the firm away from the public. When things calmed down, he would return to the public and freeze them out of the remaining shares with a reverse split.

"I'll offer, say, a half-million up front and you will carry back a noninterest-bearing note for the balance.''

"You go straight to hell!''

The phone slammed down in his ear.

Leaning back in his chair, Durant rolled the cigar between

his thumb and forefinger, then puffed contentedly while he waited for her to call back.

Gloria dropped her head in her hands and covered her face with shaking fingers. Every instinct screamed at her, demanding that she telephone the police. But Durant had called it correctly. If she brought in the police, a swarm of reporters would surely follow. The scandal would play for weeks, sweeping along Home Limited and La Tourraine, Durant and Von Marron, and possibly Nestor Brothers as well. The sleaze tabloids would resurrect the old nonsense about the curse of the Von Marron diamond. Remy's death would be rehashed, and Lulu's stay at Les Eaux, and Bobby's reputation. A storm of speculation would whirl around Robby, seeking to learn the identity of his father. Her photograph would appear on the front cover of every newspaper in the world. As a result, her publicity-shy clients would evaporate like morning mist.

Her fingernails dug into her scalp.

"Can I get you anything, Miss? A drink perhaps?"

"No. Thank you, William, no."

Because her nerves would not allow her to sit still, because she could not bear to remain near the telephone, she ran out of the house and paced restlessly across the estate grounds. The sea breeze blowing against her wet swimming suit chilled her skin, but she didn't notice. She circled the stables, lingered for a moment beside Remy's grave, then she returned to the empty beach.

She kicked along the edge of the water, her mind racing to find a solution that would allow her to beat Durant.

One option was to call his bluff. In this scenario, she proceeded as planned and phoned the trustees tomorrow morning with the tender offer. Within forty-eight hours she would own enough stock to demand a seat on La Tourraine, Durant and Von Marron's board. The majority voting block would be hers. She would call a board meeting immediately and eject Durant. He would be finished. At that moment Robby would cease to be of any value to him, and he would release her son.

But would he? Or would he punish her by arranging for Robby's disappearance to become permanent? She didn't think even Durant would resort to murder, but if he chose to release Robby into the streets of a European capital the result would be the same. At age seven Robby would not know how to contact her or Margaret. If he survived, he would vanish into one of the roving bands of homeless street urchins. She would never find him.

Rejecting this option, Gloria backtracked in her mind.

All right, start again. Look for a different approach. Was it possible to link Durant to the kidnapping? A moment's reflection indicated such a link was possible but unlikely. Durant was canny enough, careful enough to keep his involvement at a far remove. In all probability the actual kidnappers had no idea of the principal's identity. If by some miracle the English and American officials were able to eventually trace an involvement to Durant, the evidence would have to be irrefutable or he would slip through the system unscathed.

Durant had beaten her.

For several minutes she stood at the edge of the shore and watched while her feet turned icy red as cold water swirled around her ankles.

Durant's demands could be met, that was not a problem. She would buy back the firm's shares from Home Limited, then sell them to Durant. The transaction would deplete her personal fortune by at least fifty million. If Durant reneged on his note, as she expected, she would lose another fifty million. Minimum.

Lifting her head, Gloria stared at the horizon and let the breeze tangle her hair and cool her hot face. One hundred million dollars against the safe return of her son. There was nothing to consider, no real decision to make.

Turning on her heel, she crossed the sand and returned to the house, then she dialed the telephone.

"You win," she said when Durant came on the line. His laugh blinded her, and she sat quickly before her knees collapsed. "Where is my son?"

"You Von Marrons are so impatient. In due time, my dear Gloria. All in due time."

"You get nothing until I have my son. Not a single share of stock."

"You forget who's in control. You're in no position to make demands. You'll get our son when I have my stock. Not before."

Gloria covered her eyes with her fingers and made herself draw a deep breath. "That is not acceptable. I can't do anything until tomorrow. I'll have to buy the shares from Home Limited, which will require time to arrange financing. Liquidation of assets, sale of property, something." She waved a hand. "I can't do it overnight. I'll need at least a week, possibly longer."

"What is or is not acceptable is my decision, not yours."

"Win—for God's sake. Robby is only seven years old. He's never been away from home before. He's with strangers and probably terrified. Don't do this! I've told you I'll sell at seven dollars a share. I'll do whatever you ask. Just let Robby go, I beg you."

His voice was low and pleasant. He was enjoying this immensely. "Now, that wouldn't be good business. If I release the boy immediately, I have an idea you might change your mind about our agreement. You call yourself a businesswoman; you can understand my position. Plus, arranging the financing may not require a week. After all, you're motivated."

She heard him exhale, pictured him smiling around a cigar.

"When I've got the stock—you get the boy."

She swore, fighting the nausea that rolled across her stomach in cramping waves. "At least tell me he's safe. Tell me he's being cared for."

"Your touching but tardy display of motherly concern is duly noted." He laughed, then the line went dead in her hand.

She didn't know how many minutes elapsed before she hung up the buzzing phone and pushed to her feet. She pulled herself upstairs and stood in a shower with the water turned as hot as she could stand it, then she wrapped herself in an old robe and sat before her bedroom window to wait for Monday.

Goddamn, he felt good. His defense was unfolding precisely as he had anticipated. Aside from protecting the firm, he would end with enough shares in La Tourraine, Durant and Von Marron to ensure that a bastard like John Peterson could never again mount a serious challenge against him. The sheer beauty of the plan lay in the fact that he would accomplish everything with a capital expenditure of only half a million dollars. It was the greatest coup of his career, the only flaw being there was no one to observe his brilliance. No one would ever learn of it.

The bottom line was, he had saved his firm.

Nevertheless a dark threat waited behind the silver lining. He had stopped Home Limited's raid, but he remained vulnerable to attack from other raiders. The new infusion of stock would offer greater protection, but he wasn't safe yet. Early next week, he would direct the firm's attorneys to the problem. They would reexamine the trusts, analyze the points of vulnerability. He would instruct them to install a series of bullet-proof defenses. In fact, he owed Von Marron a debt of gratitude because her attempted raid had opened his eyes to a possibility he hadn't seriously considered. Now aware, he would protect against fu-

ture threats. Revitalized, he returned to the living room with a
spring in his step and a smile on his face.

Relief softened the anxiety in Chissie's expression. "Gloria
changed her mind, didn't she? She isn't going to buy La Tourraine, Durant and Von Marron."

He bent to kiss her hair, tried to remember when they had last
made love. Things were going his way, and he felt like celebrating. Perhaps tonight. "It seems you were right, my dear.
Gloria has indeed changed her mind."

"I'm so glad, Win. I hoped she would. I simply couldn't
imagine our Gloria doing something like that."

They both turned toward the door as Gardner burst into the
room unannounced. Chissie stood from the sofa and stared at
him before she rushed forward. "My God, Gardner. What's
happened? What's wrong?" She touched his cheek, peered into
his eyes.

He looked at his father. "I was with Gloria when the call
came from Lewes. Is it true? Are you responsible?"

"Not in front of your mother. Chissie, leave us." He had not
anticipated this complication. A rush of anger tarnished his mood
of celebration. From the beginning the Von Marron bitch had
tried to involve Gardner and poison his son against him. It wasn't
only the past for which he sought redress. What she had done
to drive a wedge between himself and his only son had person-
alized his hatred.

"I don't understand." Chissie looked from Durant to Gardner. "You were with Gloria today? She just phoned—"

"This does not concern you, Chissie. Get out." Durant raised
his voice. "Now." He waited until she left the room, reluctantly, biting her lips, then his brows meshed and he spoke in a
tone of low fury. "How dare you burst in here and frighten your
.mother?"

Gardner's eyes were red-rimmed, a button was missing from
his shirt, and he was wearing shorts and tennis shoes, for Christ's
sake. He looked like shit.

"Gloria's son has been kidnapped. She believes you're responsible. Tell me it's not true. Tell me you didn't have anything
to do with this."

"I'm here. Her son is in England." He smiled and shrugged.

"That's not good enough." Gardner shoved him backward
with the heel of his hand, and Durant jerked, too astonished to
experience yet the anger that would follow. It was the first time
he could remember a threat of violence in this household.

"Don't fuck with me." Gardner's eyes narrowed; he spoke between his teeth. "No vague answers. Are you involved or not? Yes or no?"

"This is between Gloria and me. Stay out of it. This doesn't concern you."

Gardner shoved him again, harder. "Yes or no."

A lifetime had elapsed since those long-ago days of brawling in the oil fields. He was no longer a young man. Regardless, Durant paused to weigh his chances against his son before he opened his fists and raised his palms. "Take your hand off me," he said coldly.

"The truth. Are you involved or not?"

"There's no need for violence. All you have to do is ask; I've never lied to you."

That Gardner hesitated before he lowered his fists and stepped backward indicated how deeply the Von Marron bitch had influenced him.

"Then answer me. Did you arrange to have Gloria's son kidnapped?"

"You saw the newspapers. I'm sure Tobler telephoned you. You know what she was trying to do."

"So help me God . . ."

"All right—yes. I've got the boy. He's safe; he's being cared for. No one is going to hurt him."

"Oh Christ!" Gardner stared, then turned toward the windows and covered his eyes. "I didn't want to believe it."

"Listen to me. You know what happened in the market last week, but do you know what happened to La Tourraine, Durant and Von Marron? We were savaged. It was a goddamn fucking nightmare. Overnight the firm lost sixty percent of its market capitalization. I lost two-thirds of my personal fortune. I can rebuild, but I need time to sort out the carnage. Gloria Von Marron saw what was happening. Shit, she's been waiting for this moment for years. She swooped down like a vampire eager to suck what blood remained. She took advantage of the firm's lowest point." He spread his hands. "Surely you understand I couldn't allow her to steal my firm."

"But—kidnapping?" Gardner's lip curled back from his whisper. "Abducting a child?"

"What else was there? All these years she's been waiting to use that kid against me, I merely turned the tables and got there first." He spoke to Gardner's back as Gardner walked to the windows and stood looking down at Park Avenue. "Of course

I regret having to use the boy, but there isn't an alternative. This is the only way to win.''

How dare his son walk away from him in disgust?

"This is business," he said sharply. "Before you take a superior posture, perhaps you'd like to explain how this is different from you snatching Che Arnand's mother and kid? It's all right for you to do whatever is necessary to protect your firm, but not all right for me to do the same? Is that your position?''

"Che Arnand is a thug and a murderer. An extortionist and a terrorist. Gloria is none of those things.''

"The hell she isn't. Did she approach me with a legitimate offer? Did she make a single attempt to sit down and negotiate? Shit, no. She took. Like the Von Marrons have always taken!''

Gardner turned from the windows. "Did you rape her?''

"Is that what she told you?" They stared at each other. "I didn't rape her; she wanted it. Don't turn away from me. You wanted the truth, so listen to it. She all but invited me into her room that night. She knew what she was doing.''

"You're saying she didn't resist?''

"Some woman like to be overpowered; that's how they get it off. Yes, she pretended to resist, but it was no rape. Win Durant doesn't have to rape a woman to get laid, for Christ's sake.''

Gardner clenched his teeth. His voice was strained. "And the boy?''

"She told you I was the kid's father, right? I figured that one years ago. The boy is her ace in the hole in case she can't get La Tourraine, Durant and Von Marron any other way. The minute I'm gone, she'll trot out the kid and swear I was the father, therefore he's entitled to share in my estate. That kid has been a grenade from the beginning. It was only a question of who pulled the pin first. Me or her.''

"The message you left in Lewes admits you're the father.''

"Don't be stupid." Durant waved a hand. "She may believe that—I don't.'' His laugh was ugly. "A long time ago I hired an investigator to dig into that time period and find out who the kid's father really is.''

Gardner stared at him, his fists opening and closing at his sides.

"You want the truth, Gardner? You want to know who the father is? Just how much truth can you stand?''

"Say it.''

"You are.'' Durant's smile was as hard as his laughter. "There's your truth. You haven't seen the boy or you would know. He looks like you.'' The look on Gardner's face made him laugh again. ''You're the only man she dated during that time period. At Cambridge after her graduation, remember? It's all in the file. You were observed coming out of her apartment the night she graduated, probably the night she got pregnant. You were seen kissing her in the hallway outside her door in the wee hours. A passionate kiss according to the witness.'' Durant winked. ''You were there a week before I was, pal. The only reason you weren't set up to take the fall is because she has more to gain by going after me.''

''You son of a bitch,'' Gardner whispered. His face was pale. ''I didn't touch her in Cambridge. I wanted to, but I didn't. All we did was talk. We talked about her dream of taking a position at La Tourraine, Durant and Von Marron. She wanted to work with the legend of Wall Street. She wanted to work with 'Uncle Win'.'' His jaw clenched. ''I wasn't with her until years later. You want the truth? The truth is, you raped her and you fathered her son.''

A moan came from the doorway, and they both jerked toward the sound. Chissie lay slumped against the door, her face gray, her eyes washed of color. She stared at Durant.

''Not Gloria,'' she whispered, ''not Lulu's daughter. Oh God, how could you?'' When she opened her eyes again, they were dull with pain. ''Get out. Be out of here within the hour, Win, or I'll call the police and have you thrown out.''

A chill shot to his toes. Chissie was his respectability, his social entrée. Without her, every door in town would slam shut against him.

''How long have you been standing there? You don't believe any of this, do you?''

''You raped her. Oh God.'' She pressed a hand to her stomach. ''One hour, Win. That is all.'' Moving like an old woman, Chissie turned down the hallway.

Durant swore violently. He didn't need this shit in the middle of everything else. He would make things right with Chissie; he always had before. But the timing couldn't be worse.

Disgust filled Gardner's eyes. ''Where is Gloria's son?''

''You lied about Cambridge.'' It had to be a lie. Robert Winthrop Von Marron was not his child. He had not abducted his own child.

''Tell me where the boy is, or by Christ I'll phone the police right now!''

''I don't know where he is. And don't threaten me, Gardner.

This isn't your problem. If Gloria wanted the police on this, don't you think she would have phoned them herself?''

"If you don't know, you know who does."

"Can you really think I'm so stupid that I would involve myself in the details of a kidnapping?''

"Call the middle man and tell him it's over. Tell your thugs to release the boy."

"I couldn't even if I wanted to. My contact is out of the country on a long vacation." Durant's lips pulled back from his teeth as he watched Gardner's fist come down and shatter the sofa table. Chissie's glasses and her novel crashed to the floor beside a Staffordshire lamp.

Gardner shouted. "There has to be a signal, something to tell them when the deal's completed. What is it?''

The signal was an ad in the *London Times*. "Nothing has changed. No one is going to steal my firm. I won't allow it. She gets the boy when I get the stock."

"The firm. It's always the goddamn firm! The firm justifies anything, doesn't it? Nothing else was ever important, not mother, not me, not common decency. Just the goddamn firm!''

"The firm did pretty well by you, or would you rather have grown up as I did? Living in a tarpaper shack, breathing the stink of a leaking cesspool. You're damn right the firm is important. I gave my life to La Tourraine, Durant and Von Marron so you and your mother wouldn't have to live the life I did. So you could have all the things I only dreamed about!''

"Bullshit. You never gave a thought to mother or me. What you did, you did for yourself. You built the firm to satisfy your own ambition and greed, and you used anyone and anything along the way. Nothing was illegal or unethical if it benefited you or the firm."

"That's business. That's the American way. You do what you have to do."

They stared at each other across the shattered table. When Gardner finally spoke, his voice was cold. "I am going to find that child. And this time you'll take responsibility for what you've done. If that means prison, that's what you're looking at. You can't kidnap a child and call it business. You can't excuse rape and kidnapping by claiming it's the American way. No.''

"If you take this thing public, you'll destroy your mother and your precious Gloria."

"I think they're both stronger than you believe." Gardner slammed the foyer door behind him.

"Sir?" Abrams peered into the living room, looked at the table and the lamp on the floor.

"Get out. Take a long walk."

He poured a stiff drink, waiting for his temper to subside, waiting for Abrams to let himself out the penthouse door. Standing over the shattered lamp, he rehearsed what he would say to Chissie. She loved him; they had spent a lifetime together. There was no need to create a scandal. In the end, she would persuade herself he was telling the truth as she had always done before.

Irritated by the necessity of a scene, he followed the hallway to the double doors leading into their bedroom.

"Chissie. Darling—"

"No talk, Win, not this time. I mean it. I want you out of here in . . ." She glanced at the diamond watch he had given her for their thirty-fifth anniversary. "In thirty-eight minutes."

"What you overheard is a lie. If you'll listen, I can explain."

When he started toward her, she lifted her hand from the folds of her skirt. She was holding the .38 revolver he kept in the drawer beside the bed. As far as he knew the gun had never been fired. He doubted she knew enough to release the safety.

Resisting an impulse to smile at her show of melodramatics, he concentrated on what the gun indicated. This incident was not going to be like the others. This time she was not going to buy a glib excuse.

"All right," he said, spreading his hands in a conciliatory gesture. "It's true I had a moment of weakness. You've seen Gloria; you know what she's like. She came on to me. She seduced me, and I admit I was weak enough to fall for it."

"You're wasting time, Win."

"It was just that once. And that was—what?—six or seven years ago. For Christ's sake, Chissie. You're too sensible to throw away a lifetime because of one quick screw that didn't mean a damn thing."

For an instant he believed he had convinced her and he started forward. Then her expression changed. She pointed the gun in front of his feet and pulled the trigger.

"Jesus Christ!" The bullet charred a small hole in the Portuguese carpet. He thanked God the apartment below was vacant.

"It isn't going to work this time, Win. Gloria wasn't the first or the last. I've deluded myself for the last time. You've got thirty-two minutes."

He stared at her in open-mouthed disbelief. She had shot at him. His wife had fucking shot at him.

"Tomorrow morning I'll see Bradly Whitmore. Call and let him know who your lawyers will be." She kept the gun aimed at his groin. "I'll keep the penthouse and the town house in Paris. I'll expect a generous settlement. As a condition of the divorce, you will set up a trust equal to Gardner's and mine for Gloria's son."

Sweat dampened his temples and his upper lip. Her hands were shaking, and she was swinging the goddamn gun around like it was a toy. "Give me the gun, Chissie, then we'll talk."

She closed her eyes and fired again. This time the bullet passed between his wrist and his thigh. It was only by the grace of God that she didn't hit him.

"Jesus H. Christ! Will you put that down before someone gets hurt?"

Standing, she advanced toward him, holding the gun in front of her in hands that shook so badly it scared the living shit out of him. He moved backward.

Her lips pulled up from her teeth. "I think you had better leave now. Right now. I'll have Abrams deliver your things to your club."

He stared at her. This was no time to attempt to reason with her. Later, when she had calmed down, he would talk to her. At this moment she was capable of shooting him. He saw it in her face. Christ, she *wanted* to shoot him. He lifted his hands in a parody of surrender.

"I'm going. I'll telephone you later."

"Don't."

Chapter 21

GARDNER RETURNED to his hotel suite, took a shower, and changed his clothes. After placing several telephone calls, he threw some things into a bag, drove directly to JFK and took a seat on the first flight departing for London.

He had the first-class section nearly to himself as there were only three other passengers, all of whom had retreated behind newspapers. After ordering a drink from the flight attendant, he turned to the window and withdrew into himself.

His father and Gloria. The image lay only a pulse beat away. Each time he thought of it, fresh shock and revulsion wrenched his stomach. What his father had done was unthinkable, unforgivable. Like a stone hurled into a dark pond, ripples generated outward from Win Durant's act of violence. Bobby, Lulu, his mother, himself, Gloria and her son, they had all been affected directly or indirectly.

Finally he understood why Gloria had sought refuge at Goose Point instead of pursuing a position at La Tourraine, Durant and Von Marron as she had intended. Now he understood the lengthy period during which she had appeared to vanish. Finally, wrenchingly, he understood why she had not confided in him. She had tried to protect him, believing the truth would cause a permanent rupture between himself and his father. As it had.

Leaning his head against the back of the seat, he closed his eyes. After a time he made himself face the realization that the only woman he had ever loved was the mother of his half brother.

His teeth ground together, and the taste of ashes rose in his throat. Christ. He swallowed his drink quickly, signaled for another.

Where was the child now? What type of scar would this experience leave on the boy? And Gloria. What was she doing?

What was she thinking? Did she understand why he'd had to leave her? This disturbed him as deeply as the abduction, that his personal shock and anguish had driven him away when she needed him. He had left her to face the fear and anxiety alone, as she had faced so many shocks alone.

When the plane banked and began its descent toward Heathrow, he glanced out the window with a feeling of relief, glad to escape his thoughts.

Nigel Watson, Home's vice president in charge of North Sea Operations, met him outside Immigration. One of Home's limousines wisked them to Nigel's club where they were shown immediately to a private room. Gardner noted tones of muted maroon and navy, artfully if haphazardly arranged furnishings bearing the glossy patina of centuries. Portraits of the founding club members hung in gilt frames suspended from the ceiling.

"Breakfast?"

"Just coffee."

"Shall we get to it then, as you Americans like to say?"

Tall, expensively but conservatively dressed by Benson and Clegg, Nigel Watson appeared more a denizen of The City than a man intimately familiar with the rough world of drilling. Gardner and Nigel had worked together in the South American jungles and he knew Nigel to be younger than his white hair indicated, harder than his Eton and Cambridge background might suggest.

After the waiter served them coffee and had withdrawn, closing the door behind him, Gardner rubbed a hand over his eyes, then looked at Nigel.

"What have you got?"

"The abduction occurred at a Sunday church picnic taking place at a park near the Tilbury home. A woman pushing a baby carriage approached the Tilburys and distracted them momentarily. When they returned to the play area, the boy was gone."

"The baby carriage was a set-up?"

"It appears so. According to our source, the Tilburys didn't immediately realize what had happened. They raised an alarm and several people assisted in searching for the boy. Then, rather abruptly it seemed to our witness, the Tilburys ended the search by explaining the boy's nanny had taken him home."

"That's when they must have guessed the boy had been kidnapped."

"At present, Mrs. Tilbury is in a doctor's care. Her neighbors believe she has suffered a stroke."

"Has she?"

"We'll know by this afternoon. It's possible she's isolated herself and is awaiting another contact from the abductors."

"Did anyone actually see the boy taken? Did they notice a car? Anything?"

"We're taking it slowly, moving with care as you instructed. The agency we're using has been instructed to learn what they can without alarming anyone. So far, we have no information regarding the actual abduction. Perhaps by the end of the day I can report something more concrete."

"Thank you, Nigel. You've accomplished a great deal already."

"Gardner—the authorities should be notified."

"That isn't my decision to make."

"I understand the difficulties involved. However, there's only so far a private firm can proceed with something like this. Assume they do locate the boy. What then?"

"I'll do what I can to persuade the principal to involve the police." They both knew to whom he referred, but neither mentioned her by name. A dozen questions flickered behind Nigel's direct gaze, none of which he asked. "For the moment, let's assume no authorities will be involved."

"Home has two thousand employees in England. The boy's photograph could be distributed among them, but it's a long shot. Plus, we could not rely on discretion. I think our best approach is to continue the search for the woman with the baby carriage. But Gardner—again, I feel compelled to stress the need for official assistance."

Nigel was right, of course. Gardner rubbed the stubble appearing on his jaw. Once the police were on it, the reporters would be also. "I'll speak to the principal."

Nigel nodded. "Please extend my sympathies. It's a rotten thing, this."

Gloria watched the dawn climb out of the Sound. Pink and gold pressed at the dark horizon, rippled across the water. Twenty minutes later a shaft of sunlight illuminated the trophy wall behind her, spotlighting rows of blue ribbons and silver statuettes.

This time she had lost.

Standing, she placed her hands against the small of her back and stretched cramped muscles as she studied the trophy wall.

All of her life she had focused on winning. And what pleasure had it brought her? Precious little. Winning had never been enough. The ribbons fading on her wall had not won Lulu's attention or interest, nor had they persuaded her parents to spend more time with her. Similar rows of tombstones embedded in lucite crowded the cabinet behind her desk. They had won respect and envy, but not friendship.

How important was winning? Did it really matter that Durant had won and she had lost?

As short a time as a week ago, she would have answered the question with an emphatic yes. But yesterday the world had spun upside down and something she had lost sight of long ago had spilled out.

Winning didn't matter. In the broad scheme of things, winning was a small event. Insignificant. Today's victory was merely tomorrow's statistic. One small number on a page filled with numbers that no one would ever tally.

People mattered. Relationships mattered. Robby mattered most of all. At what point had she forgotten?

A tiny moan closed her throat as she thought of Robby. Releasing the obsession to win, to beat Durant, had resulted in stripping away justifications she had held firmly in place for years. The harsh light of guilt glared on tender areas she had shielded by staunchly defended justifications.

She had failed Robby. She had denied him, had put him out of her life.

As dawn spread Goose Point in golden shadows, Gloria stared out the window and recalled a lonely childhood. By extension, she recognized Robby's childhood, as neglected and confused as her own. She had sentenced her son to repeat history. Robby Von Marron was growing up in a distant country without his mother and with no knowledge of a father. He had not spent a single hour at Goose Point, his home. He had no sense of family or of his own identity and background. She had been absent for his first pony ride, his first school play. She had been too busy to share the important events in her son's life. His mother was a beautiful stranger who appeared for birthdays and Christmas.

"Oh God." Tears spilled over her lashes.

What she had done was inexcusable, unforgivable. How could she have been so blind? How could she have convinced herself that revenge was more important than her son? The selfish wasted years unreeled before her thoughts, impossible to retrieve. A desperate urge not to allow another day, another minute, to pass without her son tightened her fists. She could not alter the past, but she could change the direction of the future. If only she knew where he was. Frustration and helplessness drained her strength. She had to find him; she had to find him now. To hell with the scandal, that had only been an excuse. Nothing mattered but Robby. She needed him and he needed her.

She wiped the tears from her eyes with an angry motion and reached for the telephone, jumping when it rang under her hand.

"It's Gardner."

"Gardner." His face rose in her memory, his expression twisted in shock and revulsion. Her shoulders dropped. She had lost him, too.

"Gloria? Are you there? I'm in London with Nigel Watson. I've taken the liberty of ordering a private investigation. Some progress has been made, but Nigel and I believe the authorities should be involved."

He was in London? "I agree. I was about to phone them myself when you called." She covered her eyes with her hand. "As you're there, will you act in my behalf and contact Scotland Yard immediately?"

"You know what will happen. We'll request discretion, of course, but there's certain to be a leak. The reporters will be on the story by this time tomorrow. Your photograph is going to be in all the scandal rags."

"That doesn't matter. Just find Robby. I know—I've spent years avoiding a scandal. But I was wrong, Gardner. Nothing is important except Robby."

"Have you heard anything more from Margaret? We have a report she suffered a stroke."

Gloria closed her eyes and listened to his voice. He sounded so close, and she needed him so much. "Yes, I've spoken to the doctor. The danger is past, but I'd rather Margaret and Edmund weren't disturbed unless it's absolutely necessary. They're taking it very badly."

"Then we'll need—"

"I'll be on the next plane. First, I have to speak to my attorneys. To meet your father's demands, I have to buy back Home's shares of La Tourraine, Durant and Von Marron."

Gardner finally spoke into the silence. "You're going to meet his demands then? Is that what you want?"

"I want my son." Her voice broke. "Oh God, Gardner, I keep thinking about him. He's so little. He must be so frightened.'' She pressed the back of her hand to her eyes. ''I'll do whatever it takes to get him back.''

''Will you consider this? Talk to your lawyers and instruct them to begin the financial arrangements, but tell them you expect the process to take several days.''

''It will. The financing could require as long as a week.''

''That will give us some time at this end. If we locate Robby before you buy back the shares and sell them to my father . . .'' His voice hardened and turned cold. ''I will personally deliver the tender offer to the family trusts. I telephoned mother before I left and she agrees. She insists on phoning the trustees to urge them to accept the tender.''

''Chissie?'' Pain blurred her whisper. ''Oh God. I didn't want her to know.''

''When this is over, Gloria, she wants to see you. She's afraid you won't talk to her.''

''Of course I'll talk to her; Chissie was never part of this.'' The tears wouldn't stop. Lifting the hem of a Pratesi wrapper, she pressed it to her eyes.

''We were all part of it, Gloria.''

In the silence, she struggled to control her voice. ''You talked to him, didn't you? Gardner—are you all right?'' She continued to see his shock, remembered him backing away from her.

When he finally answered, he sounded older and very tired. ''It's a shock to discover people you love aren't the people you believed they were. Your secrets have rocked my world, Gloria.''

''I'm the same person I've always been.''

''I'll work it out. I'm just not there yet.'' He paused, then his voice softened. ''How are you holding up?''

''I . . . I'm fine.''

''Liar.'' She imagined him smiling, wondered if he was. ''Nigel is keeping a line open for you at his office. Mrs. Braithwaite will phone if there's anything new at this end. If you learn anything or have any questions, call Nigel's office. Let them know when you'll be arriving so someone can meet you.''

Someone. ''Gardner . . . ?''

''Yes?''

She bit her lip, lowered her head. ''Nothing. I just . . . thank you.''

''There's nothing to thank me for. I need to find Robby as badly as you do, Gloria. Maybe finding him will help right the balance. I don't know.''

She hung up the telephone, waited a moment, then dialed her attorneys.

The instant he walked through the heavy doors and entered the firm, Durant felt the tension bunching his shoulders loosen and shift toward anticipation. His spine straightened and his chin firmed. It had always been this way. The firm, his firm, possessed a magical capacity for rejuvenation. Immediately, his energy focused and his mind sharpened.

Granted, losing Chissie was surprisingly more painful than he had imagined. One didn't spend thirty-seven years with a woman without learning to care for her. But he would manage. If society closed its golden doors against him, other important doors would remain open because he was the premier rain-maker, the legend of Wall Street. As long as he controlled La Tourraine, Durant and Von Marron no one would dare shut him out. And as long as he controlled La Tourraine, Durant, and Von Marron, he possessed vast power. He would not lack for someone to share his bed.

The rupture with Gardner was in many ways more painful and distressing than his estrangement from Chissie. Like all fathers, he wanted his son to admire and respect him. That Gardner had backed away in disgust and contempt angered and bewildered him. Half the world esteemed and respected Win Durant. Why didn't his son? Why couldn't Gardner recognize the present situation was merely business? One did what one had to do. He had to save La Tourraine, Durant and Von Marron. It was that simple and uncomplicated.

The phone rang the moment he sat down at his desk.

"Is this Winthrop Durant?"

"Who the hell is this? How did you get the number for my private line?"

"This is a payback for a favor you did me once. I don't like owing a shit like you, so listen. The SEC indicted Albert Whitley Stone on charges of insider trading. Stone's trying to cut a deal, and one of the names he gave the SEC is yours. Something about a dummy apartment and an answer phone. A chain of people, some of whom Stone knows. The SEC moved on it over the weekend. Your ass is in a sling, pal. And it couldn't happen to a more deserving guy."

"Who is this? Wait a minute . . . ." Durant stared at the dead phone. Jerking forward, he punched a clear line and dialed the number of the manager at the apartment house.

"Mr. Smith?" the manager hissed through missing teeth. "Yeah. I dint have no way to get hold of you or I'da called. Some guys was here and tossed your place."

"You let them in? I *told* you never to let anyone in but me."

"Hey, asshole. They had a warrant."

Durant slammed down the phone and swiveled to face the windows. Bright autumn sunlight sparkled across the Bay. How in the hell did Stone find out about the apartment and the answer phone? It wasn't possible. But apparently it was; it had happened. The next question was immediate. What had the SEC found on the answer-phone tape? And how long did he have to cover his ass?

Lucille Ivory rapped on his door and peered inside, her eyes wide, her face pale. "Win, there's a man from the FBI out here with a subpoena for your personal computer files."

"Get one of the firm's attorneys up here. Now."

His life was unraveling. Chissie, Gardner, now the SEC and the FBI. His foundation was crumbling slowly beneath him. He gripped the arms of his chair and felt a slick of moisture appear on his forehead. Remain calm, he commanded himself, wondering where the hell his antacid tablets were. Don't overreact. The SEC was fishing; they didn't have a thing. He would work his way through this, he always had before.

The important thing was, and it was vital to keep this thought in front of him, he had the firm. The firm would see him through.

Gloria stepped off the Home jet wearing a Russian sable over a black sweater and Armani trousers. Her silvery hair lifted in the damp evening breeze. For once she didn't care if a roving newspaper reporter saw past her dark glasses. It no longer mattered. During the flight she had decided that if the authorities did not locate Robby within forty-eight hours, she would call a press conference and use the reporters as they had used her most of her life. She would release Robby's photograph and within twelve hours his picture would appear on the cover of every tabloid in the world. Someone would recognize him.

This decided, she directed her attention to the group of men waiting at the base of the ramp. She recognized Nigel Watson standing in front of two men she assumed were inspectors with the Yard.

Gardner was not there.

Nigel Watson shook her hand, studied her face, then escorted her to a waiting limousine. The two men, Inspector Evanly and

Inspector Caley, joined Gloria and Nigel in the car before it pulled away from the plane.

"We're doing everything we can, Miss Von Marron." Inspector Evanly examined the Bentley's interior, then looked at her. He held his hat on his lap. "Mr. Watson's team has turned over their preliminary findings, and we've verified the information. We're confident we'll locate your son very soon."

"We have a line on the car used in the abduction," Inspector Caley added. "Thirty minutes before your plane landed, Gardner Durant telephoned from Lewes. His people have located the woman with the baby carriage. The Lewes force is escorting her to London."

Gloria closed her eyes and dropped her head backward. "Hurry," she whispered.

"We're trying."

"Will Gardner be returning to London?" She needed him so badly. For too long she had relied on herself. She had learned not to trust those she loved to be there when she needed them. But Robby's abduction had left her exposed and vulnerable. She saw her self-reliance for what it was. Loneliness.

"I wouldn't know, Miss."

She nodded and tried to smile when Nigel pressed her hand.

Durant let himself into the penthouse and passed through the living room toward the butler's tray.

"Christ, what a day," he said, nodding to Chissie. He swallowed a glass of Scotch, not bothering with ice. Setting the empty glass to one side, he used the silver tongs to drop two cubes into a fresh glass then lifted the stopper from the Baccarat decanter.

Standing abruptly, Chissie brushed past him without a word, switched off the television, and reached for the telephone.

"You can't say hello, for Christ's sake?"

She spoke into the telephone. "Bradley? He's here. I thought you were going to obtain a restraining order."

Durant stared at her. She wasn't buying his bluff.

"Yes, I will. Immediately," she said. "Thank you, Bradley. I appreciate it."

"All right, Chissie, that's enough. We need to talk," he said when she hung up the phone. "We can work this out." She walked past him like he was a piece of furniture, leaving a drift of Cabochard behind. It was the same fragrance she had worn the night he met her, the fragrance she had worn for forty years.

"I don't want a divorce." He spread his hands in a plea. "I need you."

With some amazement he recognized he was admitting the truth. He genuinely could not imagine his life without Chissie. She was a stabilizing influence; she was his continuity, his history, his audience. Without Chissie, who was left to understand the significance of his accomplishments?

"Chissie, please." Embarrassed, he noticed his hands were shaking. "Don't do this."

Abrams appeared in the foyer to drop Chissie's fur wrap over her shoulders, then he scurried out of sight without glancing at Win. Durant felt as if he had suddenly become invisible. Abrams wouldn't look at him; Chissie wouldn't look at him.

"Bradley will arrive in a few minutes with a restraining order. He will have a policeman with him." Chissie spoke to a point somewhere behind him. Her dark eyes were hard with pain and anger. "Don't telephone. Don't send more flowers or jewelry. Don't come here again."

She stepped out the door and left him standing in the foyer feeling like an intruder in his own house.

"Shit!" Bradley Whitmore had been hot for Chissie for twenty-five years. Durant could picture them. Whitmore, solicitous and sympathetic, inviting her to dinner to discuss what a bastard Win Durant was. Chissie, the betrayed wife, her dark eyes brimming with tears.

He hurled his glass of Scotch at the door.

Continuing to feel like an intruder, he went into his bedroom and removed an armload of clothing from the closet. The roses he had sent her protruded from the bedroom wastebasket. She hadn't even taken them out of the florist's box. The .38 was lying on top of the bedside table.

After a moment's thought, he shoved the .38 into his shaving kit. He didn't want her shooting him when he returned for the rest of his things.

Bradley Whitmore and a plainclothes policeman stepped out of the elevator when the doors opened.

"You're wasting our time, Whitmore," he snapped, looking at the restraining order Bradley Whitmore slapped into his hand. Looking straight ahead, Abrams stepped past him onto the elevator, carrying Durant's luggage. "Chissie isn't going through with this."

"I think she will, Win." Whitmore gave him a smug shit-eating grin. "When Chissie reads the file we're putting together on you, nothing on earth is going to get you through the door again.''

The elevator doors closed, stirring a chill current of truth.

Gloria couldn't sleep. After an hour she abandoned the effort and went into the suite's living room to stand beside the windows. A light mist dampened the pavement below and wrapped halos around the streetlights.

Her son was out there somewhere.

Shortly before midnight Inspector Caley had telephoned to tell her the woman with the baby carriage had arrived from Lewes. They knew Robby was being held somewhere in London. They hoped to know more before morning.

Dropping her head, she rubbed her eyes. She knew she should try to sleep. She hadn't slept since the nightmare began. Dark circles smudged her eyes; tiny lines framed her mouth. Her body ached.

If they found him—no—*when* they found him, she would never again let her son out of her sight. During the hours of torment, she had kept herself from despair by planning their future together. They would return to Goose Point. She would resign her position with Nestor Brothers and spend the rest of her life trying to make up for the lost years.

A sob caught in her throat. She knew so little about him. She didn't know his favorite foods or what television programs he liked. She didn't know what made him laugh or what frightened him at night. Her fingernails dug into her thigh.

And she had dared to think of Lulu as a careless mother. Next to her, Lulu had been a model of motherhood, every child's dream mother.

Mired in guilt and self-flagellation, it was only gradually that she became aware someone was knocking at the door to the suite. Shoving back her hair, she stumbled across the room.

''Gardner!'' When she saw him, she swayed forward and collapsed into his arms, sobbing. ''Oh God. God. I've done everything wrong. I don't know anything about my son, Gardner. I've been so blind, so goddamn stupid!''

He pushed the door shut with his foot and held her, stroking her hair as she sobbed against his shoulder.

''If I have another chance, I'll never let him out of my sight, I swear it. I'll quit Nestor Brothers. I'll devote the rest of my life to being the kind of mother I wish I'd had. I'll make this up to him somehow. I swear I'll make it up to him!''

"Shhh." When she quieted, he gently raised her chin and studied her face. "When did you sleep last?"

"I've missed you so much." She wiped at the mascara streaking her face. "I'm so sorry, Gardner, so sorry you had to know any of it. I didn't want to hurt you."

"I know." He kissed her forehead, ran his thumb along her cheek and finally he smiled. "Is this where you walk into the Sound and swim toward Europe?"

"Self-pity?" She closed her eyes and shook her head, trembling. "Is that what I'm doing?"

Bending, he lifted her and carried her into the bedroom. "Get some rest." He placed her on the bed and stretched out beside her, guiding her head to his shoulder. She was still trembling when he took her in his arms.

"The inspector said you conducted a house-to-house search for the woman with the baby carriage."

"We'll talk about it in the morning. Sleep now."

"Gardner? I love you." Her voice was thick and fuzzed with fatigue. "I've always loved you. I'm glad you're here."

"Try to sleep, squirt."

He held her until her breathing finally deepened and slowed, then he eased her head to the pillow and pulled the blanket over her. He kissed her forehead before he went into the living room and poured a drink at the bar.

Sitting in the darkness, he thought about everything she had said. In time, she would understand that smothering Robby could be as damaging as absence. He believed in her intelligence and her practicality. Eventually, she would establish a balance to meet Robby's needs and her own.

He stretched his neck against his hand and looked toward the ceiling, feeling his own weariness. For the last few days he had functioned on two levels. One level of thought dealt with the present and the search for Gloria's son. The second level wrestled with personal applications.

His parents would divorce. He would never see his father again; he had known that when he left the penthouse. Words had been spoken that could be neither forgotten nor forgiven. The past, in the person of Gloria's son, would always be with him. There was no possibility of a reconciliation.

Sitting in the darkness of a London hotel room, he gradually came to terms with his grief. Slowly and painfully. Then, as the sky brightened outside the windows, Gardner Durant turned his thoughts toward the future, testing himself against what would be required.

Gloria battled out of the soft warmth of sleep when the telephone rang. Pushing up on her elbows, she shook her hair and blinked at the clock. A quarter to five. For a moment she couldn't remember where she was, then she came fully awake, and her stomach tightened. The pain returned behind her eyes.

"This is Gardner Durant," Gardner said into the bedside telephone. Leaning forward, he touched her hand, mouthed the words that coffee was on the way. He lifted an eyebrow. "Alf Cowper? No, I'm sorry, I don't recognize . . . wait a minute. Cowper may be with an investigative firm Home Limited used a few years ago. Walt Tobler will have that information." He repeated Tobler's telephone number into the telephone, then listened a moment before he reached for the note pad on the table and scribbled an address. "I've got it. Edgeware."

"Gardner?"

"We'll meet you there as soon as possible."

"They've found him? Gardner?"

He took her hands. "Caley believes Robby is being held in a house in Edgeware. About twenty minutes north of London."

"Oh, thank God! Thank God!" Tears flooded her eyes, and her head dropped. Her lips moved in a silent prayer of gratitude, then she twisted across the bed and jumped to her feet. For an instant she stood frozen as if unable to think what to do next. Then she threw open the closet. "Is he all right? Has anyone seen him?"

"A woman who lives across the street saw a boy yesterday whom the police believe is Robby. He was fine."

Gardner sucked in a breath when she flung off her robe. God, she was beautiful.

"Who is Alf Cowper?" Naked, she tossed aside one dress after another, unable to make a decision. Finally she swore in frustration and threw a green silk blouse and cashmere skirt across the bed. Bending, she fumbled into her lingerie.

He felt the stirring of an erection and wondered how old they would be before the sight of her body failed to arouse him. Eighty? Ninety?

"The woman with the baby carriage—her name is Lila Trow—talked last night," he said, watching her dress. "An American named Alf Cowper hired Trow's brother and boyfriend to abduct

Robby. She told the police she isn't certain, but she thinks Cowper was acting for someone else.''

Gloria paused to look at him. ''It's all coming apart, isn't it?'' she asked softly. ''If they find Cowper, they'll link him to your father.''

''Yes.''

''You may not believe this, but—I'm sorry.''

He examined her face and eyes and saw the truth. She had grown toward a new maturity during the last terrible days. ''So am I,'' he said quietly. Glancing at his watch, he calculated it was midnight in New York City, late but not too late to telephone Walt Tobler.

''Unless you object, I'll instruct Walt to make the tender offer to the family trusts today.''

Gloria lowered her hairbrush and looked at him in the mirror. ''Are you very sure, Gardner?''

''I'm sure.''

''It doesn't matter anymore,'' she said.

''La Tourraine, Durant and Von Marron is still a sound investment for Home Limited.'' He met her eyes in the mirror. ''As the firm's president-elect, I advise Home to proceed with the offer.''

''Then you'll accept the presidency?''

''Yes.''

She moved to the side of the bed and gently touched his face. ''For so many years, all I thought about was revenge. I sacrificed everything and everyone I loved. I beg you not to make the same mistake.''

''This is business,'' he said, his eyes hard. ''My father would be the first to understand.''

She remained in the room while he spoke to Walt Tobler. Then, when he dialed Win Durant's private line, she stepped into the bathroom and quietly shut the door behind her.

Win Durant's hands were shaking as he hung up the telephone. It was over. He continued to hear Gardner's cold voice in his ear, in his mind. What his son had said stunned the breath from his body. He could not breathe.

The tender offer to the trustees would be made today. Scotland Yard had Alf Cowper's name. By this time tomorrow, certainly by the next day, the authorities would have Durant's name and whatever evidence they required.

He had lost the firm. The pain was physical and he swiveled

his chair, bending away from it, staring at the darkness outside his office windows.

Without question this had been the worst day of his life.

Abrams, that little prick, must have been gossiping as everyone seemed to know Chissie had shot at him. As he walked through the firm, pockets of silence opened before him and closed behind him, followed by a hiss of whispers and muffled snickers.

A few minutes before five, Bruce Mosley from the SEC telephoned to arrange a meeting for tomorrow morning. "We have a few questions," Mosley said. "You have the right to have an attorney present." Durant noted the absence of "sir" or "mister" and accepted the omission as significant. The SEC had something; the bloodsuckers were on to him.

All day pieces of his world had been crumbling beneath him. Gardner's call had knocked the last bit of solid earth from beneath his feet.

The trustees would accept Home Limited's tender offer. In a few hours the firm would be gone. He had lost.

For a moment he did not move, did not blink.

When all was said and done, a man's life amounted to only a few minutes. A few minutes, that was all; the rest was filler. A minute here, a minute there. Maybe five significant minutes in a lifetime, and those were the minutes by which a man was measured and remembered.

In the end no one would recall that Winthrop Durant had once ruled the most powerful Street in the world. No one would remember the megamillion-dollar deals or the testimonial dinners. He would be remembered as the nobody from Oklahoma who blew the big one. The man who lost it all to a Von Marron.

Desperate men commit desperate acts, make stupid mistakes. He had been desperate and consequently he had lost. The party was over.

Standing, he walked to the bar and poured himself another large tumbler of Glenlivet. This time he carried the bottle back to his desk. Before he leaned backward in his chair and crossed his ankles on his desktop, he lit a Havana Corona and rolled the sweet smoke over his tongue.

Oddly, he felt calm.

His wife had left him; his son despised him. The SEC and the FBI were hot on his ass; it was only a matter of hours before he was arrested on kidnapping charges. He had lost the firm, and he had nowhere to go.

He drew on the cigar and exhaled slowly as he studied the lights glittering across Manhattan's dark skyline. He had owned this town. It had been his. His enemy, his lover, his vassal.

He missed Bobby Von Marron. He wished Bobby were here. It would have been good to sit in the darkness with Bobby and remember old times.

When the bottle of Scotch was three-fourths empty, he opened his desk drawer and removed the gun. He checked to make certain it was loaded, then he laid it gently on his desktop before he poured the last of the Scotch and stubbed out his cigar.

He had no regrets. It had been one hell of a ride.

They dashed through the Connaught's lobby and outside to the waiting limousine.

"There are some things that have to be said before we reach Edgeware," Gardner said as the Bentley pulled from the curb. It was still early, the traffic was light. "Look at me, Gloria." He took her face between his hands. "I love you. Nothing that's happened has changed that."

Tears brimmed in her eyes. "I thought I'd lost you, too."

"I'm sorry I left you to deal with this alone."

"Oh Gardner, you don't have to apologize. I know what a shock it must have been, discovering—"

"Tell me you love me."

"I love you. I've always loved you."

"Then marry me, Gloria."

She covered his hands with her own and searched his face, his eyes. "Can you accept Robby?" she asked in a low voice.

"I've thought of little else for several days. I'm prepared to love your son as much as I love his mother."

She closed her eyes and released a long breath. Then she brought his hands to her lips and kissed them.

"There are two things you and I must agree on, Gloria." He caressed her cheek with his fingertips. "We will never discuss my father. His name will not be spoken in our home."

"Agreed," she whispered.

"And Robby must never know I'm his brother."

"Oh Gardner." Tears sparkled on her lashes as she lifted her mouth for his kiss. "I love you so much."

Ahead, the street had been cordoned off. When the limousine glided to a stop behind the police cordon, Inspector Caley appeared at the door and assisted Gloria out of the car.

"Our men entered the house a few minutes ago. We expect them to come out in just—"

The door to a narrow, two-storey house banged open and two men stumbled outside, hands clasped on top of their hands. Inspector Evanly and three men followed. Evanly led Robby by the hand.

"Robby!" Jerking away from Inspector Caley, Gloria ducked under the cordon and ran forward, her sable flying behind her. He looked so small. So rumpled and bewildered and small. She fell to her knees on a patch of yellowing grass and opened her arms.

"Mummy!" An instant later she felt his slender body in her arms, his hands around her neck, holding tightly. "Mummy, those men took me away."

"I know, darling, I know. Was it terrible?" Weeping, smiling, she smoothed his hair, kissed him again and again. Her hands flew over his face, his shoulders, his trembling body, searching for signs of mistreatment and finding none, thank God.

Leaning back from her, he peered solemnly into her wet eyes. "I tried to be brave, Mummy."

"I know you did, darling. It's all right now. It's all over. Mummy's here, and I'm never going to leave you again."

Holding on to her neck, he laid his cheek against her fur collar and looked toward the people standing by the cordon and the police wagons. "Where's Aunt Margaret and Uncle Edmund?"

"They're waiting for us in Lewes. We'll visit them for a day or so, then we're going home, Robby. We're going home."

She saw a half-dozen people duck under the cordon and run toward her. Flashbulbs exploded, and Gardner swore above her head. Robby held tighter to her neck, and his eyes widened as the reporters converged on them.

Gloria stroked his cheek and drew a breath. From now on Robby would be the focus of intense media interest.

"Darling, these people want to ask us some questions. Don't be afraid. I want you to be as brave now as you were earlier. Can you do that?"

His dark eyes were shy and trusting. "Yes, Mummy."

Standing, she clasped his small hand and leaned to touch Gardner's sleeve. "It's all right," she said quietly.

"You're certain?" Gardner looked at her a moment then moved back a step.

He had never been more proud of her. She straightened her

shoulders and faced the reporters with a cool, patrician gaze. She held her silvery head high as flashbulbs exploded around them.

"Who's the boy?" someone shouted. "Is it true he's a Von Marron?"

"Did you pay a ransom?"

She kept her arm around Robby's shoulders, holding him close to her side and she glanced up with a quick smile as Gardner's arm slipped around her waist. Then she turned and looked directly into the cameras.

"This is my son." The exhaustion melted from her expression, and her smile was luminous. "My son." Pride glowed like gray fire in her eyes.

"*Your* son? Good God. Who's the—"

Gardner interrupted. "You heard the lady. This is Robert Von Marron Durant." Reaching past Gloria, he leaned down to Robby, smiled at the boy then swung him up to his shoulder. "Our son."

"You're the boy's father?" Cameras whirred, pens raced across notebooks. "Gardner Durant, isn't it? Are you and Miss Von Marron engaged?"

"And about to be married. Someone has to make an honest woman of her." He winked at Gloria and she laughed and gave him a radiant smile. "Now, ladies and gentlemen, if you'll excuse us, my son has suffered a terrifying ordeal and needs rest. This family wants some privacy."

Shielding Gloria from the shouted questions and the blinding flashbulbs, Gardner led her toward the limousine, carrying Robby on his shoulder.

Once they were inside, Robby looked up at him, his dark eyes wide with fascination. Gardner sucked in a breath. It was like looking at himself at the same age. "Are you really my father?"

"I'm really your father."

"I never had a father before," Robby said, suddenly shy. Twisting on the seat between them, he looked up at Gloria. "Are we really going to your house, Mummy?"

"It's your house, too. Yes, darling, we're going home." She kissed his hair and looked at Gardner above her son's head. Tears of happiness swam in her eyes, turning them luminous. "We're all going home."

"Have you been in a plane before?" Gardner asked.

Robby shook his head, staring up at him with large eyes. "Can I bring Winston? Winston is my puppy."

"Of course. Did Mummy tell you that Goose Point has a stable? How would you feel about a pony?"

"If you don't mind, sir, I'd rather have a brother."

Gardner grinned then looked at the magnificent woman laughing up at him. He loved the sound of her laughter.

"I think we can manage that," Gloria said softly. Her wonderful eyes made love to him.

"Your mother is always right," Gardner said. A small hand curled into his palm, and he felt a tightness in his chest. "If your mother says you can have a brother, then it's as good as done." He smiled. "Everyone needs a brother."

When he looked at Gloria, she was smiling through a blaze of tears.

"I love you," she whispered. "I love you both so much."

The first thing she would do when they returned to Goose Point was throw away the statuettes and fading ribbons. She didn't need them anymore.

About the Author

Carolyn Bransford was born in Salt Lake City, Utah, and later attained a B.A. degree in French Literature. She spent several years overseas, studying art and theater, before entering the world of Wall Street. She has spent the last eighteen years as an adviser to wealthy individuals.

Ms. Bransford resides in New York City with her Welsh Corgi, Topper.